SOMETIMES GOD WHISPERS

SOMETIMES *God Whispers*

A Journey of Faith, Loss, and Redemption in the American Frontier

June D. Peterson

LIBRARY OF CONGRESS CONTROL NUMBER: 2024920004
PAPERBACK ISBN: 979-8-9916065-0-9
DIGITAL BOOK ISBN: 979-8-9916065-1-6

To all those who believed in me.

"They that wait upon the Lord shall renew their strength, they shall mount up with wings as eagles, they shall run and not be weary, they shall walk and not faint."

— ISAIAH 40:31

CHAPTER 1

INGE

Inge shivered despite the sunshine spilling over her shoulders. Her mind had difficulty accepting the feelings that infused her. *It would soon be over. Then what?* She glanced around the little Lutheran church that overflowed with friends and family. A quiet titter filled the room with heads together smiling and whispering. Everyone was dressed in their finest. Enormous bouquets of late-blooming flowers in vibrant red and gold lined the altar. Light streamed through the stained-glass windows giving the room a cheerful, festive air, entirely appropriate for a wedding.

Inge gazed out the church window through a blur of tears. Colorful leaves danced past the glass in the fall breeze. Her fists clenched so tight that her fingernails left imprints on her palm. *I waited my entire life for this day.*

Luke followed the pastor to the front of the church. Freshly shaved, cowlick carefully plastered to his head, and face pink from a vigorous scrubbing, he was ready to begin a new life. Every inch a rugged farmer, Luke was tall and strong. It was his gentleness Inge loved. She never stopped believing one day... one day they would wed.

Inge's mind flooded with pictures of the boy who was her best friend. Half a lifetime ago she realized she loved Luke, not as a playmate, but something more, something deeper. Before that, they played in the creek, caught frogs in the pond, and climbed trees. That summer everything changed. Fourteen was too young to understand such things, but she knew he was the one. On sunlit afternoons, lying in the soft grass as leafy shadows danced across their faces, they shared their grown-up dreams. She could still feel his arm creep around her shoulder, drawing her close. Looking into her eyes, he said, "We'll get married someday." And she believed him.

Today, Luke was getting married, but not to her.

Inge rose with the congregation as the organist performed the wedding march. The bride slowly walked down the aisle, clutching her father's arm. The pale gray wool dress with tatted lace on the collar and cuffs complemented her shapely form. Her dark hair was carefully twisted under a colorful *brudekrone*, her grandmother's bridal crown. Always beautiful, today she was radiant. Her effervescent personality and sincere heart attracted people to her like bees to honey. Of course, Luke chose her. She was everything Inge was not.

When the congregation sat, Inge sank deep into the pew. *How could I have been so foolish to believe that childhood promise? Just look at Alice. And look at me... a gangly string bean.* Alice was always the center of attention and never short of admirers. *Why did she have to pick Luke?* She could have had anyone. Wiping a tear that leaked from the corner of her eye, Inge prayed that Luke would look her way and realize his mistake.

"Inge, are you all right?" her mother murmured. Helga squeezed her daughter's hand and slipped her a handkerchief.

Inge covered her mouth. Her stomach lurched when Alice's father released his daughter into Luke's care. *I should leave. I feel sick.*

The cross above the altar shone with a clarity she hadn't noticed before. Though made of wood, its polished surface reflected light from the window and the beams penetrated her heart like shards of glass. Ignoring the vows spoken by the bride and groom, she pleaded,

Lord, I don't know if I can watch Luke and Alice begin their life together.

Positive that every glance in her direction was filled with pity, she stared at her hands as they worked themselves into knots.

Inge had barely finished her prayer when the pastor pronounced the couple man and wife. Luke escorted his bride down the aisle, pride nearly popping the buttons off his shirt. Inge nodded as they passed, refusing to look at them. Exiting the pews, everyone pushed forward to congratulate the newlyweds. Sidestepping the eager crowd, Inge sank into a corner seat. The bride and groom. The happy couple. She watched Luke tug at his collar and blush at comments from his boyhood friends. Alice flushed with elation. Excited chatter rippled through the room. Weddings were a joyous event. The beginning of a new family, a new generation, but not for Inge.

"*Tante, tante.*" Inge glanced behind her. "Uppie." She obliged, pulling her toddling niece into her lap. Tiny arms wrapped around her neck. Inge inhaled her sweet baby smell, nuzzled her golden curls, and pressed her soft body tightly against her chest. Would she ever know the embrace of her own child?

"Baby Rose," she whispered. How much longer would she be Baby Rose? This dear, sweet child who loved her unconditionally would grow up and be married herself one day. The loving embrace wrapped her with a sense of loss.

Wriggling free, Rose placed her sticky fingers on Inge's cheeks. "Wuv yu." Inge pulled her close again. Glancing up, she caught Luke watching the two of them. Was that a look of regret or was she imagining it?

"Back to your *Mor,*" Inge said, reluctantly giving Rose back to her mother. "*Tante* has to help *Mormor* cut the cake."

Her mother had not only baked the *kransekake* but had been invited to serve it after the ceremony. As a close friend of the family, Inge felt obligated to help. Why had she clung to Luke's words all these years, even when she had felt him drifting away?

After removing the top layer of the wedding cake, Inge stepped back and allowed her mother to present the first slice to the newlyweds. "It's good luck, you know," Helga said to the couple. "The first slice brings many blessings to your new life."

Inge sucked in a deep breath and stepped forward. "Congratulations to you both. I wish you all the best." It was all she could get out.

"*Takk.*" Luke nodded his thanks.

Luke and Alice laughed as they fed each other the first bite of cake. *It should have been me sitting there! I waited all these years.* Inge blinked rapidly, then pulled her eyes away from the couple.

"Oh, *Mor*. How could I have been so wrong to believe Luke and I would marry one day?"

Drawing Inge close, Helga said, "I wish I had an answer for you. I do believe if God closed this door, He will open another." Without her mother's underpinning strength, Inge couldn't imagine being able to endure all this.

Luke and Alice. She closed her eyes to shut out the revelry, but it persisted behind closed lids. *Would this day never end?*

There was no one else for her. Suitors had not beaten a path to her door, and the few who did were sent away. What would fill her life now? Caring for her parents until... and then what? Emptiness.

Inge's face hurt from an afternoon of forced pleasantries. She cut the *kransekake*, nodded, and smiled as guests accepted her offering. Watching the cake slowly disappear slice by slice was like watching her dream sink slowly below the horizon and fade into darkness.

CHAPTER 2

INGE

APRIL 1895

When did she get old? Childhood seemed like yesterday. It had been a carefree, happy time with little thought as to what lay ahead, but now her future consumed her like an insatiable hunger.

Flickering lamp light spread a soft glow over the attic room. The steep roof, the small window, and the bed piled high with warm quilts were all so familiar. Would this be her life from now on? Tomorrow, on her thirtieth birthday, it would be official. She would be a spinster.

She jerked the bun loose from the back of her head and vigorously brushed her blonde hair. Inge ran her finger lightly over her nose, feeling the bump she blamed Luke for. He had dared her to climb the tree, and in a less than graceful dismount, she'd broken her nose. She cleared the fog from the window and gazed at her reflection. There were no wrinkles yet, not even crow's feet near her eyes. She had high cheekbones, fair skin, and blue eyes, but none of it was put together in a manner considered beautiful. Dropping her hand, she watched the condensation cover the glass again, the dewy window softening her features.

Lord, You do understand this loss I feel, don't You?
This need to... I don't know.
I always thought Your plan for me was a home and family.
Evidently, I was wrong.

She blew out the lamp and crawled under the quilts, burying her head deeply in the pillow.

INGE AWOKE to the rattling of stove lids below in the kitchen. Her mother fed wood to the fire to prepare her favorite breakfast, *pannekaken* smothered with thick cream and sweet berries. The hot cast iron griddle sizzled, and her *mor* hummed as she prepared the batter.

Inge came down the back stairs into the kitchen and slipped up behind her mother to give her a quick hug. "*God morgen, Mor.*"

"Ah, Inge. Happy birthday! I remember where I was thirty years ago today." Her mother lifted a container of flour from the cupboard bin.

"Now *Mor*, I am sure you can't remember back all those years," Inge said.

"*Ja*, I remember exactly what happened." She sifted flour into a bowl sitting on the worn kitchen table. "It started at about six o'clock in the morning—"

"Now, Helga, you know your memory is getting worse every year." Her father's eyes twinkled as he set a pail of fresh milk on the counter. "Besides, you have told it so many times that the girl must have it memorized by now." He placed his calloused hands around Helga's ample waist and kissed the top of her head.

"Ja. Ja, I suppose she knows it well by now," Helga agreed. "But Peder, you were there, and you remember how special it was to hold our first child in your arms."

"For you, my dear Helga, there is nothing more special than babies," he said, teasingly chiding his precious wife of thirty-one years.

Inge watched her parents as their love filled the room. This is what she wanted. This would have been her life with Luke, one filled with fun, teasing, family... and babies.

"Ja. Tonight, the whole family will be here. It will be such fun to have everyone together." Helga smiled as she flipped the pancake.

"Ja, it will," said Peder, "but I have a day of work to finish before the celebrating begins. I'll see you tonight." He strained the milk into the separator and headed back to the barn.

"*Mor*, can I ask you something?" Inge settled in to eat her breakfast. "I love being here with you and *Far*, but I feel there should be more to my life." Unbridled thoughts flowed into words. "Everyone my age is married. I will never have a husband and family." Her food became tasteless. "Life feels so... so meaningless." Inge cut her pancake into tiny pieces, stirring in the berries until it became purple mush.

"Meaningless? What do you mean?" Helga stared at her. "You're our daughter, a part of this family. You belong here." Helga punctuated each word with a wave of her wooden spatula. "What on earth would you do if you left?"

"I don't know. I keep thinking there must be something for me out there." She cupped her face in her hands and leaned her elbows on the table. "I... I feel lost sometimes. Alone."

"Oh, Inge. I know Luke's marriage was a big disappointment, but God has a plan for your life. You must trust Him." Helga slipped her arm around her daughter's shoulders and drew her close.

Inge buried her face in her mother's apron. "Does He really have a plan for me?" She leaned into her mother's welcoming embrace.

"Ah, my precious child, when God speaks, you will know." Helga tenderly stroked her daughter's hair. "Believe me, you will know."

Ja, maybe her *mor* was right. But Inge had been so sure about Luke, and she had been so wrong.

I trusted You, Lord.
I waited for You to bring Luke back to me, and You didn't.
Can I trust you again?

HER MOTHER COOKED much of the day, and the house was filled with the aroma of fried chicken, fresh bread, and apple pie. The dining room table was stretched to its full length, set with Helga's best lace cloth and delicate, cornflower blue dishes. Squeezing nine adults around the table would be cramped, but Inge loved the closeness of her fun-loving siblings.

When the family arrived later that evening, Inge did her best to join in the teasing and laughter. What had she been thinking this morning? This was a good life, and it was the only one she had ever known. Why wasn't she content with being a daughter, a sister... or even the dreaded spinster aunt?

"Let's gather. Come, come." Helga's voice rose above the animated chatter. "It's time to eat."

Everyone scrambled for a place, filling chairs and stools. The smallest children balanced on their parent's laps, and the older ones sat at the kitchen table.

"Ja, Peder, you will please pray for us?" Helga asked.

Peder cleared his throat. "Dear Heavenly Father, we come before you with gratitude in our hearts. As we celebrate the life You have given us, we praise You for all You have provided. Amen."

Conversation flitted around the table, nearly getting lost in the din of so many voices. "*Far,*" Sven said, "I saw Jacob Johannson in town today. He received a letter from his brother, Karl, the one who is in America."

"And this was good news, ja?" Peder asked.

"Some good, and the rest not so good. Karl's wife passed away recently."

"I heard his brother died some time back, too," Peder said.

"It was just a few months after they arrived," said Sven. "He has four boys, you know."

"Ah." Peder nodded. "It must be hard, first losing his brother and now his wife."

"But it seems his farm is doing well. He swears by that Dakota country. He says it's the richest land in all the world. Nothing like the rocks here in Norway." Sven reached for another helping of chicken. "He is hoping to remarry. He wanted Jacob to ask after Alice Tilson. Of course, Karl didn't know she married Luke a while back."

"Ja, Alice. She's expecting a little one soon," said Helga. "I saw her at church just last week."

Inge swallowed hard, food sticking in her throat. A new family was beginning, and she was still here at home with her parents. Inge's vision narrowed to her plate as she tuned out the rest of the discussion. Her thoughts turned to the recent widower. Ja, he had lost his wife, but he still had his children. That was more than she had.

Following dinner, the family retired to the parlor. Amid the teasing and laughter, Inge felt her niece tugging on her arm. "Play for us, *Tante*," pleaded Sven's youngest daughter. "Please. I want to dance."

"Ja, little turnip. I would love to have you dance for us." Inge sat down at the piano. The keys were cool and smooth, and her fingers lightly flitted across the yellowed ivory. When she was a young girl, her parents had scrimped and saved to buy this old piano. It had become her special haven, where she found comfort and peace.

After an evening of celebrating, the sleeping children were wrapped in warm blankets for the trip home. Inge waved as the last birthday wishes floated through the night air. Long after the wagons disappeared, she relished the feelings of unconditional love from her family. But was that enough to fill her empty soul?

Once her parents had gone to bed, Inge wandered through the quiet, empty house. Ending up at the piano, she resumed playing. This time, though, she found that the music that usually lifted her spirits now filled her with melancholy. Fingering the keys, her mind wandered back to the many happy wishes of the day. Suddenly, her frustration boiled over, and she pounded the keys.

"I refuse to just exist!"

The vehemence of her own words shocked her as much as the discordant sounds from the piano. Was it the mention of Alice Tilson's name that stirred her feelings? More likely, it was that Alice and Luke would soon have a family, and she would never know the love of a husband and children. Resignation rested on her shoulders, sucking away the joy of the evening.

The next morning, Inge sifted more flour into the bread bowl. A thought niggled at the back of her mind, but she couldn't quite nail it down.

Make yourself clear, Lord.

A sudden, strong feeling swept over her, a realization that made her knees buckle. She collapsed into a chair. Dough clung to her fingers as she steadied herself against the table. In all her many talks with God, Inge had never felt the power of His presence as much as she did at that moment. Breathing deeply, she waited, but the feeling did not leave her. She resumed kneading the bread. *Nie, God would not ask me to take such a huge leap of faith.* Each punch and fold of the dough pulled and tugged at the thought tumbling through her head.

Lord, this makes no sense.

She placed the dough into a bowl to rise and pulled the flour-covered remnants from her fingers.

Lord, would You ask me to do something this... outrageous? I know I prayed for Your intervention, but...

CHAPTER 3

INGE

Pulled from a deep sleep later that night, Inge's eyes snapped open, searching the darkness for images that lingered on the back of her eyelids. She saw a long table with children whose faces escaped her grasp, though she knew they were hers. Leaping from the bed and barely feeling the cold floor, Inge lit the lamp and pulled out her Rosemall-decorated writing box. Her fingers traced the delicately painted flowers. God's answer was clear. After scrounging for pen and paper, she began to write before the picture faded.

Dear Mr. Karl Johannson,

Now what? What do I tell a perfect stranger about myself? Do I say that I'm a spinster, and I am applying to be his wife?

Lord, this is ridiculous.

Did she even know what she wanted in a husband? Most likely, she would want someone like her father. Although he rarely said the words, it was clear how much he loved his wife. His touch was tender, and his words were gentle. They were two parts of a whole.

I don't remember ever meeting Karl, but since he is from around here, we may have acquaintances in common. Maybe that's a good place to start. She plunged ahead.

> My name is Inge Olafson. I think perhaps you won't remember me, but my father is Peder Olafson from St. Charles. He has a small farm outside of town. Your brother, Jacob, mentioned you were hoping to find someone to come to America to care for your family and perhaps eventually marry. I am willing to do such a thing.

Her fingers cramped from clutching the pencil. A man seeking a wife would look for someone who could... who could what? What kind of man sends for a wife? Inge's thoughts ran headlong into a stone wall. *Why is he doing this? Why am I doing this?*

Inge's shoulders tensed as cramps worked their way up her spine.

I can cook, I love children, I'm a hard worker... and I desire to have a home, a family, and a husband. Is that enough?

Oh, God, is this the right thing?

Inge jumped as the tension in her hand snapped the pencil in half.

If this is not Your will, he will never answer.

She dug through her box for another pencil and continued her letter.

I am thirty years old and have much experience running a household and doing farm chores. I have never married. I love children. I am a church-going person and believe deeply that God is in control of my life. I would ask that you pray about this matter.
Sincerely,
Inge Olafson

Folding the letter, she placed it in an envelope. What if he said yes? Would she have the faith and courage to go? What kind of life would she be stepping into? It could be wonderful or... She couldn't imagine anything else. This could be the way for her to have a home, a family, and a husband. She chuckled to herself. At least no one else would know her shame if he said no.

CHAPTER 4

INGE

"Inge," Peder called. "There is a letter for you. From America." His brows raised as he handed her the envelope. "Who do you know in America?"

Inge stared at the letter. It had been weeks since she had summoned the courage to mail it. She had convinced herself that even if Karl had received the letter, she was not what he had in mind for a wife. She was disappointed some days, but most days she felt relief at his lack of response.

Avoiding her father's questions, Inge retreated to her attic room. Studying the envelope with its large, somewhat crude handwriting, she hesitated. Here was the answer. She gripped her stomach. She wanted to know, but she also didn't want to know. Her hands trembled. She could throw it away and pretend she never received it. What good would that do? The answer was yes or no. *If yes, then I will marry. If no, then I will continue living here.* Withdrawing the single sheet from its envelope, she carefully unfolded it.

Miss Inge Olafson,

I received your letter. I have a small farm with a comfortable house in the Dakotas in America. My wife died several months ago, leaving me with four sons to raise. They are four, nine, twelve, and sixteen. I could use help with them.

It is better to come before winter as travel is hard then.

Karl Johannson

Inge stared unseeingly at the paper. She really hadn't expected him to answer. Was he asking her to come? Why would he answer if he didn't want her to come? Gripping the letter, she re-read it. Was he offering her a home or a job? There was no mention of marriage.

Could she do this? She would have to leave everything she had ever known.

God, I believe You have opened a door.
Provide me with the faith and courage to move forward.

CHAPTER 5

INGE

Three months had passed since Inge had answered Karl's letter. Now she clung to the small cot in the windowless room as her stomach turned with the heaving of the ship. Forcing herself to think about something else kept her mind off the nausea. She listed all the things that could go awry. *What if I am not what Karl wants for a wife? What if I don't like him? What if... what if?* She prayed fervently for peace.

The lamp light bounced off the walls, casting shadows that cavorted like demons. Shapes turned and curled as they danced to the metallic echoes that stole into the room from the engines. The air was rank with smoke and grease. She kept the chamber pot close to her bed.

Lord, I pray I have made the right choice.

To avoid more conflicting thoughts, she sat up, retrieved a sheet of paper from her writing box, and began a letter.

July 10, 1895

Dearest Mor and Far,

I will try to write a few lines tonight. It helps to keep my mind off the rolling of the sea and my stomach. Mor, I don't remember ever feeling so ill. It's awful. I have not yet been on the deck, but I understand that the weather has not been good. Maybe tomorrow will be better.

The accommodations on board the Campania are wonderful compared to the steamer trip to Port of Hull. It was standing room only for two very long days. How they could pack that many people on board is beyond me. Here I have a cramped room I share with another woman that I have not yet met. It is not ideal, but it's much better than the feeder ship. My quarters are comfortable enough. We each have a cot and a small space for our belongings. Unfortunately, the room is dark and damp. If I want to read or write, I must use a light, even in the middle of the day. I can't believe I will be in America in a little over two weeks. I am anxious and excited all at once.

With that, Inge put the letter on her bedside table and pulled the blanket close around her shoulders. Lying down eased the nausea and eventually, she drifted off to sleep.

July 11, 1895

I know I won't be able to mail this until I get to America, but I want to share my trip with you. You will get a whole book filled with my adventures on board this ship.

I met my roommate late last night. The commotion would have awakened the dead. She and a man were screaming at each other in the corridor. Even though I could not understand the words, I felt her anger and frustration. She shoved the door open and fell face-first into her bed. I lay awake the rest of the night. She was still asleep when I left this morning. I must admit that I found her behavior disturbing. I am sure she was drunk, and I have no idea what all the yelling was about.

Today the sea is still. As I strolled on the lower deck assigned to the second- and third-class passengers, the sky was the clearest blue I have ever seen. The crisp air tastes of salt, and, at last, my stomach seems to have settled. The ship is filled with interesting people. I wish I could understand what they are saying. I can see I need to learn some English. Otherwise, it will be a miracle if I can find my way once I get to New York.

INGE'S ROOMMATE rose shakily from her bunk. "*God ettermiddag,*" Inge said. "My name is Inge Olafson."

"Stella. My name is Stella." Her voice was gravelly, and she reeked of alcohol.

The woman's brown hair hung limp around her shoulders. Her dark eyes were downcast, and her shoulders curled protectively inward toward her chest. Her clothing needed a good washing, as did her body.

"Thank goodness you speak Norwegian," Inge said. "It is a relief to know we can talk."

Stella looked up and nodded slightly. "English, too."

"How fortunate you are," Inge said. "I must learn some English if I hope to find my way once I get to America."

Stella leaned forward, her breath rank. "And just how do you propose doing that?" Her tone dripped ridicule.

"Ja, well, I'm not sure," Inge said. Leaning back on her cot to avoid Stella's breath, she knew her hopes of learning English in two weeks, even if she had a teacher, were nothing but wishful thinking.

A shrewd smile crossed Stella's face. Gazing at Inge from behind a veil of tangled hair, she said, "Maybe I could teach you a little."

"You would do that?"

"Why not? You don't have much time, but I can teach you enough to get by. I don't suppose you could pay a little for my help?"

"Ja, I can pay a little." Inge's heart leaped at God's provision once again.

STELLA'S SHRILL voice and lack of patience left Inge reeling. *I'm not ignorant. Why is she making this so difficult?* To Inge's relief, Stella departed late in the afternoon. As she kneeled beside the small bunk, her eyes burning from holding back tears, gut-wrenching prayer poured forth.

Lord, I felt this was an answer to prayer. It was, wasn't it?

Doubt assailed her, battering her faith. The scrambled letters Stella had written on the paper glared at her. "This is impossible. I'll never figure it out." Grabbing the paper the lesson was written on, she heaved it across the room.

I am with you.

Inge's head jerked up. Her eyes darted around the small room. The words had been clear. Had she heard them or were they in her mind? Picking up the papers, she slumped on her cot and tried to work on the lesson.

God, this doesn't make any sense. Can't You do... something? I cannot learn this. I am willing, but...

Do you trust me?

"Of course, I trust You. You are God," Inge said with more confidence than she felt. For the first time that she could recall, she had little choice but to trust Him. Panic rose in her throat, closing off her air. Her hands shook. Feeling hot and cold all over, she wondered about her decision. On her way to a foreign land to marry a man she knew nothing about, to spend the rest of her life... doing what? Waves of uncertainty attacked her. She was completely alone for the first time in her life. Burying her head in her hands, she cried out, "Oh, God, what have I done?"

She picked up her Bible, a family treasure from her mother, and fingered the worn cover. The tattered pages brought comfort. The list of family births and marriages and the scent of the weathered leather drew her back to her home. Her *mor's* favorite verse filled her mind. "And we know that all things work together for good to them that love God, to them who are called according to His purpose."Clutching the book to her chest, Inge inhaled the words. "All things." It didn't say some things. It said all things.

The door opened. Inge flinched as Stella entered the room.

Glancing at Inge, Stella asked, "What are you reading?" When Inge didn't respond, she pointed at the book. Inge held out the Bible. Stella took it from her and thumbed through the pages.

"Do you believe this?" she asked in Norwegian.

"Ja," Inge replied. "I believe." Her story erupted out of her as she explained why she was on the ship, where she was going, and how God provided for her.

When Inge finally wound down, Stella snorted. "Why do you think God had a hand in all of this? Looks to me like you had a chance to get something you wanted, and you took it."

Inge's mouth dropped open. "God answered my prayers," she stammered.

"Maybe this soon-to-be husband of yours is so ugly that he can't find anyone to take care of him. Maybe that's why he had to send all the way across the ocean for a wife. Or maybe he just wants a slave for his farm. Or maybe he isn't even a farmer. Maybe he's a thief or murderer or a... a who knows what? How can you be so sure God spoke to you?"

Inge's mouth slammed shut. She had never considered such ideas. Karl was from her homeland. It was true that she didn't know him, but he had family in St. Charles. *Could it be that Stella was right? Nei... it couldn't be.* She squeezed her eyes shut and tried to block these new thoughts from her mind.

"Are you telling me you packed your bags and left a nice home to follow some silly notion of getting married?" Stella ranted. "I know something about such dreams. I was once young and innocent myself. But life isn't easy, and you do what you must to survive. If there is a God out there, he shouldn't allow bad things to happen to good people." Stella paced the room. She took six steps forward, wheeled around, and marched back. "Your *wonderful* God had my parents marry me off to an old man when I was only fourteen. He beat me for years. One night he tried to kill me, so I ran away. I have been running and hiding ever since." The words came out in explosive bursts. "I thank God I have no children. Your God has me selling my body to survive. Do you think I like doing that?" Stella beat her hips with her fists. "Men are animals! They don't care about you. They use you. Even your parents use you. My father got money for me. My wonderful, church-going father sold me." She wiped tears away with her fists. "He gave me a Bible as a wedding present, for all the good that did me." She slumped onto her cot and curled her body into a fetal ball.

Inge sat stunned. She gripped the edge of her bed as she watched Stella wrap her arms tightly around her body and rock back and forth. Was it possible? Did parents do that to their children? *Nei,* she must have misunderstood. Slipping in next to Stella, Inge prayed.

Oh Lord, give me the words and the wisdom.

She tucked her arm around the collapsed figure. Stella slowly crept into Inge's lap, her sobs turning into whimpers.

God, You put me in this place for this reason. Show me... show Stella Your presence.

Inge held her until she quieted. Sitting up, Stella wiped her face with the hem of her skirt. Drawing in a deep breath, she said, "I will teach you to read from your book."

Stella dug into her bag and produced a small Bible, this one in English. Holding the Bible out to Inge, Stella said, "It was the last thing my father gave me, the last piece of my childhood I still have. I suppose I hoped, someday... Never mind. I will teach you English... and you will teach me about your God."

"I can't pay you much," Inge said. "How much do you need to get to America without... you know?"

"Don't judge me!" Stella glared at her. "I do what I have to, and I plan to get to America with money in my pocket. Without it, they will send me back."

"Maybe I could give you more," Inge said. "Would that make a difference?"

Stella sighed. "Inge, you don't understand. I know the thought of selling my body repulses you. It repulses me too. But when you have nothing else, you do what is necessary. Once I get to America, this life will be forgotten. I will start over, new and clean. No one will ever know what I did to get there."

"There is only one way to be renewed," Inge said softly. "Jesus can do that for you."

"So I've heard." She scoffed at the idea, but her eyes held a longing Inge couldn't identify. "I promise... once I'm in America, I will be a different person."

INGE LAUGHED out loud at the little boy's squeal when he caught the ball. He threw it back, sending Inge into a sideways rush to catch it. Finally, Inge held up her hands. She was tired. Sitting next to his mother, Inge asked in broken English, "Going. Where?"

The woman smiled and chattered. "My husband is in America. We are coming to join him. He has a job on the docks, and he wrote that he found a small house for us. I miss him so much. I doubt little Tommy will even remember him."

While she didn't understand all the words, Inge felt the longing in the woman's voice. "Married. In America." She pointed at herself.

The woman clasped Inge's hand and squeezed it. Her face beamed with good wishes.

Inge smiled. Would she be able to understand this woman's joy someday?

July 15, 1895

It has been an interesting few days. My roommate, Stella, and I have become, well, if not friends, then at least friendly companions. She is trying to teach me English, and we are using the Bible to help me learn. It's a long story, but God has put me where I am needed. Stella has so many questions. I pray for wisdom so that I might help her understand. I will do what I can, and God will have to do the rest. She has confided in me about her unhappy life, making me ever so grateful to have all of you.

Speaking of family, I hope that Karl's children will like me. To build a family like ours would give me such joy. It will take some time, but I can be patient. My thoughts waver between the promised excitement of my new life and all the barriers I have yet to face.

This morning on the deck, I made friends with a little boy who is about four years old. We played a bit of peek-a-boo and threw a ball. I can't wait to meet my boys. I am already thinking of them that way—my boys. I suppose the older ones won't need much tending, but the little ones especially will need me. I think God intended me to be a mother.

The ocean has been quiet these last few days. It's a bit unsettling, though, to look out each day and see nothing but water. I feel so small in the grand scheme of things.

Inge found a sheltered corner on the lower deck, out of the wind. It was an ideal place to watch life on board the ship. Surrounded by third-class passengers like herself, she was fascinated with the diversity of dress and language. First-class occupants passed by on the upper deck, the women in their colorful frocks and elegant headwear. Most of the men wore beaver top hats and heavy wool coats.

More than anything else, Inge loved to watch the children. The thought that she would never see her nieces and nephews grow into adulthood saddened her and caused homesickness to tug at her heart. *I must focus on my new life.* In only four more days, she would be in America.

From her corner near the lifeboats, Inge soaked in the warmth of the sun. She sensed a restlessness among the passengers. Many leaned on the balustrade as if willing the coastline to come into view. Others engaged in stirring conversation punctuated by excited gestures. Obviously, Inge was not the only one eager to get to America. It would be soon now. She shivered in the cool breeze, wondering what lay ahead.

July 20, 1895

I played with my little friend again today. I tried to visit with his mother. We were able to convey some thoughts to each other, even though my English is very limited. I need to practice, and she seemed to understand that. It's so frustrating to not visit with others.

Stella says I am making progress with my English. It's easier to read the words than pronounce them. I can read a little from Stella's Bible now. I certainly won't be fluent in four days, but I am feeling slightly more comfortable with the idea of trying to communicate once I get to America. Stella says she will help me get to the train station. She has been so

*good to me these last several days. I must apologize if
I gave you a bad impression of her.*

&

DISCOLORED BUILDINGS and wharves filled the shoreline. Inge
pushed her way closer to the rail, wanting a glimpse of this new land.
From this distance, she couldn't make out individual people, just activity. This was not the beautiful place she had envisioned. The sky hung
heavy over the city. Chimneys poured black smoke into the air, and all
the buildings looked weathered and gray.

If she stood on tiptoe, Inge could see Ellis Island. They would have
to pass through there before they could set foot on American soil. Inge
prayed that all her papers were in order. Stella shared stories that she
had heard about some who never made it past the island but were
returned to their native land instead. Most were sent back because they
lacked enough funds to support themselves. Others were refused for
health reasons.

July 24, 1895
*We are here! I can see the shoreline of New York
and the magnificent Statue of Liberty. What a wonderful
symbol for a country. It will take some days for all
of us to pass through Ellis Island. With Stella's help,
this hurdle will be much easier. How I thank God for
her. Stella says she will stay in New York and look
for work as a housekeeper. I pray that she will find
honest work with good people. Please pray for her
always. She still hasn't placed her faith in God, but I*

think she is considering it. She asks many questions, and I hope I am providing godly answers.

I am anxious to get off the ship and be on my way. While I am not frightened, the unknown is daunting. Once on the train, the trip to North Dakota will only take a few days. Thoughts of this new life are staggering. What will Karl be like? I pray he is a godly man. And his boys, I envision them as little gentlemen, but I am sure they are normal, busy boys. I have such grand dreams. At the same time, I have no idea what to expect. Enough of my rambling for now. I must get my belongings together so I will be ready when it is time to disembark. How I wish you were here to share this with me.

CHAPTER 6

INGE

Inge clung to Stella's arm as the mass of people pushed forward. She could hardly stand, and keeping track of her belongings became a monumental task. Would they never get through to the inspectors? They had been on the island for two days. The stench from the crush of human flesh alone was unsettling. The facilities were poor, they lacked fresh water, and the personal services reeked. The food available was expensive, so they had eaten nothing except the few things they had brought with them. Many people appeared sick and were coughing. Stella said it was consumption. Others suffered from painful eye infections. A blanket of odors, languages, and bodies wrapped around them. They did their best to isolate themselves, but it was almost impossible.

"Hurry. It's nearly our turn." Stella tugged at her arm as they inched their way to the front of the line. "Just stay with me, and I will interpret for you."

Stella stepped up and presented her papers. The inspector asked numerous questions. Suddenly, an officer pulled Stella aside. With a firm grip on her arm, he steered her away from Inge. "I'll be right back," she called over her shoulder.

Horrified, Inge watched her friend disappear. She felt a jostling from behind her, and then a man shoved her forward. Craning her neck, Inge searched the crowd for Stella. Another insistent push from behind brought Inge to the inspection area. The official asked her something, and she shook her head. His gestures indicated he wanted her papers. After scrutinizing them, he asked, "You are going to get married?" Inge recognized the word married and nodded vigorously. Her heart hammered as if it was trying to escape her chest. What would she do if they took her away? They had already removed several others from the line.

Lord, don't let me say the wrong thing.

The man studied her intently for a moment and then ushered her through the other side of the detainment area.

She was out. She was free. She sucked in a deep breath of fresh air, then froze at the sight of the throng of immigrants before her. Deciding to follow the rest of the crowd, Inge worked her way toward a ferry that would take her to the mainland. But what would she do then? How would she ever find her way without Stella?

Unsure of what to do, Inge disembarked from the ferry and decided to wait on the dock for Stella. She said she'd be right back. Inge sat with her belongings as others pushed past her. The flow of people never stopped. How would she ever find Stella in this crowd? Occasionally, someone familiar-looking would appear, but when she called out, a stranger would turn and stare at her. *What am I going to do? Where will I go?*

Inge waited until dusk. *I have to move on. I can't sit here in the dark.* She pressed her fingers against her nose and squeezed her eyes shut. Her heart beat rapidly as she slowly stood and scanned the thinning crowd one last time. Not knowing what else to do, she grabbed the handle of her trunk. It lurched behind her, bouncing on the cobblestones as she followed the flow of passengers down the street.

CHAPTER 7

INGE

July 26, 1895

Dearest Familie,

The last couple of days have been the most frightening of my life. I became separated from Stella, so
I've had to find my own way. There are masses of
people everywhere, pushing and shoving, shouting and
making gestures that I am quite sure are not
hospitable. I have never felt so alone. But God is good.
As I was trying to find the train station, I saw a
shop with rosemall paintings in the window. I stopped,
praying someone there could speak Norwegian. The most
wonderful woman was behind the counter. She took me
in, offered me food and a place to sleep, and then she
helped me with the train schedule and tickets. The train
will take me to Chicago, then Minneapolis, and then on to
Bismarck in the Dakota territory. She even wrote down

my travel plans if I was unable to explain my needs to someone. Only God could have placed such a wonderful person in my path. She also agreed to post my letter to you about my adventures on the ship.

I miss you all so much. Please keep me in your prayers.

❧

Because she was uncomfortable on the hard wooden bench, Inge often stood and walked down the corridor of the swaying train. She needed to stretch to keep from becoming even more stiff and sore. Finally accepting the need to sleep, she joined others who were stretched out on the floor between the seats or in the aisle. The constant rumble of the wheels had a lulling effect, until the whistle blared, indicating a stop to take on or drop off passengers. Most people rose to unblock the passageway, but some refused, forcing the exiting passengers to step over them. Inge was grateful for the longer stops where they could walk around and purchase food.

July 27, 1895

This is the most interesting land. In rare instances, it reminds me of Norway, but for the most part, it is vastly different. We passed through wooded areas and then into grasslands. The grass was nearly as tall as the train. Never have I seen such grass. The farther west we go, the fewer trees there are. The grass has become shorter and shriveled to a golden brown. The heat is nearly unbearable at midday. I do hope Karl's land *isn't like this.*

I am looking forward to a place where I can bathe and wash my hair. The train is so dirty. Soot from the engine blows in through the open windows, but we must have the windows open. Otherwise, we would expire from the heat. Others have black faces, and I am sure I look no better.

I must change trains today. I pray I have no problems. If all goes well, I should be in Bismarck tomorrow. I don't know if anyone will meet me. If no one is there, once again God will have to provide.

Please continue to pray for Stella. I worry about her.

FORTUNATELY, the train depot was not far from the riverboat landing and Inge found a young man to carry her trunk to the edge of the river. There was a large hotel in the opposite direction of the ferry landing, but Inge had depleted most of her funds. She had given as much as she could spare to Stella. Not sure if she could afford both a room and the boat fare, she decided to spend the night in the shelter of the sacks of wheat stacked up near the shore. Shoving them into place, they made a surprisingly comfortable bed after the hard floor of the train. The waterfront was quiet except for the low of cattle and croaking frogs. After the crowded conditions, noise, and soot of the train, these accommodations seemed inviting, almost cozy. Despite being alone on the dock, she felt no fear, just vague loneliness.

After punching the sacks of grain to make them more comfortable, Inge finally laid down. The sky was filled with so many stars that their light was bright enough for her to see the steamboat tethered to the pilings. What would her future hold? Her *mor* and *far*, along with their warm and welcoming home, were gone. Would she ever see her family again? Maybe someday she and Karl and the children could go back to visit. Inge sighed. That probably wouldn't happen for a long time, if ever. Seized by the realization that her family was half a world away, tears trickled down her cheeks. *Lord, did I make the right decision?* What if this doesn't work out? She had barely enough money left for her fare tomorrow.

I am following your will, aren't I, Lord? I did hear Your voice, didn't I? What if Stella had been right? Was it my desire that had led me to this place?

She pulled her shawl over her head to shut out the thoughts.

CHAPTER 8

INGE

July 31, 1895

Today I am on a sternwheel ferry boat heading down the Missouri River to the town of Taylor's Landing. Karl's farm is somewhere near there. Many people in this area speak Norwegian, so it's been relatively easy to find my way. I'm not sure why people from home would favor this place. It's hot and dry, and everything is brown except for near the edge of the river. The land is incredibly flat. I see a few farms along the water with small houses that appear to be constructed of mud or crude bricks. A few are made of logs. I do hope Karl's house is bigger than these, especially with four children.

The heat has been unbearable, and the wind blows continually. It's a relief to be on the boat, for the air is cooler over the water. As I was waiting for the *ferry last night, I did manage to wash myself some in the river. I still look a sight, but hopefully, I will have a chance to clean up before I get to Karl's place.*

I am nearly there. My new life is just around the corner. Pray for me always.

Your Inge.

Inge set her letter aside and listened to the muddy water lap at the sides of the flat-bottomed ferry. Sitting on a crate in the shade of the wheelhouse, Inge regarded the gray-brown hills that sloped to the water's edge. It seemed like such a desolate, empty place. This was the land that was supposed to hold so much promise. Thick clouds of gnats swarmed around her face. Sweat rolled in small rivulets down her back, and grit stuck to her fingers when she wiped her brow.

The boat chugged slowly forward, and apprehension crawled up her spine each time the wheel sliced through the water. *What if Karl decides not to marry me?* That thought had always hung in the back of her mind, but she chose to ignore it. Inge drew in a deep breath and leaned back against the wall. She centered her thoughts. What would this new life be like? Karl was about five years older than she was. She didn't know much about him, except that he had four boys and had lost his wife. *Is he a good father? Had he been a good husband? Is he kind and gentle or rough and unforgiving like this land?*

She pictured Karl waiting on the porch of his roomy home with his boys lined up on the steps. The house's white paint gleamed in the sun, and flowers surrounded the gate, painting a welcoming picture. The boys would politely greet her as their new mother. Karl would be overjoyed that she had finally arrived.

The ferry's piercing whistle startled Inge out of her reverie. She scolded herself. *Nei. I expect too much.* But it was difficult to not wonder about the future. The boat slowed and began turning. *I can't be there already. I need more time to... to figure out how to approach Karl and introduce myself.*

As the boat gently slid up the planks that served as a dock, Inge stared at her surroundings, her feet nailed to the deck.

"Hey, lady! Lady!" a crewman yelled. His gruff voice startled her. "You gotta get off *da* boat now." He pointed to the shore.

Inge picked up her bags and tugged at her trunk. After watching her struggle for a moment, the man threw up his hands, grabbed her trunk, slung it over his shoulder, and headed up the gangway. Inge picked up her small bags and stumbled up the bank behind him. Once on shore, he dropped her trunk in the dirt and marched off.

Inge surveyed her surroundings. It was a significant walk to the businesses in the center of town, most of which were ensconced in single-story structures and lacked paint. Horses were tethered to hitching posts along the dirt street. The boardwalks were empty. Where were the people?

Unable to manage the trunk, she left it on the shore and approached the nearest building. Stepping inside the open front door, she welcomed the cooler air. As her eyes adjusted to the dimness, she noted shelves lined with food tins, sacks, tools, and household items. The sharp smell of vinegar pickles tickled her nose.

"Can I help you find something?" A smartly dressed woman closed in on her. "I said, can I help you?"

"I... I... find... " Inge struggled to remember the English she had learned. "I... "

"Well, spit it out. I can't help you if you don't tell me what you want." The woman's nose wrinkled as she took in Inge's bedraggled appearance.

Inge stepped back. The more she struggled to speak, the louder the woman became.

"Samuel, I need you. There is another of *those people* who don't speak English. You take care of her." The woman spun on her heel and left Inge pressed against the counter.

Tears brightened Inge's eyes. *I may not understand the words, but her attitude is plain.*

A man's soft voice came from the other direction. He was trying the guttural sounds of a language Inge didn't recognize. She shook her head. Trying again, he switched to Norwegian.

"What can I do for you?"

"You speak Norwegian. Oh, thank You, God." Inge clutched his hands.

"Yes, I do. It's helpful in my business to speak a little bit of several languages. And, fortunately, I seem to have a gift for that. It makes doing business much easier. My name is Sam."

Inge dropped his hands as if they were hot rocks and stepped away from the counter. "Pardon me. I am Inge Olafson. I need to know how to get to Karl Johannson's place with my trunk. Is it far?"

"Well, it's too far to carry a trunk, that's for sure. Why don't we get it, and I can store it for you?" Sam ushered her out the door toward the dock.

Inge could see the questions glinting in Sam's eyes. Nobody needed to know why she was here... not yet. The news would spread fast enough.

After placing her trunk in the back room, Sam provided directions to the Johannson's place. She would need to head west on the road next to the river for about five miles until she came to a large cottonwood tree. From there, she would follow the lane north to the homestead.

Following the road out of town, the rutted, weed-infested trail made walking difficult. Brambles grabbed at her, tangling her feet. Clouds of dust rose from each step, turning her skirt a dull gray. The road closely paralleled the river, and often sunny reflections glinted through the leafy foliage. A breeze from the water occasionally wafted by, but it only teased her with its damp smell.

Lightheaded, she considered stopping. *I haven't eaten since last night,* she realized. This was the longest five miles she had ever walked.

Sweat streamed down her cheeks, and she stumbled, dropping her bags. *I can't go any further.*

How would she ever find the right large cottonwood tree? They were all towering and thick as washtubs at the base. Tripping, she braced herself against the nearest one. Her skin was on fire, and her lungs burned. Even the shade of the immense cottonwoods didn't lessen the heat.

Just for a few minutes, she told herself. *I'll rest for just a few minutes.* The river beckoned until she could no longer resist. Finding a place where she could access the water, Inge clamored down the steep riverbank and found herself on a narrow shoreline. She took off her shoes and immersed her feet in the cool water. Leaning back against a shaded fallen tree, she soaked in the welcoming damp sand and cool breeze. It felt so very good. Relaxing, she closed her eyes.

Oi da! I fell asleep. She jerked her feet from the water and stared at her skirt. It was soaked past her knees and had become a muddy mess. Getting her stockings on was impossible, so she slipped her bare feet into her shoes and stuffed the stockings in her pocket. The crumbling wall of dirt hadn't looked insurmountable when she slid down it. But now, each time she grasped a protruding branch or root, a shower of loose dirt cascaded down onto her. Slowly working her way up, she finally slithered over the top on her belly, collapsing on the edge of the bank and gasping for breath. She stood and examined her clothing, then shook her head to rid her hair of twigs and dirt. After brushing some of the dirt from her dress, she scooped up her bags and rushed back to the road.

Just down the trail, Inge spotted *the* cottonwood tree. It was massive, and it towered over all the others, with a trunk the size of a wagon wheel. "I guess I needn't have worried about finding the tree," she muttered. A narrow, uneven lane forked to the right.

She wiped her face with the edge of her skirt. *How can I present myself to Karl like this?* Just around a bend in the road, she glimpsed a two-story barn, a couple of small outbuildings, and a low squat house consisting of logs and those strange-looking mud bricks. A lone cow near the barn mooed a greeting, or perhaps she just needed milking.

Suddenly, the weight of her decision, the long trip, and her ragtag appearance felt heavier with each step forward. *I can't do this.* Within sight of her future, Inge strained to hear from God. There was no reassuring voice, and no calming thought came to her. God seemed absent from this place. Inge slowed her pace even more as she neared the house. Insects hummed in her face, the setting sun hit her eyes, and her faith faded with each step. What she sought—peace from God—was not to be found.

Approaching the door, loud voices from the inside filtered to her ears. A woman's high-pitched tone rose above the rest. *Maybe this isn't a good time.* As she raised her hand to knock, the door flew open. The force knocked Inge backward off the porch, slamming her to the ground. Engulfed in a cloud of suffocating dust, she gasped for air, but her lungs would not fill. Desperate to draw a breath, she struggled against the hand under her head. Her eyes burned from the layer of grime that had settled on her face. When the air finally entered her lungs, she coughed uncontrollably. Tears poured down her face as she fought to catch her breath. Someone was pounding on her back. Unable to speak, she tried to move away, but the strong hands refused to let go and instead pulled her to her feet. The woman's frenzied chatter swirled around Inge's head. Four boys stared at her from the steps, their mouths agape.

"What's all the ruckus about? Maggie, will you quit yelling..." The voice came from inside the house. Then Inge saw him standing in the doorway, wearing a hat pulled low on his head that concealed much of his weathered face. The short, barrel-chested man stared at her.

Wheezing, Inge extended her hand. "I am Inge Olafson. You were expecting me?"

The man studied her for a few moments, then stepped off the porch, brushed past her, and strode across the yard.

CHAPTER 9

INGE

After thrashing in bed for most of the night before falling into a restless sleep, Inge woke exhausted and more confused than ever. The woman had taken her to a small log cabin a short distance away, jabbering the entire time in a language Inge didn't understand. The constant onslaught of words pelted her like a hailstorm.

Now her head swam with questions. What happened yesterday? Was that Karl and the boys? Who was the woman? Had he married someone else?

The woman had brought her a pan of warm water and towels. Grateful, Inge sponged herself down. There wasn't much help for her hair. A good brushing would have to do. Inge had nearly finished dressing when the woman appeared at the door with a cup of coffee. She waved her hand toward the table. Bread and jam had been laid out for breakfast. Inge tried to smile as the chatter overwhelmed her.

"Maggie." The woman pointed at herself.

"Ja, Maggie," Inge repeated. "Inge Olafson."

Inge recognized a few words, but even with hand gestures, she had no idea what Maggie was saying. Someone here had to speak Norwegian. Karl was from home, so he must speak the language. But he didn't want to talk with her yesterday. Had that even been Karl? Utterly confused by the man's reaction, she acknowledged she had been an eyesore, but it couldn't have been that bad. Surely, he was expecting her. He had written for her to come. How could he just walk off and leave her standing there?

There was a knock at the door. Maggie jumped to answer it, welcoming a tall, slender man. He respectfully removed his hat and ducked slightly to enter. Maggie babbled, her expressive hands drawing pictures in the air. He held up his hand, and she reluctantly quieted.

He nodded to the women.

Maggie began talking once again. Speaking softly, the man told her something that clearly puzzled her.

She backed up and looked questioningly at him before placing the coffee pot and a cup on the table. She lingered at his elbow until he finally shooed her toward the door. She stood in the doorway, uncertainty clouding her face.

Inge watched their interaction. Who was this man? Was this Karl? Maybe the other man left because he really wasn't expecting her. Had she gotten the wrong house?

Seating himself, he slipped into his native Norwegian. "Miss Olafson, I would like to welcome you to Taylor's Landing. My name is Tim Anderson. I am the pastor and schoolteacher in this area."

Inge slumped back into the chair, placing her shaking hand over her heart. At last, someone she could talk to.

The pastor continued, "I understand you had a very interesting day yesterday. I dare say you were a shock to Karl. Karl is... how should I put this? Let's just say he doesn't react well to surprises, and you were a bit of a surprise. Karl finally admitted he had written to you, but since he never heard back, he assumed you weren't coming."

Tears streamed from Inge's eyes. "I... don't know what to do." She covered her face with her hands. Feeling a touch on her shoulder, she looked up and saw that he was offering her a handkerchief. She drew in several deep breaths. "Did I misunderstand? I have the letter. I can show you. And I replied that I was coming."

"Well, there might have been some confusion on both your parts. For one thing, Karl never got your reply." He reached out and took Inge's hands. "Maggie says you can stay here, for the time being. By the way, Maggie is Karl's sister-in-law. She has been a great help with the children after his wife's passing last year."

"What did Karl say... about me?" Inge hiccupped.

"Not a lot. I plan to visit with him once I leave here." He studied her face. "May I ask... did Karl ask for your hand?"

"Ja. I guess." Inge chewed on her bottom lip, avoiding his eyes. "Well, I thought he did."

"There is no rush to decide anything." He leaned back in his chair. "Take some time to get to know Karl and the children. Are you willing to stay and see if things work out?"

Inge nodded.

"Shall we pray?" He lowered his head. "Father, please make things clear to Inge and Karl. Guide them, Lord, and whatever comes to pass, may it bring glory and honor to Your name. Amen." Rising from his seat, he offered Inge his hand, clasping hers warmly. "I have enjoyed meeting you."

Opening the door, he turned and said, "Inge, why don't you consider coming to school? I always need help, and you could learn English at the same time. I often have parents come and learn along with their children."

Inge said nothing.

"Well, think about it. We'll talk later."

As he closed the door, she wanted desperately to call him back to help her sort this out.

Oh, God, what have I done?

CHAPTER 10

INGE

Over a week had passed, and since Inge was unable to question Maggie about the circumstances, she spent much of her time gazing down the path toward Karl's home, hoping for a glimpse of the children or their father. Occasionally, she would see someone in the distance or hear the children playing, but no one came to see her. When she tried to communicate her concern to Maggie, all she got was a pat on the hand.

Maggie was puzzling. Much shorter than Inge, she was slightly plump but strong and solid. Aside from her constant talking, she was interesting in other ways. An unruly mass of flaming red hair escaped any attempt to confine them in a bun. Inge rather liked the way the curls framed her soft, round face. The freckles that cascaded over Maggie's pert nose added a delightful touch to her rosy cheeks. Emerald eyes flashed when she was excited or angry. However, Inge found her eruptive personality mystifying. Her temper could flair at the drop of a hat, and just as quickly, it was over as if nothing had happened. How could anyone be that changeable?

Several times Inge tried to write to her family. Pride would not allow her to reveal her predicament. She refused to worry them. Lying was out, so it seemed better to say nothing at all. Maybe soon, when it all worked out, she would explain to her parents. But right now, she had to make sense of it herself.

WITHIN A WEEK, Inge settled into a routine of helping with the cooking, laundry, and preserving the garden produce. Her one respite from the stifling heat was the freshwater spring in the coulee behind the barn. Once Maggie had shown her where it was, it became Inge's haven at the end of the hot August days. Several times in the last week, she had headed for the spring just before dark. The water entering the pool was icy cold, but the far edges of the pond had warmed in the heat of the day. Grassy banks lined the pool, and a thicket of wild plums created a natural screen for a private bathing area. Shedding her sweaty clothing and immersing herself in the tepid water eased the tension that bound her. With the advent of darkness, the frogs broke the silence with a chorus of songs. Even the air smelled different, somehow fresher. This place was nothing like Norway, with its staggering mountains and green land, but the spring brought a small taste of home to her lonely soul.

Inge's hands flailed on the surface of the pond sending water droplets high into the air.

Frustration tore at her like a hook in a struggling fish. *Lord, I'm so confused.* While her circumstances worried her, the spiritual emptiness inside crushed her. The safety and security of God's arms seemed far away. Surely God was here in this forsaken place. He had to be.

Looking up, she immersed herself in a night sky so thick with stars you could walk into them. *I had a plan. I thought I would have a husband, wonderful children, and a comfortable home.* It never occurred to her that God's plan might come with some variations.

Lord, forgive me. Make the way clear for me to follow Your way instead of mine.

With that said, Inge dried herself and headed back to the cabin. The faintest whisper of peace wrapped gently around her shoulders. God would take care of her, of that she was sure. But what was the next step?

Entering the kitchen, Inge found Maggie still awake, darning socks by the lamp light. With a few words and many signs, she announced, "Going to school."

CHAPTER 11

INGE

On Sunday, a little over two weeks after arriving, Inge dressed in a dark skirt and white blouse and joined Maggie as she walked to church. Others joined them along the mile-long trail. Some nodded politely while others openly stared at her. Inge lowered her head and trudged forward, avoiding the curious looks. The worshippers filed into the schoolhouse that also served as a church for the Sunday services. Seating herself in the back, Inge observed the churchgoers as they entered. Most were couples with young families, but there were also a few women who were alone with children. The youngsters bounced in their seats, unable to settle down. Parents gave scathing looks or whispered through clenched teeth to bring order to their broods. Inge covered her mouth to hide a smile as a little boy near her pulled the pigtails of the girl in front of him. His mother reached behind him and gave his ear a twist.

The service began with a song. The tune was unfamiliar, but Inge's musical gift allowed her to hum along. *Where was Karl and the boys?* She had assumed he would be a church-going man, but now she wondered. Her mind drifted during the sermon in English. *This is not what I envisioned.* She bowed her head. The sound of shuffling along benches brought Inge back to the present. People were leaving. The service was over. A few people spoke to her. Not understanding, she simply nodded and smiled. Quietly standing next to Maggie, she listened to the conversation that flowed around her. *Will I ever understand what people are saying?*

"*Velkommen.*" A woman smiled at her. The rest of the greeting in English was lost on Inge but being welcomed in her native tongue lifted her heart as she shook the offered hand.

Inge eased her way toward the pastor who stood just outside the door talking to the crowd. "Ah, Inge, how are you doing?" he asked in Norwegian.

Shyly, she shook his hand. "I'm fine."

"Why don't you have a seat inside? Once I have greeted everyone, we can take a moment to talk."

She nodded and re-entered the building. The school had been converted for Sunday services by adding a beautifully crafted wood pulpit at the front. Parishioners had seated themselves at the desks or on benches during worship. The chalkboard had been wiped clean, and the books and slates sat neatly on shelves to the side of the teacher's desk. The sunlight flooding the room created a cheerful space for the schoolchildren. A potbellied stove in the back would provide heat once the weather turned cold. Inge leafed through the pages of a book left on the desk. Other than her Bible, she had nothing to read. And she missed her music. She hadn't realized how much until this morning. There was an ache in her hands to run up and down a keyboard once again.

"So, Inge, how are you... really?" She turned and encountered pale blue eyes filled with concern. Being able to talk to someone lightened the weight she carried. A bright smile filled her face. Taking her hand, the pastor said, "I talked with Karl this week. He thinks that the two of you need time to get to know each other." He led her to a chair near the desk.

Her body stiffened and the smile disappeared. "Pastor Anderson..."

"Please call me Pastor Tim."

"Pastor Tim." She began again, "How can we get to know each other when he doesn't even come to see me? And I have not seen the boys since I arrived. Maggie talks all the time, and I don't know what she's saying. I have no one to talk to, and I don't know what God wants me to do..." Her voice cracked. "And Karl and the boys were not in church."

"I'm sorry. I'm sure this is difficult." Pastor Tim dropped his head and stared at the desktop for a moment. "Inge," he said, looking at her. "Karl is a good man. I have no doubt that he loves his boys, and I know losing his wife nearly killed him."

"I want to be a mother to the boys. I dreamed of it," Inge said. "They're the reason I came to America, along with being a wife."

"Give it time. Pray and let God lead you." Pastor Tim rose to his feet.

Inge jumped up. "I want to come to school."

He beamed. "That's wonderful. School starts in two weeks. However, there is much preparation to be done before we open. If you would like to help with that, I would be grateful for extra hands. Come over most any afternoon and we can begin lessons."

THE NEXT COUPLE of weeks were filled with preserving fruits and vegetables. Even though the work was hard, Inge found satisfaction in being useful. One afternoon in the middle of cutting corn from a cob, she spied a small face peaking in the door.

"Pa said to come here," the boy said tentatively. Around four years of age, he was hardly bigger than a button. With unkempt blond hair, light blue eyes, and a dirty face, he shyly rubbed his bare feet on the floor.

Putting down her knife, Inge kneeled to face the boy. "*Hallo.*"

"Hello," he mumbled.

"Inge," she said pointing to herself.

"I know who you are. You're my new Ma. Pa told us we might have a new Ma." The boy struggled in broken Norwegian.

"Your name?" She pointed at the boy.

"Billy," he said as he settled himself on a chair at the end of the table.

He studied Inge with puzzled eyes. "You don't look nothin' like Ma. How can you be my Ma when you don't even look like her?"

She wiped her hands on her apron and pulled a cookie from the jar on the cupboard. A wide smile split the boy's face as he reached for it. She longed to reach out and tousle his hair and wipe the smudge from his cheek. *Someday I hope to be your mother.*

CHAPTER 12

KARL

Karl sat in a rocker on the porch, deep in thought as the last of the evening's light faded away. The setting sun left a rosy glow on the western horizon. The moon was up, but the sky was not dark enough to reveal stars. It was the only time of day when he had a few minutes to rest and think. With harvest here, the work was never-ending, and, if he admitted it, he relished being preoccupied with something besides Inge. It was soon the first of September. She had been here a month. What was he going to do?

Oh, Sigrid. How could you leave me? The pain nearly caused him to double over as he thought of his wife. She had been his life, and God had seen fit to take her. It wasn't right. She should not have died. Other people survived the influenza, less deserving people. He had not attended church since Sigrid's death, nor had he been receptive to visits from the pastor or the neighbors who tried to comfort him.

He ran his hand through his sparse hair. What had possessed him to answer Inge's letter? *Was I that lonely or wallowing in self-pity?* Since he heard nothing in return, he assumed she changed her mind. Then one day she was on his doorstep. He didn't want to marry again. Memories of Sigrid, that's all he needed.

Pastor Tim told him to take some time to get acquainted with Inge, but he couldn't make himself walk over to Maggie's house and... and what? Did he think God would provide another Sigrid? Maybe he did. He had his brother ask about Alice Tilson, probably because she reminded him of Sigrid. Maybe it would be better if a new wife was different.

Sigrid had been small and a little plump. Karl used to pick her up and twirl her around in his arms until she giggled helplessly. There was always a red ribbon in her dark curls, and he loved to tug at it to annoy her. She delighted in teasing him. Whenever she was hiding something, that brief twitch in the corner of her mouth gave her away. He went along with her pranks because he loved seeing her dissolve with laughter, like the time she had put burrs in his boots. She nearly rolled on the floor when she saw his socks full of stickers. He winced as the memories brought both comfort and pain. The boys missed their mother, too, but his loss was so raw that he found it difficult to respond to their sorrow.

Inge, well, Inge certainly wasn't Sigrid. She was tall and rail thin, almost bony-looking. Her face lacked the softness that was Sigrid's trademark. She... he didn't know... she just wasn't right. However, on the practical side, he needed someone to care for the house and children. He couldn't rely on Maggie forever. Perhaps this was an opportunity? Yes, it could be. Maybe he should hire her as a housekeeper. She would need money, and he needed help. He would be able to at least keep part of his commitment.

"That's it." Relief flooded over him. He didn't have to marry her, but he could provide employment. "Yes, that's what I'll do. Tomorrow, I will speak to her."

CHAPTER 13

INGE

The next morning, as Inge was in the middle of canning beans, Karl showed up on the doorstep. Startled when he cleared his throat, she spun to face him. Her hand flew to her breast as her heart jumped in irregular beats. Brushing her limp hair from her face, she tugged at her damp dress and adjusted her dirty apron. Sweat dribbled down her brow. *Oh, nei, I look like somebody's housemaid.* "*God morgen,*" she stammered.

He stood in the doorway, hat in hand, his head hanging so low it was hard to discern his features. 'Forlorn' was the only word that came to her mind. Not nearly as tall as Inge, he had a broad chest and narrow hips. His hair was thinning, and he had a tan line where his hat rested on his head.

"Is Maggie around?" Karl asked in Norwegian.

"*Nei.* She's in the garden."

"I see you're busy," he mumbled. "Could I come by this evening, and we can talk?"

Inge nodded.

"After supper then?" He put on his hat and disappeared in an instant.

He was finally coming to talk to her, but he didn't seem very excited about doing it. *He never even looked at me.* Looking down at her dirty dress and running her fingers through her damp hair, she wondered how Karl always managed to see her at her worst. *Tonight, I will have to make the best impression I can. I'll put on the new dress my mother made for me. Ja, I will wear the new blue one.*

"What's the matter?" Inge was still standing there when Maggie returned with another large pan of beans.

"Karl..." Inge tried to find the words to tell Maggie that Karl was coming to see her. "Come tonight."

"Karl's coming to see yeh then? 'Bout time he decided to do something." She plopped the beans in her lap and began snapping them. "We'll finish up here and get yeh all fancied up for tonight. I thought he'd never get around to talking to yeh." She went on and on.

While most of the words went over her head, Inge understood the excitement in Maggie's voice. *This is a good thing. But what will we talk about? Maybe my trip? Or the boys? I want to know about the boys.* Her mind filled with a thousand questions.

By evening, the ceaseless wind had sucked every drop of moisture out of Inge's body. Even a trip to the spring hadn't helped. By the time she worked her way into her new dress, she felt wilted again. She pulled her hair to the top of her head and fastened it with tortoiseshell combs. Looking in the small mirror that Maggie provided, Inge gasped at the woman who stared back. A sunburned face, a peeling nose, and lips that looked like crinkled paper. She rubbed her nose, picking at it until it was nearly raw. *I look like a half-scaled fish. I can't... I just can't. Not tonight.*

"Inge?" The door to her room cracked slightly. "Karl's here," Maggie said.

Inge looked up. She waved Maggie off. "*Nie.*" She threw herself on the bed and buried her red, peeling face in the pillow. *I don't want him to see me looking like this.* "Nei, nei!"

CHAPTER 14

KARL

"Women," Karl muttered as he stood on the steps after Maggie told him Inge refused to come out of her room. *I thought this was what I was supposed to do... get acquainted.* He walked down the path toward his house. Stopping short of the steps, he hurled his hat across the full length of the porch, bouncing it off the railing. How could he offer her a job if she wouldn't even speak to him? Karl stopped. *Does she think I'm going to marry her? Of course, she does. That's what she came here to do.* He mounted the steps and plunged himself into the old wooden rocker. *How did I get myself into this mess?* He slammed his hands on the arms of the chair.

Why did I write to her, and what did I say that made her think I wanted a wife? The chair creaked in protest as he leaned back. Thoughts swirled through his head. Her letter had arrived on Sigrid's birthday. His pain had been so deep he couldn't face his family that day, so he had secluded himself in a small cove on the river. Peace and solitude were what he wanted, but he didn't find them there. Somehow the quiet allowed his memories to gush like water from a breached dam. He couldn't get away. There was nowhere to escape from those last moments of her life. The fever had spiked until her skin had an unnatural redness. Each breath had been a struggle, rattling in her chest and never bringing the air she needed. Occasionally her eyelids fluttered. He talked to her but doubted she heard what he said. He told her over and over that he loved her. That he couldn't go on without her. What would he do alone? How would he raise the boys? He prayed for a miracle.

Why had she died? His beloved Sigrid should have been at his side. They should have grown old together. She always wanted another baby, a girl after four boys. She had said she wanted to raise a beautiful daughter. Sometimes they even talked about having grandchildren. Life was going to be filled with joy and laughter. It was going to be good.

The flu had run throughout the small community. So many had gotten sick. And Sigrid, as always, played nursemaid to those who were ailing. It was part of her inner being to help others. Taking that from her would have been like cutting off her limbs. God had given her a servant's heart. Karl had worried about her but knew she would help even if he forbade it. Many of those who died were the elderly or sick, but not his Sigrid. She was strong and healthy.

When the flu seemed to have run its course, she became listless and tired. Then the fever rose so high she became delirious. First, it was a small cough, then it blossomed into convulsive hacking that caused her to double over. He was relieved when it finally eased until he realized that she was slipping away from him. He prayed, he bargained with God, and he begged for her life. She became more still until her breath was a whisper, and then it stopped. For the first time in weeks, she looked peaceful. He couldn't even cry. He wanted to howl and break things, but he simply sat there holding her hand until it was cold.

Karl wiped his hand across his face and was surprised to find it wet with tears. After all these months, now he cried. Grief was a strange thing. Perhaps that day, the day Inge's letter arrived, he had been trying to bury his pain by thinking it was time to move on. No, he could never move on, and he could never replace Sigrid with another woman. What had he told Inge in his letter? Surely, he wouldn't have asked her to marry him, would he? Had his mind been so numbed that he made an offer he couldn't possibly fulfill?

Whatever he had done, she was here. Yesterday it had seemed plausible to ask her to be his housekeeper and take care of the boys. Today he realized that she would not be willing to accept that. She was hoping for a husband. But all he could offer her right now was a job. What if she refused? Then what would he do?

CHAPTER 15

INGE

Long before the sun rose the next day, Inge lay awake, staring at the ceiling. She had been thinking, praying, and condemning herself for reacting the way she did the night before.

Lord, I wanted to talk to Karl, but when given a chance, I hid. Why? Did I hide because I looked awful, or do I have reservations about marrying him?

She forced herself out of bed. *How can I face Karl after last night?* Blinking, she held back the tears. "Oh, *Mor*, I miss you so much. I need your wisdom." She leaned against the bedpost as her memories filled her with homesickness.

By the time Inge sought her first cup of coffee, Maggie was in the kitchen up to her elbows in bread dough. Inge knew the threshing crew would arrive today, which meant massive amounts of food would have to be prepared to feed ten to fifteen men. How would they ever manage?

Wagons rolled into the yard mid-morning. Before anyone knocked, Maggie yelled, "Come on in." Three women entered, carrying baskets and boxes. Setting them on the table, they pulled out hams, vegetables, and pies. Relief poured through Inge as she realized they were there to help. It was not so different from how work was shared in her homeland.

Maggie pointed at a sack of potatoes, and Inge gathered a knife and pots and began peeling. Left out of the bantering between the other women, Inge retreated to the background. Fully aware of the sidelong glances, she was sure they were talking about her. *I must learn some English... soon.*

A large woman with dark hair and deep brown eyes tugged on Inge's arm. She picked up the sack and indicated that Inge should bring the pots. She led Inge down the path, approaching Karl's house.

"My name is Vada. Vada Slocum. You must be Inge," she said in slightly accented English.

"Ja, Inge," Inge said. She glanced at the woman and noted that she was tall, even in bare feet. Heavy with an ill-fitting dress and dirty apron, she didn't seem to fit with the others.

As she entered Karl's house, Inge absorbed every detail. The large kitchen accommodated a long table with benches. *This is the table I saw in my dream!* A cookstove took up the far corner surrounded by several black cast iron pans hanging on the wall. Cupboards with bins resided between the window and the wood box. Near the door was a sink with a pump. The room was cheery and comfortable, with colorful red curtains gracing the tops of the two windows. Across from the table was a door leading to the parlor. *What a wonderful home for a family.*

Vada spoke softly and slowly, and somehow Inge understood some of what she said. After stoking the stove, they finished peeling the potatoes and put the pots on to boil. They picked the last of the garden vegetables and then prepared them for the midday meal. Last, they set the table with mismatched dishes and utensils, cramming in as many settings as possible.

Small talk flowed between the two women despite the language barrier. The easy conversation reminded Inge of her mother. Not that Vada looked like her *mor*, but a familiar gentle spirit filled her. For the first time since she had arrived, Inge felt at ease.

"Do you read?" Vada asked, holding her hands like an open book. "I want to read."

Inge didn't know what to say. She assumed most people could read. "School." Inge pointed in the direction of the schoolhouse.

Vada glanced down and shook her head. "Can't. No school." Placing her hand over her heart, she said, "I know God here, but I long to read His word." She looked at Inge. Her dark eyes begged for understanding.

Inge clasped her hands in a prayerful stance. "Pray. You learn."

AT NOON the rest of the women arrived at Karl's house with bowls, platters, and pots. The table creaked with the weight of the food. After the last of the crew washed up in the trough by the well, they took their seats and silently filled their plates. The food disappeared before the platters made it to the other side of the table. Bowls were refilled over and over. Once the men were satisfied, the women passed pies, and each man helped himself to a large slab of dessert. Then the crew relaxed and planned their afternoon's work over the last cup of coffee.

Karl had not even glanced her way. But then she had not gone out of her way to interact with him either. Inge wasn't sure if the men were aware of her relationship with Karl. They seemed focused intently on the harvest.

Inge brought out the two dishpans and poured hot water into both. With so many hands, it wasn't long before things were back in order. With the work done, the women each took a plate and helped themselves to the remaining food. Despite the hard work, hearts were light, and the room filled with laughter. Inge picked up tidbits of what was being discussed. Softly touching her shoulder, Vada led them to the porch. Inge leaned back in the rocker, grateful to rest for a moment.

"Children?" Vada asked, pretending to rock a baby.

"*Nei*. You?"

"Five. The two boys are helping in the fields and the girls are at home."

Inge nodded. How would she ever explain her circumstances to Vada?

"Where... live?" Inge wanted to know.

Vada shrugged, gesturing in the general direction of the river. "You?"

"Maggie." She pointed toward the cabin.

"Here. You will live here one day." Vada waved her hand over the house. "God told me."

THE LONG DAY of feeding harvesters had taken a toll on Inge. A soak in the spring was tempting, but the bed seemed more inviting. Intending to lie down for just a moment, she drifted into an exhausted sleep that lasted the night. The clamor of machinery woke her early the next morning. The crew was moving on to the next farm. She stared out the window at the steam engine pulling the thresher. The monstrous beast belched black smoke into the air and clawed its way slowly over the prairie. The sharp teeth on the metal wheels dug deep into the sod, leaving a broken, torn path behind it.

It was another day of cooking, this time at a different place. Inge dragged herself out of bed. *Lord, strengthen me. Get me through one more day.* After brushing the wrinkles out of the dress she'd slept in and changing her apron, she joined Maggie in the kitchen and began peeling apples and filling piecrusts. Little Billy wriggled in his seat at the end of the table. Occasionally, Inge would offer him a slice, which he accepted with a big grin. *He is every inch a little boy. He is just a little boy without a mother, but I need him as much as he needs me.*

Nearing the noon hour, Karl's next youngest son arrived at the door with the wagon. Maggie loaded the food into baskets and carefully packed them in the bed. Climbing up on the seat, she took the reins. "Make sure the food doesn't bounce all over the place," she yelled over her shoulder. Billy had the privilege of sitting on the seat with Maggie while Inge and the older boy sat at the end of the wagon bed, dangling their feet over the edge.

Inge offered her hand. "Inge," she said.

"Arnie. Well, it's Arnold but everyone calls me Arnie," he responded, barely touching her fingers. He dropped his head and focused on his bare feet as they caught the tops of the tall grass.

Inge studied the boy's profile. One day soon he would grow into his gangly arms and legs. His straw-colored hair had just enough curl to make it cling to his face, his eyes were a clear blue, and his smile revealed slightly protruding teeth. Given time, he'd probably grow into them too.

"Good... meet, Arnie," Inge said, struggling with English. "How old?"

"I's ten, goin' on eleven in December. Ma used to say I was her best Christmas present, seeing as how I was born on Christmas Eve."

"Birthday!" Inge exclaimed. "Same as Jesus."

He nodded. "It's nice all right, but sometimes people forget with all the Christmas stuff going on."

"Birthdays... special." Inge lapsed into Norwegian as she tried to share how her parents retold the story of her birth each year.

Arnie listened intently. It was clear from the expression on his face that he'd picked up some of the language from his parents. "That sounds really nice." They sat in silence for a while, until the boy decided to speak again. "Why did you come here?"

Inge's mind raced. Why had she come here? The answer seemed so simple when she began this trek, but now she wasn't sure she had an answer.

"In Norway, I pray for family," she said. "Your father answered the letter. I come and... and... be family."

"Oh," he said. "You gonna marry my Pa?"

Inge chewed on her bottom lip. Was she going to marry his father?

A bump sent the food sliding. They grabbed the baskets to keep them upright. Inge slid forward. Holding the food in place, she wondered if she even wanted to marry at this point.

"We're almost there," Maggie said. In the distance, Inge saw a sod brick shelter with grass growing on the roof, making it almost indistinguishable from the prairie surrounding it. Pulling up in front of the building, Maggie hollered a greeting. Four girls ran out of the house, followed by a tall, lean woman with graying hair and weathered skin.

"Inge, yeh remember Hulda Hobbs. She helped at our place."

Inge nodded.

Parking the wagon near the house, Arnie unhitched and tethered the team to the wagon wheel. He removed the wagon's sideboards to create a table by laying the boards across two sawbucks. Once done, they transferred the food from the wagon to the makeshift table.

Inge scanned the horizon. There was nothing here but this small hovel partially set in the side of the hill, not a tree, not another building. There was nothing but miles and miles of grass in all directions. Where were the fields and the crew?

As more people arrived with food, Inge entered the house to help. In the dimness, Inge scanned the single room. It was furnished with two beds on one end, a table with benches, and a stove on the other. The only light, other than the door, came from a small window covered with oiled paper instead of glass. Hard-packed dirt served as flooring. The confined space smothered her. *I can't breathe.* Grabbing a pot of venison stew, Inge retreated outside. She exhaled, releasing her panic. *I could not live like this. The isolation is terrifying, and the cramped, dark house is suffocating. Thank You, Lord, that Karl has a decent home.*

The crew wandered up from behind a small hill, dragging their feet. Most filled their plates without speaking or washing up. They sat on the ground and ate their meal. After eating, most of the men slouched against the wall. Inge carried the large, blackened coffee pot to each man and refilled his cup. Like the others, Karl didn't even bother to look up when she offered more coffee. *I wish he would look at me. I want to make up for refusing to see him.*

Inge looked up as a gust of wind billowed her skirt. She could see a low-lying bank of deep purple clouds filling the horizon. Reluctantly the men rose and headed toward the fields. Despite their exhaustion, Inge could sense their determination to get the grain harvested before the storm hit.

The limited water supply made cleanup a challenge for the women. The Hobbs hauled barrels of water from the river for household use, and they used it sparingly without wasting a drop. *How can they survive like this with no water? I don't even see an outhouse.*

On the ride home, Inge tried to question Maggie about Vada. She looked forward to spending more time with the woman. Why wasn't she there today? "Vada," she said.

"She wouldn't be welcome," Maggie said.

"Why not? Helped... Karl's."

"Hulda thinks them Slocums are river riffraff. Doesn't want them around her place."

"River riffraff?"

"Folks that live by the river, poor folks. Live from hand to mouth. Don't have no desire to better themselves. Most are given to drink. Good, God-fearing folks don't associate with them."

Inge understood most of what Maggie said, and she mulled over the information. Some people are... are what? Less than others? *It wasn't like Hulda lived in a palace. Who was she to judge?*

They pulled into the yard and unloaded the wagon. Hot, tired, and dirty, Inge headed for the spring. After a thorough scrubbing, she leaned back, her head against the grassy bank. The cool air created goosebumps on her exposed, wet skin. She shivered and submerged, reluctant to leave this sanctuary. Gratitude filled her.

Lord, this place is a gift, my haven from the world. Here I can cast my cares at Your feet and soak in Your presence.

Her body floated to the surface. She hung there, suspended by the water.

Thank You for my chance to talk with Arnie today. I hope he and I will be friends. Lord, I don't understand about Vada. She's one of Yours, isn't she? She loves You. Of that, I'm sure. So why is she shunned?

What is riffraff anyway?

It was dark by the time Inge followed the path back to the cabin. The lamp glowed softly on the table, but Maggie was already asleep. Inge blew out the flame and stretched out on her bed. As tired as she was, her mind swirled in ever-widening circles. *What if Karl doesn't marry me? Could I end up like Vada? Am I riffraff too?*

CHAPTER 16

INGE

Inge's hands gripped the wagon seat to prevent being thrown off as Maggie drove down the rutted road toward Taylor's Landing. This was her first visit to town since she arrived a little over three months ago. Where had the time gone? Now that it was October, they needed to stock up on supplies for winter, such as coffee and spices, as well as cloth for new clothing.

After dropping several sacks of wheat at the mill to be ground into flour, Maggie parked in front of the store and tied the team to the railing. Dodd's Mercantile was much as Inge remembered. A large counter filled one end of the room, while the shelves lining the walls overflowed with cans, bottles, and tools. To her right, a table with bolts of plain wool and cotton caught her eye, especially the roll of blue calico. Barrels of dried fruits, salted meats, and pickles lined the doorway. The mixture of vinegar, spices, and leather gave the store an interesting and pleasant odor. Inge inhaled and tried to sort out the smells.

A jarring voice behind her asked, "Can I help you?"

Inge spun around to face the same woman she had met when she first arrived. She opened her mouth, but words failed her. Taking a step back, she tried to remember her limited English. The woman's brown hair was pulled so tight into a bun that it seemed to stretch the skin on her pale face. Thin lips and a narrow nose gave her a sharp, irksome look. She was attired in a beautiful green dress, but it did not hide her angular body. Inge shook her head and retreated another step.

"Oh yes, you are one of those. Sam, you need to talk to this woman." With that, she turned to attend to someone else.

"Don't mind Clara." A quiet voice came over her shoulder. "She has little patience, I'm afraid." Sam smiled at her. "What can I do for you?"

Inge was again relieved that Sam spoke Norwegian. "I'm with Maggie. She's shopping for Karl Johannson."

"Oh, I remember you. What has it been, a month or two since you arrived? Your trunk is still here. Did you want to take it home with you today?"

Inge nodded. *My hope chest. For when I married.*

"How are things going out at Karl's?"

Inge shrugged. "Harvest is finished. We're getting ready for winter."

He nodded. "Can we expect a wedding soon?" His smile held a hint of mischief.

Startled, Inge ducked her head. Heat rushed up her neck. "I must go." *Everyone in town knows why I'm here, and they probably also know Karl isn't rushing to marry me.*

Once outside, she pulled in several sharp breaths to regain her composure before heading down the walk. She noted that a blacksmith shop, a hotel, a restaurant, and a saloon filled this street. The red, white, and blue pole in front of the barbershop lent a little color among the drab, gray buildings. As she passed the restaurant, Inge noticed people visiting as they enjoyed their meal. Staring at them, she hungered for a genuine conversation with anyone.

A claw-like hand grasped her shoulder. The cackling voice whispering in her ear raised the hair on the back of her neck. She whirled about to face a small man in filthy clothing. He cackled again. Was he laughing? Who was he? As she retreated, he pressed closer, his face inches from hers. With a slouched hat pulled down over his ears, she could barely see his milky blue eyes. His grin held only a few blackened teeth. He chortled and jabbered while backing Inge into the wall. Her fingers dug deeply into the slatted wood to keep from sliding into a pile on the boardwalk.

"Jingles," a voice called. "Leave the lady alone."

"Pastor Tim. Pastor Tim," Jingles rattled. "How is God today, Pastor?"

"God is always good, Jingles. You know that. Now why don't you go inside and tell Helen I said you could have a piece of pie on me?"

"Sure. Sure. Pie. I like pie. Like pretty ladies, too. She pretty, ain't she? Ya, ya. Pie." With that, Jingles shuffled into the restaurant.

"Inge, are you all right?"

Inge had never been so glad to see a familiar face in her life.

"Jingles is harmless," Pastor Tim said, speaking Norwegian. "He has his problems, and most everyone in town watches out for him. Rumor is that many years ago, he fell from a windmill and has been touched in the head ever since. The hotel provides him a little room in the back, and Helen makes sure he eats. But he does love to be around people. And I guess he can be a little frightening to someone who doesn't know him."

"Ja, I see." Releasing her grip on the wall, she brushed the small slivers from her hands.

"Walk with me, and I will show you around." He took hold of her elbow, and they continued down the street. Settling on a bench in front of the barbershop, she relaxed and relished their laughter and small talk.

"So, have you and Karl decided anything yet?" Pastor Tim asked.

"I don't know." Sheepishly, she related her reaction when Karl came to visit her. "When I saw him at harvest, he refused to even look at me. Is it me? Or maybe he just doesn't want to be married."

"I wish I could... could do something." Pastor Tim's eyes seemed troubled as he reached for her hand. "Karl should… he… You deserve to be treated better."

Acutely aware of the warmth of Pastor Tim's hand and the strength of his fingers enclosing hers, Inge pulled her hand free. She clutched her hands together as warmth rose in her body.

Pastor Tim cleared his throat and leaned back. Changing the subject, he said, "You can see what's here." She tried to follow his gestures and put a name to each place he pointed out. "Have you been to the mercantile?" he asked. "They have just about everything that you might need." Pastor Tim glanced at her face. "Oh. I see you have met our Clara."

She nodded. *More times than I wanted to.*

"Well, I wish I had a good explanation for people like Clara. I must remind myself that God loves all his children, and with Clara, I must remind myself often. Don't take her too seriously," he said. "There isn't much we can do except love her."

"But Sam is such a nice man." Inge covered her mouth, wishing she could take the words back.

"It's hard to figure, isn't it?" He was silent for a moment. "But love is a funny thing."

Inge wondered if Pastor Tim's thoughts included her. Love had nothing to do with this relationship she was contemplating. *I hope he doesn't judge me too harshly.*

"I had better be on my way," he said. "Here, let me help you up."

"Ja, Maggie is probably waiting for me. Oh, my—" Inge stumbled as she stepped from the boardwalk into the street. Looking down, she saw she had tripped over a bare foot. In the shadows, Inge saw a girl. Matted black hair covered her face. She wore a brown misshapen sack for a dress.

"What?" Inge bent over to see if she had hurt her. The girl scrambled backward on all fours, jumped to her feet, and ran off. Inge started to follow but felt Pastor Tim's hand on her shoulder.

"Let her go. She's a half-breed that lives down by the river."

"Shouldn't we help her? She's just a child."

"Her Pa drinks. He runs everyone off who tries to help. Her mother was a Sioux Indian. She died sometime back. The child pretty much runs wild." Breaking eye contact, he gazed at his feet. "Well, I had better get on with my errands," he said. "It was good to see you, Inge." With a wave of his hand, he turned up a side street and strode off.

Inge looked in the direction in which the child disappeared. Was she some of this riffraff too? Reluctantly, she turned and left. She crossed the street and followed the walk past a small shop with bonnets in the window. She stopped and admired the hats, some with colorful ribbons and one with beautiful blue-green feathers. She continued past the saloon, which was quiet this time of day. A man with a white apron was sweeping the floors, scattering the sawdust into the street. With a discrete sidelong glance, Inge looked through the open doors. Polished to a high shine, the bar reflected light from the windows. Behind it, bottles and glasses lined the wall. Tables covered with upended chairs filled the center of the room. The scent of fresh sawdust entered her nostrils. And then she heard it—the tinkle of piano keys.

She stopped. The urge to go inside nearly overcame her, but she knew proper ladies did not enter such places. Drawn by a desire to find the source of the sound, she slipped down the side street to the rear of the saloon. Through the partly opened door, Inge caught sight of the edge of the piano. She retreated, leaning against the building in the shadows. Closing her eyes, she fingered invisible keys on her skirt. The seduction of the instrument twisted her insides. Temptation rested on her shoulders, prodding her to enter.

CHAPTER 17

INGE

With October at hand, preparations for the winter filled Inge's time, in addition to the laundry, cooking, and farm chores. She had yet to get to school, and she had attended church just once. Where music had once brought her peace and happiness, the discovery of the inaccessible piano in the saloon left an aching void. Karl was keeping his distance, and she only saw the children from afar. At least Maggie's constant chatter helped improve her English, although she still stumbled to express herself.

Inge entered the chicken coop and wrinkled her nose as the odor of the droppings rolled over her. She held her breath as long as possible before drawing in a short gasp that made her eyes water. Pulling her apron over her nose, she searched the nests for eggs.

I don't mean to question You, Lord, but since I have arrived in this... this place, I fail to understand anything You are doing.

I will never leave you or forsake you.

Leaning her head against the nesting box, her emotions—fear, loneliness, homesickness—overflowed like a cascading waterfall.

I want to trust You. More than anything, I want to trust You.

"Inge," Maggie yelled from the house. "I need the eggs. Get some meat and cheese from the icehouse, too."

Sliding her hand gently under the clucking hens, Inge quickly gathered the warm eggs and headed to the icehouse. The building was buried deep in a hillside. Inge pulled open the north-facing door. The icehouse was still cool, even though most of the ice had melted. She grabbed a large chunk of smoked venison and some cheese and hurried to the house. Setting the things on the table, she started to take off her wrap.

"Here." Maggie pushed a plate of food into her hands. "Take this down to Karl and Billy."

What? I can't. One look at Maggie's determined eyes and pursed lips and Inge knew she lacked no choice in the matter.

By the time she arrived at Karl's, her hands were shaking so badly that the bread and meat nearly fell off the plate. *What if Karl is here?* She knocked softly. Hearing nothing, she turned the knob. The door creaked on its hinges as she pushed it open. The house was quiet. After depositing the plate on the table, curiosity overcame her, and she entered the parlor. She ran her hand over the sleek brown horsehide sofa that was worn in places from long use. A large wooden rocker looked inviting and comfortable, just right for rocking small children. A potbellied stove, surrounded by ashes and wood chips, would warm the room nicely. Inge picked up one of the carved wooden animals scattered across the braided rag rug. Beautiful details seemed to bring the cow to life in her hand. She could see children playing in this room, filling it with laughter. A woman's touch was evident in the pictures hanging on the whitewashed walls. A flower pot rested on the sill of the large window, but the plant was nothing but a memory. *I could be happy here. It feels like a home. Fill it with love and laughter and it would be all I ever wanted.*

"Karl not there. I left food."

Maggie spun around, her eyes sparking like a newly kindled fire. "That's it! I've had it. The two of yeh are going to talk and settle this matter once and for all." Her words crackled like oil in a hot pan. "Tonight, and every night from here on out, we're all having supper together at Karl's table. The two of yeh will talk, or I will lock yeh in the icehouse till yeh do!"

Inge had often wondered why they didn't eat together. Maggie always took food to Karl's but returned to the cabin to eat with her. Why wouldn't Karl take advantage of something as simple as a meal to get acquainted?

As the sun dropped toward the horizon, they toted a large kettle of vegetable stew and several loaves of fresh golden bread down the hill. Inge stopped before the steps. A shiver went down her spine.

Maggie turned. "Yeh comin'? It's this or the icehouse."

Reluctantly Inge followed Maggie into the kitchen and put the stew on the stove to warm.

Inge set out bowls and placed butter and jam on the table. She looked up as the three older boys burst through the door and stopped in their tracks at the sight of her. David, Ben, and Arnie. Maggie talked of them often, but Inge had not met the two older boys.

"Ah, boys, supper's about ready." The boys stood silently, staring at the two women. "Go! Get yer chores done," Maggie said shaking a wooden ladle in their direction. The boys backed out the door. Through the window, Inge could see their heads come together as they headed to the barn.

Inge rolled her shoulders as her neck and back tightened. This felt wrong, but Maggie seemed to think it was the only way to bring them all together. She watched as Karl rode his horse up to the barn, with Billy hanging on behind him. Lifting the boy down from the saddle, he sent him off to the house. Before he could unsaddle the horse, the other boys converged on their father.

Billy burst through the door, interrupting Inge's study of those in the yard. "Hey, Maggie, what's for supper?" Maggie gently slapped him away from the hot stove. Seeing Inge near the window, he said, "Oh, hello Mam."

"That's what he calls yeh… Mam," Maggie said. "Billy, yeh go wash up before we eat."

Billy dutifully headed for the washbasin. He barely dampened his hands and face before wiping all the dirt on the towel. It wasn't long before the other boys returned from the barn, cleaned up, and took their places at the table.

"Where's Karl?" Maggie asked with her hands on her hips.

"He's coming. He had something to finish in the barn before he came in," Arnie answered.

The boys sat stiffly with puzzled looks. Inge took an empty seat near the head of the table and murmured, "*Hallo*, boys."

"We can't wait all day for yer Pa. He wants cold food, so be it." Maggie slammed the pot of stew on the table and pulled up a chair. "Well, go on. Help yerselves."

The boys filled their bowls. Only Billy spoke, jabbering about his time spent with the neighbor children.

"Trixie's dog is gonna have puppies. I want one. Do you think Pa will let us have a puppy? I wonder what they will look like. Trixie says they can't see when they're born. Do you think they'll be that way forever? She has a frog too. She keeps it in the water trough. It's so big it won't even fit in a bucket."

"Billy! Shut up." Ben's voice was low and menacing.

Inge cringed as she saw Billy's face fall. She saw no need to be harsh with the little one. This was the first time she'd had a good look at Ben. He was at that age when his body was trying desperately to reach adulthood. It didn't take much imagination to see he would be a very handsome man one day. Sun-streaked light brown hair fell over his eyes. Those clear blue eyes, set under fine brows, were striking. His attempt to grow something fuzzy under his slightly upturned nose amused her. He would be solidly built like his father. But his handsome face also carried a shadow of something else. Whatever it was, it made Inge uncomfortable.

David appeared to be the caretaker of the rest. He patiently helped Billy cut his meat and butter his bread. *This bunch could be a handful, but what I wouldn't give to care for them.*

Arnie's sweet, shy smile welcomed her. Maybe the time she spent with him at harvest had formed the beginning of a relationship. It would take time to get to know them, but she was sure they could become a family if only Karl would make the effort.

The door squeaked, and a cold draft swept in as Karl entered the kitchen. He hung his hat and coat on a peg near the door and took his seat at the head of the table. He scowled at Inge, his eyes smoldering like untended embers, but he said nothing. After filling his bowl, he shoveled the food in his mouth as if starved, then wiped his face on his sleeve.

Squirming in his seat, Billy asked, "Pa, do you think we could have a puppy? Trixie says they'll be really good dogs."

"We don't need no dog. He would just get into the chickens and cause trouble." Karl's voice cut the air like a bullwhip. Billy shrank back and stared at his father for a moment. Then blinking back tears, he looked down and stirred his food. David slipped his arm around Billy's shoulders and gave him a squeeze.

"And you don't need to be babying him," Karl said to David. "Life ain't always gettin' what you want."

"Karl!" Maggie pounded her fist on the table. "That's no way to talk to your son."

Inge spent the rest of the meal surrounded by a wall of silence that was broken only by the scraping of spoons against the dishes. She was grateful for the quiet. She didn't know what she would do if Karl lashed out at little Billy again. After dinner, she and Maggie set out dishpans and washed the dishes as the others moved to the parlor.

Maggie scrubbed a bowl and handed it to Inge. "Forgive Karl, Inge. He really isn't a bad man," Maggie said. "I suppose it was a bit much to see yeh sitting in Sigrid's place at the table."

Inge dried the dish as thoughts churned in her head, drowning out Maggie's chatter. *How can I marry a man who is so unkind to his own children? How could he be so severe with Billy? He's just a little boy.*

Cleanup finished, Inge wrapped herself in a warm covering and slipped out the door to escape the disturbing atmosphere of the house. The spectacular sunset filled with intermingling shades of mauve and ochre surrounded her as she walked down the drive. A thick layer of golden leaves carpeted the ground. Reaching the river's edge, she seated herself on a fallen tree. In the water, small whirlpools spun fallen leaves in ever-tightening circles until they disappeared beneath the surface. *Life rolls on like the river, but I'm stuck in an eddy, spinning around, going nowhere.*

Raising her face toward the heavens, she cried aloud, "God, I want an answer! This is not the picture I had of the man I would marry. Is this where you are taking me?" Her shoulders shook, and tears slipped down her cheeks. She wrapped her arms around her legs and rocked back and forth, her face buried in her knees. Time stopped. Suddenly shivering, she realized the air was now much cooler, and the sun was well below the horizon. She pulled her shawl tighter around her shoulders. Despite the cold, she didn't want to leave this place. She found solace in the encroaching darkness.

"You all right?" Inge jumped at the sound of the voice. In the deepening shadows, she made out a form. A woman emerged from the trees.

"Vada. What are you doing here?"

"Checking the fish trap. I didn't want to interrupt your time with God, so I waited." Her tone was soft and melodious.

"You... think I'm an awful person... feeling sorry for myself."

Vada shrugged and seated herself on the ground across from Inge. "We all hurt sometimes."

"Oh, Vada, I don't know..." Words would not come out of her mouth. They sat in the stillness and watched the moon rise over the river. The silence was comfortable, and Inge found Vada's acceptance reassuring. Moonlight danced off the water, creating ever-changing silver ribbons. So much beauty in such an unwelcoming place.

"Sometimes God whispers," Vada said softly.

"What?"

"Often, we are so caught up in the big things in life that we can't see the small blessings around us. God doesn't shout at us. Most of the time, He whispers. And if we are not still, we miss it."

Inge stared at Vada. Her hands gripped the rotten bark of the tree beneath her. Cold night air stole under her shawl and down her back in an icy trickle. She trembled. *Am I missing something?*

Inge heard her name. She turned to Vada. "They're looking for me." Vada was gone. Again, she heard her name being called. Inge pushed her way through the dense undergrowth toward the sound. "Here. I'm over here."

Karl loomed in front of her. "How dare you wander off." His voice rose with each word. "Just what were you thinking traipsing off alone? I have better things to do than tramp through the woods in the middle of the night looking for you."

"I wasn't lost—"

"I don't want to hear it," Karl snapped. "I don't need this... this... aggravation. I should have never answered your letter. I don't know what I was thinking. Why don't you just... just go? Leave. I don't want you here. You hear me? I don't want you here."

Inge gasped and froze. Had she heard him correctly? Outrage filled her veins and anger boiled up, straining to be released. Shoving her way past Karl, she ignored the sharp branches as they grabbed at her. She tripped and fell, scraping her hands on the hard ground. Picking herself up, she continued to push frantically through the dense undergrowth. How could she have ever thought that God wanted her here? When she reached the road, Inge pulled up her skirt and ran to Maggie's cabin.

The door to her room shook on its hinges as she slammed it with both hands. She leaned against the frame for a moment, her breath coming in short pants. Collapsing on the bed she pounded her pillow, sending loose feathers flying. Humiliation clung to her like a filthy blanket. How did she get herself into this predicament?

Inge heard a soft knock. Maggie slowly opened the door. Inge grabbed a cup containing a few late-blooming wildflowers and heaved it at her. The cup shattered against the wall, barely missing Maggie's head. Maggie jerked back and quickly closed the door. Staring at the broken glass and the scattered flowers, Inge covered her face with her hands. *Why am I acting this way? What's wrong with me?* She slid down the side of the bed onto the floor. *Lord, what am I going to do? Where will I go? I don't understand any of this. How could I have misunderstood Your urgings?* The wood floorboards bit into her back. *Well, I wanted an answer. Now I have one.*

CHAPTER 18

INGE

S lowly, Inge opened her eyes and gingerly rubbed them. It was impossible to lift her head from the pillow. She felt like she was swimming in mud. The verbal injury of last evening cut deep. Rays from the sun shone in the corner of the window, the beams falling on her Bible. Reaching across the bed for it, she wondered if God had an answer for last night. As she held the book tightly against her chest, it felt warm, almost alive. She opened it and her eyes fell upon Jeremiah 29:10. "For I know the plans I have for you, declares the Lord, plans for welfare and not for calamity, to give you a future and a hope," she read aloud. The words 'plans,' 'future,' and 'hope' jumped out at her. All things she wanted, prayed for, and desired. However, she had found none of them. All she felt was frustration and discord. She flipped through the pages to her favorite verse.

"Now faith is the assurance of things hoped for, the conviction of things not seen."

— HEBREWS 11:1.

Lord, am I putting all my faith in things seen *and not the hope provided by You? What was it Vada said? Sometimes God whispers. This doesn't feel like a whisper. It feels like a fence post across my back, crippling me and driving me into the ground.*

After splashing cold water on her face, Inge changed her dress and cleaned up the broken cup and dead flowers on the floor.

Where will I go from here?

To start with she would apologize to Maggie for breaking her cup and nearly hurting her. Opening the door, she glanced around the kitchen. Maggie was not there, but the coffee was ready. She could smell the comforting aroma. After pouring a steaming cup, she stepped out onto the small porch. She wrapped herself in a wool shawl and then settled into the creaking rocker, clutching the cup to warm her hands.

She couldn't continue to stay here. Karl made that abundantly clear last night. Even though she knew her family would gladly welcome her, asking for help would admit failure. It would mean that she had failed to understand God's calling and failed to listen to the wisdom of her parents. Until she had exhausted all other efforts, she would not ask her family for help.

Still, she needed to get away from here. She needed a job and a place to live. *I can cook, clean, wash, and iron, there must be some need for those things in town.* She mentally ticked off a list. She was only an adequate seamstress, so that was not an option. *I can't teach because I don't speak English well enough.* That would leave out working in a store too. *I could give lessons, but I have no piano.* She fleetingly considered the piano in the saloon. Parents would never send their children to such a place.

Maggie appeared in the doorway. Her eyes were bloodshot, and her freckles stood out like fly specs on a white sheet. "I... I guess I need to... oh, I made such a shambles of last night."

"Nie. It was me. Should have told someone I leaving," Inge said. "Cup. Sorry broke it. I know... you meant well." Inge shook her head. "Won't work. Karl not want... hate me."

"Oh, Inge. I don't think he knows what he wants."

"Nie. Told me to leave. Don't know what I've done." Her shoulders sagged and her chin dropped against her chest. Cold stiffened her fingers, the warmth of the coffee gone. Setting the cup aside, she pulled the wrap closer.

"He doesn't hate yeh," Maggie whispered. "He just can't let go of Sigrid." She exhaled deeply. "Either can't or won't."

Straightening, Inge turned her gaze toward Maggie. "Tell... about her".

"I didn't know Sigrid well. I had just married Nels and we were setting up our place. We talked some but were never close. I always felt she disapproved of my shipboard romance with Karl's brother. A year later influenza broke out. So many people died, not just Sigrid." Her eyebrows knitted together. "She was funny, always playing pranks on people. And she loved her children. Their house was full of laughter and noise, as yeh can imagine with all those boys. Karl acted like a little boy too. He would wrestle and tease those children mercilessly... and they loved it. Now he barely notices them. My heart breaks for them boys. They not only lost their ma, they lost their pa, too."

Inge nodded.

"It's a sad thing," Maggie continued, "to lose yer wife. What's sadder is to see the man Karl's become."

"You lost... husband," Inge said.

"Nels and I met and married on the ship coming over. It was love at first sight, I guess." She smiled wistfully. "Shortly before Sigrid passed, the men were logging, and a tree fell on Nels, killing him." Her face clouded at the memory. "Karl was handling the saw and I think he blames himself. It wasn't his fault... but still..." Tears threatened, but she blinked rapidly to keep them in check. "So, I guess I just fell into caring for the boys. But what they need is a mother and a father." Maggie wiped her eyes with the corner of her apron and rose to go inside.

Inge followed her. She refilled her cup and sat down at the table. "Maggie, I... work. Cook, wash..."

"Oh ya, there is plenty of work around here for sure," Maggie said. "Don't know what I'd do without yeh."

"*Nei*!" Standing so abruptly that her chair wobbled, Inge pointed down the road. "Go town. Find work. Go home."

CHAPTER 19

INGE

The following morning Inge headed down the road toward Taylor's Landing. The trees lifted their naked arms to embrace the crisp, clear autumn sky. The unseasonably warm October temperatures and sun on her face emboldened her. She hummed to herself.

Lord, why do I feel in such high spirits?

This lightheartedness surely contradicted the unknown path before her, but she embraced it, nonetheless. *The decision's been made. I must follow God's lead. He will provide.* For the moment, that conviction provided courage.

From atop the small rise near Taylor's Landing, she had a clear view of the town. A wide road ran from the waterfront to the main street, then branched off into several side streets lined with houses. Drawing in a deep breath, Inge decided her first stop would be the mercantile. She could communicate with Sam, and he, being a part of the business community, might know where she could find work.

The door to Dodd's Mercantile stood open. She entered and, for a moment, was blinded in the darkened interior. As Inge's eyes adjusted, she saw Clara behind the counter, her eyes filled with undisguised scorn. Pulling back the curtain to the storeroom, Clara yelled, "Sam. You're needed out here." She then turned her back to Inge and began visiting with two women looking at the rolls of fabric.

Inge rubbed her hands up and down her skirt as she waited for Sam to emerge from the back of the store.

"Ah, Inge." Sam's quiet voice slipped into Norwegian. "How are you?"

"*Hallo*, Sam. It's nice to see you again," she said. Looking at the floor, she blinked rapidly.

Sam took her elbow and guided her to a quiet corner. "What's the matter? How can I help?"

Regaining her composure, she unraveled the story of her decision not to marry Karl. "I was wondering if you knew of anyone in town that might need help. Cooking, cleaning, laundry, or... I can't stay with Maggie indefinitely, so I was hoping to find a place to stay, too. Is there... do you know..." Her voice faded as Sam shook his head.

"I'm sorry, Inge. I can't think of anyone needing help right now. Things slow down around here in the fall and winter." He frowned. "You can always check with the hotel. Or... no, I don't think you would want to work there."

"Where? I'll do anything."

"Lena, over at the saloon, mentioned that she needs help. Seems her barmaid ran off and got married." He shook his head. "But I don't think a saloon is for you. It isn't fitting for a lady."

"Ja, I suppose not." She thanked Sam and headed toward the hotel.

She went from business to business only to be met with a shake of the head. Some couldn't even be bothered to speak to her because of her broken English. With each rejection, the disappointment she felt heaped more weight on her shoulders. *How many times have I heard no? Somewhere in this town, someone must need help.*

Jingles was seated in front of the barbershop. Inge crossed the street to avoid the awful little man. Rounding the corner, she noticed the young girl she'd seen on her previous visit, now huddled on the boardwalk's edge. She was wrapped in a tattered blanket, and Inge could see now that the girl was older than she had thought, perhaps in her mid-teens. Slowly, Inge approached until the girl began backing away. "*Hallo.* What's your name?"

Incredible dark eyes stared at her. Layers of dirt, or maybe bruises, tarnished the girl's olive skin. High cheekbones, a straight nose, and a full mouth gave hints of possible beauty, but it was hidden by a tangled mass of black hair spread around her shoulders like a shroud. Inge could not get past her haunted eyes. Beautiful and expressive, they were filled with fear and mistrust, flitting about like those of a feral animal. Inge tried to calm her, but as she moved forward, the girl scurried down the alley. Inge stood at the end of the boardwalk staring after her. How could a child survive like this? Where was her family? Surely someone must care about her.

Having exhausted the businesses in Taylor's Landing, Inge sat down on the bench near the post office. The only place left was the saloon, and she couldn't work there. But she didn't know what being a barmaid entailed. It wouldn't hurt to ask, would it? Slowly, she walked down the street. The saloon's two-story façade, with its large windows and double doors, was the most imposing building on the street. Inge paused before the door. She could not make herself go in. Instead, she rounded the building and went to the back, where she had glimpsed the piano on her last visit to town. Huddled in the alley, Inge forced her feet to approach the door. They wanted to run in the opposite direction. Just when she was about to bolt, a musical voice asked, "Can I help you?"

Inge whirled around and faced a small woman with blonde hair and dark eyes. Soft, childlike features with plump cheeks and a turned-up nose gave her an elfish look.

"What can I do for you?" she asked.

Inge stared at her. She was so tiny, barely coming up to Inge's chest, yet she was a grown woman.

"I'm Lena. Lena Calhoon."

"Inge Olafson," Inge stammered. She accepted the hand Lena offered, bending forward to shake it.

"It is nice to meet you, Inge Olafson." Her voice tinkled like chimes. "You are a tall drink of water," Lena said. "Or maybe I am just a wee sip." She laughed uproariously at her joke. "Now, what can I do for you?"

"I... I understand need help in the... store," Inge finished lamely. She couldn't even bring herself to say saloon.

Lena gazed up at her. "What can you do?"

"I cook, clean, do laundry... whatever you need me to do."

"What I need is a barmaid. Can you pour drinks, take money?" Lena asked.

"Never done such work. Can learn."

"Why do you need a job? You don't look like a working girl." Lena was blunt.

"I... I came to marry. He does not want to. Need money get home, so I work." As an afterthought, she added, "Place to stay too."

"I see."

They stood awkwardly in the side street. Inge squirmed as Lena studied her. "Why don't you come in and we'll talk a bit," Lena said. "I have something to finish. It will only take a moment."

Inge forced herself to step over the threshold and prayed no one saw her enter. A storeroom filled with bottles, kegs, and other items greeted her. Firewood and sacks of sawdust lined the wall near the door, giving the room an earthy smell that disguised the odor of stale beer. From the doorway, she could see the piano. Slowly, she inched her way toward it. It was beautiful. The wood shone like glass. Inge slid onto the stool and ran her hands over the cool, polished ivory. Tentatively, she began to play. Closing her eyes, she let her fingers caress the keys. Each note filled an empty spot in her soul. Suddenly aware she wasn't alone, Inge felt more than saw Lena and two strange men watching and listening.

"It would appear you have other skills besides those you claimed," Lena said with a grin.

"I'm sorry, couldn't resist." She stood and repositioned herself by the door. "I love music and..." She managed a weak smile.

"Come back to my office and we'll talk." Inge followed Lena to a small room just off the storage area. "Please sit."

A small desk, two straight-backed chairs, and assorted piles of books, bottles, and papers filled the cramped room. Cleaning off a chair, Inge took a seat. "Don't know about barmaid, but I could clean... or whatever else. Which isn't what you need, is it?" Her voice faded. "Can't serve drinks. Sorry." She rose to her feet. "Thank you for talking to me."

"Sit down." Lena's voice was surprisingly commanding. Obediently, Inge sat. "I have an offer for you," she continued. "But I want you to seriously think about it before you decide."

Inge nodded.

"What kind of music can you play?"

"I... I play any kind."

"I will pay you to play for my customers on Friday and Saturday nights for... let's say, four hours each evening." Lena laid out her idea. "But it will have to be lively, none of this sad stuff or hymns. No hymns. You think about it and let me know next week." Lena appeared lost in thought. "I can clean out this room if you want to stay here."

Work in a saloon? Maybe. But live in a... a bawdy house? Surely not, Lord.

CHAPTER 20

INGE

By Sunday morning, Inge's bed was a twisted heap of quilts. Sleep hadn't come that night. Her thoughts flitted from the job offer to the impropriety of it. What would Karl think? Then again, what did his opinion matter anyway? He'd be rid of her, and she'd be done with him. She prayed, but no clear answer was forthcoming. As the horizon brightened with shades of pink and blue, she rose and dressed for worship services. She lit a fire in the cookstove and put on a kettle for coffee.

Stepping outside, she inhaled the crisp late October air. After a summer of stifling heat, it felt invigorating. This was more like home, the one she would return to soon. She settled on the step to watch the sunrise. Her breath lifted in puffy clouds before her face as she whispered, "Lord, I prayed for a job. You provided, but how can I be sure this is what You want?"

Suddenly, the sun sliced the horizon, and in a single instant, the day began. *"From the rising of the sun unto the going down of the same, the Lord's name is to be praised."* That was the truth. Every day the sun rose. The seasons came and went. God was faithful. He did not change.

Her face shone in the warm light of the first rays of the morning. Her journey had just begun, and only He knew where it would take her.

By the time Maggie appeared, Inge was nursing her second cup of coffee at the kitchen table. Pen and paper in hand, she prepared to write to her family. Other than a few terse notes, she'd been reluctant to share her circumstances with them.

> October 1895
>
> My dearest family,
>
> I apologize for not writing more often since I arrived here in this Dakota land. Maggie, Karl's sister-in-law, keeps me busy with preserving fruits and vegetables and household chores. With four boys to care for, laundry and cooking are never-ending.
>
> Karl's boys are special, especially Billy, the youngest one. I am thinking of attending school with the children to help me learn English.
>
> A most interesting woman named Vada lives nearby. She seems to be wise when it comes to God and His word. I am getting acquainted with others also.
>
> I found a piano. I am going to play for the owner in the evenings. I didn't realize how much I missed my music.

Inge paused chewing at the top of her pen. These were lies, not total lies, but certainly not the complete truth. Just how much should she tell her parents? Why should she say anything? Perhaps this would be her secret to carry home. As much as she wanted to pour out her heart to them, it might be better if they never knew.

I will add more later. It's time to leave for church. I love you all and miss you very much.
Your loving daughter.

INGE TROD briskly over the prairie toward the combination school and church building. Sitting on a small rise about a half-hour walk from Karl's, the building blazed white in the distance. The stiff breeze was raw, and she quickly chilled despite a warm coat. The golden prairie lifted and fell in the wind until she felt like she was at sea. On the western horizon, a heavy, overcast sky held the promise of a change in the weather. The wild harmony of ducks and geese came from the river as they prepared for their trip south. Winter would be here soon, and she looked forward to it. It would be a new season in the land and a new season in her life. Would it bring fruitfulness or drought?

Turning into the drive that led to the school, Inge noted a few wagons near the building. She followed the people filing into the church and found a seat at the rear of the room. Opening her Bible, she read a few verses. They brought back so many memories that filled her mind. Gently closing the book, she hugged the Bible close to her chest. It had been her grandmother's, then her mother's, and now it was hers. Somehow, just holding it made her feel closer to her family. Would she ever be able to pass the book on to her daughter? She had always wanted a little girl. A child of her own would be an answered prayer. Tears pricked her eyes, and she blinked them back.

"Inge, what's wrong?" Looking up, Inge stared into Pastor Tim's concerned eyes.

"I'm fine," she answered, slipping into Norwegian. "I was just thinking of my *mor* and *far* and feeling homesick. I miss my family so much." She sighed. "I feel so isolated here without family to surround me."

Moving to one side, Pastor Tim sat down beside her and lowered his voice. "I'm sure it's difficult to leave your home and come to a strange place alone. But new place or not, God is the same everywhere."

Inge nodded. She wondered how much she should share with him. "I think I misunderstood what God wanted me to do, and now I find myself in a hard place."

"One thing about God, is that He loves us despite our mistakes." Pastor Tim smiled and patted her hand. "And sometimes He takes those very things and creates something wonderful. He will not disappoint you, Inge." He squeezed her hand before he stood and headed for the pulpit.

Inge looked around at the many faces, all of whom appeared to be so confident and comfortable with each other. The adults chatted, and the children laughed and ran up and down the aisle. She watched the parents with their children as they tried to shush them and make them settle down. Closing her eyes, she tried to imagine what it would have been like to come to church with Karl and the boys. She would have been a part of this scene. Billy would be squirming and talking a leg off anyone who would listen. Inge smiled at the picture. The other boys... She shook her head. It was not to be.

A hand touched her shoulder. Inge looked up and encountered a smiling face. "Mind if I sit with ya?"

Inge nodded. "Ja, that's fine."

"My name is Tossie. Tossie Sellers." She held out her hand for a firm handshake. Tossie appeared to be close to Inge's age. She spoke with a vague accent Inge did not recognize.

"Inge Olafson."

"Nice to meet ya. You new here?"

Inge nodded.

"We just moved here this summer. We're from the Ohio River valley. My husband, Jim, heard about this free land, and he was off and running, dragging me and the boys along with him." Tossie seemed to be even more talkative than Maggie, if that were possible. But Inge didn't mind. It was wonderful to share a seat with someone.

"Lester. Boys. You set down now. There's no running in church," Tossie yelled at three boys who finally settled next to her.

Everyone quieted as Pastor Tim raised his hands and began the service. Inge eyed her pew partner as they sang the first hymn. Tossie's clothing was a blaze of mismatched colors and patterns. She was even wearing her apron in church. While rather plain, she had a lively smile and outgoing personality. Inge's heart lifted. She wasn't the only new person in the area.

CHAPTER 21

INGE

Inge rose early on Monday morning. She planned to attend school and then head to Taylor's Landing to accept Lena's offer. *It will be wonderful to play again, to feel the music pour from my fingers.*

"Maggie. Going school and then town." Inge said, as she seated herself at the table.

"I was planning on yeh helping me pick grapes." Maggie pulled a cup from the cupboard and filled it with coffee. Settling herself opposite Inge, she said, "If we don't pick soon, the frost will ruin them."

"Well, uh..." Inge stammered. "Might have a job. I stay in town. But I help when can."

"A job? Where'd yeh find a job?" Maggie asked.

"Rather not say. Not hired yet."

Maggie's smile fell, and her eyes clouded with disappointment. "I doubt yeh'll have much time for me with a job and all." She stood up abruptly and turned her back to Inge. "But I'll manage. I always have."

"You upset?"

"No. Certainly not. Why would I be upset?" Maggie frowned.

"Karl not marry, so must go," Inge said. "You generous with home and friendship but can't stay."

"Ya, well, I suppose yer right. But I will miss yeh. I was so hoping Karl would come to his senses and see what a good wife yeh'd be, and good mother too." Maggie sighed. "Some days I'd like to box his ears to get his attention."

"I see you, Maggie. Won't be far, just in town." Inge looked longingly at the door. As much as she wanted to get going, she couldn't abandon Maggie on such short notice. "We pick grapes today. Now." Inge smiled. "I wait to go to town."

After breakfast, Inge gathered buckets and headed toward the river to harvest the grapes. Maggie gave her clear directions to the place where the vines grew thickest. The autumn air was cool, and a wisp of smoke tickled her nose. The fallen leaves rustled as she pushed her way through the trees on the undefined path leading to the water's edge.

Dear Lord, You provided. It's not what I expected, or even what I wanted, but I have a place to stay and a way to care for myself. Thank You.

Reaching the riverbank, she turned and made her way through the underbrush until the heady scent of ripe grapes filled the air. She gazed upward. The vines covered several trees. They also crept along the ground and smothered nearby bushes. Grateful there was so much fruit within her reach, she began to strip the vines of their bounty, quickly filling her buckets. She pulled the grapes from the stems and filled her mouth, letting the juice trickle down her throat and then licked her sticky fingers, enjoying the sweet tang that bit her tongue. Glancing down, she laughed out loud at the sight of her purple-stained hands and arms. She looked like she'd fallen into a wine barrel.

Curious, Inge explored farther down the edge of the river. Picking her way through the tangled ground cover, she was amazed at the variety of berries clinging to the trees and bushes. She discovered crimson wild rose hips, tiny orange berries lagging close to the ground, and heavy dark blue clusters hanging over her head. But she found the waxy white bunches on the brush to be the most interesting. She had never seen white berries before. She would fill a vase and enjoy their colors now that the trees were bare. A patch of scarlet leaves caught her eye. The last of fall's glory, she could add them to branches and brighten up her room. Bending over, she picked a handful of the vibrant stems.

"Don't do that." Inge jumped back, nearly tripping on her own feet. Vada emerged from the trees. "You need to wash your hands with soap and water," she said. "Right now."

Inge's heart continued to pound, but she was relieved to see it was Vada. Glancing around, she started back to her buckets. "Ja, I will do that when I get home."

"No! Come with me." Vada took ahold of Inge's upper arm and steered her through the trees to a small wooden shack. It blended so well with the surroundings that Inge might have walked right by and never noticed it.

"What did I get into?"

"Poison ivy. Not too bad this time of year but in the summer it's nasty. I've seen people swell up like a fat pig from touching the leaves," Vada said. "And you have never had anything itch like that will itch. Eventually, your body gets used to it, but with someone new like you, it can be awfully bad."

Inside, Vada gave her a piece of lye soap and a pan of water. "Now, wash good." Dutifully, Inge scrubbed her hands and forearms. "When ya get home, ya wash those clothes and try not to touch them until they've been boiled a while. Have a seat. I'll get you a cup of coffee."

Inge sat on a crude bench before a table made of rough-hewn boards. Glancing around the room, she noted two beds in one corner covered with quilts that were worn and none too clean. A large crate near the stove served as storage for the meager dishes and cooking utensils. Inge counted two large cast iron pots and four or five plates. For such a large family, the clothing hanging from pegs on the wall was sparse. Light filtered through the cracks in the walls, creating streaks of sunlight on the dirt floor. Vada poured coffee from a pot on the stove and placed a cup in front of Inge. Bringing some for herself, she settled on the opposite side of the table.

"I see you's picking grapes. You making juice?" Vada asked.

"Ja, when I get back." As she raised the cup to her lips, Inge noticed the dirty rim. She rubbed the lip of the metal cup with her finger, wiping off as much of the grime as possible. She sipped and found the coffee to be interesting, if indeed it was coffee. Though the right color, it was bitter and tasted of wood.

A child screamed, but before Inge could rise, Vada grabbed the little girl who burst into the room. "What's the matter?" Vada asked. She held the child close and rubbed her back.

"Billy's chasing me."

Billy? Billy was at home with Maggie. Inge looked out the door but saw nothing.

"He knocked me down." The child whined. "He's mean."

"Shh. Did he hurt you?" Vada examined the girl as she talked. "I think you'll be fine." Vada had the child sit on the bench next to her. She handed her a crust of bread. "This is my littlest one, Elizabeth. She's four."

"*Hallo*, Elizabeth," Inge said. "Glad you fine." A beautiful child with big brown eyes, she was barefoot and wore a stained, patched dress that was much too big for her. Tears cut streaks down her dirty face, and her dark hair was tangled with leaves and twigs. But under all of that, Inge could see a bright, obviously very active little girl squirming in her seat.

"Who's Billy?" Inge asked.

"He's the goat. He gets a little ornery now and again. But he never hurts 'em much."

"Where are the other children?" Inge dug through her memory trying to recall what Vada had told her about her family at harvest.

"They's in school. Ragna just started this year. Jake is eight, and

Frankie is ten. My husband's oldest boy is eighteen, but he don't live here no more. He run off a couple of years ago. His ma died when he was about seven, and he never took to me after I married Gabe."

"And your husband?"

"He's hunting right now. We need the meat for winter."

Inge held her cup with both hands but was having a difficult time drinking the strange-tasting brew. At ease in Vada's presence, she longed to share her news with a friendly face. Drawing in a deep breath, Inge said, "Vada, I found a job. I move to town."

"So, things are not working out with the marriage?"

"*Nie*. Karl not want to marry me. I not what he expected." Karl's rejection of her was more than she could share right now. "But God provided for me."

"How's that?"

Inge described the position she'd been offered. When she finished, they sat in silence for a minute.

Vada shifted on the bench. Her face had a pained expression. "Inge, do you think this would be pleasing to the Lord?"

Inge's back stiffened. She had expected Vada, of all people, to understand.

Vada continued, "God says we are not to be foolish but are to understand His will. Do you think God would want you to work in such a place?"

"I prayed. God provided. I not turn down the thing I prayed for." Inge lifted her chin and her voice rose slightly.

"Perhaps you need to pray that God makes His will known to you." Vada's voice dropped. "The devil can easily lead us astray, especially when we's scared."

Inge stood, thanked Vada for her hospitality, and left the ramshackle building without a backward glance. Why would Vada say that? Surely, she saw that this job was an answered prayer. She couldn't possibly understand Inge's plight. Inge retrieved the grapes and pushed her way through the trees headed for Maggie's cabin. Her skirt caught on broken branches, slowing down her furious pace. The more she thought about Vada's comments the angrier she got. *How dare she tell me what to do? Look how she lives. Dirty. Starving. Like she checks with God before she does anything. I certainly don't need someone like her telling me what to do.* She slammed the grapes down on the porch. Maggie turned at the sound.

"You right about river riffraff," Inge said. "I stay away."

Inge stomped from the house toward the spring, fuming under her breath. Too cold to bathe, Inge rested on a stump nearby and listened to the water gurgle as it tumbled from the rocks and fed into the pool. White mare's tails streaked through the upper sky giving it a mystical appearance. Inge smiled. Her *far* often quoted the old proverb, 'Mare's tails and mackerel scales make lofty ships to carry low sails.' It meant a storm was on the way. Maybe there would be more than one storm if she accepted Lena's job.

Lord, I miss our time together in this quiet place. It's a place where You and I can sort things out together.

Thoughts bounced around in her head. Angry that Vada had challenged her faith, she now found doubt crouching on her shoulder, whispering in her ear. Could Vada be right? She didn't feel comfortable in Lena's saloon, but God had provided a job and a place to stay. And she would be able to play the piano. Besides, it was her only option, unless Karl changed his mind. What if he did? After the other night, she couldn't even consider marriage to a man who was so cruel to his children. But then there were the boys. She could so easily love those boys.

CHAPTER 22

INGE

That evening after supper, Inge and Maggie relaxed in the rockers near the stove. The only sounds in the room were the creaking of the chairs and the ticking of the clock. These last few months the women had fallen into a friendly companionship. Maggie didn't feel the need to talk incessantly, and Inge found the silence pleasant. Their time together was comfortable and satisfying.

"Go school tomorrow and then town," Inge said. "Back before supper. Bring you anything?"

"I don't think so," Maggie said. "Karl will be taking the wagon to town before long to pick up the flour and the last of the supplies for winter. I'll send a list with him."

Inge nodded. Leaving here was going to be more difficult than she thought. Maggie had been there from the day she arrived, supporting and encouraging her. Inge's shoulders drooped. She hadn't expected to feel the loss of Maggie's everyday presence.

"I think I'll go to bed. It's been a long day," Maggie said as she stood. "If you're going to school, yeh will have to get up early. There are chores to be done before yeh leave." She smiled. Not her usual cheery smile, but a little wry and sad. "Sleep well."

Inge awoke before daylight and hurriedly dressed in the cold room. She prepared lunches for herself and the boys, separated the cream from the milk, and brought in meat from the icehouse for supper. The sun had not yet peeked over the horizon when she and the boys began their trek to school. Trudging along the path that was trampled into the prairie, the group was unusually quiet.

"Do you enjoy school?" Inge asked of no one in particular. The boys kept walking without answering. "Is the pastor a good teacher?"

Arnie looked up and nodded slightly. The conversation would not come easy, if at all.

Nearing the school, Ben and Arnie ran ahead to meet friends but David slowed his pace and walked alongside Inge.

"Why are you going to school?" he asked. "Didn't you do that as a child?"

"Ja, I did. But here... here I need to learn English better. And I should know something of this country, don't you think?"

In his mid-teens, David was tall and gangly. His appearance was a contrast to the other boys. His dark, wavy hair, hazel eyes, and quick, shy smile reminded Inge of her brother.

"I suppose," David said. "Do you want to marry my father?"

Inge's breath caught in her throat. "Ah. It isn't so much that I don't want to marry him. I think he does not want to marry me."

"Maybe." David remained quiet for a time. "But he needs you. We all need you." With that, he hurried ahead and ran up the steps into the school.

Inge stopped abruptly. What did David know that she didn't? Her feet caught in the tall grass as she slowly approached the school. Did Karl need her?

The bell rang just as Inge arrived in the yard. The children ran for the door, entering the classroom and taking their places on benches at the tables. Inge slipped in quietly and took a seat in the rear of the room near the potbellied stove. She watched Pastor Tim as he prepared his books and wrote an assignment on the blackboard. A handsome man, he was tall and slim with a relaxed demeanor. He seemed to fill the space with his cheerful personality. His nearly white-blond hair tended to fall over his face and Inge found it endearing when he absent-mindedly brushed it out of his eyes. He knocked on the desk, gaining everyone's attention.

"Good morning, children," he greeted them. "Please stand and let's recite Psalm Twenty-three."

Benches scraped the floor as the children stood and began, "The Lord is my shepherd…"

Inge listened closely and nodded in agreement with the words. A half a lifetime ago she sat in a classroom reciting Biblical verses, too. Some things hadn't changed. The faces were fresh and eager, filled with anticipation. She needed this. It felt good to be around the children and the instruction, and it felt good to experience the freedom of being on her own.

"Today, we will begin with spelling. Please get out your slates." Seeing Inge, Pastor Tim nodded and winked.

The morning progressed from spelling to arithmetic. The pastor broke the children into groups with the older ones helping the younger. At recess, he approached Inge. "I'm glad you decided to come." His blue eyes twinkled. His personality was vastly different from when he was playing his role as pastor on Sundays. Here he was lighthearted, gently teasing the children as he helped them when they struggled. He handed her a slate and said, "Just do what everyone else does. You'll catch on quickly." With that, he herded the students back to their seats.

Inge observed the rest of the morning, trying to follow the lessons, but the children often distracted her. David and two other boys appeared to be the oldest, followed by a mix of girls and boys in the middle, and one little girl in first grade. That must be Ragna, Vada's daughter, for she was a picture of her sister, Elizabeth. She tried to figure out which of the boys were Vada's but failed. Bold and bullying, Ben appeared to hold sway over many of the other boys. Arnie kept to himself and read quietly. David sat off to one side, absorbed in his lessons. The others were typical children, wriggling, giggling, and waiting for recess when they would be free to play. Before Inge knew it, it was noon. The children grabbed their lunchpails and headed outdoors. Pastor Tim seated himself next to Inge, and they shared their lunch.

"So, what do you think? Is it making sense to you?" Pastor Tim asked, unwrapping his bread and kippers.

"Pastor Tim…" Inge lowered her head as a flush crept up her cheeks. She still didn't know how much she should confide in the pastor. "Things are not working out with Karl."

"Oh, Inge. I'm sorry. Is there anything I can do? Should I talk with him?"

"*Nie.*" She related as little as possible of what Karl had said in the woods. "But it will work out. I intend to go home when I have earned enough money."

"It's troubling, that's for sure." Pastor Tim leaned back and searched her face. "But I can't say it's a complete surprise. When I heard Karl sent for you, I wondered…" His words trailed off. "Karl's cut himself off from the neighbors, the community, and even his family, from what I hear."

Inge nodded. "He doesn't want me here. I can never be a replacement for his wife, so it's best that I go home."

"Will you continue to stay at Maggie's until you leave?"

"Well, perhaps part of the time. My work in town will require me to stay there a few nights a week."

"You have a job? Doing what?"

A sudden squabble on the steps drew Pastor Tim's attention away from Inge. He stepped away to settle the children in their seats and resume their lessons.

As the day progressed, Inge began to fidget. No matter which way she turned, her skin burned. Unable to stand the discomfort any longer, she abruptly left school in the middle of the afternoon.

Stripping off her clothes as soon as she entered the cabin, she dipped warm water from the cookstove's reservoir into a pan and scrubbed every inch of her body. It only seemed to irritate her skin more. Fiercely rubbing her eye, she felt it begin to swell. What was happening to her? Dressed only in her chemise and drawers, she wanted to rip those off too, as well as her skin. Suddenly Vada's warning leaped to her mind. She'd forgotten all about washing the poison ivy out of her clothes. "Isn't this a pretty kettle of fish," she said, clawing at her neck.

While she was wringing out a cool cloth to cover her eyes, the door opened. "Oh, Maggie—"

Inge turned to see Karl stiff as a post in the doorway. She quickly grabbed a towel from the table and tried to cover herself as she darted behind the wooden rocker. Heat filled her body, rising until it exploded at her hairline. *Nei.*

Karl took off his hat, then hastily slapped it back on his head as he spun around and left the room, slamming the door behind him. Inge's heart hammered as she stood in shocked silence. Retreating to her room, she sat on the bed and replayed the scene in her mind. What had Karl been doing here? Why hadn't he knocked? She groaned. Once again, she had appeared as a bumbling idiot in front of him, a half-naked bumbling idiot at that.

There was a soft knock at the door. "It's Maggie. Can I come in?"

"Ja. Come in."

"What happened? I just saw Karl on a dead run heading for the barn. I thought perhaps something was wrong."

"Ja, as usual, something is wrong." Inge wrung her hands. "I... I was getting cloth, and I thought it was you. In my undergarments and Karl came in..." Her breaths came in great gulps.

The bed sagged as Maggie sat down beside her and slipped her arm around Inge's shoulders. "Shh, it's fine. It isn't like Karl hasn't seen a woman in her undergarments before."

"But... not me!" Inge's chest caved inward as she hugged her upper arms. "Every time he sees me, I'm a mess or causing problems. No wonder he doesn't want to marry me. Nobody would want to marry me." She flung Maggie's arm away.

"Well, I don't think that's true." Maggie shook her head and stood.

"Maggie, don't go. Sorry. Not your fault."

"Yeh know, I've been thinking, and it might be better if yeh weren't here. Maybe yeh getting a job might help Karl see things rightly." Maggie shrugged her shoulders. "I don't know anymore."

Scratching her arm, Inge remembered her condition. "Maggie, I think I have poison ivy."

"Let me see." Maggie examined Inge's arms and neck. "And I think yeh have a good case of it too." Maggie headed to the kitchen. She rummaged through the cupboard, finally pulling out baking soda. "I'll make some soda paste. That will help some."

Inge nodded. She didn't care what it was, she just needed something to help with this horrible crawling sensation that rolled over her body. There was no escape from it.

Maggie smeared the white paste on all the red, weeping spots. "The soda will draw out and dry up the blisters. But it will still itch. Scratching makes it worse, so don't scratch."

"How long?"

"Oh, it should get better in a few days, a week at the most." Maggie gathered up the bowl and clothes. "Yeh may want to stay in here and wear as little as possible. Clothing only aggravates it."

Inge clutched the quilt to resist the urge to scratch. With her head buried in the pillow, a muffled moan escaped her lips. *Why did Karl have to walk in when I was half-naked? His timing is... well, it's inconvenient.*

CHAPTER 23

INGE

After a week of seclusion, the rash was nearly gone. Inge's eye was still inflamed, but at least she could see out of it now. Arnie had come by after school each day to help her with reading lessons. He was a quiet and solemn boy who acted very mature for a ten-year-old. The loss of a parent would probably do that to a child. He brought his favorite book, *Tom Sawyer*, and they read it together, chuckling at the antics of the characters. But the highlight of each day was when Billy came to visit. He would sit by her side and listen as she practiced reading aloud.

"You're getting better, Mam." He would nod earnestly and pat her hand.

It was impossible not to love Billy. His ceaseless questioning often tickled her. He was curious about everything, and his laugh often bubbled forth from the slightest thing. For a four-year-old, he was also insightful, sensing when Inge needed comfort. She longed to take him in her arms and hold him. *He is ministering to me when I should be caring for him.*

INGE BEGAN the next week with every intention of attending school and then going into town to accept Lena's job offer. But when Billy came down with a runny nose, followed by a bad cough, Maggie brought him to the cabin to keep an eye on him. His listlessness tugged at Inge's heartstrings. Her desire to care for the little boy overwhelmed her, so she decided that a few days wouldn't matter. If God wanted her to have the job, He would make sure it was still available.

"He has to drink," Maggie said, handing Inge a cup. "I'll fix a mustard plaster for his chest to help the cough."

Inge stroked the boy's head. He was warm but didn't have a raging fever. She held a cup of warm sassafras tea to his mouth. "Drink this, Billy."

He sipped the liquid, then gagged and spit it on the floor. "Nooo."

"I know it tastes bad," Inge said. "But it will help you feel better. You want to feel better, don't you?'

He nodded and sipped again, clamping his hand over his mouth until it went down.

"Mam," he whispered.

"Ja, Billy."

"Will you read to me? From your book? You sound like my ma when you read from your book."

"Of course." Inge reached for her bible and began reading in Norwegian from the Book of John. She had discovered the boys could understand Norwegian, though they only spoke it haltingly.

"No. I want to hear the story about the giant. You remember... and the little boy?" Billy looked at her, his eyelids drooping. "Can I sit with you?"

Inge smiled and welcomed him into her lap. Sitting in Maggie's big rocker, she flipped to the story of David and Goliath. "It is a good story, ja?" She began reading, and soon Billy closed his eyes and nodded off wrapped in her arms. He was so precious and so innocent.

Lord, let me mother these boys. They need me, and I need them. You can change Karl. I know you can.

By the next day, Billy was feeling better. While the cough still lingered, he bounced around the house like a playful puppy. These last few days with the boys had filled Inge with a yearning and a hope she thought was gone, and when Billy snuggled deep into her lap with his ear to her chest, Inge fanned that spark, coaxing it to life. Maybe someday they might be a family. God could work miracles. She was sure of it.

CHAPTER 24

INGE

Inge sat in the classroom throughout the morning. She could see that she had made strides with reading in the last week and a half, but she had much more to learn. As she and Pastor Tim shared their lunch, Inge read aloud to show him her improvement.

Pastor Tim clapped his hands. "Your reading skills are so much better. At this rate, you will be reading and speaking like the locals soon."

Inge beamed from his praise. "I must thank Arnie. He came every day and helped me."

"I missed you last week." He grinned. "I understand you had a bit of a, uh... predicament."

Inge felt heat rise in her cheeks. "It was my fault. If I had paid attention to what Vada said, I'd have been fine."

"We've all suffered from poison ivy at one time or another." He laughed out loud. "I wondered why you squirmed so on your first day of school. I figured my teaching was boring you."

Shyness stole over Inge. She avoided his teasing eyes by looking out the window.

Pastor Tim cleared his throat. "How do you know Vada?"

Inge told him of her meetings with the woman. "She seems very wise, and she knows God's Word, but I don't know how. She told me she can't read."

"That family's a mystery. The children come faithfully to school. They are bright, beautiful children. But I've never seen their parents." A thoughtful look crossed his face. "Would you take me to their place sometime?"

"Ja, sure. I think I can find it again."

"One of these days I will drop by Karl's, and you can show me where she lives."

"Ja, sure, that would be fine," Inge said. "If I'm there."

He gave her a puzzled look as he rose to ring the bell.

Inge stood too. "I'm heading into town now to take care of some business. I'll try to come back as often as I can," she assured him. "It will depend on work. There is always plenty of work to be done, you know."

CHAPTER 25

KARL

Karl leaned back in the rocking chair near the wood stove in the parlor. Harvest was over, the boys were in school, and it was the season for winter projects. Holding a diamond willow branch in his hands, he slowly let his knife find its way down each side of the stick. The diamond patterns stood out as distinctly as if he had carved them. Nature had placed them perfectly, and he didn't plan to change any of them, just enhance the beauty God created.

Billy played with his toy animals near the firewood box. He was such a bright, cheerful little boy. Karl loved him dearly. A thin fog of dread descended over him. If he loved his boys too much, perhaps God would take them too. Just like He had taken Sigrid. He stared out the window with thoughts of his wife constricting his throat. Memories were better than reality, better than anything that he could expect to experience again.

Karl jerked his hand back. Blood dripped from his finger. The knife had slipped and nicked his knuckle. He put the cane down and wrapped his handkerchief around his hand before easing back into the rocker to nurse his finger. The cut would heal in a matter of days. Why did it take the heart so much longer to mend?

He had to get out of the house. It was suffocating him. Sigrid was everywhere and nowhere. He bundled Billy in a warm coat and hat, and they headed outside. A pile of unsplit firewood beckoned him. It was the perfect thing for working these unsettled feelings out of his system.

Karl's thoughts meandered as he handled each chunk of wood and swung his axe to reduce it into usable pieces. He tried to avoid thinking about Inge. He couldn't begin to name the feelings she churned up in him. Was it anger? Guilt? Or maybe fear? Maybe it was fear that he might lose Sigrid completely. His wife's face was already fading from his memory, and that frightened him.

The axe bit deep into a large block of wood, so deep he couldn't pull it out. Rage surged through him. How dare Sigrid leave him! How was he supposed to raise a family alone? It wasn't fair. None of it was fair. Karl placed his foot on the chopping block, using pressure from his leg to help release the head. It wouldn't budge. He jerked at the axe handle until the blade finally broke loose from the wood.

Then last week, as if things couldn't get any worse, he'd walked in on Inge half-dressed. He was flabbergasted, and it felt like he stood there for hours before he absorbed what he was seeing. He probably should apologize. The tiniest smile curved his lips as he pictured her trying to hide behind a towel.

Karl swung the axe again, determined to split the log. He couldn't replace his wife with a stranger. What would Sigrid think if he did that? Deep down, he knew. Sigrid would want him to continue living, to marry again so he wouldn't be alone. And the boys needed someone to look after them. Maybe he would marry again if he found someone as special as Sigrid. But Inge, she was a... a... He didn't know what she was. He hoped that eventually she would give up and move on. Making her his housekeeper was probably not going to work. He doubted she would accept that offer. He removed his hat and wiped the sweat from his brow. Even after he had exploded at her in the woods, she stayed. Getting rid of the woman was like removing cockleburs from your socks. Even when you were sure the stickers were gone, the tiny unseen barbs would work their way under your skin. Her ability to do that irked him. He regretted yelling at her, but admitting he was wrong was out of the question. It might give her hope. Women thrived on hope, and he couldn't have that.

His axe bit deeply into the log, the splintered pieces flying in every direction. "God, what do you want from me?" he shouted into the wind. Billy looked up from playing with the cat and stared at his father. Karl waved his hand dismissively at the boy and leaned heavily on the axe handle. Sweat dripped from his face, and his lungs ached from the exertion. He shivered as the wind chilled his overheated body. Why had he cried out to God? Was it a last resort? While Sigrid had loved God with all her heart, he had mostly gone to church and professed faith to please her. He sighed wearily. Would he ever be happy again? Did he even deserve to be happy? He knew now that happiness wasn't something he could hold on to. No matter how tightly he grasped it, it slipped through his fingers like water, leaving only the damp film of memories that eventually dried up.

He buried the blade deep in the wood and stood up straight. Something had to give. *Will it be me or Inge? I don't think I have the endurance to outlast her patience.*

CHAPTER 26

INGE

Later that afternoon, Inge knocked on the back door of the saloon. When no one answered, she opened the door and peeked in. There was no one in sight, but she could hear voices coming from the front. She forced herself to step over the threshold and hesitantly sought out the source of the laughter.

"Ah, Inge. I thought you had forgotten about me." Lena's voice was softly melodic in the shadows of the open room. "I'm glad you came back."

The man at the bar grabbed a broom and began to upend the chairs so he could sweep the floor.

Lena led Inge to the office area at the back. "I cleaned it out for you," she said, waving her arm around the room. Inge eyed the space. The only difference was the addition of a narrow cot in one corner. It was still crowded with assorted papers, boxes, and books. There would barely be space to sleep.

"Well, what have you decided?" Lena asked as she sat at the small desk and leaned back in her chair.

Inge's instinct was to beat a hasty retreat. This didn't feel right. She swallowed her apprehension, cleaned off a chair, and sat down.

Holding the chair's papers in her lap, she asked, "How often want me to play?"

"I have been thinking about that. I get my biggest crowds on Friday and Saturday nights. How about we start with those two nights?"

Inge nodded.

"You could sleep here those two nights and then spend the rest of the week at your other place," she continued. "Or you can live here if you want. What do you think?"

"How much pay?"

"Let's see. If you play for four hours or so each night, I will pay you five dollars a month."

Inge nodded again. Considering what she would be doing and the time involved, she was sure this was more than generous. It would take her several months to save up enough for a ticket home, but she could do this for a short period of time. But what would Karl think of her? It didn't matter. She couldn't wait around forever. She needed money whether she went home or not.

"Ja, good. I accept."

"When can you start?" Lena asked.

"Today is Tuesday. Maybe Friday?" The sooner she went to work, the sooner she could leave this place.

"That would be wonderful. Remember, lively music, and... well, do you have any other clothing? Something a little more... more colorful and interesting?" Inge looked down at her plain brown skirt and fingered the buttons on her dark striped shirtwaist. "And your hair... it's beautiful, but so severe. Maybe something looser?"

"Ja, sure," Inge mumbled. "I see you then." *Does she expect me to dress like she does, with ruffles and flounces and low-cut necklines? I don't think so. I may have to work here but I'm no... floozy.*

Friday arrived before Inge knew it. None of her meager clothing seemed suitable for a saloon. She saved her gray wool dress for church, but the rest of her clothing was more appropriate for housework and had seen hard use since she'd been here. She settled on a deep blue skirt with a white blouse. Next, she considered her hair. Even as a young lady, she had worn her hair in a bun at the base of her neck. What could she do differently? As an experiment, she pulled the front back, braided the long strands, and wrapped it like a golden crown around the top of her head, with the rest flowing loosely down her back. She stared at her reflection in Maggie's small mirror. This would work. She admired her reflection. *Maybe I should do this more often.*

Inge was still suffering from Maggie's stinging rebuke after she had confessed the nature of her job, so she hoped to steal quietly out of the house. Determined to see this through, she intended to be there every week despite Maggie's and Vada's feelings about it. Unable to put off her departure any longer, Inge finished filling her small bag with necessities and dressed warmly to prepare for her long walk to Taylor's Landing.

"So, yeh haven't come to yer senses yet. How can yeh go work in that detestable pig sty?" Maggie asked. "Yer as bullheaded as Karl."

"Ja, I go," Inge's voice faltered. So much for sneaking out without a confrontation.

"Do yeh realize what this'll do to yer reputation?" Maggie pulled herself up to her full height, placed her hands on her hips, and stared up at Inge.

They'd been over this—many times. Maggie was outraged at Inge's stubborn stance, and Inge refused to give up the only chance she had to care for herself.

But what if Maggie was right?

Lord, what if this decision follows me for the rest of my life?

CHAPTER 27

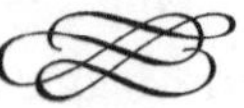

INGE

After two weeks, Inge developed a routine. She spent Friday and Saturday in town, attended church on Sunday, and then went back to Maggie's for the rest of the week. Initially, she planned to live at Lena's, but after her first couple of nights, she realized she couldn't stay there every day. The room was cramped and cold, and she hated the noise and smell coming from the saloon. Humbly, Inge had asked Maggie if she could spend part of the week with her at the cabin. Even though their relationship was still somewhat strained, Maggie was gracious enough to welcome her back. When possible, she attended school. It was the highlight of her week. Not only was she learning and spending time with the boys, but Pastor Tim was thoughtful and kind. They never seemed to run out of things to talk about.

As for working at Lena's, while she loved playing the piano, she felt uneasy and out of place in the rowdy environment. Her music failed to fill her as it once did. The customers left her alone, and, surprisingly, there were some who seemed to appreciate her tunes. But once finished for the night, she escaped to her room as quickly as possible.

INGE HAD BEEN at the piano for an hour entertaining those who had braved the cold on Saturday night. The few men in the saloon were deeply engrossed in a poker game near the potbelly stove. Cold crept into the room despite the roaring fire, leaving Inge chilled in her far corner. She shivered and closed her eyes to block out her surroundings. But the loud voices at the card table couldn't be shut out.

Inge began a lullaby by Brahms. She longed to play a hymn, but Lena had been quite clear about that. The soft and comforting lullaby was close, though. Forcing her cold fingers to move along the keys, an uneasy feeling crowded in on her. This was wrong. She didn't belong here.

Oh, Lord, I hope I haven't misunderstood you again.

"Hey, lady. Why don't you pick up the pace a little?" Inge felt a hand on her shoulder, then it drifted down her back. She flinched. "It's cold outside. Let's warm it up in here," said the man behind her.

He squeezed closer and pressed his head against her cheek, rubbing his whiskery chin across the side of her face. Hot breath on her neck reeked of beer and tobacco. Inge stifled a gag. Her fingers froze on the keys. The length of his body pressed closer to her. The brim of his hat poked the side of her head. Every inch of her body felt charged with revulsion.

Inge leaned forward to escape the man's grasp. Just as she was about to slip off the stool, his arms swung around her, holding her in place. Why didn't someone help her? Surely the card players would come to her rescue. Where was Lena?

Oh Lord, help me, please!

"Roy."

Inge felt the man stiffen.

"Roy, be a good boy and back off. Leave her alone."

Carefully, Roy removed his arms from around Inge and slowly backed up a few steps. Inge slid off the stool and bolted for the storeroom. Her heart thudded in her ears as she clung to the door frame in the shadows and watched the man slowly turn to face Lena.

Lena smiled. Lying on the counter was the biggest double-barrel shotgun Inge had ever seen. Slowly Lena caressed the stock, encircled her finger in the trigger, and traced the length of the barrel with her other hand. In Lena's small hands, the gun looked like a cannon. Roy watched each move with fascination, his eyes never leaving the weapon.

"Now, Roy," Lena said quietly. "You don't want to upset old Maude here, do you? She gets right crotchety when my customers don't behave nicely." Lena continued smiling, but it touched no part of her face except her lips. "She might like to see a little action. What do you think, Roy?" She shifted the position of the gun, letting her finger remain loosely on the trigger as she swung the barrel around to point toward Roy.

Raising his hands, Roy backed across the room. Dropping into his chair, he placed both hands palm down on the table. "No, ma'am, I sure wouldn't want to upset old Maude," he said, his face draining of color. The card players pushed their chairs away from the table and moved to the other side of the room.

"That's good. She can make a real mess when she's upset. How about you finish your beer and then you go home?" Lena's voice remained soft and quiet, but there was an intense current underneath it that electrified the room.

Roy nodded.

"And Roy, you spread the word that no one bothers my piano player. Is that understood?"

He nodded again, beer slopping from the glass as he raised it to his mouth.

"Thank you, Roy. Now please apologize to Inge," Lena said. Her grip on the gun never relaxed.

"Yes, ma'am." Roy swallowed hard. "I'm sure sorry, Miss Inge." He took one last gulp of his beer and fled the saloon, letting in a gust of cold air before the door slammed behind him.

Inge clutched the door frame with both hands. The power Lena brought to the room stunned her.

"Inge, come here. Have a seat," Lena said.

Inge coaxed her wobbly legs to the table and fell into a chair. Lena placed a small glass in front of her filled with a golden liquid. "Drink it."

Inge shook her head. The sharp smell of alcohol rippled through her nose. "*Nei*. I... I can't." Still shaking, she rubbed her face where Roy's whiskers had left a burn. Unable to meet Lena's gaze, she had to get out of there. She felt dirty all over.

"I said drink it." Lena's voice left no room for disobedience.

Inge's hand trembled as she picked up the small glass and took a sip. Flames ripped down her throat, and she coughed until her eyes watered. She wheezed and fought to draw in a breath.

"Go on. Drink it all. A shot of brandy is good for the soul on occasion."

Inge attempted a smaller sip with much the same result.

"Throw it back. Won't burn so much that way. Hold your nose if you have to."

Oh, Lord. I can't drink this. I can't be here.

Inge looked at Lena and then at old Maude on the bar. *What have I gotten myself into?* Holding her nose, she downed the drink. It seemed to be the lesser of the two evils.

Inge clung to the edge of the table, shuddering as the brandy went down. She fought to get a breath. When it came, she coughed until it felt like her lungs would come up in pieces. Then warmth began to spread through her mid-section. She could feel her tense muscles relaxing slightly.

"Now you just sit here for a bit." Lena leaned back in her chair and eyed the poker game. It was quieter than it had been before. Old Maude seemed to have a calming effect on everyone.

Inge stared at the tiny woman sitting with her. This was a woman who threatened to shoot a man and forced a drink on a woman. Who was she?

"Lena." Inge's voice was hoarse. "Would you have shot him?"

Lena leaned close to Inge's ear. "Of course not. Old Maude wasn't even loaded." She smiled conspiratorially. "But we won't tell them that. I have a reputation to uphold."

Inge's eyes widened. *What reputation?*

CHAPTER 28

INGE

After her harrowing night at the saloon, Inge was all too ready to leave Lena's place on Sunday morning. As she walked the three-and-a-half miles to the little country church, the icy fingers of a bitter November wind tested the layers of her clothing. By the time she arrived, her hands and feet were numb with early frostbite.

Inge stumbled in the door, willing herself to put one foot in front of the other.

Pastor Tim looked up from feeding wood into the stove. "Inge, you look half frozen." He held her up as he led her to the potbellied stove in the center of the room.

"Ja," she said. "That I am."

"Here, sit." He pulled a chair close to the heat. Removing her shoes, he massaged her feet to restore circulation. She winced as the feeling returned to her toes. He tucked her feet near the stove and turned to her hands, rubbing them gently. Inge, suddenly conscious of the warmth of his touch, drew away.

Pastor Tim stepped back. "Ah... I better get more firewood." Pushing his hands deep in his pockets, he backed away.

Inge heard wheels creak on the frozen ground outside. The door burst open, and Hulda Hobbs and her four girls entered.

"Mornin'," Hulda said to Pastor Tim. "It's a nippy one out there today. I expect the weather could turn bad before we know it." After hanging her coat on a peg, she caught sight of Inge behind the stove. "Oh, I didn't see you there." Her eyes lit on Inge's raised skirt and stocking feet. "You two here alone?"

Inge's face grew warm. She quickly pulled on her shoes and covered her ankles with her dress.

"Yes, Inge arrived just a bit ago. She was chilled to the bone when she got here," Pastor Tim said. "I've been trying to warm her up."

"I can see that." Hulda raised her brows.

Only a few others braved the cold and wind to attend worship. The Williams family nearly filled the church with their lively brood, and Tossie Sellers flitted around the room like a colorful butterfly. In the short time Tossie had been in the area, she seemed to have made friends with everyone. She had a gift, one Inge wished she possessed.

Following the sermon, Pastor Tim made an announcement. "Remember to set aside Thanksgiving Day when we celebrate grateful hearts, good food, and fellowship with our friends and neighbors. This year we will meet at the Williams farm. We'll need extra hands to clean out the barn and set up tables. So, if you can help, please see me and we will get a work party together."

Inge nodded. Memories of *Hosttakkefest* filled her. It seemed every land had a special day to express gratitude.

Because of Your provision, Lord, I will be on my way home in a few months. Give me the strength to work at Lena's long enough to get there.

Before Inge knew it, Thanksgiving had arrived. Maggie prepared the wild turkey Karl had shot for the occasion, and Inge fixed a large container of winter squash sweetened with honey. That, along with several loaves of bread and a few pies, was their contribution to the meal.

Karl drove the wagon up to the cabin and helped load the food. Once the baskets were settled, Inge and Maggie climbed up to join the boys who were already snuggled under heavy blankets with heated stones at their feet.

In the wagon, seated between David and Arnie, little Billy crawled into Inge's lap. A pang of regret tugged at her heart. The loss of what might have been would always be a weight on her shoulders. This was the family picture she longed for—everyone laughing, snuggling together, and heading for a neighborhood gathering, except for Karl. He had completely ignored her when they loaded the food. *Can't he see this is where I should be, not at the saloon?*

Karl pulled up to the front of the Williams's weathered two-story barn. Everyone grabbed pots and baskets and hurried inside. The floors had been swept clean, and sawhorses covered with boards created tables. After covering the makeshift surface with quilts and cloths, Inge and Maggie laid out their fare as others continued to pour through the door with more food. Soon the table overflowed with venison, turkey, ham, potatoes, breads, vegetables, and desserts. Delicious odors floated through the air mixing with the musky smell of hay, feed, and animals. Inge drew in a deep breath. Now this felt like her home in Norway.

Even though it was cool in the barn, everyone was dressed warm enough to be comfortable. Stoves at each end of the building warded off most of the chill. People rapidly filled the benches lining the sides of the room as everyone continued visiting and laughing.

Inge welcomed the clamor of voices and the squeals of the children, remembering those times as a child when they had held barn raisings. It was hard work, but fellowship with friends and neighbors made it a special event. The chatter and the jesting—it was the sound of home. An unexpected wave of emotion rolled over her, tightening her chest.

Tears burned her eyes. She hurried toward the door, running headlong into Pastor Tim.

He grasped her arms to keep her from falling. "Inge, is something wrong?"

"I... I... it's nothing." Inge pulled away and ran outside. She rounded the corner of the barn where she found a quiet spot sheltered from the wind and prying eyes. Blinking rapidly, she filled her lungs with cold air while she did her best to rein in her feelings. She longed to belong and be part of this scene. The ride had refueled her thoughts of having a family. She thought she'd buried those dreams, but the yearning never left.

"Inge, can I do something to help?"

Pastor Tim's voice startled her. Inge turned to face him. Her chin quivered, and her vision blurred. Her breath came in hiccups. Pastor Tim reached out and pulled her into his arms. His embrace released her tears. He gently held her, stroking her back, until they subsided. Her cheek buried deep in his rough coat, she inhaled the smell of damp wool and wood smoke. Good earthy smells, just like her *far. Oh, Far, I wish I was home.*

"Inge, what's wrong?" he whispered in her ear. "Did someone do or say something to upset you?"

"*Nei, nei.* The festivities brought back memories. I miss my family so much. I have no friends, no one." The folds of his coat muffled her words.

"You know that's not true," Pastor Tim said. "You have many friends. Don't you consider Maggie your friend? And me?"

"Well, Maggie has been very good to me," Inge said. "But she is part of Karl's family, and our relationship has been strained of late."

"What of the other ladies at church?"

"None of them seem to want to have much to do with me. We can't communicate. I'm an outsider."

Pastor Tim chuckled. "They were all outsiders at one time or another. All these people have come from somewhere else, me included. I tell you what," he said. "Why don't you find just one person you'd like to know better and then pursue a friendship."

Inge nodded. Suddenly aware she was wrapped in the pastor's arms, she leaned back and lowered her head, hoping the shadow of the building would conceal her hot face.

"I'm sorry to burden you with my problems." She sniffed and wiped her eyes with her sleeve.

"Believe me, it's not a burden," he said quietly. "That's what I do—care for the flock." He reached up to smooth a stray strand of hair that had come loose from her bun. His fingers lingered on her jawline for a long moment. Inge retreated another step. Pastor Tim quickly dropped his hand to his side. He dug in his pocket and produced a handkerchief. "Here, wipe your face. We should go in. It's soon time to eat."

The moment they entered the barn, Ernie Williams called out, "Hey, Pastor. We're hungry. Say grace so we can eat."

Pastor Tim raised his hand to call for quiet and prayed over the food. "Lord God, You are a gracious and giving God. You have provided all we have here today—the food, the family, and the friends. Fill our hearts to overflowing with gratitude for the gift of Your Son. Amen."

The hair on the back of Inge's neck tingled. Her eyes swept the room until she saw Hulda Hobbs near the door with a knowing smirk on her face. Inge looked away and wiped her nose before she joined Maggie on a bench near the stalls.

The crowd elbowed for a place in line to access the food. Inge and Maggie squeezed into an open space and filled their plates. Returning to their seats, they balanced their overflowing dishes on their knees as they ate.

"Mmmm... isn't this ham wonderful?" Maggie rolled her eyes and licked her lips. "And the cherry pie is a real treat."

Inge nodded. The mashed turnips slathered in rich butter, just like her *mor* used to make, filled nearly half her plate. With one taste she was back home in *Mor's* kitchen, surrounded by the sounds of her mother's laughter, her father's gentle teasing, and her nieces and nephews bounding through the house. *I want to go home.*

When their stomachs were full and content, she and Maggie leaned back against the wall and watched the activities. Boisterous children bounded around the room, with Arnie and Ben joining them as they scrambled up the ladder into the loft. A shower of fine dust floated down as they jumped in the piles of hay overhead. David was chasing a rambunctious Billy. Where was Karl? Inge caught sight of him sitting alone near the milking stalls on an overturned bucket, his plate perched on his knees. His shoulders were hunched, and his head hung only inches above his plate as he slowly ate. He looked pitiful. Why didn't he join his friends or even the boys?

All around the room, adults stood talking in small clusters. Some played checkers on make-do tables, and a few women sat quilting or knitting. With Christmas just around the corner, Inge knew that every free moment would be used to finish gifts for family and friends. What would Christmas be like here? She was certain it wouldn't be anything like home, and she found the whole idea distressing.

Inge had hoped Vada and her family would be here, but she didn't see them in the crowd. If there was anyone she had connected with since her arrival, it was Vada. Despite Vada's blunt remarks concerning the saloon, she wanted to know the woman better. There was a certain unexplainable kinship between the two of them. While she didn't see Vada, she noticed Hulda holding court in the center of a group of women. Who knew what little tidbit Hulda was sharing with them?

At the far end of the barn, musicians readied their fiddles, a guitar, a banjo, and a concertina. After a few squeaks and moans, the group launched into a lively polka, followed by a waltz. It didn't take long for the floor to fill with enthusiastic dancers. Inge and Maggie watched the participants while their feet kept time with the music.

"Excuse me." A short, rotund man with a bald head and a huge handlebar mustache stood before them. "May I have this dance?" he asked as he looked directly at Maggie.

Maggie smiled nervously. "Ah... I suppose." She clenched her hands together. He gently took her arm and whisked her onto the dance floor. Inge watched as they whirled and dipped. Despite his girth, the man was light on his feet. By the third dance, Maggie's face began to light up the barn like a lamp in a dark room. Inge's hand crept to her neck. Bittersweet envy caught in her throat, but she couldn't take her eyes off the couple. After several dances, Maggie staggered back to the bench to catch her breath.

"Could I get you ladies something to drink?" Maggie's partner bowed slightly in front of Inge. "My name is Gustaf Schlick."

Inge nodded. "Inge Olafson."

He returned with three glasses of punch, handing one to each of the women. Friendly and outgoing, with a deep, rich voice, his gaze never left Maggie's face as he sat down next to her. His dark brown eyes matched his mustache, and his full, ruddy cheeks reminded Inge of a circus clown. From his devoted attention, he was obviously captivated by Maggie. Maggie giggled when Gustaf took her hand. *What an interesting match. Maggie deserves to have someone in her life.* Feeling like a fifth wheel, Inge excused herself and wandered to the stove by the door. She warmed her hands and watched the fun from afar.

"How are you doing?" She turned slightly at the sound of Pastor Tim's voice.

"I'm better now. I apologize for earlier." She returned to watching the crowd.

"Inge, as a single woman, I am sure you feel left out of many things," he said. "But keep in mind what I said about seeking a friend."

"Ja, I will do that," Inge said as she noticed Hulda off to the side eyeing them. *Does that woman have nothing else to do but keep track of me?*

Pastor Tim touched her elbow. "Would you like to dance?"

Inge gaped at him. Dance? She glanced Hulda's way again. *May as well give her something more to talk about.* Pastor Tim's hand enclosed hers, and she allowed him to lead her onto the floor. Although she wasn't a polished dancer, Inge managed to keep up with Pastor Tim as he led her around the large open area. Waltzing around the room like dandelion fluff in a breeze lifted her heart, and at that moment, she felt desired. Maybe even a little beautiful. They continued until she was out of breath. Pastor Tim led her back to her seat and sat down beside her.

"Thank you, Inge." Pastor Tim inhaled deeply. "It's been a long time since I've enjoyed myself this much."

Inge nodded. "Me too," She placed her hand over her chest as she pulled air into her lungs.

Inge caught sight of Karl across the room. Alone, he slowly rubbed his hands up and down his thighs as he watched them. Did it bother him that she was dancing with someone else?

Maggie and Mr. Schlick sailed up to them. "Pastor, I want you to meet Gustaf. He is new in town. He's a... a carpenter," she said. Maggie's sparkling eyes were glued to Gustaf's face.

Inge slipped her hand over her mouth to hide her grin.

"Hello, Pastor," Gustaf boomed. "It's nice to meet you. Yep, I'm new to the area. Maggie is kind to call me a carpenter. I'm an undertaker by trade, and I also build coffins. The two tend to go hand in hand. I'm sure you and I will work together from time to time."

"Nice to meet you." Pastor Tim stood to greet the man. "And I hope we don't do that much business together. I'd like to keep my flock alive and well." He grinned. Gustaf laughed loudly, bowed at the waist, and whisked Maggie back onto the dance floor.

"They make an interesting couple, don't you think?" Pastor Tim asked.

Inge nodded and swallowed hard. Jealousy sat on her shoulder, and she couldn't seem to brush it off.

Chewing on her bottom lip, Inge stood. "I need to gather up the dishes. It's nearly dark, and we'll head home soon. Thank you for a wonderful afternoon." She hesitated for a moment before she turned toward the table to begin gathering the kettles and placing plates and bowls in baskets.

"Here, let me take that." Karl took the basket from her hands. His kind offer filled her with a slight expectation as they quietly walked across the yard to the wagon. Depositing the containers in the back, Karl spun around. "Just what are you trying to do? Make a complete fool of me?" His face darkened, and his blue eyes were as cold as the frozen ground. Inge reeled back as if he had slapped her. She grasped the edge of the wagon bed to keep her knees from buckling.

"I overlooked your *job* at the saloon, and now you make a spectacle of yourself cavorting with the pastor." He pivoted and stomped toward the barn. "I'll get Maggie. We're going home right now."

Speechless, Inge shivered in the cold. Karl's words stung. She climbed into the back of the wagon and pulled the blankets up to her chin. A strangled sob escaped her lips. She wanted to justify her actions, but she doubted that Karl would listen or care what she had to say. Communicating with him was like talking to a doorknob. She tried to convince herself she'd done nothing wrong, but deep down there was a grain of truth in what he had said. She did work at the saloon, and she had danced with the pastor. And she enjoyed it.

Maggie and the children crawled in the back of the wagon and curled up under the quilts. Karl urged the horses into a strong trot, and the wagon bumped its way over the frozen ruts. Even little Billy snuggled in her lap didn't lift Inge's spirits, and Maggie's excited prattle about her budding romance was the last thing Inge wanted to hear.

Karl stopped in front of the cabin to unload the wagon. Inge stood in the shadows for a moment. She needed to escape Maggie's enthusiastic chatter before she exploded. She raced to the outhouse. Her eyes watered from the odor as she hid in the cramped shanty. The building stunk. Karl's attitude stunk. Everything stunk. But she refused to cry. There was no understanding that man. He told her to leave, and now he was acting like she was his property. *Make a fool of him? How am I making a fool of him?* A gust of cold air filtered through the cracks in the walls. As angry as she was with Karl, she was even more upset with God. He had fed her dreams, and then he had thrown her overboard. These last few months she had flailed about, adrift in a sea of confusion, struggling to keep her head above the surface.

"Are you testing me, Lord?" she yelled. "I am not Job. I don't want any part of Your test. I followed Your direction, and now I have nothing." The wind wailed. "How could You do this to me?" Inge pounded her fists against the door. It flew open revealing Maggie standing on the stoop.

They stared at each other for a moment before Inge pushed her off the path into the bushes and ran to the cabin. The bedroom door shook as she slammed it.

Moments later there was a soft knock. "Inge, what happened to upset you so?"

"Go away. Leave me alone." Inge meant it. She was done with people, done with trying to fit in, and done with... everything. She was even done with God unless He did something soon besides slapping her down when she tried to follow His lead.

I've listened for what I thought You wanted. But obviously, I have misunderstood. I'm trying, Lord, but You are going to have to make Your will much clearer. I'm willing, but I can't do the right thing if I don't understand what You want from me.

She threw herself on the bed. The faster she could leave this place, the better.

CHAPTER 29

INGE

The day after Thanksgiving, as she walked down the road toward Taylor's Landing, Inge asked the Lord's forgiveness for her outburst the night before. It wasn't God's fault Karl was such a *dumme tosk*. She mulled over their latest encounter. Why did she even care what he thought? He wasn't going to marry her, and besides, she was leaving soon. So why did his attitude bother her? She didn't like the saloon, but it was only a means to an end.

Then there was her interaction with Pastor Tim yesterday. What had she been thinking when she agreed to dance with him? Was it Pastor Tim's attention, his comforting ways, or the need to have some fun that seduced her into acting so foolishly? *But was it foolish? We just danced. Karl had no right to judge me.*

Catching her foot on a branch, Inge nearly fell. Where was she going? So busy rehashing recent events, she missed the turn onto the main road into town. Fluffy snowflakes cartwheeled around her. The dark, bare trees combined with the new snow gave the landscape a bleak feel. If only she could find a clear path forward—good or bad, wise or foolish, based on truth or delusion—to something she could hold on to. Reality and dreams were rarely paired, but she still longed for them to come together.

The silent woods sent shivers down her spine. Inge turned and hurried back toward the main road. A faint column of smoke rising above the trees drew her attention. She must be close to Vada's place. Maybe she should stop and say hello. Ja, she would do that. She would pursue a friendship, just like Pastor Tim had told her to do.

Inge knocked on the door and waited. Inside, a bench scraped against the floor. After a moment, the door cracked open. Vada's eye and nose appeared. "Oh, you are home," Inge said. "Thought I'd stop and visit." Vada gazed at her but didn't respond. "Can I come in?"

The door slowly opened. The space was dark with only a low burning lamp on the table offering minimal illumination to the room. A sack covered the window, eliminating any light that might have entered on this cloudy day.

"Have a seat. I'll get some coffee." Vada's measured words were slightly slurred. She kept her back to Inge as she gathered two cups and the coffee pot from the stove.

Inge settled on the bench next to the table. "Where is Elizabeth?"

"She's here," Vada said. "You can come out now, Elizabeth." There was a scuffling sound behind her. Inge turned to see the child crawling out from under the bed. She ran to her mother and clung to her leg. "Everything's fine." Vada soothed the child. "It's just Inge. You remember her?" With her face buried in her mother's skirt, Elizabeth nodded her head.

"What's going on? Why was Elizabeth under the bed?"

Inge's question hung in the air unanswered.

Vada turned. Inge could see bruises covering one side of Vada's face. Inge pressed her lips together, catching a cry before it could escape. The blackened eye, swollen nose, and split lip left the woman nearly unrecognizable.

"What happened?" Inge whispered, rising from her seat. She grabbed the coffee pot and cups from Vada's hands and put them on the table. "Here, you sit," she said, pulling out a seat. Vada groaned and leaned on the table. Inge helped her lower herself onto the bench.

Kneeling in front of her, Inge could see the bruising was severe, and her nose might be broken. "Are you hurt anywhere else?" Vada's hand fluttered near her ribs. Inge pushed in several places, causing Vada to cry out. "Don't think your ribs broken, maybe cracked. Vada, you see a doctor."

"No. I'll be fine. I just need a couple of days to get back on my feet," Vada mumbled between shallow, raspy breaths.

"*Nei*, not fine. I get a doctor."

"No, please. No doctor."

"Where's your husband?"

Vada looked startled. "He's gone... for a while. We'll get along. The children will be home from school, and they can help me."

Inge returned to her bench, still clasping Vada's limp fingers across the table. "How did this happen?"

"I tripped. Near the river. Lost my footing and fell over the riverbank. Landed on some rocks. Stupid of me. So clumsy." Each word out of her mouth was painfully slow and garbled.

Inge stared at her but said nothing. Vada rubbed her throat, then drew the collar of her dress together and held it tightly closed. Inge leaned forward and pulled back the collar. Large bruises in the shape of a handprint wound like a noose around her neck.

"What's this? These bruises... did someone...?" Inge sought words to express her horror as she looked at Vada. "Who did this?"

Vada covered the side of her face with her hand. "No one. I'm just clumsy." Her lips drew into a thin line, causing her split lip to bleed. She shifted in her seat and glanced at the door. "I want you to go now."

Inge stared at her. It was clear that the woman hadn't fallen.

Vada rose from the bench. "Please. Go."

"I can't leave you like this. You're hurt."

Vada opened the door, her eyes pleading. "You can't tell anyone. Do you understand me? No one."

"Why not?" Who could she tell? The woman needed help.

"Go. Tell no one." Vada gave her a small shove toward the door. "Promise me."

Inge pulled her coat close and stepped outside. "I'll come back in a few days." The door slammed behind her.

Inge's mind raced as she climbed the trail back to the main road. Vada's husband had to be responsible. She needed to tell someone, but who? Maybe she could go to the sheriff or Pastor Tim? Vada didn't want her to say anything, but what about the children? Would they be safe? Vada needed to get out of there and go somewhere her husband wouldn't find her.

The mournful wind in the trees only inflamed her feeling of powerlessness. With one last backward glance, Inge picked up her pace and hurried to get to Lena's saloon before the drifting snow became a full-blown blizzard.

Inge's mood was dark and unsettled when she arrived. She loosened her hair, changed her blouse, and grabbed a quick bite of cheese and bread before she headed to the piano. The evening seemed to drag on forever. She wanted to play a dirge to express her despair. Thoughts pounded her like hailstones. Each strike revealed more possibilities concerning Vada's fate. There was nothing she could do, nothing at all. Inge sat upright as the realization struck her. Feeling ashamed, she dropped her head until it touched the surface of the piano. She had the ability to do one thing, the most important thing—pray. Instead of trying to fix things on her own, she should be turning to God. She shook her head slowly. Her fingers moved along the keys. Lena wouldn't be happy, but she was going to play a hymn. She whispered the lyrics like a prayer.

"When peace like a river attendeth my way, when sorrows like sea billows roll, whatever my lot, thou hast taught me to pray, it is well, it is well, with my soul."

CHAPTER 30

INGE

Inge awoke with a start before dawn broke Saturday morning. What was that? Except for the wind moaning under the eaves, the saloon stood silent. She listened for the sound that had roused her. It was indistinguishable at first, but it became more familiar as she waited. Slowly, it filled her from the inside out.

Be still and know that I am God.

The words didn't make sense to her. *Or maybe I don't want to hear them.* Inge shivered. Her room had grown cold overnight. She hurriedly donned layers of warm clothing. Lena had paid her last night, and she could feel the coins in her pocket. She intended to spend some of it on a small gift for Vada.

The warmth of the mercantile welcomed Inge when she stepped inside. As she browsed through the goods, her fingers stroked bolts of brightly colored cloth, traced the lines of elegant teacups, and examined shiny red apples. While tins of food or spices would surely be appreciated, they didn't seem personal enough. Her eyes stopped on a scarf of the most incredible sky blue she'd ever seen. It was as soft to the touch as newborn skin. However, the price gave her pause. It was nearly half of what she'd earned. Inge put it back and continued to wander down the aisles, but eventually, she found herself drawn back to the scarf. If she spent her wages on this gift, she would have to work longer to build up her resources to return to Norway.

Is this foolish, Lord? I need the money, and this is so frivolous. Vada has no need for such an impractical gift, but it's so beautiful.

I will provide.

Thank You, Lord.

Inge gathered up the scarf and presented it at the counter.

"That's a little fancy for you, isn't it?" Clara raised her eyebrows. "It's silk, you know."

Fingers of heat rushed up her cheeks. "Ja, I know," Inge stammered, lowering her head. "It's a gift."

"And who would you know that would deserve such an expensive gift?" Clara folded the scarf and wrapped it in brown paper.

The woman's words cut deeply. Blood pounded in Inge's ears. Her eyes blazed and she sensed her mouth was about to boil over. "Everyone deserves a special gift now and then. Even the likes of you."

Clara's jaw dropped and her face froze.

Appalled at her own actions, Inge swept the change off the counter, grabbed her package, and hurried out of the store. Some people never failed to amaze her. How could kindhearted Sam be married to such a mean-spirited woman? Even so, what had she been thinking snapping at Clara? She hadn't been thinking at all.

Striding down the boardwalk, Inge was appalled at her reaction to Clara's nasty remarks. Her hands tightly grasped her package, and she kept her eyes glued to the walkway. What had she ever done to Clara? Why did Inge allow her to get under her skin?

A sudden impact with a man nearly knocked Inge off the boardwalk, sending her bundle careening into the street. She stumbled and collided with the hotel wall, grabbing the man's arm to keep from falling to the ground. She finally managed to grab the overhang post, regaining her balance.

"Sorry," Inge gasped, stepping back and tugging at her coat. "Didn't see you."

"Pretty Lady." Jingles' mostly toothless mouth formed a huge smile. "Pretty Lady."

Picking up the scarf that had fallen from the wrapping, Jingles moved to the edge of the boardwalk. "Come. Meet my friend." Jingles tugged at her sleeve. Inge grabbed the scarf and brushed his arm away before she looked up. The girl stood in the building's shadow.

"Raven. Come meet Pretty Lady," Jingles said. He pulled on Inge's sleeve again. The girl sank deeper into the gloom. "Pretty Lady is my friend. You like her. Her's nice."

Inge's eyes widened and her stomach clenched at the sight of the girl. She was dressed in filthy rags, her hair was a snarled mess, and her face was streaked with dirt. She had to be freezing without a coat. The girl refused to look at Inge but sought Jingle's face for reassurance.

Inge held out her hand and spoke softly. "*Hallo*, Raven. My name is Inge." The girl backed away. "Raven is a beautiful name. Nice to meet you."

Jingles whispered. "Her don't talk much. But her a nice girl."

"I'm sure she's a wonderful girl." Inge smiled at her.

Not wishing to further frighten Raven, Inge returned to the boardwalk. An almost imperceptible flutter brushed her shoulder. Inge turned and Raven's outstretched hand floated softly over the blue scarf.

"It's beautiful, isn't it?" Inge said. Raven's fingers lingered on the soft material, caressing it as lightly as a spring breeze. Inge held it out. The girl dropped her hand and stepped back. "It's fine. You can have it."

Raven's eyes darted to Jingles's face. Seeing a slight nod, she snatched up the scarf and disappeared down the alley.

"Her's a good girl," Jingles murmured again. His hand stroked Inge's arm before he turned to enter the hotel.

What just happened? The scarf had been for Vada. There was no reason to give it to Raven, but it felt right. She had to do something to help this child.

She longed to gather Raven in her arms and take her home. The girl deserved so much more. Inge stood there staring at the empty alley. She stepped off the walk wanting to follow her.

Wait.

Wait?

Waiting would only cause more pain. Maybe Lena could take Raven in. It wasn't ideal, but at least she would have shelter in the saloon.

Inge struggled through four long hours at the piano that evening. Each note reminded her of Vada and Raven and their painful predicaments. Her music lacked the melodious sound that usually flowed from her fingers. No matter how hard she tried, she couldn't find the right notes. From behind the bar, Lena sent questioning glances her way. She played where her feelings took her, and tonight, her concern for Vada and Raven far outweighed what other people might think.

As she prepared to leave the saloon on Sunday morning, Lena stopped her. "You want to tell me what's going on?" she asked. "You seem to have been elsewhere these last two days."

"It's fine. I'm fine," Inge said. "Problems. Friends have problems." She clenched her jaw. She certainly couldn't tell Lena about Vada's injuries after the recent experience with Old Maude.

"Your appearance tells me different." Worried lines creased Lena's face. "If you ever want to talk, well, I've heard it all. I am your friend, Inge. You know that, don't you?"

Should I tell Lena? What could she do to help? Vada doesn't want me to interfere. I feel so helpless. What if her husband does this again? What if he hurts the children?

Inge gave Lena a grim smile. As much as she longed to confide in someone, she felt obligated to honor Vada's wishes. Prayers that God would protect Vada and the little ones rose from deep within.

CHAPTER 31

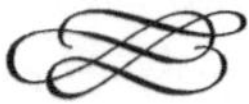

INGE

The long walk to church in the freezing weather brought her hands and feet near to frostbite each week, no matter how warmly she dressed.

"Lester, move back. Let Inge get up to the stove." Tossie Sellers yelled at her son. Dutifully, Lester retreated, and Inge gratefully stepped into his place. Holding her hands close to the heat, she absorbed the warmth.

Once everyone settled in their seats, Pastor Tim opened the service with prayer. The songs and messages seemed to come in bits and pieces between Inge's wandering thoughts.

"One thing we are often guilty of," Pastor Tim said, "is jumping to conclusions. It's easy to misjudge things when we have no true knowledge. Jesus came to testify to the truth. As His children, we need to do the same."

Inge's thoughts jumped immediately to Hulda Hobbs and her gossip. Inge was glad to see she wasn't there. Was it possible the pastor's words were aimed at Inge herself? Visions of Vada's bruised face filled her mind. Now that she thought about it, she had no proof Vada's husband had hurt her. But who else could it have been?

Following services, Inge selected the faint trail off the main road. She was intent on visiting Vada before returning to Maggie's cabin. The path had drifted over, and plodding through the knee-deep snow exhausted her. Overheated and out of breath, she approached Vada's small ramshackle house, stopping short of the structure to survey the setting. She didn't wish to barge in and possibly make things worse.

Seeing no movement in the area, Inge approached the door and knocked. The sound of little feet tapped across the floor, and then the door opened a crack. Inge looked down to see Elizabeth's small face peeking out.

"*Hallo*, Elizabeth. How are you?" Inge asked. "Is your mother here?" The girl nodded and opened the door wider. Inge entered and blinked in the semi-darkness until her eyes adjusted. Vada sat at the table. The rest of the children were lined up on the bed.

"Come in. Sit, please. Frankie, get a cup of coffee for Inge," Vada said. "I'm glad you came. I wasn't sure you would."

"I said I would come." Inge gave Frankie's arm a reassuring squeeze when she placed a steaming cup on the table.

"Children, please see to the chores. Bundle up. Make sure the goats have water and check for eggs."

Inge watched as the children slipped on their coats and went to do their mother's bidding. Elizabeth stayed behind, clinging to Vada's skirt.

Several shades of purple still covered the side of Vada's face, and Inge noticed she winced when she took a deep breath. "What can I do to help you?" Inge asked.

"Nothing. We'll be fine." Vada tried to smile, but her scabbed lip turned it into a lopsided droop. "But it's very nice to see a friendly face."

Leaning back, Vada pulled an object from her lap and laid it on the table. Curious, Inge reached for the article made from animal hide. The fur, soft as a kitten, had been sewn together with small, fine stitches into mittens.

"I'd like you to have these." Tears glistened in Vada's eyes. "You are a good friend. The only one I have had since I've been here." She swiped at the corner of her eye.

"Oh, Vada." Inge's throat constricted. She gripped Vada's hands. "You are my only friend, too."

Tears slipped down Vada's cheeks. "We're a pair, aren't we? A couple of lost souls in the wilderness."

"But we have each other. God answered our prayers, didn't He?"

Vada nodded. "I am so grateful for Him and for you."

Inge swallowed hard and found her voice. "These are beautiful. Did you make?" Inge ran her hand along the soft fur.

"Gabe runs a trapline in the winter. I tan the hides myself."

Inge thought for a moment. "Could you make for Karl's boys before Christmas? Not much time but need gifts. I work now, so can pay."

"I can make them for you," Vada said. "But I won't accept your money. You're a friend. I can't take money from a friend."

"*Takka.* Boys will be pleased," Inge said, "and I will pay for them."

"So, you're working at the saloon now?"

Just as Inge opened her mouth to explain, the door burst open. A tall man with a scraggly beard and long dirty hair stood in the doorway. He carried a rifle. He wasn't pointing it at her, but the gun's presence was unsettling.

"Who're you? What you doin' here?" he growled looking at Inge.

Throwing his gun on the table, he leaned forward to study Vada's face.

"And you. Look at you." Vada flinched as he laid his hand on her shoulder.

Inge stood. Before she could say a word, he whirled and barked at her. "You. Get outta here. Now."

Vada raised her hand, waving her away. Inge barely got outside before she heard raised voices. Should she leave? Would they be safe?

"Lord, please don't let him hurt her or the children. Please," Inge prayed fervently.

CHAPTER 32

KARL

Karl rested his head against the cow's warm flank. Steam floated upward from each squirt of milk as he filled the bucket. Now and then, he would aim a stream at the cats. It lifted his spirits to watch them try to catch the milk in their mouths. Feeling a little more generous than usual, Karl poured some of the fresh milk into a pan. "Enjoy it, fellas. 'Tis your Christmas present."

Christmas would be upon them in a few days. Karl had loved *Jul* when they celebrated as a family. Sigrid always made sure the boys had gifts and she would prepare all their favorite foods from the homeland. Karl got into the spirit by cutting the tree. A wry smile crossed his face as he recalled the family laughing together as they decorated it.

Sigrid had made *julekurvers* filled with hard candy for each of the boys. It had been nearly impossible to keep them out of the small heart-shaped packages until *Jul* arrived, but Sigrid loved every moment of teasing them with the tempting treats. They wove the long golden straws Karl had saved from harvest into stars, and the boys would string popcorn and rose hips. Sigrid tied colorful bows to the heads of wheat before placing them on the tree. Karl's fingers slid down the side of his face to cover his mouth. There was something disturbing about a warm recollection knowing it was only a memory. Why did these thoughts keep haunting him?

Karl carefully strained the milk into a clean bucket and took it to the icehouse. The cream would rise to the top and they would have fresh, thick cream for their Christmas *rommegrØt*. Maggie had informed him that she had invited Gustaf for Christmas Eve supper. In a way, he was grateful. When others were around, it eased his sadness. However, if Maggie had also included Inge in their celebration, it might not be so comforting. Any magic in Christmas this year would come from Maggie and Gus. Karl was pleased that Maggie had found someone, but he found it also troubled him. How would he manage if Maggie left?

"How are you doing, Karl?" The voice startled him.

Pastor Tim stood at the icehouse door. Karl's back stiffened and his hands gripped the bucket until his knuckles turned white. He had no intention of discussing his problems with the pastor. Religious types thought they had answers for everything. God could fix it—right? Karl brushed by Pastor Tim and strode to the barn. He had things to do. He needed to feed Bossie and clean her stall.

"Karl, you can't avoid me forever," Pastor Tim said following him. "We... you and I need to talk about Inge."

Karl spun on his heel. "We don't have to do any such thing," he sputtered. "This is none of your business anyway."

"Well, in a way, it's become my business. Inge has come to me for... for advice and comfort. She feels terribly alone and isolated."

"And that's my fault? Look at what she's doing... working in a saloon. Just what every good woman should do."

"It's not like you left her a lot of choices, Karl. You did tell her to leave," Pastor Tim answered softly. "And I don't believe she is doing anything wrong. She is just trying to survive under difficult conditions."

"Why does she need a job anyway? I provided everything she needed." Karl grabbed a fork and tossed the dirty straw away from the stall. "She has a roof over her head and food to eat."

"You provided for Sigrid, too. The difference is your attitude. You loved and cared for your wife. Inge feels unwanted."

"You have no right to bring Sigrid into this. This has nothing to do with her." Karl's voice cracked.

"But it does, Karl. It does." Pastor Tim stepped aside to keep from being covered in muck. "I know you loved Sigrid, but she's gone. You must move on. If you don't, you will destroy your life, the children's lives, and Inge's future. You need a partner, the boys need a mother, and Inge needs a family. Please, Karl, Christmas is coming," Pastor Tim pleaded. "Reach out to your family. They need you. Don't kill the little joy and love that's left."

Karl continued stabbing at the straw with the fork, his back to Pastor Tim. Finally, he heard footsteps retreating from the barn. Breathing a sigh of relief, he turned and saw Pastor Tim mount his horse and ride out of the yard.

He doesn't understand what it feels like to lose someone, and some of this is his fault too. Dancing with my wif— Inge on Thanksgiving like he was courting her.

A shudder ran down his spine. He narrowed his eyes and scanned the entire barn. Karl knew he heard something. The words, ***I sacrificed for you*** were imprinted in his mind. He flung the fork. It barely missed the cow and stuck in the hay. Had he not seen Pastor Tim leave the yard, Karl would have blamed him for this unseemly trick. Even as his eyes searched the stalls and the loft, he knew the barn was empty. He recognized the voice, but he refused to deal with it right now.

CHAPTER 33

INGE

nge balled up her shirtwaist and threw it across the bedroom. It fluttered to the floor without touching anything. She wanted to break something just to hear the glass shattering. Maggie's happiness impacted her every time she turned around. *Oh, Lord, forgive me for even thinking such things. Why are my relationships so complicated? Who am I fooling? My relationships are nonexistent.* Karl wanted no part of her. She had avoided Pastor Tim since the dance, and it left a sizable gap in her life. He understood her. His boyish grin and sometimes droll sense of humor had made her laugh. She missed him more than she thought possible. But she wasn't sure if it was appropriate to... to what, encourage him? Or would she just be duping herself into believing he cared?

Maggie talked about Gus incessantly. Inge couldn't bear to hear one more word about the man. She wanted to be happy for Maggie— and she was—but her own disappointment undermined her at every turn. Now, she discovered, Gus would be coming to Christmas Eve supper. Gustaf's attention had Maggie dancing on air while Inge pounded out tunes in a saloon filled with disreputable characters.

Inge hadn't pictured her first Christmas in America like this, being left out, alone, and discouraged. In her daydreams, she envisioned all the things that made *Jul* special would be here, in her new home. But there was nothing like that.

❧

INGE APPROACHED VADA'S DOOR, listening for any sound inside. She knocked. Her bag bulged with Christmas trinkets and candy for the children. It was the least she could do to provide a little Jul joy for them. The bright winter sun created a diamond-encrusted blanket of snow before her. Even the trees were decked out for the holidays with glittering frost adhering to every branch. But the winter beauty didn't cheer her.

The door swung open and four beaming faces peered out.

"Come in, Inge," Vada said as the children held the door. "I have missed seeing you." Vada's spirits seemed upbeat, even joyous, a stark difference from Inge's last visit.

"I'm well. How are you?" Inge asked staring intently at Vada's face. The bruising was nearly gone.

"It's good. Everything is good," Vada answered.

The children giggled behind her. Turning, Inge beheld the small cedar tree covered with beautiful angel ornaments made from feathers, pieces of cloth, and fur, along with seedpods. It looked out of place in the shabby room.

"Isn't it wonderful?" Elizabeth asked as she grabbed Inge's hand and led her to the tree. Her eyes shone with excitement. "Ma told us about the angels that came when Jesus was born, so we made angels to put on our tree." Her fingers gently caressed one of the figures. "Jesus was a baby, you know. Just like the one in Ma's belly." She chattered on. "I want to name the baby Jesus. Don't you think that would be a good name?"

"Ah... ja, Jesus is a wonderful name." Inge looked questioningly at Vada.

Vada blushed and then softly smiled.

"This is true?" Inge asked.

"Ya. Ya, it is."

"When? When is the baby due?"

"In the spring. The children are so excited. I don't know if they can wait that long." Vada extended her hand to Inge. Leading her back to the table, they sat opposite each other.

Inge clasped Vada's hand. "What does your husband think about a new baby?"

"Well, he doesn't know yet. He's been out on the trapline but should be home in a day or two. He wouldn't miss Christmas with the little ones," she said. "This will be a nice gift for him, don't you think?" A smile lit up her face. "Oh, speaking of gifts, I have something for you." She placed four pairs of mittens on the table. They were stunning, with cream leather palms and brown fur on the backside. "They're beaver, so they should keep the hands warm and dry."

"Oh, Vada, they're beautiful," Inge said as she felt the leather and slipped her hand into the soft lining. "But didn't bring money to pay you. Won't get paid until the new year."

"No, no. I want nothing. Please, just take them. Consider it my Christmas present to you."

"*Takk*. And I pay you. Too special to give away." Inge tried to be firm. "And that reminds me why I stopped." She pulled bags from her small satchel. "These are for the little ones." She handed over small packages wrapped in brown paper to each of the children. "But you have to wait until Christmas to open them." Small fingers probed the packages and then hugged them to their chests. The expectation on their faces lit up the dark room.

"And this for you." Inge handed a bag to Vada. Inside were four oranges. They had been expensive, but Inge wanted to get her something special.

Vada rubbed the outside of the fruit, held it to her nose, and inhaled the citrus odor. "Oh Inge, it has been many years since I have had an orange. Thank you so much." Rising, she engulfed Inge in a massive hug. "You are a gift from God."

"*Nei*, I'm the one blessed," Inge whispered. "I was so lonely. You an answer to my prayers."

Vada smiled. "Merry Christmas, Inge. May this be the first of many for our families."

Pulled in by the joy emanating from that small dwelling, Inge stayed longer than she intended. Still worried about what would happen when Vada's husband returned, she found Vada's lack of concern puzzling.

"Vada," Inge said as she rose to leave. "You will send one of the children if you need anything, won't you? I mean, with your condition and all."

"Oh, Inge, I will be fine." Her face beamed. "God built me to have babies."

"Ja, but still…" Inge's voice trailed off. "Something could happen. You could *fall* again."

"There's no danger. Believe me." Vada hugged her close for a moment. "Gabe will be home soon. He will be so happy to hear my news."

"Have a wonderful Christmas." Inge managed to smile weakly as she stepped outside.

I hope he is, Lord. I pray that Gabe is happy to hear the news.

CHAPTER 34

KARL

The following afternoon, Karl glanced out the barn door and saw Inge heading to the icehouse. Her shoulders sagged as she trudged through the snow. Now and then she wiped her eyes with the back of her mittens. For one inexplicable moment, Karl's heart went out to her. Quickly looking away, he stifled the feeling. He couldn't think about Inge. Muddling his way through another Christmas without Sigrid was enough for him to handle right now.

It had taken two days of fighting his demons to admit Pastor Tim had been right. He must consider his family. Determined to change, Karl had been working on gifts for the children, except for Billy. He had something special for Billy. Would his effort be enough to make up for last year when he hadn't even acknowledged the holiday? The boys must have been so disappointed. Would they forgive him? Should they?

Karl ran his thumb over the honed edge of the axe, glistening and sharp. It was time to cut down the Christmas tree. The solid gray sky pressed down on him as he dragged his feet through the shin-deep snow. He loved this land, but he could live without the endless wind. Today it had teeth. The snow skipped and swirled upon the ground like shifting sand. His thoughts were a burden, each one laying a greater weight on his shoulders. He needed to resolve this problem of Inge. After all his years of marriage, he still didn't understand women.

Now that Maggie had Gus, smiles and giggles gushed out of her like she'd downed a bottle of Lena's finest, while Inge seemed needy and cold. No, not exactly. She was too serious, too determined, and too hell-bent on getting hitched. If not to him, then maybe the pastor. That disturbed him too. He wanted her to leave but knew it would be months before she had earned enough for passage back to Norway. Anything could happen in that time. Maybe he should help her. He heaved a deep sigh. *It's my own fault she's here.*

Maggie had been a godsend over the last year. With her nearby to help with the boys, he'd managed after Sigrid died. Had he really managed? Maggie had not alleviated his loss, but she had relieved him of much of his parental responsibility. A blind man could see that she and Gus would marry soon. With Maggie gone, he would have to fend for himself. Should he marry again? It was plain, even to him, that Inge would be a good mother to the boys. And they seemed to have taken to her. But is convenience a good reason to marry?

Reaching the small cedar grove, Karl selected a tree about five feet tall and began to chop at the base. With each blow, his indecision resurfaced in waves. *God, if you're real...* Whack. *Help.* Whack. *Me.* Whack. The force of the blows quickly toppled the tree. Karl fell to his knees, winded, then sat back on his haunches before leaning against the fresh-cut tree. He slid down and huddled in the snow. The wind howled through the trees and pushed swells of snow down the gully, creating a drift that began to build behind his back.

A battle raged within him. How could he possibly betray Sigrid by marrying someone else? His breathing slowed, the snow tethering him to the ground. Unaware of how long he lay there searching for answers, sleepiness tugged at his eyelids. Weariness crawled up his body, so calm and so serene, like a warm blanket. He didn't feel the cold. He felt only peace, the most peace he had felt since before Sigrid died. He wanted to stay here, wrapped in this cocoon.

A branch from the downed tree pricked his nose as it whipped in the wind. The fresh odor of cedar filled his lungs. He was engulfed by memories of Sigrid lighting candles on the Christmas tree, the scent filling the entire house. And then she was there, her features as clear as day. But her usual lighthearted bearing had been replaced by sorrow. Reaching out, she gently touched his cheek, and all the suffering etched on her face flowed into his body. He expected warmth and softness, but only disappointment and pain filled him.

Sigrid smiled softly. "Truly, truly, I say to you, he who believes has eternal life." Then, as quickly as she appeared, she vanished.

Suddenly Karl understood the sadness that filled her eyes. It was him. He had caused it. Sigrid would always be with him, but his lack of care for the boys had broken her heart.

Intense shivering drove Karl to rise to his knees. His very bones seemed to clatter as he thrust upward through the snow and fought to get his feet under him. He fumbled with the rope, trying to tie it to the fresh-hewn tree, but his fingers wouldn't bend. He couldn't feel the cord. Finally, the tether became entangled in the branches enough to hold the tree fast. Forcing himself upright, he staggered toward home. With each step, life became more precious. Each time he fell, Sigrid's image floated before his eyes. He managed to walk a few steps. He fell again, and again. He had to get home, for the sake of the boys. And for Sigrid. He had to celebrate Christmas with his family, and if God was gracious, perhaps this feeling would last longer than just one day.

CHAPTER 35

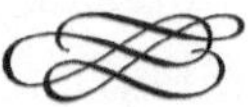

INGE

Christmas would arrive in a couple of days. Inge had always excitedly anticipated the holiday, but this year she struggled. Even though she would participate in the family celebration, she still considered herself an outsider. Maggie's invitation to bake cookies today had lifted her spirits some. But as much as she desired it, she would never be a part of this family.

The door burst open, hitting the wall with a resounding bang and filling the kitchen with a gust of cold air. Maggie dropped her pan and flour scattered across the floor. Karl pitched forward, grasping the door jamb to keep upright. His face, which was mostly hidden by his cap, was unnaturally white. His legs buckled, and he slid down the frame to his knees.

"Inge! Help me!" Maggie grabbed Karl as he slumped forward. "Take his other arm."

Together they dragged him to the rocking chair near the stove.

"Take off his coat. I think he's nearly froze to death." Maggie said.

Inge unbuttoned his coat and freed his arms.

"Get his boots off." Maggie reached for a large dishpan hanging on the wall behind the stove. "See what kind of shape his feet are in."

The alarm in Maggie's voice drove Inge into action. She kneeled and unlaced Karl's shoes. They wouldn't budge when she pulled. She pushed up his pant legs to loosen the boot around the top but recoiled at the touch of his ice-cold flesh. Sitting down on the floor, she braced her feet against the chair and tugged with both hands. The boot and sock came free with an eerie sucking sound. His foot was as white as the snow outside the door.

Maggie gently placed his feet in a pan of tepid water. Karl moaned.

"Dip those towels in the warm water and bring them here." Maggie wrapped Karl's hands in the warm cloths. "Stoke the fire and put some blankets in the oven."

Inge rushed to get the wool blanket off her bed. She folded it as small as possible and put it in the oven. Grabbing another from the sofa, she warmed it in front of the stove for a few minutes before wrapping it around Karl's body.

"We need to get a hot drink in him. Is there any coffee?"

Inge shook her head.

"Then water will have to do."

Inge tried to hold his head upright. Much of the water dribbled down his chin before he finally swallowed.

Karl tried to focus his eyes, but they glazed over and rolled back in his head. Cradling his head in her arm, Inge patiently poured sips of water into his mouth.

"Sig... Sigrid." His words came in pieces. "See... you."

"Shhh. Everything is fine. You home now." Inge wiped his chin with the corner of her apron.

"Sigrid here." He feebly pushed her hand away. "You're not Sigrid."

"*Nei*, I'm not."

Maggie kneeled on the floor and prodded his feet. "Can you feel this?"

He nodded slightly.

Maggie pulled the blanket off him and replaced it with the warm one from the oven.

Violent trembling seized Karl. His hands shook like leaves in a storm and his teeth chattered until Inge thought they would fall out.

"Good," Maggie said. "Yer body is trying to warm itself up."

Inge added more warm water to the basin and gently massaged Karl's feet. His cheeks were still white, along with the tip of his nose, but the blush of color returning to his extremities meant he probably wouldn't lose his fingers or toes.

"Karl, I want to get yeh to bed," Maggie said, holding up his head and speaking loudly. "Can yeh walk?"

Karl grunted and tried to lift himself from the chair. Inge pulled his arm over her shoulder and helped Maggie as he stumbled to the bed.

"Cover him," Maggie said. "I'll be right back."

Inge tucked a warm blanket around Karl and added a quilt. Would he survive this without aftereffects? The boys would be devastated if they lost their father. She couldn't let that happen. "God, you are in control here. I ask for Your touch to bring healing to Karl's body. He has suffered enough," she whispered, gently touching the white spots on his face.

Maggie returned with a bottle. Pouring a small amount into a cup, she lifted Karl's head and poured it down his throat. Karl inhaled deeply and then coughed until the bed shook.

Inge recognized the smell of brandy. Eventually, he quieted, and the color returned to his face. *Thank You, Lord.*

"He knows better than to be out in this cold for any length of time. It must be close to twenty below zero." Maggie paced the kitchen, her hands fluttering like a bird looking for a place to rest.

Inge pulled her toward the table and forced her to sit. She returned with two cups of freshly brewed coffee.

"No," Maggie said pushing the cup aside. "Gimme that." She reached across the table, grabbed the bottle of brandy, and took a long drink.

Slamming it down on the table, Maggie placed her hand over her heart and cleared her throat. "Better. That'll calm me nerves," she said in a hoarse whisper.

She didn't cough. Did that mean...? Inge's eyes opened wide. *Nei*, certainly not.

"Don't look so surprised." Maggie chuckled. "A little brandy is good for yeh now and again."

Ja, it seems to be the cure for almost anything.

CHAPTER 36

INGE

While Karl rested, Inge and Maggie filled the rest of the afternoon making *pepperkake*.

"He'll be fine, don't you think?" Maggie rolled the ginger dough into a flat sheet.

Inge nodded. She had been praying unceasingly since Karl had crashed through the door. Taking a knife, Inge cut star and tree shapes out of the dough. She poked a hole in each for a string so they could be hung on the tree.

"Yeh are praying, aren't yeh?" Maggie pulled a pan of light, crispy cookies out of the oven and shifted them onto a towel. "I reckon he could use a dose of prayer 'bout now."

Inge nodded and offered a hopeful smile. She could pray. Nearly losing him to the cold had brought up new feelings. Her heart felt full and empty at the same time. It was full of compassion for Karl's loss but also empty because she could never be the person to heal his hurt. He wasn't a bad person. She now understood that he drove her away to avoid his own pain. He didn't hate her, but neither could he accept her.

The boys arrived in the neighbor's sleigh after school. The heady aroma of baking cookies greeted them. Billy bounced around the room jabbering about the fun he had at the school Christmas party. Dropping their books and lunch pails in the corner, they all stared longingly at the treats on the table.

"There's a tree outside," Arnie said. "When can we put it up?"

"Hush." Maggie put her finger over her lips. "Yer Pa is resting. He 'bout froze fetching that tree."

"Is he going to be all right?" David asked.

"Ya, but he must warm up a bit. He's tucked in bed for now."

"Can we see him?" Ben asked.

Maggie shook her head. "Yeh boys get the chores done. Maybe he'll be up by supper time."

Inge stirred the soup bones that had been simmering on the stove. She dropped potatoes, carrots, and turnips into the heavy broth. Perhaps she could get Karl to eat a bit when he woke up.

"Can we put up the tree?" Billy asked. Maggie held up her wooden spoon when he tried to snatch a small piece of cookie. "Please?" he said, quickly withdrawing his hand.

"Maybe tomorrow," Karl said.

Inge jumped at the sound of his voice. He leaned on the doorway between the kitchen and parlor for support. The color had returned to his face, but his hands still trembled.

"What're yeh doing up?' Maggie asked, hovering over him like a mother hen as he seated himself at the table. "And what were yeh doing out in that weather?"

"Things are a little fuzzy," he said. "I don't remember getting home."

"Yeh almost didn't make it. Yeh were out of yer head when yeh got here."

"I must have cut a tree." Karl rubbed his hand over his forehead as if trying to push the cobwebs away.

"Inge, check his hands," Maggie said. "Let's hope he won't lose the use of them."

Inge sat a hot cup of coffee in front of Karl. She reached for his fingers to examine the frostbite areas. Though they were red and swollen, there didn't seem to be permanent damage. He didn't pull away as she prodded the darkened spots that were beginning to blister. Aware that his eyes followed her every move, she avoided his gaze and concentrated on his skin.

Drawing away, he used both hands to steady the cup. Even then coffee splashed out as he lifted it to his lips.

Something was different. Inge couldn't put her finger on it exactly. He seemed less hardened and angry than he had before. Despite the frightening ordeal and his obvious weakness, he appeared relaxed and softer somehow.

Lord, I don't know what You have done, but I ask for You to continue to heal Karl—inside and out.

LATE THE NEXT AFTERNOON, the boys burst into the kitchen with their hands and pockets full of treasures they gathered on their hunt for Christmas tree decorations. Karl had remained behind and, with help from Maggie, had managed to nail two boards to the tree's trunk so it would stand.

"Hey, Mam," Billy said. "See what I got?" He held out a fist full of cockle burrs stuck to his mitten.

"Ja, I see," Inge replied as she carefully peeled the mitten from his hand. "They are very... uh... interesting."

Billy grinned, jumping up and down in front of the tree, his pink face glowing from the cold. His enthusiasm was contagious. Inge felt her heart warm at the thought of Christmas.

After supper, Maggie handed out needles and thread to the older boys, and they began stringing the red rose hips while the women quickly washed the dishes. Maggie stoked the fire before she put a pan on the stove to heat. It had to be good and hot before adding the popcorn.

"Arnie," Maggie called. "Yeh come shake the pan for me. Don't let it burn." Arnie took the handle in one hand and kept his other on the lid while he shook the kernels and listened for the first pop. He beamed from ear to ear as the popcorn lifted the top off the pan. Soon they would have fluffy strings of white popcorn covering the branches.

Inge took in the scene before her. Arnie proudly placed his newly acquired bird nest on the tree. David worked quietly in the corner with some willows. And Ben mercilessly teased Billy. Karl reclined in a chair near the potbellied stove, watching the activities. A slight smile graced his face. He blinked rapidly now and then, wiping the corner of his eyes with his handkerchief.

David kept rambunctious little Billy occupied, Arnie worked to please everyone and Ben, well, he was a mystery. Coming of age and losing his mother around the same time were bound to create intense feelings, but his relentless teasing of the others, especially Billy, bordered on cruelty. As for little Billy, who wouldn't love him? Filled with giggles and smiles, joy trailed after him like a sweet-smelling aroma.

"Billy. Come here," David said. Billy ran and leaped into his arms. "Here, hold this. You can help me." He lifted the child, and Billy carefully placed the star, woven from the willows, on the top of the tree.

"It's bootiful, isn't it?" Billy clapped his hands. "Do you think baby Jesus will like it?"

"He will love it," Maggie said. "Now the best part." She brought out the cookies from their hiding place. "Be careful or the cookies will break. We can't put broken cookies on the tree."

"Maggie?" Billy's small hand pulled at her skirt. "What do we do if they break?"

"Why, I guess we have to throw them away," she answered with a straight face.

"Nooo, we eat them."

"No, she's right," Ben said. Taking a cookie and breaking it in two, he went to the door opening it a crack. "See? You can't eat it. I threw it out."

"Nooo," Billy cried, pulling on the door. Ben then dangled the two pieces in front of his face. Billy stretched up his little arms to grab them. "Please, Ben. Don't throw them away. Please."

"Ben stop!" Maggie said. "Let's get these cookies on the tree." David threaded string through the holes and tied them off. He handed them to the others, who hung the cookies carefully on the branches.

Grateful that Maggie had called a halt to Ben's tormenting, Inge didn't understand why Karl hadn't done something about it. Was he blind to Ben's actions, or did he not care?

Oh, Lord, I want to be the one who hugs these boys, who laughs when they say something funny, who comforts them when they hurt, and who offers advice.

Despite everything, she still wanted to be their mother.

CHAPTER 37

Early in the morning two days before Christmas, Maggie and Inge took the team and wagon down the snow-covered road into Taylor's Landing. With their feet resting on heated stones and an extra quilt over their laps, they were comfortable despite the cold.

The clatter of the horses' feet against the frozen ground turned Inge's thoughts to home. If all went as planned, she would be back in Norway by next Christmas. What would she do once she got back to her home? She hadn't thought ahead any farther than to leave here and return to the safe arms of her family. She could picture the Christmas celebration that was happening there tonight, with her parents, siblings, and the children gathered around. Inge could almost smell the spices, the fruit pies, the fresh bread, and even the fishy *lutefisk*. Her mouth watered thinking about it.

She would miss the hugs from family and the reading of the Christmas story. Would she be able to do that this year? Her nieces and nephews always listened intently as if they had never heard it before. She could see the sad expressions on their faces as Mary and Joseph were turned away from the inn and then their wonder as the baby was placed in the manger. A sad smile twisted the corners of her mouth. Would they have music this year with her absent? Would they miss her as much as she missed them?

Maggie stopped in front of the mercantile, breaking into Inge's reverie. "I have to make another stop, and then I will be back."

Clinging to her small change purse, Inge entered the store, welcoming the warmth and the festive air. She searched the room for Clara, not sure she could face the woman after their last encounter. She let out a sigh of relief when she didn't see her.

Inge had mittens for the boys, but what could she get for Maggie or Lena? What about Karl? Would it be appropriate to buy him something? If only he would accept the healing of God, he would have the peace and comfort he desired the most.

Finally deciding on candied fruit for Maggie and a small box of hard candy for Karl, Inge sought something appropriate for Lena. Perhaps a small sack of sweets and a holiday wish would be enough to let her know how much Inge appreciated having a job. After gathering her packages, she walked down the boardwalk to the saloon. Even though it was still early in the morning, Inge knew Lena would be at work. She skirted around the building as always and came in the rear. She still found it impossible to enter through the front door. As expected, Lena had her head buried in the previous night's receipts.

"Merry Christmas, Lena," Inge said from the doorway. "Here, brought some candy."

Lena stood and took her gift. "Why thank you, Inge. I've not gotten into the Christmas celebration much lately, but I do like candy. My sweet tooth, you know." She smiled. "This is very thoughtful of you."

Inge nodded. She was always uncomfortable in the saloon, but now that it was the Christmas season the feeling was even more intense than usual. Shifting from one foot to the other, she had a troubling urge to flee.

"Wait a minute." Lena went behind the bar and returned with

something clasped in her fist. "I want you to have this." She unfolded Inge's hand and dropped the object into her palm. It was a cameo broach. An exquisitely carved, cream-colored rose lay nestled in a round, pink stone surrounded by gold filigree and attached to an artfully crafted golden chain.

"Can't take," Inge gasped. "Beautiful, but too much."

"Consider it a gift from a friend to a friend," Lena said. "You have brought me such joy listening to you play. I can't tell you what it means to me." Inge wasn't sure, but she thought a fleeting shadow passed over Lena's face. "Please take it. It would mean a great deal to me if you would."

Inge gazed at the necklace in her hand, then closed her fingers around it. She nodded at Lena and stepped out the door into the alley. Despite Lena's chosen profession, the woman had a generous and caring heart.

Inge thought of Raven as she passed the hotel. On such a cold day, perhaps she stayed inside. Had she ever gotten a coat? Did she even celebrate Christmas? Jingles wasn't in his usual place on the bench in front of the building either. Inge now realized he meant no harm to anyone. He was just Jingles. But he still made her uncomfortable. The wind had picked up, whipping her skirt into a frenzy. They needed to head home soon.

Inge stood near the mercantile's potbellied stove as she waited for Maggie to return. The holiday spirit pervaded the room. It was full of neighbors visiting, shopping, and searching for last-minute items. Sam's cheerful presence set the tone. His knack for making everyone feel welcome was a natural product of his humble nature. His face was lit with a smile, and his eyes danced as he reached under the counter to pull out some little thing and deftly slip it into a child's hand. In turn, he would receive a huge grin, or a shy smile, or sometimes a hug in payment. Clara advised women on their selection of cloth, buttons, or even spices for baking. Her face was all business and seemed chiseled from rock. Inge stepped behind the stove, grateful Clara remained occupied with customers and didn't notice her. Gentle Sam and stone-faced Clara. How could two such different people end up married?

"Are you ready?" Maggie's voice startled her. "I think I have everything I need."

"Ja, ready. Colder and wind blowing."

"The wagon is out front. Do you have packages?"

"Just this." Inge held out the few things she had purchased.

Maggie looked like a cat that had caught a canary, and she was not about to let it sing, at least right now. Her eyes danced and she bit her lip to hide her smile. Inge waited for her to burst out with her news. She surely couldn't keep a secret for long, or could she?

They placed their packages in the back of the wagon and climbed onto the seat. The rocks were cold, offering no comfort for their feet. Wrapping the quilt snugly around themselves, they headed toward the farm. The temperature had dropped, and the wind drifted loose snow across the road. Inge hunched in her coat and tucked her hands under the blanket. Maggie urged the horses into a trot, and the wagon bounced mercilessly over the frozen wheel tracks.

As they pulled into the lane toward the house, snow began to fall. Not large fluffy flakes, but tiny, hard ice crystals driven by the wind. Inge ducked her head and pulled her scarf over her face to protect it from the stinging snow. Maggie stopped in front of the barn, and Inge stepped down to open the door. The odor of hay and animals wafted out. While still cold inside, it was better than being out in the wind.

Were You born in a place such as this, Jesus? No one has even mentioned Your name. We cannot have Christmas without You.

The icy pellets clinked against the barn, echoing her unanswered questions.

CHAPTER 38

INGE

Julaften, the eve of Christ's birth. Inge inhaled. The house smelled like Christmas, roast goose, apple pies, and fresh bread. Maggie still carried that silly smile on her face as she dashed from the stove to the table, always keeping her eye on the window. Certain all this giddy grinning had something to do with Gus, Inge wondered how much longer she could keep her secret without exploding.

The boys scampered in and out of their room wrapping gifts.

"Can't do this!" Billy threw his present on the floor.

"Let me help you," David said, giving the little boy a hand tying the string. "There you go." All smiles again, Billy placed it among the other packages.

Karl opened the door, letting in a blast of cold air. "Can someone help me with these?" The boys rushed forward and took the bundles out of his arms. "Put them under the tree." He sounded almost jovial. "And no peeking." He laughed aloud.

Who is this man? He was certainly not the Karl that Inge knew. She had sensed a change in him after he nearly froze to death, but this still confounded her.

"I'll be right back." Karl ducked out the door. "I have one more thing to do."

Inge glanced at Maggie, who cocked her head to the side and raised her eyebrows. He returned in a few minutes, shed his coat, stoked the stove in the parlor, and settled into a chair.

The fire crackled. The clock ticked. Maggie's spoon dinged against the pan as she stirred the gravy. But the laughter coming from Karl and the boys sent goosebumps up Inge's arms. What had brought on this change? Was he finally getting over his grief, or was he merely putting on a good show for the holiday?

A sharp rap startled Inge. Maggie fairly jumped out of her skin as she rushed to open the door.

"Come in, come in," she said, beaming at Gus.

Karl greeted him with a handshake. "Let me take your coat."

Gus pulled Karl aside and whispered something in his ear.

"Ya, sure. Should I bring the boys?"

"No. We can manage." Gus turned and sniffed the air. "We'll be right back. It smells wonderful. Oh, I brought guests with me. Two more. I hope that won't be a problem?"

Maggie shook her head, her mouth agape.

Inge grabbed more plates and added them to the table setting. Two additional people would make it crowded, but they would manage. She knew Maggie expected Gus, but the other two were a mystery.

Gus and Karl were back in less than fifteen minutes. Jingles followed them as they entered the kitchen. Inge was surprised but glad that Gus had brought him. She realized he probably had no family. Jingles stopped in the doorway and tugged at someone behind him. He stepped back outside and eventually coaxed Raven into the room.

Inge's hand flew to her heart.

Thank You, Lord, for bringing this child to us for Christmas.

Inge smiled and stepped forward to greet her. Raven's eyes were immense and filled with panic. Shrinking away, she backed into the closed door, both arms crossed over her chest.

Inge stopped. "Jingles, why don't you and Raven warm up in the parlor while we get the food on the table?"

Jingles took Raven's hand, patted her shoulder, and drew the girl into the next room. She held back but finally followed Jingles. Inge pulled chairs near the stove for them.

A fleeting look of displeasure crossed Karl's face as he watched them sit. Sliding his chair closer to Gus, he resumed their conversation. *He could at least acknowledge them. This isn't a night to be rude.*

"Did you know they were coming?" Inge asked Maggie once she returned to the kitchen.

Maggie shook her head. "Just Gus. He's the only one I asked." She pulled Inge off to the far side of the room. "He loves me! He told me this morning when we were in town." The words gushed out like water dumped from a bucket.

At last, the source of Maggie's ebullient attitude. Inge wasn't surprised. The two of them had been inseparable since Thanksgiving. "Wonderful. Glad for you." She clasped Maggie's hand and put a smile on her face.

"It's wonderful, isn't it?" Maggie's smile widened. "I never thought I'd feel this way again."

"God knows," Inge said, "and He provides."

The women dished up the potatoes, gravy, vegetables, lutefisk, lefsa, and Irish soda bread, as well as pickles and relishes. Gus volunteered to carve the goose.

"Come, it's time to eat," Maggie called.

Gus sat at one end of the table and Karl at the other. The rest squeezed together on the benches. It took considerable persuading, but Raven finally settled between Jingles and David, with Maggie seated next to Gus. Inge sat on the other side, next to Karl, with the other three boys. Karl gave her an odd, sidelong glance as she sat down. Of course. This was Sigrid's place. She slid out of her seat and scooted in on the other end of the bench, pushing the boys down toward their father.

Maggie looked up. "Karl? Are yeh going to bless the food?"

"Ya, sure." Karl shifted in his seat, cleared his throat, and stared at his plate. "God... it's another Christmas." Silent for a moment, he continued, "Thank you for the food... and for the family." His voice quavered. "Amen."

The room filled with the clinking of dishes, laughter, and cheerful chatter—a hum that filled Inge's heart.

Poor Raven. She curled in upon herself until Inge thought she might fall off the bench. Her eyes remained downcast as she traced her finger along the edge of the blue scarf wrapped tightly around her neck.

The poor child wore a dress much too large for her. It hung on her gaunt frame, giving her the look of a scarecrow. Someone must have taken pity and given her a cast-off. Inge was glad to see the heavy leather moccasins on her feet come up to her knees.

David spooned up her food. She grabbed small bits with her fingers and used bread to sop up the rest. Her head hung so low that her hair often dipped onto her plate. Sensitive to the girl's lack of table manners, David shook his head slightly when he saw that Billy was about to point them out.

Jingles jabbered throughout dinner. He ate noisily, talking as he chewed and clearly enjoying all the hubbub. Gus regaled them with tales of his undertaking business. Maggie remained silent. Her face was warmly flushed as she cast shy glances at Gus and hung on his every word. Karl quietly watched the festivities. The smile on his face had not quite reached his eyes.

Let him release his sorrow, Lord, and become the father the boys need.

Maggie looked at all the satisfied faces. "Shall we wait until later for the dessert?" A collective groan came from those at the table.

Arnie and Ben joined in the dishwashing, only because they

knew they wouldn't get to open gifts until everything was cleaned up. Karl, Gus, and Jingles settled in the parlor. David and Raven sat in a corner near the tree. David kept his distance, speaking softly to her. Even though her arms were still crossed over her chest, she didn't seem as frightened as before. Inge had yet to hear her speak a word.

"Are we done yet, Maggie?" Billy whined, tugging at her apron strings. "I wanna open my presents."

"Go gather everyone and we'll begin." The boy was a whirlwind of excitement as he scurried off. Inge pulled her Bible from the shelf near the cupboard. A gold chain peeked from between the pages. Uncertain whether to wear the necklace Lena had given her, she had placed it in her Bible for safekeeping.

Billy squirmed and poked at the packages. Ben and Arnie eyed the gifts, their eyes shining in the lamplight. The adults settled themselves on the horsehair sofa and chairs appearing to be almost as excited as the children. Uncertain if she should join them, Inge held back.

"Please," David said. "Sit on the sofa."

After sitting down next to Maggie, Inge cleared her throat. "Read Christmas story?" she asked, looking at Karl for approval.

He nodded.

"In Norwegian, I read." Inge opened her Bible to chapter two of Luke. Even though she was sorry that Gus and his guests wouldn't understand, she plunged ahead. "'And it came to pass in those days that there went out a decree from Caesar Augustus, that all the world should be taxed.'" She continued through the chapter describing the birth of Jesus. Even Billy stopped wriggling and listened attentively. God's gift of His Son, wrapped in a swaddling cloth, and lying in a manger, affected everyone in special ways.

Following the reading, David and Billy passed out the packages. They took turns opening their gifts one at a time.

Inge opened a small scroll from David—a poem. Beautifully written, it brought tears to her eyes. Arnie and Billy had drawn a picture of the family, and it included her. She swallowed the catch in her throat and thanked them.

Maggie produced a round box for Gus. "Merry Christmas," she said.

Gus pulled off the lid and pushed aside the paper. "Maggie, it's the most handsome hat I have ever seen." He slipped the felt wool bowler onto his head. It fit perfectly and the dark color matched his mustache.

"I thought it would give yeh an air of distinction when yeh officiate at funerals," Maggie said. She blushed and lowered her eyes as Gus took her hand.

The boys thanked Inge for their mittens. Karl's choice of gifts for the children surprised everyone. David received a finely tooled leather cover for his journal. Ben's hunting knife had an exquisitely carved deer horn handle. Arnie received a flute that had been whittled from a creamy piece of ash. And little Billy got... nothing? There was no package for him. Tears welled up in his eyes as he watched his brothers enjoy their gifts.

"Don't I get a present too?" He looked at his father.

"Oh, Billy. Didn't you get anything?"

The little boy shook his head, tears threatening to fall.

"Well, let me see. Maybe I forgot it outside. We can't have you going without a present."

Billy's face lifted with expectation.

Karl opened the door and pulled a small crate covered with a canvas inside the room. "Here it is. I knew I had something for you."

Billy rushed over, pulled off the covering, and peered between the boards. He plopped down beside the box with a bewildered look on his face.

"Go ahead, you can open it," Karl said.

The boy removed the lid and was greeted by a ball of black and white fuzz with a red tongue and bright shining eyes. "A puppy. It's a puppy," he whispered.

"He comes with responsibility," Karl said. "You must feed him, keep him out of trouble, and train him to be a good dog."

Inge doubted the boy heard anything his father said. The little dog leaped into his arms and slobbered all over his face. The two of them rolled about, Billy laughing and the puppy yipping. Even Karl joined the rest of the boys on the floor as they played with him.

Inge laughed aloud as she watched their antics. Unexpectedly, she realized it had been a long time since she had genuinely laughed... an awfully long while since she had experienced real joy. That awareness tempered her feelings toward the scene before her. She wasn't part of this, so it was better to not get overly emotional or attached. *But it's probably too late for that.*

"Wait up, there's one more gift... for my Maggie," Gus shouted above the din. "Grab your coats. We must go up to the cabin."

Billy refused to put his puppy back in the crate and join the others. "I will stay with him," Inge said. "No need to go outside."

"Oh, no yeh don't," Maggie exclaimed. "Everyone is going to see my present. The dog will be fine for a few minutes."

Inge took the quilt from the sofa and gently placed it around Raven's shoulders. The girl pulled it close, rubbing the soft flannel edging against her chin. Jingles put his arm around her and led her out the door.

Billy reluctantly put the pup back in the box. Slipping on their coats, they followed the others up the path to Maggie's. A few snowflakes glided to the earth. Billy raced ahead, dodging here and there to catch one on his tongue.

"I got one," he shouted. Running to Inge, he opened his mouth. "See?"

"Oh, Billy, that must have been a big snowflake," she said. Grinning, Billy bounded away to join the others.

What had Gus gotten for Maggie? It must be big if they had to unload it at the cabin. Judging by the starry looks in their eyes, Inge was sure that they would marry soon.

The rest were waiting at the door for Inge to catch up with them. "You all wait here while I go in and light the lamps," Gus said. With that, he disappeared into the house and soon a warm glow crept out the windows.

He cracked the door open and said, "Maggie is first, then the rest of you can come in."

Once everyone was inside, Gus whisked the canvas off a large wooden box that was suspended between the seats of two chairs. Maggie's gasp was audible. A hush settled over the rest as they stared.

"I used the finest of woods and polished it with special oils, which is why it's reflecting the light so beautifully." Gus stroked the red cedar as if it were a baby. "Notice the rounded corners. Takes a lot of work to get them perfect." He lifted the lid to display the top. "I inlaid white ash in the design of a prairie rose because I knew it was Maggie's favorite flower." He put his arm around her and pulled her close. "I did not want my remarkable Maggie to have anything but the absolute best," he said. "What do you think?"

Inge looked at the others in stunned silence. Was it what it appeared to be? Because it appeared to be a coffin. Maggie's mouth hung open and her eyes reflected something akin to alarm. Her mouth snapped shut, and she pushed away from Gus, keeping him at arm's length.

Jingles stepped closer and touched the inlaid rose. "It's right purdy, Gus," Jingles said. "Hows come you put a rose on a coffin?"

Gus's jaw dropped. "Oh no! It's not a coffin. It's a hope chest. A big one that we can fill with all our hopes and dreams," he said. He put his hands on Maggie's shoulders and looked into her eyes. "Because I am very much hoping she will marry me."

Maggie was speechless, but her smile and tears, along with her nod of ascent, were enough for Gus. He enveloped her in an enormous hug and twirled her around the room.

Covering her mouth, Inge backed out the door and headed toward the bench beneath the plum thicket. Brushing off the snow, she sat down. Giggles erupted, turning into hysterical bursts until her sides hurt. *Not a coffin? Looked like one to me.*

Suddenly aware she wasn't alone, Inge's eyes strained in the darkness at the figure coming toward her. She recognized Karl once he got closer.

"What's so funny?"

Unable to control herself, Inge waved her hands toward the cabin and collapsed in laughter again. Karl looked at her for a moment and began to chuckle. Resting on the bench beside her, the unusual gift led to more laughter.

"It really isn't funny," he gasped.

"I know." She dissolved into another frenzy of giggles.

Once the delirium had passed, the two of them sat on the bench watching huge fluffy flakes float down from the starless sky. "Snow makes a lovely Christmas Eve," Inge said.

Karl leaned forward resting his elbows on his knees. His hands cupped his chin as he stared at the feathery snow slipping quietly to the ground.

Inge rose. Now that the absurdity of it all had passed, she felt uncomfortable.

Karl reached out and rested his hand on her arm. "Please stay. I haven't laughed like that since before Sigrid died. It felt good."

"Ja, it did," she said, returning to her seat. "Been a long time for me, too."

"I'm happy for Maggie."

"Me too."

"I'm sorry," Karl mumbled as he reached for her hand.

"Sorry?" She frowned.

"Yes, sorry I am not a better man, a better father... Just sorry."

Inge didn't know how to respond to his confession.

"Pa." Billy's excited voice exploded through the curtain of snow. "Pa, let's go see my puppy."

Karl jerked his hand away and followed the little boy back to the house, not looking back or inviting her to join them. Inge remained seated without the will to get up. For one moment hope lived... then dissolved like a snowflake on her tongue.

Hunkered on the snow-laden bench, Inge prayed. "Lord, I don't know what you are asking of me. I am scared and unsure I am following Your will." She watched the flakes of snow pile atop one another. Alone, each flake was nothing. Together, they created something beautiful. "I am willing to sacrifice myself to build this family. Show me how. And give me the courage to step out in faith, and follow Your leading no matter the circumstances."

"We were about to have cake," Maggie said when Inge entered the kitchen. She had forgotten it was Arnie's birthday. Everyone gathered around the table. They clapped as he blew out a large candle in the center of the cake. He smiled and shyly looked around. His entire body filled with an effervescence that lit the room.

"What did you wish for?" Billy asked. "Tell me. I wanna know."

Arnie thought for a moment. "I can't tell you. If I tell you, it won't come true."

"That's stupid," Ben said. "It's just a wish. It ain't gonna come true anyway. Don't be such a baby."

Arnie's shoulders sagged a bit and his smile faded. Ben slapped him on the back hard enough to knock him forward a step. Why did he take such satisfaction in ruining his brother's special moment?

After everyone had retired to the parlor, Raven edged up to the table. She stared at the cake, then reached down and hooked some frosting on her finger.

"When is your birthday, Raven?" Inge asked as she poked more wood into the stove.

The girl jerked her hand behind her back.

Inge busied herself with warming the coffee and collecting cups.

"Mine in spring. I love that. New life is everywhere. *Mor* made birthdays special. Miss that. I miss my mother," Inge said. Bringing two cups of coffee, she sat down across from the cake.

"Me too," Raven said, her voice barely above a whisper. "I miss my mother, too. Never had a birthday." She looked up. "I like spring."

"Ja. Spring wonderful time." Inge went on to tell the girl about Christmas with her family. Raven listened intently but with a bewildered look on her face.

"Why do you give things to each other?" she asked.

"Well..." Inge began to talk about the gift of Jesus. Raven's brow furrowed and her face warped in confusion. Inge stopped. "Because we love each other."

"I never got a... a..."

"Gift," Inge said.

Raven nodded.

Remembering the scarf, Inge pointed to it. "Scarf. A gift."

Raven softly fingered the blue scarf around her neck. "Gift?"

Inge nodded.

The corner of Raven's lip attempted a smile.

The rest of the family wandered into the kitchen for a slice of cake. Inge poured more coffee while Maggie passed out generous squares of dessert. Eventually, only David, Inge, and Raven remained at the table. David placed a slice in front of Raven and then served himself. He placed a fork near her and then dove into his own sweet treat. Raven took a small bite. She savored it before swallowing. Inge marveled at the girl's self-control. Apparently, she wanted it to last forever.

"I think we had better head home." Gus's booming voice echoed off the walls. "It's still snowing, and we want to get back in case the wind comes up. I don't want to get caught in a blizzard. Come on Jingles, let's get going." They donned their warm clothing, except for Raven. She had only the worn blanket to wrap around her shoulders.

Inge handed a quilt to Gus. "Keep her warm."

The reflection of the gold chain protruding from her Bible caught Inge's eye. Pulling it free, Inge walked over to the girl.

Taking Raven's hand, Inge slipped the necklace into her palm. "Merry Christmas. A gift. God loves you."

CHAPTER 39

INGE

Frost unfurled its feathers on the windowpane overnight. Rubbing a spot clear, Inge glimpsed the crisp, clear Christmas Day with its dazzling display of new fallen snow. The deep, almost holy silence was broken only by the occasional snapping of a tree reacting to the intense cold. While others disliked the frigid temperatures and snow of winter, Inge found an almost sacred connection to the purity of the white landscape. A slight quiver crept up her arms. Christmas Day was always special, but today she felt something different. Today would be an extraordinary day. She was sure of it. Reluctantly turning from the window, she hurried to dress in the cold room.

Maggie's smiling face glistened as she bustled about the kitchen. "Can you believe it? Can you believe Gus wants to marry me?" She chattered like a magpie.

Inge smiled. She couldn't blame her. Love should be shouted from the highest hill.

"I must plan the wedding. Will yeh help me?" Maggie asked. "I never had a wedding with Nels. I want to do this right. Do yeh think I should make a new dress? And where should we hold the ceremony? I'm not a good churchgoer, but maybe the pastor would marry us?"

The cascade of words made it impossible for Inge to do anything but nod.

"Come. Eat. Then we'll join Karl and the boys for church services," Maggie said. "Gus will be there too." She turned pink at the mention of his name.

Getting everyone warmly bundled and into the wagon took forever. Billy's insistence that they take the puppy gave way to tears when Karl said the dog could not go to church. As they sat bunched together and covered with blankets, the heated rocks at their feet kept them warm. They sang carols as their noses reddened and eyelashes frosted in the wintry air. This was Christmas. Faith and family coming together to celebrate Christ's birth.

Buckboards and sleighs filled the churchyard. After climbing out of the wagon, they greeted friends and neighbors as they entered the building. Inge removed her heavy coat and glanced around the room hoping she might see Vada and her family.

The coat slipped from her hands. She reached for the back of a bench for support. Slowly she retrieved her garment. Her other hand groped along the wall for the coat hooks as her gaze remained glued to the front of the room. A piano sat up front. Not just any piano... her piano, the one she played at Lena's. Polished until the wood gleamed, it was adorned with cedar boughs, candles, and red ribbon. She could hardly believe it was really there. She dropped into the pew, her mouth still slightly ajar, gawking at it.

A hand rested on her shoulder. Inge turned and looked into Lena's twinkling eyes. "May I join you?" Inge nodded and slid over to make room.

Still speechless, she raised her hand toward the piano.

"I guess if I want to hear you play now, I will have to come to church." Lena grinned and gripped Inge's hand. "It seemed such a shame that everyone couldn't enjoy the piano and your talent, so I have given it to the church and school."

"What?"

"Merry Christmas," said Pastor Tim as he stepped behind the pulpit. "God has truly blessed us this year." He gestured to the piano. "Thanks to Lena Calhoon, we are now entrusted with this beautiful instrument." The congregation applauded. "Now all we need is someone to play it." He looked at Inge and motioned toward the piano.

Inge's legs refused to lift her up. Lena's hand on her elbow finally propelled her forward.

"Please, Inge. Come and grace God's house with music on this Christmas Day," said Pastor Tim.

Sitting down, Inge let her fingers run over the keys, savoring the cool, smooth ivory. Somehow, the keys felt different than they did in the saloon. She leaned back and allowed God to bring forth His music. "Hark the Herald Angels Sing" flowed through the church. The crowd sang along with gusto. She racked her mind for every carol she could remember. Lost in the moment, it was only after her fingers rested that she sensed the joy and reverence in the room.

Inge looked up from the keyboard. Karl was staring at her. Had he been pleased with her playing? Maggie giggled and Karl turned his gaze to her and Gus. His face was usually so unreadable, but now it looked naked and undisguised. He jerked his head away and loosened his collar. Inge could not help but watch as he fidgeted in his seat, his gaze always returning to Maggie and Gus. Was he... jealous of their interaction? *Nei*, that wasn't it. A longing filled his face, betraying a desire or need to... to what? There was something bothering him. It was as if he was perched on a rooftop trying to decide his fate. She had tried to understand the sorrow he experienced. Why was he so troubled today? Maybe it was because of Christmas. Holidays were difficult when you were alone, and she was acutely aware of how that felt.

Pastor Tim preached a sermon on the Savior's birth. No matter how many times Inge heard it, she was still awed that God, Himself, had come into the world as a defenseless baby. Not to redeem all of humanity but for her alone. While she knew Jesus saved everyone, for her, His gift was personal.

As the last notes of "O Holy Night" dissipated, Inge didn't move. This was wonderful. To play in church was beyond her dreams. Her hands froze on the keys. *Nei!* This can't be.

God provided this magnificent gift, but she wouldn't be here to play it.

She stumbled through the last song, her hands losing their will to play as she realized she would no longer have a job either.

How will I get home? How will I manage to earn my fare? God, I don't understand. I can't stay, and now I can't go.

"Uhm, Pastor." Gus stood. "I would like to make an announcement, if I may." Moving to the front, he twisted his hat in his hands. "Aah, I have... that is, Maggie and I... what I mean to say..." Taking a deep breath, he looked at Pastor Tim. "Would you marry us come February? That is, I asked Maggie, and she has consented to be my wife." The blush on his face spread to the top of his bald head as he held out his hand to his intended. Maggie joined him at the front of the church, her cheeks turning crimson.

"I would be delighted." Pastor Tim pumped Gus's hand. "A wedding to begin the New Year. What a wonderful surprise."

"And we'd like all of you to come to the wedding," Gus said to the fellowship as he wrapped his arm around Maggie and drew her close. The congregation exploded with cheers and whistles.

From the corner of her eye, Inge saw Karl stand and come forward. He cleared his throat a couple of times. "As long as we're having a wedding, let's make it two. I would like to marry Inge at the same time."

Inge's jaw dropped. She clutched the piano to keep from falling off the bench. *What did he say? I must have heard wrong. Married?*

Pastor Tim's eyes widened, and his mouth opened slightly. "Two weddings. What do you think of that?"

Pastor Tim's face was unreadable as he took her arm and guided her to Karl's side. He certainly wasn't as enthusiastic as he had been about Gus's announcement.

Maggie and Gus were cheering. Billy jumped up and down on the pew. The other boys were grinning, except for Ben, whose face rolled like a thundercloud. Karl fidgeted, barely acknowledging Inge at his side. What just happened? Was she getting married?

INGE

Despite being homebound because of the frigid weather, the week after Christmas flew by. Inge left the cabin only once, and that was to visit Vada.

Knocking on the flimsy door of the shack, she was relieved to see Vada's face light up when she opened the door. She pulled Inge inside and wrapped her in an enormous hug, squeezing the breath out of her.

"I missed you." She held Inge at arm's length and looked her over. "Come in. Get next to the stove," Vada said. "You look half frozen."

Inge embraced the stove to thaw herself out. How did Vada's family survive in this awful cold? Gaping cracks between the boards were stuffed with moss and grass, but even with that, heavy frost clung to the walls.

Settling on the bench before the table, Vada poured hot drinks for them both. "How are you doing?" Vada asked. "Did you have a nice Christmas?"

Unable to contain her news a minute longer, Inge burst out, "Karl asked me to marry."

Vada pushed herself stiffly upright, the coffee pot suspended in mid-air.

"Aren't you going to congratulate me?" Inge asked.

Vada lowered the pot to rest on the table and stared down at her cup.

"Well, say something." Inge leaned forward and extended her hands.

"Congratulations."

"You don't look pleased," Inge said. "I came to be married, and now I will be."

"Are you sure this is what you want?" Vada lifted the cup to her lips.

"I am. God cleared the way for me. Now have husband and family, home of my own."

"If you take this step," Vada said, "it will be for a lifetime. Our dreams don't always take us where we ought to be."

"Are you saying that this isn't God's plan for me?"

"No. I would never say that." Vada's brow furrowed. "God has a plan, but it may not be the same as yours."

Inge rose from the table. She had counted on Vada's support. Instead, her friend had thrown cold water on her wedding plans. *We both listen to the same God but come to very different conclusions.*

Which one of us isn't hearing what You say, Lord?

Inge pulled the door open. "Thank you for... for the visit." Uncertainty wrapped itself around her and squeezed her heart until it hurt.

Inge mulled over their conversation as she plodded through the deep snow toward home. There was a snippet of truth in Vada's words. A thread of uneasiness resurfaced and hung around the edges of her anticipation. Had not God opened the door? *Sure, Karl isn't perfect, but neither am I. Once we're married, everything will fall into place. Besides, I can't worry about things that might never happen.*

Memories of Luke rolled over her. She had loved him. A relationship with Karl would not have those intense emotions. What would a marriage to Karl look like? Would they be partners, companions, friends, or maybe none of those things? Could she live with... with emptiness? Was she like the woman in the Bible who had harangued the judges at the gate until they gave her what she desired? *God, surely I haven't begged until you gave me what I wanted whether it was Your will or not.* Struck by a sudden thought, she smiled. God had removed her job. Surely that was a sign she was to stay here and marry Karl.

CHAPTER 41

KARL

A new year would begin tomorrow. Karl stared at the ceiling in the barn as the wind howled around the corners and snow sifted through the occasional crack in the walls. *What on earth was I thinking? One minute I was sitting in a pew and the next I found myself getting engaged.*

He had settled in his mind that Inge would return to Norway, but now... now he had informed the entire congregation of his intentions. He couldn't very well renege on his word. He would look foolish, at the very least. To add to his guilt, Inge seemed pleased to be marrying him. He had no complaints about her cooking and housekeeping skills. The boys liked her, especially Billy and Arnie. These were all good points, but the fact remained that he had no feelings for the woman. Well, no, he did have feelings. He felt irritation that she was here and Sigrid was gone. He hated that she wanted to fill that space.

He couldn't marry her. He would betray Sigrid if he did. Karl listened to the owl hoot in the loft. The soft, mournful call filled him with weariness. He knew he was lying to himself. It wasn't true. Sigrid would want him to move on, to not be alone. He saw it in her eyes when she appeared before him that day he cut the Christmas tree. He had sensed sorrow, but also disappointment. She knew him so well. She knew he would cling to her memory and use it as an excuse to remain alone and isolated.

But he also had the boys to consider and with Maggie and Gus getting married, he wouldn't be able to rely on Maggie for... for everything. She had stepped in and become a mother to the boys. Annoyed with his reliance on his sister-in-law, he stabbed the fork into the hay and dropped it in the manger with a thump. Bossie rolled her eyes and stepped away. Women! He couldn't even please the cow.

He was tired of being alone. But would this marriage solve that problem? Might it not be worse to be married to someone you resented, someone you constantly compared to another, or someone who would fall short of your desires at every turn? Would that be fair to Inge? Could he pretend that he cared about her? Surely, she would know that he wasn't being genuine, especially after his rude treatment of her. This was all too much. His head swam with questions for which he had no answer.

Karl kicked the side of the stall. Rubbing his aching foot, he reached out to soothe Bossie as he knelt and scrubbed her udder before milking. He pulled the stool close and began rhythmically filling the bucket with milk. He had a month to figure out what he should do. What the solution might be, he didn't know, but something had to be done. Perhaps he should talk to Pastor Tim.

Not sure if that was wise, he leaned into the cow and continued milking. The two of them obviously had a wonderful time at the Thanksgiving celebration, and he found that he was slightly envious of their interaction while dancing together. Inge had laughed out loud. It was the first time he had seen her enjoying herself. He was jealous because he wasn't part of it and hurt because she seemed to like being in Pastor Tim's arms. He knew she had done nothing wrong, but he hadn't been able to stop himself from being nasty to her. Now that he was going to marry her, he should... should be able to make her happy. But he didn't know if he was able to do that.

CHAPTER 42

PASTOR TIM

Pastor Tim stood at the door of the church and watched the wagon bounce over the snowdrifts as Hulda and her two friends drove off. What a way to begin January. Being a pastor came with some difficult jobs. He tried to explain to the women that the piano was just an object. There was no reason to not keep or enjoy it. As for Lena, they were not called to judge other people by their circumstances but by their hearts. Quite sure neither idea penetrated their self-righteousness, he shrugged his shoulders and closed the door. They left as adamant as they had been upon their arrival. He wondered if he had chosen the right profession.

To top it off, they objected to Inge's marriage to Karl, as if that was any of their business.

Inge loved God and would be an outstanding wife and mother. Pastor Tim knew she had never acted inappropriately while in Lena's employ because Inge had confided to him her concerns about accepting the job. Anyone could see that she had high values and a sweet, gentle nature. From the astonished expression on her face last Sunday, he was sure she had no idea Karl intended to propose, much less in front of the entire church. Had Karl even given it much thought? Or was it another of his impulses, like inviting her to come here?

Well, whatever it was, it appeared there would be a wedding. The thought of Inge entering a loveless match disturbed him. She appeared pleased to be marrying Karl, though, even after his rejection of her. That act he couldn't understand. She deserved so much more than a marriage that lacked affection. Her determination to wed appeared to be driven by a force beyond common sense.

Pastor Tim stared through an unfrosted corner of the window-pane. Why did this bother him? Had his feelings gone beyond that of a pastor for his flock? Or was it Karl's obsession with his first wife? Why couldn't he let her go? He had to release Sigrid or this marriage would never work.

Turning from the window, he sat at his desk and tried to work on school lessons for the new year. But his mind wandered. He liked Inge. They had a lot in common. Why was she so intent on marrying Karl? Or was it just the idea of marriage and family? He could see her affection for the boys, especially little Billy. He rose from the desk and paced the floor before opening the door of the potbellied stove and throwing in a log. Sparks and smoke filled the air. He wanted to sweep her away from all this chaos. But what could he do? She had decided and it wasn't his place to interfere.

Was she more than a friend? Did his feelings run deeper than they should? The stirring he felt at the Thanksgiving gathering had filled him with confusion. She had been so vulnerable and alone. He had held her and found desire filling his body. *Oh, Lord, I can't be involved in this. It's their decision, not mine.*

CHAPTER 43

PASTOR TIM

On the following Sunday afternoon after church, Pastor Tim welcomed a visit by Karl. "It's good to see you. Inge plays beautifully, doesn't she? You must be proud of her."

Karl stood in the doorway, backlit by the sun, his face hidden in shadows. He stepped inside and stared at the floor, fidgeting with his hat until Pastor Tim thought he might tear it apart.

What can I do for you today?"

Clearing his throat several times, Karl began, "I... I wanted to..."

"Is everything all right?"

"Ya, well... I'm not sure. I mean... I need to talk to you about the wedding," Karl said, his words coming out in chunks.

"Certainly. Is there something special you want to do?"

"Well, no. It's just that... I'm not sure... I don't know..." His voice trailed off.

"Well, spit it out." Pastor Tim chuckled. "I'm sure we can figure out something. I expect the brides to have made most of the arrangements. What would you like me to do?"

"Ah... I... I was thinking that I shouldn't be doing this." Karl's words tumbled over each other in their rush to leave his mouth.

"Doing what?" Pastor Tim asked.

"Getting married."

Pastor Tim slowly lowered himself onto a bench. "You don't want to get married?" A sickening feeling rolled over him. Karl wouldn't do this again, would he? What kind of a man rips hope from a woman time and time again?

"Ya, well... it was kind of hasty on my part." Karl looked sheepish. "I'm not sure why I announced we'd be married. I don't know. It was strange... No, it... well, I can't really explain it."

Pastor Tim's heart collapsed within him. "I'm not sure what you expect me to do."

A heavy silence settled over the two men. Devoid of words, Pastor Tim ran his hand through his hair. Karl sank into the seat next to him.

Finally, Pastor Tim asked, "Why don't you want to marry Inge?"

"It was a mistake. I should have never asked her to come here. I don't know what I was thinking. I just know I can't marry her." Karl's voice cracked.

"Karl, it's been nearly two years since Sigrid passed. Think of the boys. In addition, you must think of yourself. Life goes on, and sometimes we must muddle through the best we can." Pastor Tim floundered, trying to find appropriate words.

"So, the best I can do is marry Inge? Even if I don't want to?" Karl's eyes reflected the absurdity of Pastor Tim's answer.

"Ah... well, I didn't say that exactly. Have you talked to Inge about this?"

"No. Actually, we have not talked since Christmas Day."

"That was two weeks ago." Pastor Tim's voice rose. "Well then, I'd say you had better discuss your doubts with her before this goes any further. She's a wonderful woman. Maybe she'll understand." Pastor Tim agonized over his words. How could he explain to someone as bullheaded as Karl, that you didn't jerk people back and forth like a yo-yo? "It wouldn't be right to make a decision this serious without talking to her first."

"Ya, I suppose. Talk to her, huh?" Karl's hands shook. He nervously worked at the small hole in his hat until he could shove his finger through it. "What do I say?"

"Well, the truth might be a good place to start." Pastor Tim's hand slapped the side of the pew, and it sounded like a gunshot echoing in the empty room.

Karl jumped. "Tell her the truth? What will she think of me?"

"I have no idea, Karl." Pastor Tim's harsh tone made Karl squirm. "Pray and ask God to intervene. He's the only one who can give you the words, or the feelings, that you need right now." A knot formed in Pastor Tim's middle at the very thought of Inge being rejected again. He really wanted to wrap his hands around Karl's neck and shake some sense into him.

"I suppose we should talk," Karl mumbled.

"Let me know what you decide. Soon." Pastor Tim herded Karl outside before he said something he'd regret.

Leaning his forehead against the closed door, Pastor Tim clenched his fists. How could Karl do this to her? Again. He swept his desk clean with his arm, books thudding to the floor.

Lord, You can't let this happen.

CHAPTER 44

KARL

Following his chat with Pastor Tim, Karl mulled over their visit on the way home. "Talk to her, he says. That's easy for him to say," Karl muttered. Deep down, he knew what he should do, but calling on Inge was probably the last thing he was going to do. Maybe if he didn't show up for the ceremony? Even he knew he couldn't do that. People would see him as... a cowardly heel or worse. And what would his boys think of him? No, there had to be some other way. Some way he could drive her away so this wouldn't be his fault.

After arriving at the barn, he unsaddled the horse. He busied himself with feed and water as he racked his brain for a solution. He attacked the hay with a pitchfork and flipped forkfuls into the manger for Bossie.

"Karl?" Inge's voice startled him.

What was she doing here?

"I was hoping to talk to you about... well, about the wedding plans." Her words came out in measured bursts. "How would you feel if I asked Lena to stand up with me?"

"Well, isn't that just dandy!" He jabbed the fork deep into the pile of hay. "Lena? In the wedding party?"

Inge squirmed at his tone. "Lena is a good person. We can't judge—"

"You want to have a saloon keeper stand up at *my* wedding?" Turning, Karl said, "If you have her up there, you will be alone at the altar."

Wariness opened Inge's eyes wide. "Didn't mean to upset you. Perhaps we should sit down and discuss the plans... soon."

"Ya, perhaps we need to talk." Karl threw another forkful of hay into the trough.

"When?" Inge asked. "When would be a good time?"

"Ah... I'll let you know." He had created this situation himself, but now he desperately wanted to escape it. He had to think and come up with some way to tell her the truth.

Inge nodded, opened the barn door, and slipped outside.

Karl flung the pitchfork, driving the tines into the floor. How was he going to get out of this mess?

CHAPTER 45

INGE

Inge looked at her gray dress. The weddings were less than a month away and approaching fast. Maggie had the perfect cloth stored away for a special occasion, though she had never suspected it would end up as her wedding dress. The pale green calico made her fiery hair shine like burnished copper and her emerald eyes sparkle. It also softened the ruddiness of her complexion, giving it a rosy glow.

As for Inge's wedding attire, she had decided to wear her only suitable dress rather than something new. She and her mother had made the lightweight gray wool dress before she left Norway. Though not quite as flattering as Maggie's, it was still quite acceptable. With the addition of lace at the edge of the cuffs and around the neckline, it befitted the occasion.

While Maggie's enthusiasm bubbled over onto everything she touched, Inge confined her feelings to a small box. It was easier to control them that way. She wondered about her union with Karl. At this point, what choice did she have but to marry him? Without any means to support herself, she had to do something. She couldn't stay in the cabin, since Maggie and Gus would live there after their wedding. She could visualize Maggie and Gus building a life together, perhaps even having children one day, but there was no such picture for herself. So she tried to avoid contemplating any future beyond the actual ceremony, but it was impossible not to think about it. How did Karl feel about all of this? He certainly didn't act excited about getting married. In fact, he seemed to be avoiding her.

DECIDING THEY HAD TO TALK, Inge's courage rapidly dwindled as she stood in front of the barn. She had waited a week for Karl to seek her out. Why was he avoiding her? Unless… unless he had changed his mind. Just as she was about to retreat, the door swung open, and Karl stood there with a bucket of steaming milk.

"What are you doing here?" he asked.

"You said we should talk, and I have been waiting…" Inge's voice faded.

"Ya, well, not now. I have things to do." He tried to move past her.

Inge snapped. Outrage blurred her vision and filled her ears with a roar. She grabbed his arm and shoved him back into the dim light of the barn. The pail hit the ground and milk slopped onto their feet.

"We will talk. Now!" she said, stepping to within inches of Karl's face.

Karl's mouth dropped open.

"I have waited for seven months for you to make a decision about marrying me." She grabbed his shirt, pulling him closer. "And then you make an announcement to the entire congregation. Did it ever occur to you to *ask* me?"

Karl held up both hands in surrender.

"Do you understand that I left my home, my country, everything to come here for you? Do you understand the sacrifice I made?"

Karl tried to back up, but she continued to press closer.

"I feel loss too! You miss your wife, but you have four wonderful children and a home. I have nothing."

Karl put his hands on her shoulders and pushed away from her.

She let go of his shirt and took a step back. "And now because of Lena's generosity, I can't even earn enough to go back to Norway."

Karl opened his mouth to say something.

"And that's another thing. I did nothing wrong in Lena's saloon. Why did you think less of me for that? I was trying to get out of your life."

Karl stumbled back a few steps.

"Do you want to marry me or not? Because if you don't, I will leave. Today." Inge backed up, giving him some room.

Karl turned abruptly, picked up the bucket, and hurried to the icehouse.

Watching his back recede in the dusk, Inge's shoulders sagged, her energy spent. She slammed the door against the frame. Still shaking, she sank down on the milking stool near the cow. *I shouldn't have said those things. He never said a word. What got into me?* The cow turned her head and stared at Inge's trembling body with gentle eyes. Offering a low moo, she swung her head over Inge, leaving a long string of green saliva draped on her cheek.

She wiped her face. The green slime clung to her fingers. *Why am I willing to marry someone like Karl? He's unkind, unpredictable, and who knows what else? He hems and haws like... like a groom with second thoughts.*

Inge buried her head in Bossie's warm flank. "What's wrong with me? Am I so blind that I can't see a hopeless state of affairs?"

This marriage, of course, would not be the romance she desired but more of a partnership. No, that wasn't it either. It was convenient. Could she settle for that? Luke's rejection still pained her. *Luke was everything. Karl is nothing. He is unknown, unknowable. Would I ever feel safe with him? Would I ever feel loved?*

"Bossie, what do you think?" She ran her hand over the black spot on the cow's shoulder. "I doubt you have to worry about such things."

The cow flicked her tail and continued to search for the tastiest stems of hay.

"Are you happy with a stall and feed? You seem to be."

How much am I willing to sacrifice? Would a home and children be enough? Am I being pigheaded in pursuing this relationship... or am I missing what You called me to do, Lord?

The cow lifted her tail and unloaded a pile of warm manure that splattered onto her skirt. Steam rose from the new deposit and the smell surrounded her.

"Thanks, Bossie. That's exactly how I feel."

Inge stood when she heard the creak of the door hinges. Gathering her skirt around her, she brushed past Karl as he entered. He seemed surprised that she was still there.

"Inge, I'm sorry." The words came out in a ragged whisper as he grasped her arm.

Pulling away, she moved forward. He jerked her back.

"I said I was sorry!"

"I know," she said, refusing to look at him.

Karl pulled her inside and shut the door. Standing in the growing darkness of the building, he stammered, "I... I'm sorry... for answering your letter and asking you to come here."

"I know."

"I needed someone. When I saw you, I knew you could never replace my wife." He clutched her arm tighter.

"I know," she said, prying his hand loose.

"I don't blame you if you want to go home. It would probably be the best thing for both of us."

Inge nodded.

"But, if you want to be married, we can do that," Karl said. "Or I will pay for your ticket to return to Norway."

Inge stood there, shrouded in the encroaching darkness. "What do you want me to do?"

CHAPTER 46

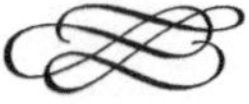

INGE

The next day Inge found herself at the school. Knocking softly, she hoped Pastor Tim wouldn't be there on a Saturday. If he was, she had no idea what to tell him. Pride would not allow her to share her feelings. She desperately needed some quiet time to pray. God had abandoned her, or at least that's how it felt. She needed to be alone.

She opened the door and scanned the room to make sure it was empty. Sighing in relief, she moved to the piano. It was the music she needed. Music would ease her confused emotions and bring some order to her thoughts. Her fingers trailed over the keys, producing a melancholy tune.

Marry Karl or go home? Since Lena had given the piano to the church, she no longer had a job. God had shut that door, and then He opened another—a marriage proposal. Karl had reiterated his offer in the barn last night. And he had given her a way out if she decided not to marry him.

Lord, I made a commitment to You, and I thought, to Karl. I agreed to marry him and be a mother to his children. To be his wife. It was an answer to my prayer. Is there a bigger picture that I can't see?

Her thoughts wandered to Pastor Tim. He was her friend. She had feelings for him that she didn't have for Karl. What did he feel for her? He had comforted her and tried to make her feel welcome with his ministrations. Was there more? If there was, should she give up her dream of a home and family because something might happen between them? She had lived all those years waiting for Luke, and it had been to no avail. *I don't want to repeat that mistake. Romantic dreams are one thing. Reality is another.*

With a thunderous crash on the keys, the notes rebounded off the walls. A yelp came from the back. Inge jumped up and stared at Pastor Tim's legs flailing in the air.

His face flushed with embarrassment as he picked himself up off the floor. "So sorry, Inge. I never meant to disturb you." He laughed. "Your last little... the loud... it startled me, and I tipped the bench over."

She returned to the piano and pulled the cover over the keys.

"What are you doing here?" he asked, straightening his jacket.

She shrugged and lowered her head.

"Is something wrong?"

She nodded and rose, moving toward the door. Pastor Tim reached out to stop her. She pulled away and slipped on her coat.

"I had to get away for a little while," she whispered.

"Yes, I suppose it is rather chaotic in the cabin." He dropped his hand. "But I don't think that's what's bothering you."

"It's fine," Inge's voice shook. "Everything is fine." She turned her back to him.

"I don't think so." Pastor Tim turned her around to face him. She began to cry. He held her as she wept, stroking her back as if she were a frightened child. "Please, Inge, talk to me."

The sobs subsided. She drew in a deep breath but remained in his grasp.

"Tell me. Tell me what's bothering you."

Pulling back, she shook her head. "I have to go." She opened the door and stepped into the cold. She couldn't talk to him now. She had to come to an understanding of God's plan.

Inge thrashed through the heavy snowdrifts putting distance between her and Pastor Tim. She begged God to answer her prayers. Her chest heaved with each breath. Thoughts battered her mind as she considered the possibilities.

If I trust You, it means pouring myself out on the barren ground and hoping that something will sprout. What if nothing grows or bears fruit?

Perhaps God hadn't spoken at all. She knew His voice could be elusive, and it sometimes tasted of her own desires. On rare occasions, His voice could be as clear as a chiming bell. Other times it was indistinguishable from the wind in the trees. After all these months, she wasn't sure she trusted that voice anymore. But today... today the words had been audible.

Do you trust me enough to sacrifice yourself?

Inge slogged along the unbroken path to the spring. Surely God would make His will clear here, in her haven. All summer the pool had been her hope-filled sanctuary. Today, ravaged by winter, the barren landscape felt lifeless. The pond, frozen and swept clean by the wind, reflected her confused thoughts. She brushed snow from the fallen tree and sat down, shifting her position to put the wind at her back. Even in the shelter of the trees, the cold ate through her many layers of clothing. She shivered.

Dark clouds scraped the sky. The branches of the bare trees tapped out messages in the gusty breeze. Did their chatter carry an answer?

Had she heard right? Did God truly want her to sacrifice herself for another? For Karl?

Her mind, wrapped in murky indecision, provided no answers. God's word had been clear. "Trust in the Lord with all your heart, and do not lean on your own understanding."

It was difficult to argue with that.

CHAPTER 47

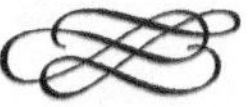

INGE

February sunshine smiled through the windows of the church on Inge's long dreamed of wedding day. Nervously smoothing her gray wool dress, she felt a little drab next to the glowing Maggie. How she coveted the joy Maggie displayed. The best she could muster was hope laced with apprehension.

Inge stood at the back of the church. The benches were decked with ribbons and bows. Cedar boughs covered the altar and the piano. Candles glowed, creating a festive air. Many hands had worked to make this a special day for the brides. A smile tipped the corners of Inge's mouth. *God is good. All the time.*

Billy rushed in calling, "Mam, I have something for you." His blue eyes sparkled with excitement as he handed her a small package. "I made it for your wedding." He jumped up and down. "Open it! Open it!"

Inge knelt and carefully opened the box. She lifted out a small nosegay made of red rose hips tied with a green ribbon. "I picked the rose hips all by myself, but Maggie helped me some with the ribbon." A grin sliced his face.

Inge leaned forward and pulled the little boy into a tight hug. "Thank you so much. So thoughtful of you." His arms slipped around her neck, and she pressed his body close to hers.

Squirming free, Billy placed his hands on either side of her face and looked her square in the eye. "You will be my real mother today, won't you? I want a real mother."

Inge nodded. "Ja, today I will be your new *mor*."

Maggie touched her arm, and Inge looked up. Gus and Karl were standing in front with Pastor Tim. The benches overflowed with friends and neighbors, all laughing and smiling. For a moment their faces blurred, and their voices became indistinct garble. The aisle seemed miles long. She looked at the door. *Can I do this?*

Inge fingered the corsage pinned to the shoulder of her dress. Billy was the one bright spot in this relationship.

God, today I step out in faith and ask You to bless my attempts to please You.

David held out his arm to escort Maggie. Inge offered her damp fingers to Billy. Someone, David probably, had slicked his hair back. He thrust his chest out as he proudly stepped up to take Inge's hand. The congregation rose as they passed by. When they reached the altar, David delivered Maggie to Gus, who gripped her hand in both of his.

Billy loosened Karl's fist and placed Inge's fingers into his father's palm. Patting their clasped hands, he smiled up at them before he returned to his seat next to Arnie and Ben.

"Today we are gathered for a very special event," Pastor Tim began. "A wedding is always notable, but today we are celebrating the joining of two couples in matrimony."

Gus beamed. Karl stared at the floor.

Pastor Tim looked at both couples. "Marriage is an institution of God. In the beginning, God created man. When He saw Adam was by himself, He created woman to be his helpmate. God did not intend for us to go through life alone, but for the relationship to be fulfilling, the two were to become one. There must be faithfulness, respect, and most importantly, love. It's openness and honesty that draws the couple into the relationship that God intended. They become complete in one another."

Pastor Tim looked at Maggie and Gus. "Maggie, do you take this man to be your husband?"

Maggie responded with an exuberant, "Yeh."

"And Gus, do you take this woman to be your wife?"

"Absolutely," Gus boomed. A chuckle rose from the congregation.

Turning to address Inge and Karl, Pastor Tim began again. "Inge, do you take this man to be your husband?"

Inge nodded. "Ja."

"And Karl, do you take this woman to be your wife?" Inge could barely hear him say his vow. Pastor Tim looked up and announced, "I now pronounce you both man and wife."

Gus grabbed Maggie and planted a kiss on her lips. Her face reddened and she leaned into him. Inge looked at Karl. Her knees weakened, and her head began to swim.

What have I done? Our relationship has none of the things a marriage should have. Lord, please...

She slipped her arm through Karl's. He covered her hand with his. She offered a quavering smile to her new husband.

The cake was not the fancy *kransekake* that her mother would have made for her wedding day, but perhaps it would still bring her luck. In fact, very little of this ceremony reminded her of the wedding celebrations back home. Looking at the two-tiered cake she and Maggie had baked, she felt a stab of pain. This was not the dream she had of her father walking her down the aisle or the faces of her family as they gathered to celebrate this day with her. She was not a blushing bride anticipating her wedding night with the man she loved. She wasn't sure how she felt about spending the rest of her life with Karl. *Nei! This is my long-awaited dream. I will not think otherwise.*

Inge watched an older couple holding hands and sharing bites of cake. Would she and Karl be like that at their age? Or the kind of couple who slipped into a corner and danced to music in their heads. Sam had brought candy treats from the mercantile for the children. He slipped his arm around Clara. She smiled and drew closer. Who would have thought? Maybe there was feeling beneath her cold, nasty exterior after all. Lena sat on the far side of the room, smiling as she placed the gifts on a table. Surrounded by friends and family, Inge wanted to believe she had done the right thing.

Eventually, the crowd thinned as the guests headed home before it got dark. Gus and Maggie slipped away, leaving Inge, Karl, and the boys alone with Pastor Tim.

"Well, you two should probably be off," Pastor Tim said. His face was drained of emotion despite a smile. He folded and unfolded his hands, finally offering a handshake. Inge had felt his eyes follow her throughout the afternoon. Was it sorrow or regret etched on his face? *Nei*, it had to be something else.

"I'll take care of the little ones this evening," David stammered. "You two can go up to Maggie's cabin for your... your wedding night." Color rose in his cheeks, and he looked at the floor.

Inge placed her hand on his arm and offered a smile. "*Takk.*"

Karl gave him a curt nod. "Well, I suppose we should be going."

Billy ran up to Inge and clutched her skirt with icing-covered fingers. "You're my mother now. Right?"

"Ja." Inge smiled and squeezed the little one. Arnie stole closer and crept in for a hug when Inge opened her arms. *My boys. I have a family.* Ben stood silently near the door with his arms crossed over his chest, his face a tightly drawn mask.

Saying goodbye to the boys, Karl walked Inge outside into the advancing darkness. "Would you like to have dinner at the hotel?" he asked as he helped her climb onto the wagon seat.

"That would be nice."

Inge's sight blurred as she watched the still figure of Pastor Tim, backlit in the open doorway, recede into the darkness as they drove away.

CHAPTER 48

INGE

Inge rose early the next morning and lit a fire that soon warmed the cabin. As she watched the flames consume the kindling, she reflected on her wedding night. Dinner at the hotel had been quiet and strained. Inge's attempt at small talk faded with Karl's lack of response. He was equally reticent on the ride home.

It felt odd to share a bed with someone else, yet the warmth of another body was strangely comforting. Heat rose in her face as she thought of her awkward attempt at intimacy. While not what she had dreamed of, she would be content. Things would get better, she was sure, especially once they settled in their home with the children.

Pans rattled on the stove as Inge prepared breakfast.

"What's all the noise?" Karl asked.

He stood in the bedroom doorway in his long underwear, looking as if he wasn't sure where he was or what had happened.

"I'm making breakfast. How would you like your eggs?" She put a cheerful note in her voice as she greeted him.

"Uh, whatever. I don't care."

By the time the food was ready, Karl had returned fully dressed.

"I suppose I should take my things down to the house soon," Inge said as she placed the flapjacks and eggs on the table.

"I suppose." Karl sat down. He focused on his plate. A slight reddening rose up his neck.

Was he embarrassed? Or disappointed with last night?

"Ja, Gus, and Maggie will be back from their honeymoon in a couple of days and will want to have the cabin to themselves."

Karl nodded as he rapidly forked the food into his mouth, washing it down with hot coffee.

"I think it's so nice that Gus plans to build them a new place in town. They can begin their life together in their own home." Inge rambled, trying to fill the stillness in the room. "Maggie says he has all the lumber ready for the builders. It shouldn't take long once they get started. At least if the weather remains decent."

Before Inge began to eat, Karl rose and excused himself. "I have chores to do, and the boys have to get off to school."

"I can do that. Get the boys ready for school, I mean." Inge rose from the table, her full plate still in front of her.

"No. I'll take care of it. You… you eat and whatever else," Karl said. "I'll have the boys bring up the wagon later to get your things." He put on his coat and left.

She stirred her eggs with her fork before scraping them into a pan for Billy's puppy. After cleaning up the kitchen, she put her personal items into her trunk. She had lived in this room for eight months. Now she was leaving its safety to move just a short way down the path into a totally new realm, one she had dreamed of but one vastly different from what she had imagined.

CHAPTER 49

KARL

Once Karl got the boys off to school, he headed outside to feed and water the livestock. The quiet comfort of the animals and the solitude of the barn gave him a chance to think.

It had been a long time since Karl had lain with a woman. Every nuance of Sigrid's body filled his mind. He knew how they fit together. Just like Pastor Tim had said, they had become one. Could he ever let her go? That wasn't the question. Did he want to let her go? Was he using her as an excuse to keep Inge at arm's length?

Their wedding night had been a bit of a disaster in his mind. He had lain beside her on the bed last night feigning sleep. She had done the same. He wasn't sure who had dozed off first. Inge was innocent. She wasn't prepared in many ways for the marriage bed. He was sure she had been disappointed. He had consummated the marriage, but it had been without feeling. Sigrid had always been so eager to embrace him, and Inge clearly didn't know what to do. And it was partly his fault. She didn't *feel* right. Long and angular where Sigrid had been round and plump. She was shy and unsure of herself, whereas Sigrid would snuggle close to his back and stroke his chest. Sigrid was famil-iar. Inge was... different.

What am I doing? I can't spend the rest of my life comparing everyone to Sigrid. She's gone. No one is going to meet her standards. He remembered her as perfect, but she wasn't. He had conveniently forgotten the little things she had done that drove him to distraction. His biggest peeve had been her faith. It wasn't that he didn't believe in God, it was that she believed God. She trusted Him completely. Inge appeared to be cut of the same cloth, and he didn't want her to be anything like Sigrid.

Inge was trying. She wanted to be here. She wanted to be married. To him. Why? He had no idea. He had been nothing but rude and nasty to her since she arrived. Why had he acted that way? Because it hurt so much to lose the one you loved. He couldn't bear that loss again. It seemed better to not feel at all than to feel overwhelming pain.

But that wasn't fair to Inge. She entered this union in good faith. She had more conviction than anyone he knew. Sigrid's faith had been... softer. Inge's was filled with determination. Is that why he kept her at a distance? He knew her faith was stronger but was she stronger in other ways? She had tenacity, he'd give her that.

God had rescued him from freezing to death. He acknowledged the strength of God in that instance, but he had let that moment of clarity slip away. He realized his need for God, but as in all things, he had a tough time trusting in an unseen being. In his desperation, he had cried out, and God had provided. God seemed to have spoken again, but he didn't want to listen.

He needed someone. He needed a wife. Could he learn to love her?

CHAPTER 50

INGE

"Stop," Inge shouted. Her clean laundry lay on the floor. Billy and Arnie hadn't been able to resist racing in and out of the newly washed clothing hanging on lines strung throughout the house. The puppy pounced on this new plaything. Grabbing a shirt in his mouth, he dragged the clothes across the dirty floor. They would have to be rinsed again. There were days when she would like to wring the puppy's neck. Inge groaned. The pump was frozen solid, so she'd have to melt more snow.

The weather had turned startlingly cold shortly after the wedding. Now, after almost two weeks, Inge's patience had grown thin trying to appease everyone. The boys were underfoot, bored, and in trouble constantly. Karl was short-tempered.

Lord, I long to be part of this family but if You don't break this cold spell soon, I may do something very unmotherly. I thought I would have time to get to know each one, not be immersed to where I must hold my breath.

"Boys," Inge said. "Find something else to do." The boys stopped at the sharpness of her tone. Their long faces broke her heart. "Arnie, why don't you read to Billy?"

"No!" Billy yelled. "I want to jump on your bed."

Inge sighed. "*Nei,* you will not jump on my bed. Now off you go." She wished she had half of Billy's energy. She'd like to jump in her bed too, but for a good long nap.

Other than a couple of quick trips to the barn each day to care for the livestock, Karl had been locked in the house, too. He either paced the floor or stared out the frosted windows. More often, he took his irritability out on the boys, scolding them for being children. Still unsure of her place, Inge walked on eggshells trying to keep the peace.

"Mam, did you know that George Washington was the first president?" Arnie asked as Inge was preparing supper.

It lightened her day when Arnie shared his school lessons with her. If he continued along this path, he would be a good teacher one day.

"*Nei,* I didn't," Inge answered. "He must have been an important man."

"Yep. He cut down a cherry tree once, but he couldn't lie about it."

"That's good. We should never lie," she said. Arnie had warmed up to having a new woman in the house. And Inge appreciated his acceptance.

Other than wanting to nail Billy's shoes to the floor to keep him out of trouble, the little boy wasn't a problem. Ben, however, delighted in provoking the others. That boy would be a challenge.

"Ben, quit it," David said as he intervened between his younger brothers.

"Make me. Go ahead. Try." Ben continued to prod Billy into running through the house.

Snatching Billy as he passed by, David secured him in a corner and entertained him with a cat's cradle. Inge sighed, grateful for his efforts to keep the little one occupied.

Occasionally Inge ventured out of doors for a few minutes until her lungs ached from the cold, but that wasn't enough to ease her trapped feeling. They needed more room. The boys had a small space with bunk beds on each side and a path up the middle. Karl and Inge's room was only slightly bigger, with a place for a bed and a small dresser. She had squeezed her trunk into a corner and had to climb over it to get into bed.

Her one joy at the end of each day was reading aloud. It brought some harmony to the family. The boys would sit quietly as they listened to the Bible stories. Even Karl seemed to pay attention. And Inge found peace in reading the scriptures. God's words were comforting, and she needed that right now.

"Roice always; pray without ceasing; in everything give thanks..."

"No, Mam," Arnie said. "It's rejoice, not roice."

"Re-joice," Inge repeated, smiling at Arnie.

She sat back when she had finished. *Do I do that? Rejoice? Am I grateful for all things? I should rejoice at being imprisoned with four high-spirited children and their short-tempered father?*

You're asking a lot, Lord.

THE COLD SNAP PASSED, and March held a hint of spring. Grateful the boys were back in school and Karl could work outside, Inge relished a rare moment of quiet. She rolled a prayer into each fold of the bread she was kneading on the table. It felt good to have some quiet time to converse with God once again.

The door burst open, and Arnie charged into the kitchen.

"Look, Mam," he shouted. "We got us a goose! Its feet were frozen in the river, so we wrung its neck and cleaned it up for supper." Pride shone from his face. He held out the carcass, freshly dressed, for her approval.

"Oh, Arnie, that's wonderful," Inge said. "I don't have time today, but tomorrow we will have a goose dinner."

Billy entered dragging a large basket. His puppy danced around his feet trying to get his nose in the container. "Look, Mam. I saved the feathers for a pillow."

Ben followed behind him. Suddenly the dog yelped, and the basket flew into the air.

"Oh, my." Inge watched a blizzard of down scatter the full length of the kitchen. The puppy raced back and forth creating a whirlwind. Inge sank into a chair.

The boy's eyes were enormous as they watched the feathers settle on everything like a layer of fresh snow. Inge had never seen them so sober. The only exception was Ben, who wore a barely disguised smirk on his face.

"What have you done?" Inge wailed. "Look at this mess."

Seeing their crestfallen faces, she wished she could take back her words.

Afraid of saying more, she handed the boys the broom, put the exuberant puppy outside, and went back to her bread. Brushing the feathers to the side, she slapped the dough around before she rolled it into loaves.

Even Billy was subdued as they cleaned up the feathers. Sweeping only seemed to make it worse, but little by little, they gathered up most of the fluff and took it outside.

"Mam." Billy tugged on her apron. "Are you gonna tell Pa what we done?"

"Ja, I am," Inge said.

All three stood in front of her, eyes downcast, uncertain looks on their faces. Even Ben had nothing to say.

"I'm going to tell him that you brought home a goose for dinner."

A long-held breath whooshed from their lungs, and they escaped to the barn to help David and Karl with the chores.

Inge placed the bread near the warmth of the stove to rise and took the goose to the woodshed for safekeeping. Small swirls of feathers danced beside her skirt as she walked. It would be a long while before the house was free of them. She sat down, placing her elbows on the table and resting her chin in her hands. Rejoice in all things, the Bible said. Looking around the kitchen, she sighed wearily. "Lord, I think I'm grateful for the goose."

Inge looked up as Billy peeked in the door. She beckoned him to come in. Arnie and David followed him.

"Mam, we're sorry," Billy whispered.

"Yes. We meant to do a good thing," Arnie said.

Looking at them, Inge's heart melted. Who could be angry in the face of such heartfelt remorse?

"I know you did, and I appreciate it." She held out her arms and Billy leaped into her lap. Arnie sidled up next to her, and Inge slipped her arm around his waist. David placed his hands on her shoulders and gave her a reassuring squeeze. She reached back and covered his hand with hers. She began to chuckle. Sucking in a deep breath, she tried to squelch the laughter, but it overflowed. The boys stared at her incredulously.

"It was an incredible feather storm, wasn't it?" she said, gasping for breath. "I think we will be picking feathers for a long time to come."

THAT NIGHT INGE placed a kettle of stew on the table along with the freshly sliced bread. Plates were filled with steaming meat and vegetables covered in deep brown gravy. The boys were unusually quiet as they took their bread and awaited the passage of the butter. The only sounds were utensils striking plates.

Karl stopped chewing and pulled a feather out of his mouth. "What on earth is a feather doing in my bread?"

The boys concentrated on their plates.

Inge smiled. "Oh, the boys brought me a goose this afternoon. I guess a feather must have escaped."

"One?" Karl pulled another from his slice of bread.

"Well, maybe two," Inge responded as she continued eating. She cleared her throat and then began to cough. Covering her mouth, she rose from the table and retreated to the woodshed as hysterical laughter threatened to escape. *This really isn't funny. And yet it is.*

When she returned, Karl asked, "Is there something going on here that I don't know about?" He glanced around the table, facing each boy. No one said a word.

"*Nei*, nothing, other than we will have roast goose for supper tomorrow night," she said. "Eat up, boys, you promised you would clean up for me tonight. Remember?"

The boys looked up and then nodded. With Arnie leading, they cleared the table, got out the dishpans, and began washing dishes. Karl shook his head, collected his carving project, and sat down in the parlor. Inge settled into a chair across from him and picked up her darning.

Karl glanced her way repeatedly, but Inge kept her head down. *I probably should tell him. Well, maybe not.* She bit her lip to disguise her smile. *Definitely not.*

CHAPTER 51

INGE

Inge looked out the window at the gorgeous April day. "I think I will visit Vada today," Inge said to Karl at breakfast. "The weather has been so nice that a walk will feel good."

Karl stopped eating. "I don't want you visiting those people."

"She is our closest neighbor, and I haven't seen her since December."

"Those people are dangerous. Stay away from them," he said. "Do you hear me?"

Inge picked up her plate and began clearing the table. Pulling the dish pans out, she splashed water onto the stove as she filled them. *Ja, I hear you.*

Waiting until Karl was occupied in the barn, Inge bundled up Billy and set off on a walk. Heavy dark clouds punctuated the sky, their cottony white tops exploding against the blue sunlit background, like they were angry and happy at the same time. She pushed her bonnet back and absorbed the warmth of the sun. This was just what she needed, and if she just happened to pass close to Vada's, what was to stop her from visiting for a minute?

Why was Karl so adamant that she not visit Vada? *He has no right to dictate who I can or can't see. He'll never know anyway.* Then she looked down at Billy. He would know eventually. Even if she swore the little boy to secrecy, Karl would find out sooner or later.

Inge carefully picked her way around the soft spots in the road. But before she could grab Billy's hand, he ran for the nearest pool of mud and water.

"Billy. Stop," Inge called. "You are too old to jump in puddles."

"Oh, no, Mam. You's never too old to jump in puddles."

Inge rolled her eyes and aimed a gentle swat at his backside. He didn't have to do the laundry.

Inge stopped atop the bank. Snow still covered all but the tops of the buck brush in the woods. In the distance, a jagged bed of ice on the river glistened in the sunlight. Did she dare? An urgent feeling settled upon her, pushing her toward the woods. She had to see Vada. The feeling was too overwhelming for her to turn back now.

She pushed through the knee-deep snow and tangled bushes. Billy floundered behind her. At times she was forced to carry him. Sweat-soaked, out of breath, and wet past her knees, she arrived at Vada's doorstep. They stomped the mud and snow from their shoes. Before Inge could knock, Vada opened the door.

"How are you?" Inge asked, looking at her swollen body. "You look like you're ready to have the baby any minute."

"I'm fair." Vada lumbered to the bench and collapsed onto it. "But it's hard to get around."

"What can I do?" Inge asked, settling Billy on a bench.

Vada gasped for breath between words. "Nothing... really. Need to... put my feet up."

"Your husband is not here?" A dark shadow of uneasiness crept over Inge.

"He's off trapping." Vada inhaled shallowly and coughed. "He said he would be back before the baby comes."

Relieved that her husband wasn't home, Inge asked, "Where is Elizabeth?" There was no sign of the child in the room.

"I sent her to school with the others." Vada hung her head. "'Tis too much to keep up with a little one."

"Are you eating?"

"Ya. The children cook some when they get home from school."

"You need better care than this."

"Please help me to the bed. I must lie down." Vada struggled to rise from the bench.

Inge offered support as she shuffled her bulk across the room. The filthy bed had barely enough blankets to keep a baby warm. Vada collapsed onto it, seized by a fit of coughing. Inge covered her with the ragged blanket.

The cold room didn't offer much comfort. Inge put her hand on the stove and found that it was cold. She kindled a fire. This hovel would be slow to warm if it did at all. A breeze through the cracks in the walls fluttered the few pieces of clothing hanging on pegs. *This is unacceptable. I must do something.*

"I am going to get help," Inge said. "You can't take care of yourself or the children." For once, she got no argument from the woman. Inge added a large chunk of wood to the fire, and then she and Billy headed up the bank, following the trail the children used to go to school.

What am I going to do? She knew Karl would not be willing to assist her. Perhaps she could go to the school and see if Pastor Tim could help move Vada to... to where? Maggie's cabin? Why not? It was empty now that Maggie and Gus had moved to their new home, so it would be perfect. She could easily keep an eye on Vada and care for Karl and the boys too.

Inge burst through the schoolhouse door. "I must talk to you," she said to Pastor Tim.

Startled, he stared at her. "Children, continue with your lessons." He joined her near the door. "Inge, what's wrong?" he asked in a hushed voice.

"I need help. Vada Slocum is in a bad way."

Billy clung to her hand, peeking around her skirt at the rest of the children.

"What do you mean?" Pastor Tim asked. "The children are here, even little Elizabeth."

"Ja, she is. Because Vada can't take care of her. The children have been trying, but she needs more than that." Inge's words stumbled over each other. "Vada is pregnant. But I think she is sick too."

Pastor Tim nodded his head. "I see."

"I was hoping to take her to Maggie's cabin. That way I could look after her."

"Would Maggie mind if you used the cabin?"

"I haven't asked her, but it's empty and close by. I really don't think she'd mind."

"I agree." Returning to the room, he announced that classes would end early. "Also, I need to borrow a rig and could use an extra pair of hands. We are going to move Mrs. Slocum to Maggie Johannson's cabin."

Lester Sellers stepped up and volunteered the use of his buckboard.

"David, would you take the Slocum children to the cabin with you?" Inge asked.

David nodded, then gathered the children together.

Ben did not follow the others but hung close to Inge's elbow. "You know Pa ain't gonna like this." His voice shook.

Inge ignored him.

"He ain't got no use for those people."

She pushed past him and moved toward the buckboard.

He persisted. "You got no right to put that woman in Maggie's cabin. They got a place, and they need to stay there." His voice rose until the others turned to look at him.

He was right. She hadn't asked Maggie about using the cabin, but she didn't have time to go to town and ask permission. He was right about Karl, too. Right now, she didn't care. Vada needed help, and that was all that mattered.

Ben caught her arm and spun Inge around to face him. His grip was tight, painful.

"You will not bring *those people* onto our place." The muscles in his jaw twitched. "Pa will throw you out with the rest of the trash." His voice bit like a sharp wind. "I'll make sure of it."

She shuddered and turned away.

INGE SLID off the back of the buckboard and opened the cabin door. David had started a fire, and the cabin was almost comfortable.

"David, would you please keep the children occupied?" Inge gripped his arm. "I need to get Vada settled."

Inge pulled blankets from the chest and covered the bed with heavy quilts while David herded the children toward the parlor.

"And thank you for getting a fire going."

Vada leaned heavily on Inge while Pastor Tim put her arm over his shoulder. Slowly, they got her inside. Vada collapsed on the edge of the bed. Inge eased her back, covering her with quilts as the exhausted woman moaned. Inge stroked her forehead, pulling her stringy hair away from her face.

"Vada, can you hear me?" She tucked the blankets closer when the woman shivered. Paler than before, sweat now beaded on her upper lip.

Inge pulled Pastor Tim aside. "I don't like this. I think we need to get a doctor."

"Could be she is just tired from caring for the family in her condition."

"*Nei.* There is something more." Inge's brow wrinkled.

"I'll contact the doctor when I get back to town," Pastor Tim said.

Once Vada seemed comfortable, Inge gathered the boys and went down to the house. She stopped at the icehouse to pick up venison for broth.

As she was leaving, Karl and Ben emerged from the barn. "I'll need that milk," she said as they neared.

Karl dropped the bucket, spilling milk over the rim. Brushing by her, he walked toward the house. He paused on the porch for a moment. "Just what do you think you are doing?"

"I am being a good neighbor," she said, grabbing the pail.

Entering the kitchen, she gathered a couple of loaves of bread from the woodshed. "David, please see that your brothers have something to eat. There is meat, milk, bread, and whatever else you can find."

He nodded.

"And bring up all the extra blankets you can find as soon as possible."

She retrieved the milk from the steps and hurried up the path to the cabin.

Inge stoked the stove, put the venison on to boil, and cut large chunks of bread for the children.

"Frankie, please fill cups with milk for the little ones," Inge said as she checked on Vada. Still pallid but not ghostly white as she had been, her face shone with perspiration, and she wheezed with each breath. Inge touched her forehead and found that she had a fever, as she had feared.

David entered with several blankets. Setting them on a bench, he asked, "Is there anything else I can do?"

"David, you are a godsend." She cocked her head toward the door. Stepping outside with him, she said, "If you could keep us supplied with firewood and water, I would be grateful. Also, if you could bring some vegetables from the root cellar so I can make soup? Oh, and David, could you take the children to school in the morning?" She gave him a wan smile. "I don't mean to drag you into this..."

"I'm glad to help in any way I can." His hand rested on her arm and offered a gentle squeeze.

Inge made sure the children had their fill of bread and milk before they settled down on the floor, each with a blanket. Ten-year-old Frankie mothered the smaller ones, gathering the quilts close around them before she laid down herself. Inge glanced at the four children huddled together under the covers. What would happen to these little ones if their mother died?

"Is Mama going to get well?" Elizabeth's sober face poked out from under the quilt. Inge sat down beside her and gently wiped the milk from her upper lip with the hem of her apron.

She stroked the girl's snarled hair. "We'll pray that God will heal her."

"Do you think God will do that?" Elizabeth asked.

"Absolutely! God loves your mama."

"I don't think He loves everybody." The four-year-old was solemn. "He loves people who don't live by the river. I don't think He loves us very much."

"That's not true, Elizabeth. Not true at all." Inge's voice rose.

"Ya, it is. I hear people talk. They say we's poor riffraff. God only likes good stuff."

Inge slipped her arms around the little girl and held her close. "*Nei*, Elizabeth. You are not riffraff, and God loves everybody the same." She could feel the child's tears wetting her dress, so she hugged her tighter. "You are beautiful and incredibly special. Always believe that."

The doctor arrived late that night after delivering a baby in town.

"I think she may have pneumonia," Dr. Whipple said after examining Vada. "She is also probably malnourished."

"What can we do?"

"Keep her warm, make sure she rests, and encourage her to drink as much as she can," he said. "The pregnancy will complicate things. Just give her time. And pray."

Wrapped in a shawl, Inge sat in the rocker near Vada's bed. A sense of foreboding loomed over her. Vada's temperature had risen, and she writhed in the bed.

Bowing her head, Inge poured her heart out to God. "Lord, You are sovereign. I cannot begin to understand how You work. Please be with this family. They need You in ways that I can't possibly understand. Assure Elizabeth that she is worthy and loved. Lay Your healing hand upon Vada. She deserves so much better." Just before she nodded off, she pleaded, "Please, God, change Karl's mind about this family."

CHAPTER 52

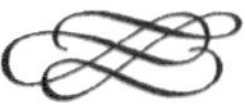

INGE

Inge watched Vada's chest rise and fall. She appeared to be breathing easier the next morning. After sending the children off to school, Inge took little Elizabeth with her and went down to Karl's house. The early morning air was crisp and filled with the smells and sounds of spring. Inge drew in a deep breath, allowing the slight breeze to refresh her. What was Karl going to say about her not coming home last night?

I suppose it would be asking too much for him to help. God, give me strength and wisdom to handle his reaction to all of this.

Inge opened the door to see Karl at the table with Billy. The child was eating nothing but a slice of bread with jam. Crumbs covered the worn plank tabletop. She guessed that had been everyone's breakfast this morning.

Karl stood abruptly, tipping over his chair. Inge jumped when it crashed to the floor. "Do you have any idea what you are doing?"

Her cheeks burned. She pressed her lips together as she swallowed her words.

"I am your hus—"

Her hand shot in front of Karl's face, stopping his words. "Billy, will you take Elizabeth up to the cabin to check on her mother?"

Billy looked at his father and then slipped out of the chair. She helped him with his coat and said, "Be careful. I will be there soon."

Once the pair were gone, she faced Karl. "You will not tell me I can't help someone in need. That poor family is starving, freezing to death, and Vada is pregnant. Would you have me just leave them?"

"She has a husband. It isn't my fault that he doesn't provide for them. They've survived up to now without anyone's help." Karl placed his hands on his hips. "They are not your responsibility. I don't want no wife of mine messing in their troubles."

Had he no feelings at all? She clutched the back of the chair until her knuckles turned white.

"Do you understand?" Karl glared at her.

Inge planted her feet squarely on the floor, her arms crossed over her chest and her gaze locked on his. "Well, *your wife* is messing in their troubles. I cannot in good conscience send them home. Vada is sick and the children are hungry. Someone must help."

Karl's eyes narrowed, his lips forming a grim line. He righted the chair, spun on his heel, and walked out, the noise of the slamming door reverberating through the room.

Inge collapsed into a chair as her rapidly beating heart assaulted her rib cage as if to escape. She wrapped her arms across her chest to hold it in. Her body trembled as she weighed her husband's outburst.

Who was this man she married? A Christian man would have welcomed the poor and downtrodden.

As far as that went, who was she? She had openly defied her husband. Her arms dropped to her sides. *What was I thinking? I should have asked nicely, though that probably wouldn't have worked either. Am I the reason Karl is so unreasonable?* She couldn't ignore Vada's circumstances, but was she forsaking her family for Vada's?

"*Nei, nei*. I can't deal with this now." Her stomach rolled, anxiety tying it in knots. "I have to... to... I don't know."

She pushed the disturbing thoughts to the side and concentrated on pulling soup ingredients, flour for bread, and a few other odds and ends from the cupboards.

When she returned to the cabin, she found Billy and Elizabeth playing with sticks they had taken from the wood box. It took so little to entertain them. She peeled carrots and potatoes, adding them to the venison broth.

I am doing the right thing, aren't I, Lord? You want us to care for each other. Why can't Karl see that? Who do I listen to... my husband or You?

Feeding two households was proving to be more difficult than Inge thought. Thank God for David. She knew she was placing an unfair burden on the sixteen-year-old by asking him to care for the boys, and it made her feel guilty. That was her job, not his.

The children arrived from school and clustered around their mother. "It's so good to see you," Vada said. She smiled as the children all talked at once.

"That's enough," Inge said. "Your mama is tired."

After gathering the children to the table for supper, Inge served the soup and bread. The children couldn't fill their mouths fast enough, so they drank the soup from their bowls and grabbed more bread.

"Slow down. Don't eat so fast. There is plenty to go around." She doubted they had had decent food for months.

"Frankie," Inge said, "can you take care of the children if I leave for a short while?"

Frankie nodded. "I took care of Mama at home, the little ones too."

"*Takk,*" Inge said. The ten-year-old girl was mature beyond her years. She wondered if she had ever been allowed to be a child.

Inge took a pot of soup to the house. Billy proudly carried the bread. It would be a little squashed but still edible. Once there, she reheated everything and prepared the evening meal.

Karl and the boys trooped in from the barn. No one mentioned the Slocums.

What had Karl told them? Lord, don't let him bring up our differences in front of the boys.

Following an uncommonly quiet supper, Inge cleaned up and prepared to head back to the cabin. She didn't dare look at Karl. What must he think of her? Silence settled over the house like a black cloud. She had to get out of there quickly.

Karl grabbed the door as she went to close it behind her. "How long are you planning to abandon *your* family for those people?"

Inge sighed. "As long as it takes."

CHAPTER 53

INGE

Exhaustion clung to Inge. *I know I did the right thing, but I don't know how much longer I can keep this up.* Caring for eight children and cooking for two families was enough to fill her days, and that didn't include laundry and caring for an invalid. She was up before dawn, and her head didn't touch the pillow until long after the others were asleep.

How long had it been since she slept in her own bed? A week? Two? She forced herself to rinse the rest of the clothes. If she didn't do something, she would fall asleep on her feet.

The children burst through the door. Did all youngsters make so much noise? She was surprised to see Pastor Tim follow them in.

"I was checking to see how everything was going," said Pastor Tim. "And I hoped for a quick visit with Vada." He raised his voice to be heard over the children's chatter.

"Please, come in." Inge straightened her aching back and summoned a smile she didn't feel.

"Is she up to visitors?"

"I think Vada would love to have some company other than me and the children."

Pastor Tim knocked softly on the bedroom door frame before entering. "Vada, how are you?" He settled into the rocking chair near the bed.

Inge closed the door, allowing them some privacy.

"Children, please go outside for a little while. Arnie, take them to gather the eggs," Inge said.

It was next to impossible to do anything with everyone under her feet, but she had to hang these clothes and then begin supper. What would it be like to have a real meal again, or a leisurely cup of coffee with a slice of pie? She would be happy to have anything besides the soup and stew they had been living on lately.

Inge looked up when she heard the bedroom door open.

"How is she doing?" Pastor Tim asked quietly, his face creased with worry. "Really doing?"

"She will need care until the baby comes. I'm not sure when that will be. It looks like it could be any day, but Vada seems to think it will be at least a month."

"How are you managing?"

"Well, I am doing the best I can," she mumbled. "I count on David a lot, but he is in school during the day."

She collapsed onto a chair and brushed off her stained apron. If only Karl could be more accepting of these events. If only he would offer to help... if only he would be more like Pastor Tim. *Nei, I can't compare. There is work to do. I need to... to... do something. Finish the wash. I think I have worn these clothes for a week. I must look a mess. I haven't bathed or even had time to breathe.* Her mind was like a tangled ball of yarn.

"Inge, you can't keep on like this for another month." Pastor Tim's voice drew her out of her stupor. "You need help. Would some of the neighbors relieve you occasionally?"

Her eyes brimmed with tears. "Do you think they might?" While she wanted to embrace that thought, she was quite sure no one was going to step up to help the Slocums.

"What about Maggie?" Pastor Tim asked.

"She just got married, and I am using her cabin without her permission. I can't ask for anything more." Inge sagged deeper into the chair and rested her head in her hands. "Vada is my friend," she said. "She needs me. But truthfully, I don't know how much longer I can continue."

Pastor Tim knelt before her and took her hands in his. "Then we will pray for God to intercede."

"I've been praying—for strength, patience, healing. All the time I pray." He rubbed the back of her chapped hands. He was so gentle, and his handling of the circumstances was so different from Karl's harsh reaction.

"But Inge, have you prayed for help?"

She shook her head. "I took this on myself, so I should be the one to handle it."

Pastor Tim lifted her chin so she could see his rueful smile. "Inge, God doesn't expect us to carry His load alone. He wants us to ask for His help, and then He is free to provide in the best possible way."

She nodded.

"So, we'll pray right now for God's provision." Still holding her hands, Pastor Tim began, "Lord, You know the position Inge is in. You know what she requires, and You can help her. Please give her all that she needs, including rest. We thank you for your grace and mercy. Amen."

"Many thanks."

"I will pray with Vada before I go," Pastor Tim said and then stepped into the bedroom.

A knock on the door broke the silence. She rose from her chair expecting David with another load of firewood.

Inge looked down at the small figure in the doorway.

"Lena. This is a surprise." She had not seen Lena since her wedding. "Come in, please."

"I stopped at the main house, but there was no one there. I took a chance someone might be up here." Lena came inside and took a seat, staring at Inge. "What have you done to yourself? You look like hell," she said. "What on earth is going on?"

Pastor Tim stepped up behind Lena. "Inge has been caring for the Slocums. Vada is pregnant and not doing well, so Inge has taken it upon herself to look after them. Unfortunately, trying to care for two families has taken its toll. As you can see, she has worn herself thin."

"How is Vada?" Lena asked. "And you?"

"We are doing well. Most of the time." Inge swallowed hard because a lie does not go down smoothly.

"Well, that's that. I'm heading back to town, and I'll see you in the morning." Lena wrapped her arms around Inge and squeezed her tight.

"In the morning?"

"You'll not handle this alone," she said, stepping toward the door. "I came to ask if you could help with Raven, but I see that you have your hands full. I'll be back."

Inge looked at Pastor Tim. A self-satisfied smile crept over his face. He shrugged his shoulders. "I had better be going, too."

Inge rubbed her forehead as Pastor Tim rode off, wondering at God's provision. And how Karl would react to it.

CHAPTER 54

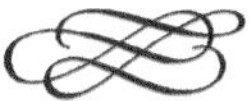

INGE

Lena's arrival about mid-morning the next day gave Inge a surge of hope. The buckboard coming up the lane was overflowing. "You boys get up here and help unload. Your mother needs help. Right now!" Lena yelled as she passed the boys in the yard.

From Karl's porch, Inge covered her mouth to hide a smile. Leave it to Lena to issue orders like an army officer, giving the boys no chance to refuse.

David grabbed Billy's hand, and they followed the wagon to the cabin. Arnie raced ahead while Ben took his time, trailing behind the others. Inge swept the last of the mud off the porch before she followed the rest.

"Haul that mattress into the bedroom. Put the food in the kitchen. Get those blankets in there too." Lena barked at them.

"Ben," David said, "grab the other end of the mattress." Ben stared at him. "Come on. I can't do it alone."

Reluctantly, Ben helped get the mattress inside. Arnie unloaded boxes of food. Billy tripped on the step with his armload of blankets and fell with them to the floor. Unable to pick them up, he dragged them across the floor. Lena snatched them from his grasp and put them on a chair.

A slight, stooped figure remained on the buckboard seat wrapped from head to toe in a blanket. Inge watched Lena gently coax the crouching figure off the seat. Wrapping her arm around the thin body, she led the person into the cabin.

"Fetch some washtubs and water," Lena said over her shoulder to David. "There will be baths tonight. We are going to get everyone cleaned up."

Inge leaned on the porch railing, the flurry of activity a whirlwind around her. Lena could accomplish more things in a few minutes than she could get done in a day. Relief filled her. And Vada would get better care now that Inge didn't have to balance two households.

Thank You, Lord, for help and for friends.

Lena returned to grab a small bundle from under the wagon seat. "Put up my horse in the barn. Make sure you feed him good." Lena slapped the reins into Ben's hand.

"I... I—" Ben sputtered.

"Go on, git," she said. "And by the way, I will need the wagon in the morning to take everyone to church." Inge followed Lena to the door. Looking back at the boys, she swallowed a smile at Ben's astonished look.

CHAPTER 55

KARL

Karl remained stone-faced as he listened to Ben rant. He should try to calm him down, but what could he say to the boy when he was just reflecting his own thoughts?

"We not only have that river trash living with us, now we have that saloon woman out here. And she is ordering us around like she owns the place. Do this! Do that! Like we're hired hands or something. You ain't gonna put up with that, are you, Pa? Who does she think she is, anyway?" Ben's words flew like bullets across the room. He paced, his arms flailed, his muscles knotted as he explained things to his father.

I can't deal with this right now. I need some room to breathe. Karl threw on his coat and headed for the barn. Once inside, he kicked the doorjamb so hard that pain shot up his leg to his knee. Toppling into the hay, he winced as he rubbed his foot. What was he going to do with Inge? He could live with the Slocums in the cabin as long as they stayed out of his way and her husband didn't show up, but having Lena Calhoon involved was going too far.

Why couldn't Inge just take care of the family and the house? She didn't have to save every sick dog that crossed her path. Sigrid had understood that, especially after her involvement with the Slocum family had nearly gotten him killed. Gabe Slocum was a dangerous... maybe deranged man. Sigrid had tried to be the good Samaritan, too, until Gabe had threatened them. Karl was lucky he came out of the confrontation unscathed. Humiliated, yes, but unhurt. Sigrid had learned her place, and she never argued with him again.

Karl clenched his teeth and moaned when he moved his foot.

He was going to have to speak to Ben. Karl could see the boy was out of control. He should be a better example, but his frustration and anger resurfaced with Inge around. It had been easier to crawl into his hole of grief, but he couldn't stay there. He was going to have to face each day head-on, though how to do that escaped him.

He lay there listening to the animals pull at the hay and chew their food. They blew softly through their nostrils as they moved the feed around in the trough. The barn owl ruffled his feathers in the rafters, and the building creaked in the wind. A hundred different choices ran through his mind, none of which seemed to be appropriate. The daylight was nearly gone when he pulled himself to his feet. He was going to have to address this turn of events. One option was to tell Inge the truth. But he wasn't ready to tell her why he didn't want the Slocums around, at least not right now.

He nearly collapsed when he stood up. Pain shot through his foot and up into his calf. Hanging on to the stanchion, he shifted to his other leg. Had he been able, he probably would have kicked the door again in anger at his own stupidity.

"She won't listen. She's bullheaded and... and... well, bullheaded." He labored his way up the rise to the cabin using the hayfork as a crutch. When he got to the step, he hesitated. He could hear laughter and splashing in the house. Not sure if he should knock, he was surprised when Lena opened the door, letting out a blast of warm, damp air. Her dress was wet, and her face flushed. He caught a glimpse of children bathing in tubs.

"What do you want?" Lena closed the door and emptied a pail of water off the porch.

"Ah... um, is Inge here?"

"Inge went home."

"Home? Oh, you mean..."

"Yes, I mean *your* home." She pulled herself up to her full five feet and put her hands on her hips. Daggers shot from her eyes.

"I didn't know."

"Of course you didn't. You were off sulking or swimming in self-pity."

Karl stared at his feet. She was right. He suddenly felt small in the presence of this snippet of a woman. She was helping and he was being critical of everything Inge did.

Lena eyed the fork in his hand and leaned closer to Karl. "If I see a mark on that girl or hear of anything amiss, there will be hell to pay. Understand?"

Karl jerked back, grimacing as he did.

"And do something with that leg." Lena stepped inside and shut the door in his face.

He eased himself down the steps and limped toward his house. Letting himself in, he saw Inge had left him a place at the table. He dropped into the chair and put his foot on the bench.

Inge appeared from the parlor. "Would you like your supper now?"

"Ya, sure." There was a huge slice of humble pie on his plate already. He may as well eat it with the rest of his meal.

Looking up, he saw all four boys staring at him. Clearing his throat, he said, "It's always good to have help in situations such as this." The words came out like chunks of stone. "And I want you boys to help with our... our... guests."

He dismissed them with a flick of his hand.

"Inge, sit." She slid onto the bench next to him. Lowering his voice, Karl asked, "What are you doing? It wasn't bad enough that you brought that Slocum woman home. Now we are entertaining the saloon keeper. Do you think about any of this? I married you to take care of this family." He drew a resigned breath. "Please tell me there will be no more of this."

Inge nodded. "But Karl, you need to know, Lena brought Raven with her. Since her father's death, she has no place to go. She needs a home. I told Lena she could stay."

Karl was silent for a moment. Then his fist hit the table so hard that it overturned the plate. Humble pie be damned! Rising from the chair, his leg buckled under him. He grabbed the edge of the table and steadied himself.

"Are you all right?"

"No, I'm not."

"What happened? Let me help you," Inge said, offering her arm.

Refusing her help, he hobbled toward the rocker in the parlor and collapsed into the chair. He groaned. The boys, as well as Inge, all looked questioningly at him.

"I... uh, I slipped and twisted my ankle," he said.

"David, bring that stool over here." Inge knelt and began to unlace Karl's boot.

"I can do that." Sweat popped out on his brow as he tried unsuccessfully to remove his shoe.

"For pity's sake. Give me your foot." Inge pulled it into her lap.

Karl leaned back. He gripped the arms of the rocker. A moan escaped his lips when Inge pulled the shoe free. Peeling off his sock, she inspected the damage. It was already swollen and taking on a nasty shade of purple. She gently pressed along the edges of the bruising until Karl jerked back.

"I think you could have broken some bones in your foot."

He gritted his teeth.

"You'll have to stay off it for a while."

Karl sank deeper into the chair. *It's her fault. If she hadn't gotten involved in all this, I wouldn't have lost my temper, and now I can't even take care of things around here. How much worse can it get? Why on earth did I think things would be better if I married her?*

CHAPTER 56

INGE

"Billy!" Inge yelled. "Get back up on the porch." Trying to keep the boys clean for church with puddles in the yard was almost impossible. What was it about little boys and mud?

David drove the wagon up to the front of the house with Lena on the seat beside him.

"Isn't it a glorious day?" Lena asked, gesturing at the green hills that the warmth of April had brought to the prairie.

Inge looked at the wagon full of children. "Who is staying with Vada?"

"Raven said she would watch her."

Arnie and Billy piled into the back, joining the clean Slocum children decked out in fresh clothing. The girls huddled under blankets, excited about showing off their new dresses and well-groomed hair, and the boys found it was more fun to tease the little girls than it was to play in a puddle.

"Yur sittin' on me."

"Don't pull my hair."

"She pinched me."

Inge listened to the chorus and smiled. It was amazing what one night of uninterrupted sleep could do for a person. She thanked God she didn't have to herd this bunch alone.

Drawing her heavy wool shawl tightly around her shoulders, she drew in a deep breath. Still cool this early in April, the sun provided a touch of warmth that would soon make the day pleasant.

Spring had arrived in fits and starts, but Inge loved everything about it. She took in the smell of damp soil, the sight of the buds on the trees, and the wonder of the crocus that defied winter and forced itself through the snow to bloom. Life was emerging from its cold grave. God provided this essence of Himself each year to remind her, not of Jesus's death, but His resurrection.

From atop the hill, Inge could see the still-frozen river. How much longer before it crept out of its banks and flooded? She couldn't worry about that now, not on such a lovely day. Sunlight graced the side of her face, leaving its warmth and peace behind. It was the first time in weeks she had spent a significant amount of time outdoors. Leaning back, she listened as Lena hummed, the children chattered, and the birds sang. *It's a new season, with a fresh start. This family... my family is my life now.*

After pulling up to the church, David tied the horse to a low branch on the only tree in the yard. The children jumped out and filed into the building behind Lena like chicks with a mother hen. She lined them up in the pew with David on the opposite end.

Lena gave Inge a little push toward the piano. "It's been a while since I heard you play."

The cold of February had been too extreme for travel; she had been so busy caring for Vada and her family. It had been far too long since she had been able to attend services. Relishing the feel of the keys, she closed her eyes and played song after song, the notes filling the small building.

A hand on her shoulder startled Inge from her reverie. Pastor Tim stood beside the bench. "As much as we love your music, Inge, I think it's time for the sermon."

Heat rose in her face as she slipped back to the bench beside Lena.

"Today is a special celebration," Pastor Tim began. "As much as we love Christmas when we remember the birth of Jesus, Easter is when we reap the benefits of the sacrifice of our Savior." Faces watched him expectantly. "Jesus has blessed us with the gift of eternal life."

Easter? It couldn't be. But it was April. Suddenly she missed her parents, her family, and her home. A lump formed in her throat. *If I was back home...* Her thoughts trailed away. She wasn't back home. She was here in her new home, with her new husband.

She had hoped Karl would change and become kinder after the wedding. Her disappointment was hard to swallow. He must have cared a little to ask her to marry him. Why couldn't he show his feelings? Why did he make things so difficult? All she ever wanted was a husband and family, and now she had it... or did she?

Pastor Tim's voice rose, penetrating her thoughts. "Have you thought about what you do with this wonderful gift?" he challenged his parishioners. "Use it. Reach out to your neighbor, to a stranger, to anyone who does not know Jesus as their Savior." He nodded toward Inge. "Will you please play 'The Old Rugged Cross' for us?"

Inge seated herself. The music flowed and the congregation filled the room with song.

On a hill far away stood an old rugged cross
The emblem of suffering and shame.
And I love that old cross where the dearest and best
For a world of lost sinners was slain.

Her fingers faltered. A sour note brought stares from the crowd.

Forgive me, Lord. I have suffered nothing compared to you.

When the service was over, people mingled before departing. Lena and Inge, along with the Slocum children, stood apart from the rest. A few people spoke, but most just nodded to them as they passed.

Pastor Tim strode over and took Lena's hand. "I'm so glad you are here. And it's good to see the children too." He continued to hold her hand as he spoke. "You know you were an answer to prayer, don't you?"

Lena blushed like a bashful child. Dressed modestly in a pastel blue muslin dress, her hair pulled away from her face with a few blonde curls escaping to caress her pink cheeks, she looked like a fetching schoolgirl.

"I hope you'll join us again," he said.

As he turned to reenter the church, Lena called out, "Pastor. Would you care to join us for Easter dinner?" She coyly tipped her head to the side. "I have a ham."

"Why Lena, that would be wonderful. What time?"

"Anytime. I'll start cooking when we get back to the cabin."

Inge watched the exchange between the two of them. Oddly, she was jealous of Lena's interaction with Pastor Tim. He gushed over her but had only given Inge a slight nod.

David pulled the wagon up to the steps and helped Inge and the little ones climb into the back. Always the young gentleman, he supported Lena as she stepped up onto the seat. Taking the reins from her hands, he directed the horse toward home.

Lena turned to Inge. "I will put the ham in the oven when I get to the cabin. Would you make the potatoes for me?"

Inge bobbed her head.

"We can work together and get a meal fixed before long. We'll eat at your place. You have more room."

"Ja, sure." But Inge wasn't sure of anything. How was she going to explain this to Karl? He already blamed her for his broken foot, for the Slocums, for Lena's intervention, and for Raven's presence.

God, don't let his irritation ruin the day. I'd be humiliated if he created a scene in front of Pastor Tim.

When they arrived home, Inge and the younger boys climbed

down from the wagon, and David drove off to take the Slocum children and Lena to the cabin.

❧

"Is there anything I can do to help?" David asked as he entered the kitchen.

Inge nodded. "Bring in more potatoes from the icehouse. Oh, and get a squash too." She pulled out bowls and pans.

"What's going on?" Karl grasped the parlor doorway, his brow furrowed.

Inge picked up a pan half-full of potatoes. "I'm making Easter dinner."

"Easter?"

"Ja, Easter." She slammed the pan onto the stove. "And we're having guests."

"Guests?" he asked.

"Ja. Guests."

"Who's coming?" His tone was clipped.

"Pastor Tim." Inge sucked in a deep breath. "And Lena." The air whooshed from her lungs, and her voice trailed off. "And the Slocum family."

Karl opened his mouth, then slammed it shut. Turning on his good leg, he limped back to his rocker.

Inge watched him retreat. There were days he felt like a pebble in her shoe, just enough irritant to keep her on edge. She wasn't even sure which one of them was the problem anymore. *I am getting as bad as he is.*

Inge cooked a mound of potatoes and honey-sweetened squash. She emptied two quarts of green beans in a pan and sliced bread. The moment Lena opened the door, the room filled with the salty, sweet aroma of ham. Inge's stomach growled. David brought in a basket filled with pickled beets, mashed turnips, scalloped corn, and plum sauce.

Inge ushered the children to the water pump and basin. As usual, handwashing turned into a water fight. Inge looked at the wet floor and closed her eyes. A knock at the door kept her from scolding the boys.

"Nice of you to come," she said as she showed Pastor Tim into the parlor where Karl sat alone. "Please, have a seat."

She stopped at the table and rearranged the plates as she eavesdropped on their conversation. Would Karl say anything about Lena or the Slocums?

"What happened to your foot?" Pastor Tim asked.

"I slipped," Karl offered curtly.

"I see. I hope it isn't serious. We missed you at services this morning, but I now understand why you weren't there."

Karl nodded.

"It was very generous to invite me to dinner. I always enjoy people, especially children. You have a houseful right now. It must give you great joy to see that lively bunch."

Inge was embarrassed that Karl ignored him. He could at least be pleasant for one afternoon.

"Gentlemen." Inge stood in the doorway. "Please join us."

"Here, let me help you." Pastor Tim offered Karl his arm.

Karl disregarded it. He rose unsteadily to his feet and shuffled to the table. Lena sat on one side with the Slocum children. Inge took a seat on the other side with the boys. Pastor Tim sat at the end opposite Karl.

"What about Vada and Raven?" David asked.

"Vada needs to stay in bed," Lena said. "And Raven... well, she isn't up to being around a lot of folks just yet. I'll bring them something when we finish here."

Inge shifted uncomfortably in her seat next to Pastor Tim. "Would you bless the food?"

"Certainly," he said. "Lord, we come before you on this day to give thanks for the sacrifice of Your Son. He gave His life that we might have salvation. I thank You for this gathering and for this food. Amen."

After the prayer, Inge rose from the table. "I'll take food to Vada and Raven now."

She filled two plates, covered them with a towel, and headed up the hill. Gently knocking before she pushed the door open, Inge looked around for Raven. "I brought you something to eat," she said, placing the food on the table.

The room appeared empty at first glance. Quiet, catlike movements drew her attention to the far corner where Raven was hiding behind the stove.

Hearing the rustle of blankets, Inge turned toward the bedroom. "Vada, are you awake? I brought dinner for the two of you."

"Not hungry," she whispered.

"You need to eat," Inge said. "If you don't, you won't get better."

"Maybe later."

Nodding, Inge backed out of the room. She slid into a seat and pushed one of the plates toward the end of the table.

"Raven, please come out and eat." Raven finally moved out of the shadows and perched on the edge of the chair as far away from Inge as she could get.

"Let me get you a fork." When she rose, Raven scooted off the chair, backing away. Inge laid the fork on the table within her reach and returned to her seat. The girl seemed so vulnerable and lonely. She needed a friend... a family.

Inge sensed something had happened since Christmas. The girl had been uneasy and timid then but not fearful. She was small in stature, probably only five-foot-two, and thin as a stick. Even her new clothing did not hide the bones that protruded along her shoulders and neck.

Although her hair was black, it reflected a reddish tinge in the light. Dark, slightly upturned eyes and high cheekbones, along with her small, straight nose and full mouth, gave her an exotic quality. Inge suddenly realized that she had never really seen her before, other than the one time at Christmas when she had been dirty and disheveled. The only other times she had encountered her, she had hidden her face or stayed in the shadows. It was distressing to see the depth of her mistrust.

Raven perplexed her. She was a beautiful young woman, but darkness hung over her. Her eyes were haunted, and though Inge wasn't sure what had happened in the girl's life, it was clear that something had driven her to a bleak place. Yet, despite it, she survived and prevailed.

Oh, Lord, open this young woman's heart so she might blossom into all you intend her to be.

CHAPTER 57

INGE

Inge was grateful for Lena's help and sorely missed her when she had to return to her saloon after a week. Raven had begun to help with the cooking and Frankie took over getting everyone ready for school. Inge prayed she would be able to manage things now.

Still bed-bound, Vada's health had improved. She was eating well and enjoyed having the children around in the evenings. Pastor Tim stopped by once a week to check on her. And if there was nothing pressing to do, Inge would read to her in the afternoons. Billy and Elizabeth would cuddle close and listen too. Even Raven eavesdropped near the door.

"I bet he was all rotten by the time the fish spit him out," Billy said after hearing the story of Jonah. "No wonder those people were scared. I'd be *real* scared."

"Rotten?" Elizabeth echoed.

"Ya, rotten, like that dead muskrat Buster brought home. Remember?"

Elizabeth solemnly nodded. "Scary."

Inge saw Raven gag at the idea of something rotten. The girl opened the outside door, sucking in a deep breath of fresh air.

"But God used Jonah to tell those people to repent. And if Jonah had obeyed when he was asked the first time, he would have never been swallowed by a big fish."

"What's repent?"

Inge's shoulders sagged with guilt. *Something I need to practice.* She slid Billy off her lap. "It's when we choose to not do something ever again."

Inge joined Raven at the door. "Are you feeling unwell?"

The girl was pale and drawn. She clutched the door frame with one hand and placed the other over her mid-section.

Inge touched her arm and Raven shrank back.

Inge wasn't sure exactly what had gone on in Raven's life as the girl rarely talked. When she did speak, it was minimal. Her name didn't befit her at all. A bird should fly free above the earth, but Raven acted more like a chained puppy.

"My stomach is a little jumpy," Raven said. "I'll be fine."

"I can make some mint tea. Do you think that would help?"

Raven shook her head. "I think I will lie down for a little while."

Inge remained on the steps to admire the vibrant spring that was flourishing everywhere in her sight. Already late April, Inge realized that her birthday had come and gone. She hadn't even remembered it. She wasn't sad that she had forgotten, just surprised at how little it mattered. Life had been so busy she hadn't had time to dwell on the family celebrations and holidays back in Norway. She felt the loss, but also felt gratitude for what she had now. She had a friend, a sister in the Lord. And there were the boys. They brought joy every day. She had to work to find things to be grateful for in her marriage to Karl, but, nonetheless, she did have a husband and a home.

Looking back over the last year, she wondered at the road her life had taken. Somehow it wasn't the path she had foreseen. It had been a year of difficulties, but God had never promised there would be no trials. *He only promised to walk that path with me.*

CHAPTER 58

INGE

Inge jerked out of her sleep, nearly falling out of bed. She had heard gunshots. Sitting up, she was convinced it wasn't a dream. There was another burst. She grabbed Karl's shoulder and shook him. "Someone is shooting at us," she whispered.

Karl groggily raised himself up on his elbows. Another series of shots reverberated through the house.

"No, it isn't gunshots. The ice is breaking up on the river. Don't worry." He rolled over. "The water has never gotten to the house."

"What? What do you mean?"

"The ice. When the ice breaks up, the river floods. Sometimes the water comes up to the barn but never to the house. Don't worry."

Inge's feet touched the cold floor. She padded to the window and searched the woods for something, anything that indicated a flood was imminent. Nothing. She laid back down, tucking the quilt around her freezing body. Along with the jarring sound of the ice, there was a guttural grinding as the floes set against each other, making it impossible for her to go back to sleep.

By morning the ice had ceased to crack and groan. Inge looked out the door often, but nothing had changed. She couldn't see any water down the lane. They lived a good half mile from the edge of the river. Surely the water wouldn't rise that much.

Later in the afternoon, Inge trudged up the small hill to Maggie's cabin. Standing on the rise, she searched the trees again for signs of water. Shaking her head, she decided Karl had been half-asleep last night and had no idea what he was talking about.

"How's Vada today?" Inge asked. Raven was busy kneading dough, so she tilted her head toward the bedroom door.

"Vada, how are you feeling?" Inge searched Vada's face as she entered the bedroom.

"I'm doing well," Vada answered. "But if I get any bigger the bed will break." She smiled wanly. "Inge, I think the baby is coming soon."

"Are you having pains?" Inge took her hand.

"No, no pains. I just feel it, you know? Like I should get ready for the birth. Gathering things—diapers, flannel, and such. Can you help me with that?"

Inge stood at the end of the bed. She hadn't even considered the actual birth. What would she do when labor began? Having a baby was a natural thing. Women did it all the time, but now she wished she had attended to her sisters when they gave birth.

"What do you want me to do?"

"I have a few things at the house. Cloth for diapers and some baby clothes. They're in a box under the bed. Do you think you could collect them for me?" she asked.

"I can go today if you think I need to."

Vada nodded. "I heard the ice crack last night. You need to go soon, very soon. The water can rise quickly once the ice is free."

The children burst through the door, filled with energy and all talking at once. They gathered around their mother, sharing their day with her.

Inge was startled by Pastor Tim's voice. He stood in the doorway. "I thought I would come by and see how Vada was doing, so I decided to bring the little ones home from school in the wagon. The road is a muddy mess, and with the ice going out soon, there is always danger."

Inge twisted her hands. "I hate to bother you." She tugged at her apron. "Vada wants me to get some baby things from her house." She moistened her lips. "I could ask Karl, but I don't know when he will be back." *And he probably wouldn't take me anyway.* "Could you take me?"

Pastor Tim ran his fingers through his hair, resting his hand on the back of his neck for some time while he stared at the floor. "This is not a good idea with the ice going out."

"Ja, so I've been told. But Vada does need her things."

Finally, he nodded. Inge fetched her shawl and climbed up on the wagon seat. He pointed the horse down the road toward the trail that led over the bank to the Slocum home. "You do know this is not a good time to be down on the river bottom, don't you?"

"It looks safe enough right now."

Heavy clouds with a greenish cast filled the sky. She felt, rather than heard, the low rumble of thunder. Shifting away from Pastor Tim in the wagon seat, Inge pulled her wrap close around her neck. It was disquieting to have him so near. This was nothing like those times at school when they had talked about everything. She longed to tell him about... *nei*, she couldn't. There was nothing Pastor Tim could do to change the choices she had made.

Near the barely visible path, Inge searched the trees for Vada's shack. Nothing seemed out of place. There was no water, just mud from the melting snow. In some places, snowbanks still lingered, hanging on the brush.

"Inge, you really shouldn't go down there. The water can rise incredibly fast, and the ice floes are dangerous. They can cut a tree in half—"

Ignoring Pastor Tim, she climbed down from the wagon and darted over the steep bank.

"Inge, wait," Pastor Tim yelled. He caught up with her and pulled her back. "I will take you to town and you can get whatever you need there."

Inge tried to break free of his grip. "It won't take a minute. I'll run down and grab the box."

"Inge, no." He forcibly grabbed her arm. "You don't understand how dangerous it is. It's impossible to outrun the water. You'll be caught in the brush and branches and drown if the ice doesn't crush you."

She had promised Vada, and she would make good on that promise. As she pulled back and tried to shake free of Pastor Tim's grasp, she slipped in the mud and fell to her knees.

"Inge, please." She read concern, even fear, in those incredibly blue eyes that were fixed on her. "Please don't go," he begged. "I can't lose you."

Inge rose slowly, her eyes never leaving his face. Her mind raced, and her heart pounded. She was unable to break the hold his eyes had on her.

Pastor Tim released her arm but not his gaze. "We have to go."

There was a faint thumping in the distance. The ground trembled, sending a quiver up her legs. Vada's shack was within sight. She could make it. She fought through the brush. The wild roses snagged her clothing and held her back against her will. Slush and mud filled her shoes, weighing her down. Just a few more steps. Tripping on a large branch, Inge looked down. Silent black water crept around her feet like a coiling snake. The grinding sound of ice impacting the trees filtered up her spine like icy slivers. Her feet were heavy as stones. Time slowed as she watched the wall of broken ice move slowly, like a giant plow ravaging the prairie. Bark was ripped from the trees, and the brush flattened. Vada's shack quivered before one side of it collapsed. "*Nei.*"

"We must go. Now!" Pastor Tim grabbed her arm. He pushed her toward the steep, slippery bank. Inge grabbed tufts of grass and small bushes, but they came loose as she tried to pull herself up. Digging her hands into the clay, she began to gain some ground. Suddenly, she felt hands on her backside that pushed her over the top. Gasping for breath, she felt Pastor Tim collapse beside her. The water swirled below, thick, dark, sinister. She watched it warily. It was a living being, destroying everything in its sight. She began to shake uncontrollably. Her legs wouldn't support her when she tried to rise. She dissolved into a pile of quivery flesh, her body inches from the turbulent water.

Pastor Tim picked her up and tossed her into the bed of the wagon. He grabbed the horse's bridle and led him to higher ground.

The air left her lungs as she hit the hard wagon bed. Curling into a fetal position, she clawed the air as her lungs refused to fill. Coughing, Inge rolled onto her back. Tears flooded down her face leaving dirty streaks. Finally, she managed to draw in a small breath.

"Did I hurt you?" Pastor Tim's voice trembled.

"*Nie*, I'm fine," Inge said, then coughed violently before sucking in great gulps of air. She pulled herself into a sitting position. Her mud-covered hands tried to brush the leaves off her wet skirt. Looking up, she saw the roof of the shack riding atop the ice wall. Vada's house was gone. How would she ever tell her?

The water continued to rise, spreading like thick molasses and oozing between the trees and bushes. She'd never seen anything so menacing. In a few minutes, it had climbed to the top of the bank. Eddies full of debris silently swirled closer and closer. Inge couldn't take her eyes away.

"We need to get going," Pastor Tim said.

Inge fingered her dirty clothing. Eyeing Pastor Tim's soiled pants and jacket, she began to laugh. Reaching out, she swiped at the mud covering his cheek. Sliding out of the back of the wagon, she glanced down at her own bedraggled body. Her laughter suddenly turned to hysterical sobbing.

Tim pulled her close and whispered, "It's fine. We're fine. It's just mud." Her body shuddered. Pulling her even closer, he whispered softly into her ear. "Don't worry. Shhhh... shhh."

Inge pulled back. "I... know." Pointing at the rapidly rising river, she gasped, "If... not for you, I would be... down there."

Drawing her close again, he murmured, "But you're not. You're safe. I'll get you home."

Her clamoring heart slowed, and her breathing returned to normal. Inge drew comfort from the strength of Pastor Tim's body. Aware of the slow rhythmic rise and fall of his chest and the warmth of his arms around her body, she felt safe. He had saved her life. She relaxed, her body naturally molding into his lanky frame. Her arms slid around his back, and she pulled him closer, burying her face in his neck. His hands stroked her back.

"Hello." A voice echoed off the trees.

Dropping their arms at the sound, Inge and Pastor Tim pushed apart.

Young Ernie Williams rode up and dismounted from his horse. "I saw the wagon and was worried that something had happened."

Pastor Tim lifted his hand in greeting. "We're fine."

"Looks like the ice is free." Ernie took in their muddy clothing. "But then it looks like you already know that."

"Ya, well, we had a bit of a scare. Inge wanted to get some things from Vada Slocum's place. We managed to get up the bank just before the water..." Pastor Tim stopped. He cupped his jaw in his hand and let out a long breath.

Inge stood by his side, unable to meet Ernie's gaze.

Ernie stared off into the trees. "You ain't gonna get nothin' from the Slocum place now. Good thing they ain't there."

"Yes, indeed," Pastor Tim said. He offered Inge a hand to get up on the wagon seat. She pulled back and climbed up by herself. Joining her, Pastor Tim turned the horse toward the Johannsons. "Thanks for stopping," he said to Ernie.

The short ride back to the house was even quieter than before. Inge couldn't look at Pastor Tim. What must he think of her? She had acted disgracefully. She was, after all, a married woman. Nevertheless, the memories of Pastor Tim's warm body and the strength of his arms continued to surround her. *Nei. This is not good. Temptation is never a good thing. I have Karl and the boys. I won't allow myself to have these... these feelings. It's wrong.*

Before Pastor Tim could alight at the house, Inge jumped down from the wagon. "*Takk*," she said. Avoiding his eyes, she raced for the porch.

Inge tried to brush the mud off her clothing. It was no use. She would have to change before she told Vada about the failed trip. She entered the kitchen slamming the door behind her. Too late, she noticed Karl standing before the stove pouring coffee.

He dropped the cup, splashing hot liquid over his fingers. "Ow." Slowly, his eyes focused on Inge. "What happened to you?"

"I... uh, I fell." Inge fled to the bedroom to change.

Returning to the kitchen, Inge found Karl seated at the table with a fresh cup of coffee. She dampened a cloth in the water bucket and furiously wiped the mud from her face and hands. She kept her back to Karl. Would he sense her embarrassment and the guilt that roiled within her?

She threw the cloth in the dishpan. Leaning her head against the cupboard, she tried to stifle the sobs that choked her throat.

"Oh, Karl. The river. I didn't know. Trying to help Vada, and I... I almost drowned." Her sobs muffled the words. "I'm so sorry."

"You went to the river alone?" His voice dropped to a near whisper.

Inge nodded slightly.

Karl rose from the table. Turning her around, he wrapped his arms around her and pulled her close to him. "Inge. I couldn't bear to lose another wife."

Inge stood frozen. The gesture only lasted a moment. Karl dropped his arms and stepped back. He awkwardly patted her shoulder.

Inge gazed intently at the floor. She pulled her arms around her chest. "I'm fine. Really." She hiccupped.

"You and the children will go nowhere near the river. Do you understand?"

Inge lowered her head. "I won't. Never again."

"Good." Karl opened the door. "Don't you know I'm trying to take care of you?" he said before he stepped outside.

Inge sank into a chair. She buried her head in her hands and shook like brittle branches in a windstorm. She felt like she was going to break. She had met Karl's concern and show of affection with nothing. However, she had fallen into Pastor Tim's arms with pleasure.

Oh, Lord, what is happening here? This is not right.

She rose from the chair and paced. The room was too small for her to outrun her feelings.

You have given me what I asked for. Why am I not content with that? I want to love Karl, I really do.

She returned to the table and laid her head on the surface. She prayed for forgiveness, hoping that Karl would never know the feelings that had flowed through her body. She begged God to give her those same feelings for her husband.

CHAPTER 59

PASTOR TIM

Leaving the house, Pastor Tim eyed the rising water as it crept past the big tree that marked the Johannson's lane. It felt ominous and foreboding. He cut across the prairie to avoid it, but he couldn't escape the thoughts that swirled in his head like the eddies in the river. *What was I thinking? Even offering to take Inge to Vada's was not appropriate. But it was a good thing I did, or she could have died.*

The warmth of her arms drawing him close burned in him. He could still feel her shudder with fear, her head nestled in his shoulder, and her breath warm on his neck. He wanted to scoop her up in his arms and rescue her from this place, from Karl, from all of it. She deserved so much more than this marriage of convenience. She was a good woman, a godly woman... and someone else's wife.

Dear God, what am I going to do?

It would be nearly impossible to dodge Inge. She played the piano for church services. He would have to face her every Sunday, or more if he continued to visit Vada. Would the rest of the congregation see the demon he was fighting? Hulda Hobbs had already sensed something between them, though she had backed off her gossiping since Inge had married Karl. Still, he felt sure his feelings were in plain sight of everyone. Concealing them would not be easy. If he ignored Inge or treated her differently, that too would be noticed by someone.

He kicked himself. Why hadn't he said something to her before she accepted Karl's proposal? But that had been a surprise to everyone, especially Inge. She probably felt she had little choice but to say yes. If only he had let her know that he was... was what? Maybe he was intrigued or interested, but even if she hadn't accepted Karl's proposal, would he have done anything? Thinking back, he recognized his penchant for avoiding decisions. It was always difficult for him to say no, so he simply did nothing. By not deciding, he allowed the decision to be made for him. Now he was forced to make a choice. Knowing this marriage would be difficult for her, he could not remain a part of her life. He cared enough to not want to hurt her chances of having the home and family she wanted so badly.

Maybe he should leave here, but not right now. He had to finish the school year. But it would be soon. Where would he go? Back to his family in Indiana? His father never understood why he left. Disappointing him would haunt Tim forever. He had never been cut out to follow in his father's lawyerly footsteps. He was too restless and too filled with a desire to serve God. He had tried seminary, but that hadn't fulfilled him either. There had been too many rules, too much dogma. His faith was not found in religion. But perhaps the seminary was the place for him now. Maybe he needed structure in his life. He knew he had to remove himself from Inge's presence. His feelings for her ran too deep for him to ignore.

CHAPTER 60

INGE

Inge regarded Vada's girth and realized that if she didn't have the baby soon, she would burst. It was nearly the first of May, and the baby had to come any day.

Inge told Vada of the high water and the destruction of her house. Vada was devastated. As bad as it was, it had been her home.

Inge read from the Book of Matthew. Vada's eyes were closed, but Inge knew she wasn't asleep. "Vada, is there anything I can do for you?"

Vada turned her head and opened her eyes. "No, nothing." She drew in a labored breath. "Reading to me is the best medicine I could ever have."

"I'm glad. If only I could do more."

"You have been so good to me." She reached out and took Inge's hand.

"What would I do without *you*?" Inge asked. Vada had given her strength in hard times, and her wisdom and understanding of God's word were always an encouragement. Vada's acceptance of her lot in life never failed to amaze Inge.

"Well, I suspect things might be better with Karl if I wasn't here," Vada said.

Inge gazed out the window, her thoughts far away. "Do you ever doubt?"

"About what?"

"That you are doing God's will," Inge asked. "Was I wrong to marry Karl?"

"I can't answer that for you," Vada's tone was hushed. "Only you know what God told you."

Inge pulled her hand free and rubbed her forehead as she closed her eyes. *Have I made a mistake?*

"Doubt is not a bad thing," Vada said.

Inge's eyes flew open. She rose and opened the window. The room was closing in on her.

"Without doubt, there is no faith." Vada smiled at her. "Sometimes our lack of faith leads us down a different path."

Inge threw her a puzzled look.

"God does not expect us to follow Him blindly," Vada said.

Inge clenched her fists, her fingernails biting into her palms. Tears pooled in her eyes, and her heart thumped like a drum in her hollow chest.

"God will always be by your side. He does not leave you because you doubt." Vada said.

"It feels like He has left me at times. Like He has given up on me." Inge swiped at the tear that trickled down her cheek.

"You are a woman of strong faith. He will *never* leave you." Vada's face clouded with concern.

"What if I misread the signs? All those times I thought He was speaking to me. What if..." Inge's voice trailed off.

"God holds your story in His hand. We all make mistakes, but God forgives and loves us anyway."

Inge returned to the chair and gripped Vada's hand. Could her friend sense her guilt?

"God's plan is bigger than what we can see. If you had not been here, if you had not answered God's call, I would probably be dead, and my children... my children..." Vada shuddered. "You saved us all."

Inge squeezed a small smile from her lips.

"*Never* say that God is not at work in your life. He is using you to build a family, to comfort others, and to be an example to your husband."

Inge sat back in the chair. "Do you think so?"

"You are a fine example of a wife and mother," Vada said with certainty.

The scent of blooming chokecherries filtered through the partially open window, their odor distinctive and overpowering. The smell surrounded her, heavy and sickeningly sweet. What would Vada think if she knew about her feelings for Pastor Tim, or her lack of affection for Karl? She could never share these secrets with Vada... or anyone. Shame flooded her. Would God really forgive her?

CHAPTER 61

INGE

One evening early in May, as Inge was fixing supper, Vada went into labor.

She gasped for breath with each contraction. "The midwife. She lives... near the river... east of town. Get her."

"Sit with her," Inge said to Raven. The girl perched on the edge of the chair, her eyes huge and her face white. "I am going to get help."

"But... but what if she has the baby when you're gone? I can't deliver no baby." Raven's voice came out in a high-pitched squeak.

"The baby won't come for a while," Inge assured her. "I'll be back shortly." She gathered up the children and took them to Karl's house.

Her mind whipped in circles trying to decide what to do first.

Opening the front door of the house, Inge yelled, "David, go get the midwife. Vada's in labor."

He raised his head from a book. "What?" he asked, looking confused. "Where do I find her?"

"It can't be that hard," Inge snapped. "Ask around. Lena would probably know." Her gaze pointed at the door.

"I'll go." Karl stood in the parlor doorway. "I know where she is. David, you watch the children."

Inge threw him a wary look. Surprised, but grateful that he was willing to help, she nodded. "*Takk.*"

At the cabin, Inge and Raven heated water and laid out towels. When they were done, Raven paced, and Inge held Vada's hand while she prayed. Vada seemed to get weaker with each contraction.

Please, Lord, let the midwife get here soon. I've never delivered a baby.

She felt panic rising in her chest. *Nei, not now. I must be calm.*

Much to Inge's relief, Karl arrived with the midwife within the hour.

He held his hat against his chest. "Anything else I can do?"

"The children... "

"Don't worry. David and I will watch them." He fidgeted with his hat and suddenly reached out and squeezed her arm. "It'll be fine. You can do this."

Before Inge could say a word, he was gone.

Vada moaned as the midwife poked and prodded her abdomen. "This'll be a hard birth. She's not strong," she said. "Get my bag."

Raven scurried to the kitchen to get the case. The midwife pulled out some small containers and had Raven brew tea. "Willow bark. That'll help with the pain some, but mostly we gots to wait til the baby is ready."

The hours crept into one another as the night dragged on. Inge wiped Vada's face with a cool cloth and encouraged her to drink the tea. Just as dawn broke, Vada gave birth to a little boy. He did not protest when swatted on the bottom. Inge released her bated breath when he finally gasped for air. She gently wiped him clean and wrapped him in a warm towel. As she was ready to lay the child beside his mother, the midwife said, "We gots another one comin'. Get me the scissors."

Inge handed the baby to Raven and grabbed a towel and the scissors. Another baby? Vada was having twins. Within a minute, the midwife was holding a baby girl by the ankles. She slapped her bottom. Placing the child on her side, the midwife ran her finger into her mouth. After a few agonizing seconds, the baby drew a breath and managed a small whimper to let the world know she had arrived.

Two babies, Inge thought. No wonder Vada had such a hard time these last few months. She quickly wrapped the second child in a cloth.

"Vada." Inge lowered her head and whispered in Vada's ear. "You have two beautiful babies. A little boy and a little girl." Vada's eyelids fluttered, but she didn't open them.

The midwife cleaned up and ushered Inge and Raven into the kitchen. "You gots to take care with her. She lost lots of blood. I be leavin' you some herbs that'll help." The midwife's face was grim. "She need be nursin' them babies real soon. I'm not likin' the looks of this."

Inge nodded. When the midwife was gone, she dropped to her knees beside the bed.

God, let nothing happen to my friend.

CHAPTER 62

INGE

"Please Vada, you must nurse this little one." It had been two days and Vada was still weak. Inge had tried to get the babies to latch on to the breast but without help from Vada, it was a struggle. She warmed cow's milk to fill their empty stomachs, but the twins still weren't getting enough to eat.

Raven nodded off while rocking one of the babies. Lack of sleep was taking a toll on them both. Being up at night and then trying to care for both families was sucking up every ounce of strength Inge had. Karl was in the fields, and the children were in school. Perhaps she should send David to town to ask for Lena's help. *Nei*, she couldn't ask for her help again. Somehow, they would manage. Cradling one of the babies, she dropped into the rocking chair beside Vada's bed. It was impossible to keep her eyes open.

The door opened and a gust of wind startled her awake. Maggie barreled through the kitchen and stood over her.

"Look at yeh!" she scolded. "Why didn't yeh send for me?"

She seized the baby from Inge's arms like a hawk snatching a chicken. "Yeh could drop this precious thing by dozing off in a chair." She paced the floor, cooing to the infant.

Inge sat with empty arms outstretched and her mouth hanging open.

"I don't understand," Inge said. "What are you doing here?"

"Just yesterday I heard from Karl that yeh'd taken in the Slocums. Which is fine with me. An empty house needs to be filled with family." Maggie continued to sway back and forth with the child in her arms. "I come to help yeh."

Still groggy, Inge blinked her eyes to make sure she was seeing right. Maggie *was* here. She wasn't dreaming.

"Yer just plain thick-headed," Maggie railed. "Why didn't yeh ask for help?"

The second baby that was nestled next to Vada began fussing. Inge reached over to pick her up.

"What? There's two little lasses?" Maggie craned her neck to peek at the little girl. "Karl didn't say anything about two babes."

"Ja, Vada had twins."

"Oh, me sufferin' self. Twins." Maggie said. "Wouldn't yeh know it?"

Maggie placed the babies in the basket. She bustled around the room straightening blankets and feeling Vada's forehead.

"Yeh be gettin' home and get some rest." Maggie laid out diapers and bottles. "Yer not needed. Go home."

Inge stood on the porch not certain she wanted to go home. Never knowing how Karl would react unnerved her. But wait, Maggie said Karl told her about the Slocums. Had he asked Maggie to help?

❧

INGE LIFTED a spoon to Vada's mouth. "You have to eat."

Vada reluctantly sipped the broth. "No more." She turned her face away.

Relief flowed through Inge to see that Vada had nearly emptied the bowl. She had been terrified the woman wouldn't survive. Now she had hope. But it would take some time before Vada could care for the babies, much less the rest of her family. Thank God for Maggie's abundant energy these last two weeks.

"Inge," Vada said. "I want the babies blessed. Can you have Pastor Tim come here and do that?"

"Blessed? Don't you mean baptized?" Inge was puzzled at her request. Babies were baptized within a few months of their birth. As far as she could remember, that was how it was always done.

"No," Vada said. "In the Bible, the father blesses the babies. It was part of their inheritance. I want my babies blessed by God." She leaned back and sank into the pillows. "Please, Inge, do this for me."

Inge nodded. "I will send a note to school with the children," she said as she closed the bedroom door.

Elizabeth and Billy sat at the table with questions written all over their faces.

"Will Mrs. Vada let us name them? Can we?" Billy begged.

"Ya," chimed in Elizabeth. "Do ya think Ma will let me play with them?"

"*Nei*. You certainly cannot play with them," Inge said sharply. "They're not dolls."

Billy looked disappointed, but Elizabeth was near tears.

"I am sure your mother will listen to your suggestions," Inge said, wishing she had been kinder.

The children were delighted when Vada finally decided on names for the little ones. With great fanfare, she considered all the names suggested by the children, but in the end chose two that were her own —Suzanne for the girl and Silas for the boy.

Their father should be here. He should be part of this naming ceremony. Vada was confident he would return, but Inge wondered. And what would she do if he did?

CHAPTER 63

PASTOR TIM

As he approached the cabin, Pastor Tim again unfolded the note that Inge had sent to school with the children. Vada had requested that he stop by to see her. He pulled up in front of the cabin, and the children scrambled down from his buckboard. Vada's children were delightful, but how was she ever going to care for two more? Arnie pushed the door open, leading the rest into the cabin, except for Ben who jumped down and trotted off toward the house.

Pastor Tim stood in the doorway with his hat in hand. "I got your message. Do you have any idea what Vada wants?" he asked Inge.

"Why don't you go in and talk with her? I'm going to get the children a bite of bread and jam before I send them off to help with chores."

He opened the bedroom door. "Vada, can I come in?"

"Please. Come have a seat," Vada said.

"How are you doing?" Pastor Tim settled in the rocker and leaned forward in the chair.

"Ah, Pastor. I have been wanting to see you."

"You have had a frightening couple of months. It's good to see that you are better." Pastor Tim took her hand. "Now, what can I do for you?"

"The babies. Did you see the babies?" Vada's voice was weak but filled with pride.

"I did. They're beautiful."

"Yes, they are. Very beautiful," Vada whispered. "God has blessed me."

"Indeed. Children are always a blessing."

"Pastor, in the Bible, fathers always blessed their children. I want God to bless my babies."

"A blessing. I'm not sure I know what you mean. We can have a baptism at the church when you are stronger and the babies are a little bigger." He released her hand and leaned back against the chair.

Pushing herself up to a sitting position, Vada said, "I want God to bless them. They are His children."

"I see." Pastor Tim pushed his hair away from his eyes. He wasn't sure he understood completely what she was asking, but what could a blessing hurt? "When do you want to do this?"

"Soon."

He hesitated. "Are you sure you don't want to wait until your husband comes home and you get stronger?"

Vada stared straight ahead. "No. Tomorrow. Can you do it then?" She was silent for a moment. "And we will do it here, with Inge and the children."

"If that's what you want, I will plan for tomorrow."

A weight seemed to lift from Vada's shoulders. He had never witnessed such a driving need to make sure God was an integral part of a child's life.

THE NEXT DAY Vada's room was filled with excited children. Pastor Tim took in the grins and expectation on their faces. Vada sat up in bed with numerous pillows stacked behind her back. Her hair had been braided into a crown atop her head, and a new bed jacket covered her nightgown. Despite being weak, Vada glowed.

"Are you ready?" Pastor Tim asked as everyone gathered around the bed. The babies were nestled in a willow basket filled with soft blankets next to their mother.

Vada's eyes brimmed with tears as she looked at the sleeping infants.

"Lord, we come before You today to dedicate these two small lives to You," Pastor Tim began. "You are the creator. You formed these two little ones in the womb. Just as Abraham, Isaac, and Jacob bestowed a blessing upon their offspring, we wish to bless these children in Your name."

Vada smiled and nodded, her finger stroking Silas's soft cheek.

"Bless their future," Pastor Tim continued. "We ask for Your protection, for Your provision, and for Your love to always permeate their lives. But foremost, we ask for You to reveal Yourself to them even now, as infants, so that they will grow up knowing You, serving You, and loving You."

With that, Pastor Tim prayed over Silas and Suzanne, placing his hand upon each one and blessing them in the name of God the Father. Afterward, the children cheered and pushed forward to see the babies.

"They don't look no different," Billy said. "Aren't they supposed to be different?"

"How do you think they would be different, Billy?" Pastor Tim asked.

"I don't know. Maybe they should have wings like angels or something."

Pastor Tim chuckled. "I don't think they will ever have wings. We didn't make them angels, we just asked God to look after them for the rest of their lives."

"You mean even when they get big, God will still watch out for them?"

"That's right, even when they are old, God will be there with them."

"I want God to take care of me," Billy said. "I get into lots of trouble sometimes."

"Well, God won't keep you from getting into trouble. You must make good choices. But He will help you when things get difficult."

Billy pondered this for a moment, then ran to make sure he got a treat.

Pastor Tim watched David deliver a slice of cake to Raven. She had not shared the celebration but had remained out of sight. Somehow watching two innocent young people beginning to know one another filled his heart. Life was not always easy, but Raven had suffered far beyond her years. She deserved a good home. He prayed she had found one with Inge and Karl.

His gaze drifted to Inge sitting in the rocker holding Suzanne against her shoulder. She nuzzled the baby's soft head. Suzanne's dark hair was already long enough to form small ringlets. Inge rolled the curls around her finger. Pastor Tim's heart ached within his chest. Knowing how much Inge had longed for a family, he wondered if Karl and the boys had fulfilled that desire. She was born to be a mother. Her face flushed and her eyes sparkled as she gazed at the infant. Standing, she put the sleeping baby back in the basket.

Inge often seemed... unhappy. Maybe a better word was disappointed. Perhaps that was the heaviest burden of all, one he might have changed if he had had the courage.

Silas began to squirm, and Inge picked him up. He turned his face into her chest and made sucking noises.

"I think this little one is hungry," she said to Vada, handing Silas to his mother. Vada pulled the nightgown free from her shoulder, nestled him close, and nursed him. Pastor Tim averted his gaze.

He approached the bedroom once the baby had been fed. "I'm going to leave. Just wanted to see if there was anything else I could do."

"Thank you so much. It was a special day," Inge said. She glanced at Vada, who had nodded off while feeding Silas. "And I know it meant the world to Vada."

For the first time in weeks, Pastor Tim felt relieved. Inge seemed to have found her place with the boys, Vada's family, and maybe even Karl. Even though it cut his heart deeply, he was pleased that she had embraced her choice. He could not stay here. Once school was out, he would leave.

CHAPTER 64

INGE

Spring had rolled into summer. The longer days of early June were already uncomfortably warm. Inge winced as she attacked the hard dirt with her shovel. Her blisters wept, but she continued to spade up the black soil. Little by little, she transformed the garden into a soft mound in which to sow her seeds. She had to plant soon if they were going to have a harvest for winter. Karl was breaking sod into usable fields below the house. Wielding a plow all day probably left his hands raw, too. She ruefully smiled. *At least we will have something in common now.*

Inge stood upright, stretching to ease her aching back. As she wiped the sweat from her brow, she noticed Vada motioning to her from the cabin.

"You deserve a few minutes of rest," Vada said. "I brought you a glass of cold water."

"*Takka.*" Inge settled into the rocker. Digging up the garden had left her more fatigued than usual. She'd be glad when the older boys were back from helping Maggie paint her new house. She could use their help.

"Inge," Vada said, worrying her apron in her hands. "I need to talk to you about Raven."

"Raven?" Inge thought things were going well. The girl was coming out of her shell, helping with the children and the house. Vada had the patience of a saint when it came to teaching her how to do household chores.

"Yes, Raven. What will happen to her when I leave?"

"Leave? What do you mean, leave?" Inge sputtered.

"Ah, Inge. I will have to go some time, and I need to know that Raven will be cared for when I'm gone."

"But where will you go? What will you do?"

"Gabe will come. I know he will. And then we'll leave."

"You may know that Vada, but I don't recall seeing hide nor hair of him around here." Irritation prickled Inge.

"He'll come. That's not my concern right now. It's Raven I'm worried about," Vada said.

"She can stay here as long as she wants, you know that."

"That's good, but that isn't what I meant. I need your promise that you'll take care of her."

"I don't understand. She's fifteen years old. She doesn't require care like the smaller children."

"That's the point. She is young and alone." Vada paused. "And I think she is with child."

"She's *what*?" Inge leaned so far forward that she nearly fell out of the chair. "Do you mean she is having a baby?"

"Yes, I think she is. All the signs are there."

"But how? When?" Inge fumbled with timelines in her mind. "She's been here since April. How could she be pregnant?"

"I don't know. I suppose it happened before she came, perhaps after her father died."

"When?" Inge sucked in a sharp breath. "When do you think the baby is due?"

"In the fall maybe," Vada answered.

"Have you talked to her about it?"

"No. I don't think she understands yet."

Inge rolled her hands into fists, revealing her chapped, red knuckles. A deluge of thoughts filled her head as she headed back to the garden. The hoe split the dirt and scattered chunks across the ground. *Nei. This couldn't be. Vada had to be wrong.* Raven had had such a hard life already and now... now to add a child. *How did this happen? She hasn't been anywhere or seen anyone since she arrived except... except David. Surely not. David would never do such a thing.*

CHAPTER 65

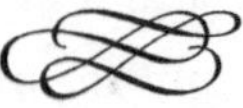

INGE

Inge stood outside the house, hoping for a breeze. Mulling over Vada's news yesterday only increased her need to pray. Raven couldn't raise a child alone. Even if she stayed in the cabin, she would need help. *I don't even want to think about telling Karl about this.*

"Mam," Billy shouted. He and Karl were coming up the lane from a trip to town. In front of the barn, Karl grabbed the boy's arm and lifted him down from the horse.

"There's a letter for you." Billy ran to the house waving it over his head like a flag.

It was from her parents. She lowered herself into the rocker on the porch and savored the feel of the envelope. Somehow, just holding it brought them closer. Closing her eyes, she clutched the letter to her chest. She pictured her *mor* sitting at the kitchen table laboring over each word. The scent of freshly baked bread filled her nostrils. The constant drip of water from the pump accompanied her *mor's* scratching pen. A smile tugged at the corners of Inge's mouth as she opened the envelope.

April 1896
Our dearest Inge,

It has been a delight to get your letters. We were especially happy to hear that you and Karl finally wed. We hope that things continue to go well for you both. The whole family wishes you a happy birthday.

Your brother and sisters are doing well. Sven has another little one on the way. That makes your mor happy. The farm is doing well, and it looks like a good harvest this year.

I wanted to let you know that your mor has been feeling poorly for some time now. The doctor doesn't seem to know what is wrong. He prescribes a tonic for the blood and rest. I would ask you to pray for her.

We love you and miss you.
Your Far

Inge read it again.

Nei, Lord. You must not let anything happen to Mor. All she needs is a touch from You.

She could not bear to lose her precious mother.

"Hey, Mam," Billy said, pointing down the road. "Who's that?"

Inge rose and stepped down from the porch. She shaded her eyes from the bright sun, but even then, she couldn't make out who was in the wagon.

As it drew nearer, Inge trembled. *Gabe. He came back. Nei. Vada can't go... not with him.*

The wheels rolled to a halt just a few feet from her. Alongside Gabe was a young man, perhaps in his early twenties, filthy and scruffy, wearing a beaver hide over his shoulders.

"I hear you got my family hid away up here," Gabe growled at her. "I come to fetch 'em."

"Ja, they're here." Inge swayed slightly. Her legs weakened. "I... I will take you." Her voice held a ragged edge. She gave Billy a push. "Go play with the others. They're down by the creek. And stay there." He looked at her questioningly, opening his mouth to ask something. Inge shook her head, and he turned and scampered off.

She had no intention of allowing Gabe to see Vada alone, not after Vada's bruises and broken ribs the last time he had seen fit to come home. Inge hoped her presence would keep it from happening now, but what would prevent it if they left? How could she keep Vada here? Her mind raced as she walked slowly up the hill. *There must be something I can do.*

Stepping into the cabin, Inge cleared her throat. She forced the words out. "Vada, there is someone to see you."

Looking up from stirring the pot on the stove, Vada's face broke into a smile the likes of which Inge had never seen. She flew into Gabe's arms and smothered him with a hug.

"I knew you'd come. I missed you so much." She was crying as she hung on his gaunt frame. "It's been so long. I thought, well, sometimes I thought you'd been kilt or bad hurt."

"Naw, I'm a tough old goat. You know that." His smile was nearly as big as Vada's as he wrapped his long arms around her again. "We ran a trap line nearly up to the mouth of the Missouri. The wagon is loaded with furs." He lifted her chin and wiped the tears from her cheek with his dirty finger. "I heard in town that the river took our place this spring."

Vada nodded. "If not for Inge, we would have been dead. She has been such a blessing, especially when the babies came."

Gabe held her at arm's length and looked her up and down. "Babies?"

Vada drew him into the bedroom. Inge hovered near the door. *He wouldn't dare hurt the babies, would he? What will I do if he... if he...*

"Meet Silas and Suzanne," Vada said. "They were born a month ago. Aren't they the most beautiful things you've ever seen?"

Gabe leaned over the basket where the children lay sleeping peacefully.

Inge held her breath.

Softly stroking each head, he said, "They's the most beautiful babes I ever seen."

Watching the interaction between Vada and Gabe confounded her. Vada was genuinely pleased to see her wayward husband. Why on earth would she be glad to see him? Inge's gut churned. This made no sense at all.

Inge noticed the young man from the wagon standing in the kitchen doorway. He bore a striking resemblance to Gabe. He was a little shorter and more muscular, but he shared enough features for her to be certain he was some relation.

"Please come in." She gestured toward the table. "Would you like some coffee?"

He pulled a chair out and turned it around, his arms resting on the back. "So, how long has that old hen and her brood been livin' offa ya?" he asked.

Inge placed a cup in front of him and instinctively pulled back. His greasy dark hair hung over his face, and his smell nearly made her gag. But there was something else. She couldn't put her finger on it until he brushed the hair away from his face. Cold, empty eyes stared at her.

"Ja, well, Vada and the children have been here since the spring flood took their home."

"It's a dern shame they weren't in it." His mouth twitched revealing a broken front tooth.

Gabe returned to the kitchen with Vada close behind.

"Oh, this here's my eldest, Matthew," he said to Inge.

Vada's face blanched. She shrank into her husband's shadow.

Inge's heart hit the floor with such force that she staggered to keep her balance. Gabe was not the one who had beaten Vada. Matthew was. And Vada was scared to death of him. Inge grabbed a chair to hold herself upright.

She glanced at Matthew. His body was draped over the chair like a dirty blanket, his face filled with a glint of satisfaction. He clearly enjoyed Vada's reaction.

Inge dug her hands into the back of the chair until small splinters pricked her fingers.

"We need to get packed up so we can head out. Daylight's burnin'," Gabe said. "Hurry now, get your things."

Vada stood frozen in the bedroom doorway.

"Come on. We need to get on the road. Matt and I found a great place upriver. It'll be needin' some fixin'. Gotta get it done this summer so you and the little ones will be settled in by winter when we head back to the trap line." Gabe slung his arm over Vada's shoulder, indifferent to her sudden change in demeanor.

"Oh... well, it will take some time to gather things up and pack them," Vada stammered. "I will have to get the children ready, wash some clothes, and..." her voice trailed off.

"No time fer that. We gotta get on our way. It'll take a week or more to get there."

Vada glanced at Inge with red-rimmed eyes that were filled with fear.

Inge stood there, wringing her hands. *Should I speak to Gabe? There is no reason Vada can't stay here until he gets the new place ready.*

"Speakin' of, where's the young'uns?" Gabe asked.

"I'll get the children," Inge said as she backed out the door. After rounding the corner of the barn, she leaned back against the rough siding for support. Panic gripped her. *I think I am going to be sick.* She struggled to breathe. Air refused to enter her lungs. She began to slide down the side of the building as her legs gave way. What could she do? There had to be some way to convince that man to leave Vada here, but how? Gabe was her husband, and he had every right to take his family with him. That wasn't even an issue right now. Matthew terrified her. Evil dripped from every pore in his body. She was sure Vada would never tell her husband what his eldest child had done. *Surely God will not allow this to happen. He must have a plan, one that excludes Matthew.*

Inge steadied herself against the wall for a moment before she crossed the corral to the creek.

"Come on, Mam." Billy laughed. "Come get wet. It feels so good."

Raven was throwing handfuls of water, and the rest were running and screaming to get away. Inge's heart ripped in pieces knowing Vada's family would soon be gone. *Lord, You can't take them.*

Blinking back tears, Inge called, "Come, children. We have company up at the cabin. Let's go."

"Who was in the wagon?" Billy asked. He was soaked from head to toe. "Are we having company for supper?"

"Hurry," Inge said. Trying to separate them from the water might have been difficult if not for the visitors.

Raven raised her panicked eyes toward the cabin. She shriveled to half her size and disappeared into the shadow of the barn. While she had become comfortable with Vada's family, she always hid from strangers.

Seeing the wagon piled high with furs, Frankie asked, "Is it Pa? Has Pa come to get us?" She broke into a run when she saw Gabe's gangly frame emerge from the doorway. "Pa, is that you?"

Gabe snatched them up in his arms as they clustered around him. Their excitement was contagious. For a moment Inge smiled, but it was short-lived. When they saw Matthew leaning against the door, the children stopped their chatter instantly. They slipped into a line behind their father. *Is the man blind? Surely, he will not put them all in danger.*

"What's a matter with you young'uns? Go on. Help your Ma get things gathered up." He gave them a push toward the cabin. "We got a lot of ground to cover before dark."

Inge entered the cabin and found Vada putting their few belongings into flour sacks.

"Take the blankets, too. You will need them." The two women collapsed into each other's arms. "Vada, you can't go. I know it was Matthew who beat you. You won't be safe," Inge whispered raggedly. "Please don't go."

Vada clutched Inge, her fingers digging into her back. "I will miss you more than anything." Tears streaked down her face as she pulled back. "But I must go. Gabe has come for us."

Leaning back with her hands on Vada's shoulders, Inge looked deeply into her eyes. "*Nei*, you don't have to go. He can trap all he wants, and you can live here with us. At least until he gets your new place ready."

"No. Gabe's a proud man. He wouldn't have someone else care for his family." She sighed. "Especially Karl."

"But what about Matthew? You can't go if he goes along. He might..."

"It'll be fine. Really, Inge, it will. Gabe won't let anything happen to us."

Right. Just like he protected you before. Inge's shoulders sagged, and her arms dropped to her side. "What will I do without you?"

"We have been a pain in your husband's backside for months now. It's time for you to become a family with Karl and the boys," she said.

"What about Raven? Have you told her about... you know?"

"No, I haven't. You can do that when I'm gone. Please watch over her."

Inge nodded.

Within a short time, Vada's family was crammed into the wagon. The babies lay in their basket, nestled in the furs. The children wrapped themselves in soft silvery skins and giggled. Vada clung to the sideboard, her feet dangling off the rear of the wagon. She wiped tears from her face and raised her hand as they drove away.

CHAPTER 66

KARL

Karl stood in the shadow of the barn door with his eyes glued to Gabe. *How dare that man set foot on my place?* Once the wagon reached the cabin, he ran to the house and grabbed the shotgun off the wall. His hands shook as he pulled shells from the cupboard. He loaded both barrels and fumbled as he shoved extras into his shirt pocket. *Gabe must be here for his family.* He forced himself to take a seat on the porch rocker with the gun across his lap. He drew in several deep breaths. *I'll be ready for him this time.* There would be no running through the woods with Gabe Slocum peppering his backside with buckshot.

He heaved a sigh of relief when he saw Inge standing on the cabin porch. Sometimes she was so much like Sigrid, it scared him. Sigrid had insisted he help that family. He had tried to reason with the man, but Gabe's hooting laughter still echoed in his ears as he had dodged from tree to tree fleeing through the woods. He would sit right here, on his own porch, with his gun loaded. He would be patient, and Gabe Slocum would not get the drop on him this time.

Karl stood as the wagon neared his house. He cocked the shotgun, his knuckles white as he gripped the stock. His knees wouldn't bend when he stepped off the porch. He drew his hat low over his face. Balancing on the balls of his feet, he made himself ready for Gabe Slocum. *Let him set one foot in my yard, and I will fill his backside with buckshot. Just one foot...*

"Afternoon," Gabe said as he halted the wagon beside Karl.

Karl nodded slightly.

Gabe stared off into the distance. "Thank ya for takin' in my family." He drew in a deep breath and studied his work-scarred hands holding the reins.

Karl shifted the gun so that it was cradled in both hands and pointed toward the wagon. His gaze never left Gabe's face. All it would take was one misstep.

"It were mighty kind of you, considering." Gabe spat a wad of tobacco off to the side of the wheel and wiped the remains from his walnut-stained beard with his free hand.

Karl stood silently. *Give me just one reason.*

"Well, we'll be on our way then." Slapping the reins against the rumps of the mules, Gabe touched the brim of his hat as the wagon started down the road.

Karl made sure Gabe Slocum and his family were out of sight before he walked up to the cabin.

Inge had collapsed into a mound on the step. Karl settled near her. Neither said a word. Inge wrapped her arms around her knees and buried her head in her stained skirt.

Karl wanted to comfort her but had no idea what to say. Honestly, he was glad they were gone, but he knew Inge and Vada had become like sisters in these last few months. Vada was probably as close to family as she had here, and now she was alone again—with him.

Inge reached for a hankie in her pocket. Her hand pulled out the letter Billy had given her earlier. "My *mor* is sick."

Karl leaned forward and clasped his hands together.

What could I possibly say? She is losing the two most important people in her life.

CHAPTER 67

INGE

It didn't seem possible that it was July already. Vada had been gone for three weeks and Inge still watched the road daily hoping she would return. Surprisingly, the tension had eased with Karl. Had Vada's presence caused him that much irritation? He was almost... almost *pleasant* some days.

"Fourth of July?" Inge didn't understand Billy's excitement.

"It's a big party with fireworks!" Billy was dancing around a chair. "We all go to town, and they have music and ice cream and just... everything!"

"Ja. Big party. For whom?" Inge asked.

"Oh, I don't know, just a big party."

She mulled this over as she rolled out the pie dough.

"What is this party that we are going to?" Inge asked as David entered the kitchen. "Billy was not helpful in explaining it."

David grinned with the same unabashed enthusiasm that Billy displayed. "It's the day we celebrate the founding of this country. Everybody gets together, and we eat, play games, dance, and just have a lot of fun," he explained. "It's like a birthday party for America."

"A birthday celebration." That she could understand.

"Do you think Raven would go with us?"

"I don't know." Inge doubted the girl would leave the safety of the cabin.

"I worry about her. Why is she so scared all the time?"

"Have you asked her about it?"

"She doesn't want to talk about herself. She is so... well, she's like a frightened little bird."

"David, I know you and Raven are becoming friendly, but before you get too... involved, there is something you should know." She motioned for him to sit down at the table.

Seating herself across from him, Inge took his hand. "David, Raven had a very rough life before she came here. She seems to want to put it behind her."

"And that's good, isn't it?"

"Well, ja. But there are some things that can't be left behind." Should she tell him? It would be common knowledge before long. It would be better for him to hear it from her. "Raven is expecting a baby."

David stared at her. "She's what? A baby? I don't understand." From his shocked expression, Inge knew he had nothing to do with Raven's pregnancy.

"She won't talk about it. In fact, I am not sure she even acknowledges her condition. I tried to explain things to her, but I don't know how successful I was."

"How do you know she is... is...?" His words came out in bits and pieces. "She would know, wouldn't she?"

"Despite her hard life, Raven is still innocent in many ways. She may understand she is with child, but there is a part of her that won't admit it. If she is having a baby, then she can't leave her past behind." Inge paused. "My heart breaks for her, and I really don't know what to do."

"When do you think the baby will come?"

"I have no idea. I can only guess. If she was... well, if it happened just before she came here, it would be in November sometime."

David stared out the open door, his body stiff as if glued to the chair. Silence weighed heavy in the room.

"I am sorry to tell you this way. You are good for her. She needs a friend." Patting David's hand, Inge said, "Think this through carefully before you talk with her. Please."

He rose from the table and made his way to the door. "Sure, ya. I will."

Inge returned to her pie and poured her frustration into the dough. Having a child was such a wonderful thing, but maybe not this time. She hated telling David, but she hoped her honesty would prevent further hurt for both.

Lord, is there no chance for this girl to have a happy life? And what of David? I know he cares, perhaps too much.

CHAPTER 68

INGE

By evening, Inge's dress clung to her as she headed to the spring. Perspiration beaded from every pore in her body, leaving dark, damp spots in her clothing. She couldn't wait to cool off. The water restored her body, and her spirit was refreshed by the stillness of the place.

She could see Raven on the cabin steps. Her head was buried in her folded arms, which rested on her knees like wilted flowers.

Ask her to join you.

I need my alone time, Lord. Besides, she's too shy.

Inge stopped before reaching the cabin.

I really need this time for myself. Time with You.

Stretching her back, she continued up the path. Even though the sun had set, the day's heat poured over her body. Sweat trickled down her brow, and she wiped it from her eyes with the back of her hand.

Fine.

It never worked to argue with God. She always lost the battle.

"I am going to the spring," Inge said as she approached the cabin. "Why don't you come?"

Raven scooted up one step. "With you?" she asked. "You want me to come with you? To take a bath?"

"Tomorrow is the Fourth of July celebration, and we will head to town early. I thought it would be nice to cool off this evening. Since I have the baking done, I can take a few minutes for myself."

"Uh, I don't know... I, uh..." She stood up and started for the door.

"You can bathe on one side of the bushes, and I on the other. That way we can have our privacy," Inge said. "Come on, it will feel good after this scorching day."

Raven nodded. Inge could see her mid-section was filling out. It wasn't obvious that she was pregnant yet, but she was rounder than before.

"Grab a towel and some clean clothes," Inge said as she turned and headed up the coulee toward the pond.

She resisted the urge to look back but listened intently. When she was nearly past the barn, she heard the door slam. Knowing the girl had stepped out of her only refuge, even if it was just a trek to the spring, brought a smile to Inge's face.

You were right, Lord. Give me the words she needs to hear. Let me be her light in this dark time.

Inge luxuriated in the cool water, splashing and scrubbing her body. With the onset of dusk, the frogs began to sing, keeping perfect time with each other. Wings whirred through the air as the barn owl flew overhead on his nightly hunt. A handful of stars twinkled on the horizon, and a sliver of crescent moon served as their lamp. She basked in nature's music and hated to get out, but darkness was creeping through the trees, turning the twilight into deep shadows.

"I'm coming out, Raven." She toweled herself off and slipped into a nightgown. "We had better head back before it gets completely dark."

Stepping past the bushes that separated the pools, Inge saw Raven struggling to get her damp body into her clothing.

"Here, let me help." She moved Raven's hair to one side, surprised the girl allowed her to do it, and then pulled the clingy dress down her body. "Raven, you have such beautiful hair." She ran her fingers through it to remove the tangles.

"You think so?"

"Ja," Inge said. "You are becoming a lovely young woman."

"David says that, too. I don't believe him."

"Why not?"

"Because he... they... people lie. They tell you nice things and then do bad things to you. I don't believe nobody."

"What about me?" Inge asked. "Do you believe me?"

The silence seemed to last forever before Raven answered, "I want to."

Inge gestured to a large fallen tree near their feet. "Please, sit for a minute."

Raven slowly lowered herself to the log.

"The pain inflicted by others can last a lifetime if we let it. It's easy to want to protect ourselves so we are never hurt again. I don't know what your life has been like up to now, but I am sure there are things that... weren't nice."

Inge reached out for the girl's hand. Raven allowed her to grasp her fingertips.

"I understand a little, like the loss of your mother, and I know it was not good with your father. But that's behind you now. You can make a new life."

Raven softly touched her abdomen. "But some things can't be

forgotten." She stared at Inge, words caught in her throat. "If I am having a baby…" Jumping up, she ran farther up the coulee.

In the near darkness, Inge followed the sounds of her sobs, finding her curled into a ball beneath a plum tree.

"Oh, Raven," Inge knelt and wrapped her arms around the girl. Raven stiffened and pulled back, but Inge refused to let go. Eventually, she yielded to the embrace.

Inge wiped the young woman's face with the corner of her night-gown. "God does not want you to suffer like this."

"I don't know God." Raven's voice was muffled in Inge's chest.

"Ja, you do. Remember when I read stories to Vada? I know you listened," Inge continued. "Remember how God saved Noah and his family? Or Esther? God put her exactly where he wanted her to be to save her people." *How will I ever explain the love of a savior to this child?*

"Those were nice stories." Raven trembled. "Vada believed them. Why would she believe after all that happened to her?"

"I believe they are true," Inge said. "Vada knew they were true, too."

"Why?"

"Because I pray, and God answers me. He knows what I need, and He provides. He sees everything I do and takes care of me."

"He doesn't take care of everybody. Nobody ever took care of me." Raven pulled back and rubbed her eyes. "And I don't want anyone to see me. I am safe if no one can see me."

"You can never be invisible to God. He's there for you, even if you don't know Him."

"Then why did He let that man… hurt me?" Sobs threatened to burst from her throat.

"We live in a world where not everyone knows God." Inge squeezed her shoulders. "And sometimes people can be downright evil."

"Vada and I talked about what happened… when she was hurt. She said it was all about forgiveness. I can't forget and I don't want to forgive." Raven sat stiffly, shivering in the cool night air. "I want him to… die sometimes."

"Raven, God does not intend for you to live with this pain without His help," Inge murmured.

She leaned back against the tree.

How can I explain forgiveness to her? I have a hard time trying to forgive Karl for his actions. I am the wrong one to bring this child to faith. I question You all the time.

I will prevail.

"You can become a new person if you put your faith in Him," Inge whispered softly. "Believe the stories. Believe Vada. Believe me."

Raven rested on her knees and wrapped her arms tightly around her body. She rocked back and forth until only tears remained as evidence of her struggle.

"Will He… take away the baby?"

Inge drew in a sharp breath. "Let's hope not. All life is precious to God. While this baby may not be what you expected, God has given you an incredibly special gift. Never forget that."

"But what will I do? How will I care for a baby?" She pushed Inge away.

"You can stay in the cabin. We'll help you as long as you need us." Inge cupped the girl's face in her hands. "Raven, God will provide for you if you ask Him. I know He will."

"I want to know God." Raven tugged at her clothing as she looked toward Inge. "Can God do that? Make me new?"

"Ja, He can." Inge drew the girl close. "Let me pray for you." She cradled the back of Raven's head in her hand as she stroked the girl's back. "Lord, God of heaven and earth, this child is Yours. I ask that You reveal yourself to her, fill her with your spirit, and heal her heart."

Raven's body slowly relaxed into Inge.

Lord, only You can do this. Please do a mighty work in this life.

"Jesus, show Raven your amazing grace and mercy. Let her know how much you love her."

Inge felt the girl's tenseness begin to fade. As she leaned back, her dark eyes reflected the scant moonlight, and Inge saw something different. There was something new in them.

I trust You, Lord, to bring this child into your loving arms.

Tears streamed down Inge's face as she smiled at Raven. God could do it. She knew He could.

CHAPTER 69

INGE

Inge awoke early the next morning. It was the Fourth of July. She lay on her side of the bed quietly praying. God had triumphed with Raven last night. She had tucked the exhausted girl into a bed covered in a blanket of peace.

Daybreak had filled the window with a soft light when she felt Karl stir.

"Are you as excited as the boys about today's celebration?" Inge asked.

Karl grunted, stretching his legs to the end of the bed.

"It sounds like it will be an enjoyable day," she said.

Karl rolled over onto his back. "Sigrid loved all the activity, the people, the music."

Inge's heart sank a little deeper into her chest. Would he never let her go? She rolled over on her side to face the wall, her guard firmly in place.

"I... I'm sorry." He reached out and put his hand on her shoulder. "I didn't mean to..." He sighed, dropping his arm. "It's hard for me. Can you understand? This marriage has been... well, difficult sometimes."

"I probably haven't helped." Inge stared at the plaster cracks under the windowsill, their paths leading to nowhere.

"Well…"

"I suppose I can be a little bullheaded on occasion."

"You do have a mind of your own, I'll give you that." Karl chuckled.

"We make quite a pair, don't we? Like oil and water."

Karl turned her body to face him. "Now that Vada is gone, let's see if we can do better."

Inge pulled back. *I still don't understand why Vada was such a problem.*

"I miss her," Inge said. Silence molded the moment. "She told me that I saved her life… and the children too."

Karl tensed, then relaxed. "I expect you did."

"And now there is Raven." Inge hesitated. There was no easy way to say it. "She's going to have a baby."

Karl sat bolt upright in the bed. "What?"

"You heard me." She pushed the pillow into a bunch behind her back as she sat up. "And *nei*, I don't know what happened."

Karl slouched back, frustration lining his face. "You are so good at this."

"What?"

"Saving the whole world. I have never known anyone who attracted the poor and lost the way you do."

"I just care," Inge murmured.

Sunlight streaked through the window as a new day dawned. Maybe this day could be a new beginning.

"I care too." Inge strained to hear Karl's faint words. "But I can't even save the things I love." His voice cracked and he drew in a shallow breath.

Karl's pain hit her as if it were her own. How could someone else's hurt cut so deep? She picked up his hand and held it against her chest.

Swiping his eyes with his other hand, he turned his head away from her. "You saved me too." He held his breath until it exploded from his lungs. "If not for you, I would have frozen to death. I wanted to die."

What was he saying? She had only done what anyone would do. Had the blizzard been his way of quitting or throwing his life away? Is that why he constantly made life miserable? Why was he telling her this now? Did he want things to be different?

God, what have You done? Was I making a difference even when I was a pain in his backside?

"Why? Why would you want to die?"

"Sigrid was gone. I was afraid if I married you, Sigrid would leave me forever." He gripped the quilt, doubling it into a knot. "You would take her away. So, I wanted... To be honest, I don't know what I wanted."

Karl's face crumbled before her. His pain cracked into tiny pieces and fell away like paint on an old building, leaving his face raw with emotion. Inge gripped his hand harder and placed his fist next to her cheek.

"I will never take Sigrid from you," she whispered. "Love is a wonderful thing, and we should hold on to it forever. Raising your boys will be the finest tribute to Sigrid's love."

She kissed his knuckles. He opened his hand and rested it on her cheek.

"Thank you. Thank you for being here, and for never giving up." He smiled weakly. "Do you think we can make this work?"

Billy's small face peeked in the bedroom door. "What is it, Billy?" Inge asked.

"Hurry! I want to go to town and do stuff."

"Then you better get dressed and help with chores. We aren't going anywhere until it's all done," Karl said.

Inge smiled at Karl before she swung her legs off the bed and began a new day with infinite possibilities.

EXPECTATIONS DARTED through Inge's mind as she packed food for the noon meal and the potluck later in the day. She questioned this drastic change in Karl. Was this the beginning of a real marriage, or was her dream simply teasing and taunting her again?

Arnie and Billy burst into the kitchen. "Hurry, Mam. We don't want to miss anything!" Arnie said. Marbles slipped from his sack and rolled across the floor. He scrambled to pick them up.

Inge grabbed the slingshot out of his back pocket. "I don't think we need to take this with us."

"Mam, are you going to play games?" Billy jumped up and down, pulling on her apron.

Inge grinned and tousled his hair. "I don't know. What kind of games do they have?"

"Well, I'm not sure. I was kind of little last time. But I know there were games. I'm going to play every one of them!"

"Then gather up your father and the rest of the boys so we can get going. I don't want you to miss anything." Billy was out the door before she had even finished her sentence.

Karl drove the wagon up to the front of the house. He and the boys stashed baskets of food safely under the seat. Arnie offered his arm to help Inge into the wagon and then scrambled into the back with Ben and Billy.

"Where's David?" Karl asked.

"Oh, he's up to the cabin mooning over that half-breed girl." Ben spread contempt on each word like thick butter on a slice of bread.

Inge had yet to understand Ben's attitude. He had a cruel streak she found unfathomable. Though he teased Billy and picked on Arnie, he ignored Inge most of the time. It didn't matter how she tried, nothing pleased him.

"I expect I'll have to do something about that one of these days," Karl muttered under his breath.

Inge looked at him. Exactly how did he feel about Raven? Or was it the baby? After this morning, she thought he had mellowed, at least a little.

He slapped the reins across the team's wide backs, and the wagon lumbered toward Taylor's Landing.

Jouncing on the seat beside Karl, Inge grappled with her feelings for this man. Even though they had lived together as man and wife for the last five months, she knew little about him.

Please, Lord, let this day be the beginning of a new life for us.

Taylor's Landing was bustling, even though it was only ten o'clock in the morning. Red, white, and blue bunting covered the hotel porch. Wagons filled every available open space, and the horses were unhitched for the day. Clusters of people gathered in the street, and laughter and chatter floated in the air.

Alighting from the wagon, Inge inhaled the excitement. She had forgotten how much she enjoyed mixing with others. While she didn't know many of the townsfolk, she looked forward to seeing Lena. Maggie and Gus would be there, too. She hadn't seen them for over a month.

The clang of metal startled her. A crowd had gathered at the horseshoe pit near the mercantile.

"I'm going to try my hand at horseshoes," Karl said as he watched the boys scatter in all directions.

"You go on. I will wander around a bit. Maybe I can find Maggie."

Inge watched Arnie in the three-legged race. She remembered lumbering through a race with Luke's leg tied to hers. Then, as now, there were more feet in the air than on the ground, but the children bounced back up and continued to hobble to the finish line. She passed near the livery where a group of men examined the horses that had been entered in the race later in the day. The money discreetly changing hands would not make their wives happy.

Colorful quilts lined the front of the hotel. Inge stopped and admired the detailed work. Needlework was not her gift. Oh, she could mend and darn, but she could never make anything as exquisite as this. She ran her fingers lightly over the intricate patterns.

"How about some pie?" a woman asked, her table filled with delicious-smelling desserts. "You can buy a piece or the whole thing." Inge shook her head.

A whole hog was suspended over the fire pit. Grease sizzled as it hit the flames, and several young boys took turns rotating the spit. The odor of roasting meat made Inge's stomach churn. She quickly retreated from the area, holding her hand over her mouth.

To escape the heat and dust, Inge wandered down to the riverboat landing. It was cooler there and the smell of damp, earthy sand filled her nose. Had it only been a year since she disembarked in this place? The air was as still and heavy as the stones that littered the bank. She turned her face, searching for a breeze. So much had happened. It almost seemed like a dream.

She scanned the hills on the opposite side of the river. This Dakota Territory was so different from her homeland, but she had grown to appreciate the uniqueness of it. Beauty could be found everywhere, from the spring wildflowers that covered the prairie to the hoar frost that clung to the trees in winter. For the first time in a long while, Inge's heart filled with hope and anticipation of the future.

"May I intrude upon your thoughts?" Inge turned to see Pastor Tim standing a short way away. Where had he come from?

"Ja, of course." She nodded as he approached.

"Sorry if I startled you. I saw you head off in this direction and thought we might chat," he said. "Memories?"

"Ja, I was thinking about the day I arrived. It seems a lifetime ago."

"What did you imagine it would be like?"

"I don't know. Foolish dreams, I suppose." She was thoughtful for a moment. "Strange, isn't it, how things worked out?"

"Inge, I want you to hear this from me before the rumors spread."

He pursed his lips. "I've decided to leave Taylor's Landing. I'm going east to finish seminary."

Inge's heart plunged to her feet as she stared across the river. He can't leave.

"Inge?" Pastor Tim touched her shoulder.

She jerked around.

"I know this is awkward, but I feel it's best for me right now." Looking down, he pulled at the pockets of his pants.

"Ja, best for you," she mumbled.

He reached for her hands, but she pulled away and turned her back to him.

"I... I can't stay," he said.

If Pastor Tim left, she would be alone again. Vada had left her, now him. A deep sense of loss crept up her body. She hugged the mooring post to keep from slipping to her knees.

Pastor Tim's concerned voice broke through her haze. "Inge, I wish things were different. You have Karl and the boys now."

"I'll be fine." That was a lie. She wasn't fine at all. Her best friend was gone, and now her... her... What was Pastor Tim to her anyway? Was he a friend, or just her pastor? Or was he the man she might have married if Karl hadn't...

Pastor Tim was right. It was better that he left. It was too late for anything else. She was wed to Karl.

She turned to face Pastor Tim. His face reflected the pain she felt inside.

"You're right." Her throat closed as she choked on her words. "It would be better if you left." He had been her confidant. She longed to tell him about this morning, about the hope she felt, and about the change in Karl. Those things were now erased by a crushing ache.

Pastor Tim looked around. He removed his hat and combed his hair with his fingers. Glancing toward the activities, he motioned in that direction. "Perhaps we should join the festivities."

Squaring her shoulders, lifting her chin, and pasting on a smile that left a lot to be desired, she said, "Ja, we probably should."

"I think the men are about to begin the axe-throwing competition. Karl's a contestant, isn't he?"

She nodded.

An enormous log had been sawed into slices, each piece set on edge to provide a target for the contestants. Inge cringed as the men hurled their heavy axes at the bullseye. Most hit the wood somewhere, but none hit the center.

"Come on Karl, it's your turn." The announcer motioned Karl forward. "You're the champ. Show 'em how it's done."

Karl picked up his axe and made a few practice swings before letting it fly. The head buried itself in the middle of the block. Cheers rose through the crowd as the men slapped him on the back.

"Ladies and gents, come back this afternoon for the last attempt to knock Karl out of the standing." The announcer's voice droned on. "He's good, but some of you are better."

INGE LAID out their dinner on the wagon bed. Hurt, guilt, and confusion circled her like a hawk after a chicken. *I must act as if nothing has happened. Forget everything except Karl's attempt to... to be a husband. I need to focus on that. God has answered my prayers, and now I must try to be a good wife. Pastor Tim will be gone and will no longer be a distraction. Ja, it will be better.*

"Karl, I didn't know you were so good with the axe," Inge said.

Karl piled pieces of meat onto a slice of bread. "My *far*, in the old country, he was a logger. I learned as a boy."

"Hey, Pa, you were a winner." Ben could hardly keep his feet on the ground as he joined them. "Teach me to throw."

"It takes a long time, Ben," Karl said. "But we can work on it."

"I want to try now. Can I?" His enthusiasm was unrestrained. "It doesn't look that hard."

"It takes a lot of discipline. We'll set up a block at home and you can practice."

Ben's lips formed a grim line and his cheekbones turned a startling white. He faced his father for a moment and then spun on his heel and stomped off.

"INGE! I have been looking for you," Lena shouted.

Inge waved as she saw Lena in a brightly colored dress push through the crowd.

"Come, let's stroll through town. I want to see the quilts and sample the pies," Lena said taking her arm.

What a pair they made walking side-by-side. Inge was tall and rangy, and the diminutive Lena only came up to her shoulder.

"How are things going now that Vada is gone?" Lena asked.

"I miss her so much."

"She was a special one, wasn't she? How is Raven handling... things?"

Inge stumbled as her foot caught on a board. She stopped. "You know, don't you?"

"I suspected. She was in a sad state when I found her behind the saloon." Lena sighed. "But I hoped for the best."

"Life is so unfair sometimes. I have to wonder where God is in this entire mess."

Lena squeezed Inge's hand. "He's there. We just can't see the end of the story yet."

The rest of the day passed with a parade, fiddle contests, and, of course, the horse race. Following a supper of pit-roasted pork and the side dishes brought by the revelers, everyone gathered for a dance.

The sun dipped below the horizon, and the air cooled. Inge noticed a group of men off to the side of the dance area tipping a jug. *I don't see Karl with them. Thank You, Lord, that he doesn't imbibe.* Several women made a beeline toward the boisterous cluster. She was glad she didn't have to be part of that confrontation.

The guitars, fiddles, and concertina created a lively tune. Seating herself next to Maggie, Inge sipped her drink and tapped her foot to the beat of the music. The dancers whirled across the open ground, lit by a bonfire and lanterns hung from poles. Maggie's face glowed in the soft light. *She's so happy. I envy her. Twice in her life, she has known love.*

Startled out of her reverie by a bloodcurdling scream, Inge dropped her cup, splashing the drink over her skirt and shoes. The music stopped with squeals and squeaks. A man rushed forward yelling, "Get the doc!"

Inge tried to push through the crowd.

Lord don't let it be one of the boys.

"Give me a rope or a belt. I have to stop the bleeding." Pastor Tim leaned over the man on the ground. "Hurry."

Inge stepped back to keep from being knocked over. She scanned the mass of curious onlookers for a glimpse of Karl and the boys.

The doctor elbowed his way through the crowd and bent over the body. The screaming had ceased, replaced by moans and whimpers. "Tie that tight around his leg," the doctor ordered. "You men, bring him to my office."

"Who is it? What happened?" Inge grabbed Gus as he pushed people aside to create an opening in the crowd for those carrying the body.

"It's Karl. He's been hurt."

Hurt? How could Karl be hurt? He was right here.

"Karl? Are you sure?" *Karl is fine. They're mistaken.*

She shoved her way through the front door, clawing at bodies that were in her way.

The doctor bellowed over the clamor in the room. "Loosen the rope, I need to find the end of the artery so I can tie it off."

Blood was everywhere. A giant red rose spread over Pastor Tim's white shirt. Its ever-expanding petals created patterns that changed before her eyes. How could it be so beautiful? A fountain spurted through the air. Everything had a lovely halo around it just before it went black.

CHAPTER 70

INGE

"Stop." Inge pushed away the hand patting her cheek. Opening her eyes, she stared into Maggie's worried face. *What am I doing on the floor?*

"Here, sit up. Yeh fainted," Maggie said. "It's Karl, remember?"

"Oh, my God." So much blood. "Where is he?"

"He's in the surgery," Maggie said.

"Wha...what happened?"

"Sh... sh..." Maggie's voice quavered. "The doctor's with him now."

Inge pulled herself up from the floor and sagged onto the bench. It had been a lovely day. She had been sitting with Maggie, listening to the music. Karl was just across the way talking with some men, and suddenly there was a piercing shriek.

Inge could hear the doctor's voice on the other side of the closed door. She rose and pushed it open a crack. Karl lay on the table thrashing and moaning. Pastor Tim leaned over him, restraining his arms. Blood streaked Pastor Tim's face. His eyes were wide with fear.

"Karl!" the doctor shouted. His hands cradled Karl's face. "Listen to me." Inge closed her eyes. "Karl! You need to hear me."

A low moan drifted across the room.

"I must remove your leg. The artery is severed, and I can't repair it."

"Nooo," he moaned.

"You'll die if he doesn't." Pastor Tim's voice rose as he tried to get Karl to focus.

Maggie reached around Inge and pulled the door closed, then wrapped her arm around Inge's shoulders.

"He's going to cut off Karl's leg." She pressed her fists against the door sill and rested her forehead on the door. "He can't do that!" Inge slapped the door with both hands.

An agonizing scream penetrated the room. Inge grabbed the knob.

Maggie pulled her back, clutching Inge's hands. "Yeh can't go in there."

"But... he... he said he's going to cut off Karl's leg. Why? Why would he do that?"

"There must be a good reason." Maggie's voice faltered.

The doctor opened the door. Inge's knees shook and she clutched a chair for support.

"Mrs. Johannson?"

"Ja, that's me."

"Here, sit." He gently pressed her into a chair.

She looked at his hands, and then her gaze ran up his arms. The man was covered in blood like he had bathed in it. What on earth was happening? This couldn't be from Karl.

"Mrs. Johannson, I am going to have to remove Karl's leg. There is too much damage to save it."

Panic raised the hair on her arms, and her hands trembled. The silence was stifling. "Why is he so quiet?"

"He is unconscious right now, and I have given him something for pain."

Inge strained to understand what he said. His words made little sense.

The doctor nodded at Maggie. "Stay with her. She will need someone." Placing his fingers on Inge's arm, he squeezed. She looked down and saw that his bloody handprint remained on her sleeve.

The hands on the clock barely moved. The bench was hard and uncomfortable. Inge broke free of Maggie's grasp and paced the small room. Voices coming from the office were muted, but the sound of the saw grating on bone sickened her. She almost wished Karl would scream. Then she would know he was alive. Shivers sliced her spine like shards of glass.

The outside door opened. "Mrs. Johannson?" Inge looked up. The man filled the entire doorway. "Ma'am?" he asked, removing his hat.

"I am Inge Johannson."

"Mrs. Johannson, I am Sheriff John Brewer."

Inge nodded. She looked up into his face. It was filled with concern and unusual kindness.

"Ma'am, we are trying to figure out what happened. Do you know if Karl had bad words with anyone today?"

Inge shook her head. "*Nei*, I don't think so."

"Is there anyone who would want to hurt him?"

"*Nei*. Sheriff, nobody will tell me what happened." Inge grabbed his elbow and shook his arm. The sheriff gently removed her hand.

"Well, Karl was hit in the leg with an axe. We found the head at the site. Don't know how it happened yet, but we are talking to bystanders." The sheriff paused. "I'm real sorry, Mrs. Johannson. Real sorry."

Inge slumped back in the seat. Maggie's arms kept her from slipping to the floor.

"An axe. Who would... an axe?" Inge whispered.

"Sh... They'll figure it out. Sh..." Maggie clung tighter.

Three hours later, the doctor emerged from the surgery. He pulled up a chair to face Inge. Blood covered his clothing, and his face was pale and haggard. Pastor Tim hovered near the door for a few moments. He glanced at Inge and quietly shook his head before he slipped outside.

"Mrs. Johannson, I am sorry about your husband." The doctor's voice was hoarse and gravelly.

"Is he dead?"

"No. No, he isn't." He drew in a deep breath. "But he has lost a lot of blood."

"You cut off his leg?"

"Yes, ma'am. He would have died otherwise. I did a lot of this during the war. It's not a good thing, but sometimes it's the only way."

Inge's body gave way. She couldn't breathe, and her head swirled like a dust devil in the fields, sucking up every bad thought that passed by. It was a dream. It had to be a dream.

"Will you take care of her?" the doctor asked Maggie.

"Ya, I will see to her."

"Karl needs to stay here for some time. I want to keep a close eye on him." The doctor's head drooped. "Pray he doesn't get an infection."

&.

The darkness outside felt oppressive, like a wet blanket weighing on her shoulders. The Fourth of July merriment had ceased. After the stifling office, with smells of medicine and blood, the fresh night air slowly cleared Inge's head.

"I need to be here." Inge pulled away from Maggie's grasp.

"I know yeh want to be here, but there is nothing yeh can do right now." Maggie tried to steer Inge down the boardwalk. "The boys need yeh. We'll go to my house. Gus and I will stay with yeh."

"The boys." Inge looked questioningly at Maggie. "Where are the boys?"

"They're fine. Lena kept an eye on them until Gus took them to our place."

"Do they know?"

"They know their father has been hurt."

Reluctantly, Inge allowed herself to be led away.

Pastor Tim stepped out of the shadows. "Inge, I'm so sorry." Moonlight shone on his blood-stained clothing. Dark streaks crisscrossed his chest. "Is there anything I can do?"

Inge stared at him. Something he could do? Her mind was blank. There was nothing anyone could do. She turned her back to him and allowed Maggie to guide her toward the waiting wagon.

CHAPTER 71

INGE

Inge sat up. Sun streamed through the window. Where was she? Memories of the day before flooded back. Yesterday had been a wonderful day until... *Nei*! She threw her feet off the edge of the mattress and tried to sort her thoughts. There was no need to make the bed, as she had fallen on top of the blanket like a toppled log.

The boys had been asleep by the time she arrived at Maggie's shortly before dawn. Inge was grateful. What would she tell them? She was not prepared for such a sudden and horrific change. *How could this happen?*

Rising from the bed, she tried to brush the wrinkles out of her clothing and make herself presentable. The doctor's bloody handprint circled her arm. That meant it was real. Every awful memory was real. She clutched the bedroom door frame, unwilling to open the door.

Please, Lord, let me awake from this nightmare.

Taking a deep breath, she turned the knob.

The boys sat at the table eating their breakfast. Arnie's face was dirty and streaked with trails of tears. Ben stared at his spoon as he stirred his cereal. Billy chattered about something he saw yesterday. They looked at her as she entered the kitchen. She wanted to run. *What am I going to tell them? I can't do this. They're just children who need their father. What if... what if Karl dies?*

Closing her eyes, she prayed this would be just another day. But it wasn't. She slowly walked across the room and slid into an empty chair at the table. Maggie appeared with a cup of coffee, and Inge took a sip. Reheated, it was bitter and strong.

"Pa's not dead, is he?" Arnie's voice cracked.

"Oh, *nei*. He's not dead." Inge tried to sort out her words. "He is still with the doctor." She drew in a deep breath. Coffee spilled from the cup in her shaking hands. She had to be strong for this family. "There was an accident. The doctor had to... to cut off his leg." A sob caught in her throat.

"What?" Ben's hands slapped the table as he leaped up from his chair. "Cut off his leg? Why?"

"Your father was struck in the leg with an axe."

"Do they know who did it?" Ben asked. His eyes darted around the room, resting on the door for a long moment before settling on her face. His eyes wouldn't meet hers. A tremor filled his body. He grasped the table for support.

"*Nei*. Last night, the sheriff didn't know how it happened. Maybe he will know more today."

Unanswered questions hung like a dark cloud over the kitchen. "I am going to see him right now." Inge pushed the chair away from the table. "You boys stay here with Maggie and Gus."

Arnie jumped to his feet. "I want to go."

"I know you do." Inge rested her hand on his arm. "But not right now."

"Mam, Mam." Billy's insistent voice tugged at her heart.

"What, Billy?"

"What are they going to do with it?" the little boy asked. "Pa's leg. What are they going to do with it?"

Inge gaped at the child. "I... I don't know."

"Well, I think we should have a funeral," he announced. "That's what you do when things die, right?"

Unable to fathom the question, Inge groped for something to say. "I... I guess we... Maybe you should ask Pastor Tim about that. I must go."

Karl was unconscious. Inge slid into the chair beside his bed. His skin was gray, his robustness gone. Her eyes refused to focus on the vacant spot below his knee.

Please, Lord, You have to heal him.

"I think he will survive." Inge jumped as the doctor's voice intruded on her thoughts. "He lost a lot of blood, but his color is a little better this morning."

Inge looked up. The doctor's features sagged down his face like soft chinking. Exhaustion stooped his back. A slight man with white hair and a mustache, he looked much older than his sixty-some years.

"I'm Asa Whipple." His head drooped. "I am so sorry that I had to do this." The doctor's voice faded as Inge focused on Karl's face.

What am I going to do? His leg was gone, but Karl was still alive. *I should be grateful for that.* She rubbed her forehead, trying to listen to the doctor.

"So far, it doesn't seem that the leg is infected," Dr. Whipple continued. "But that can change quickly. I will have to watch it carefully for the next few days."

She stared at Karl's motionless body. "Does he have pain?"

"Not right now. He's unconscious. Perhaps that's a blessing in its own way. When he wakes up, it will be excruciating. I have laudanum and opium. That will help some."

Inge hesitantly reached for Karl's hand. It was cold. She wrapped both her hands around it. He had to live. What would she and the boys do without him?

"If you are going to be here, I will try to rest. It's been a long night. If you need me, I am just in the other room. He should be fine for a while. Just watch his breathing."

Inge sat quietly by the bed clutching Karl's hand, mesmerized by the rise and fall of his chest.

As long as he's breathing, Lord, as long as he's breathing, you can do a miracle.

She sent a prayer forth with each breath.

Toward late afternoon, Inge nodded off. She had not eaten, nor had she slept much the night before. A hand on her shoulder startled her out of her half-sleep state.

"Inge, are you awake?" Lena's concerned eyes probed hers.

It took Inge a moment to remember where she was. She made sure Karl was still breathing, and a wave of relief flooded over her.

"Inge?"

Inge drew both hands over her face trying to loosen the cobwebs. "Ja. I'm just tired."

"How is he?"

"I... I don't really know. Thank God, he is still breathing. I was to watch him but I... didn't..." Inge's shoulders heaved.

"You did fine. He appears to be resting. That's what he needs to do right now." Lena's soft voice was reassuring.

Inge buried her head in Lena's mid-section. *This is my fault. If I had a better attitude, if I had been more attentive, if I had been a good wife, if I had been with him...*

"Inge, listen to me." Lena cupped Inge's face in her hands and forced eye contact. "Karl will heal. Right now, you need to rest, too, so that you can take care of him. I will stay with him for a while. I want you to go over to your old room in the saloon and sleep. And get something to eat. You will need your strength." Lena's voice was gentle but insistent.

"Can I help?" Pastor Tim stood in the doorway. His face was drawn and lined with fatigue.

"Yes, you can," Lena said. "Get her something to eat and take her to my office so she can rest."

Pastor Tim nodded. "How is Karl doing?"

Inge shook her head. Turning back to Karl, she again watched his chest move up and down.

Please, Lord, forgive me for falling asleep. Please heal Karl. Please.

"Go," Lena commanded. "I will stay with him. Go. Eat. Sleep."

Pastor Tim gently took her arm and guided her out of the room.

"I should stay. I need to stay." Inge tried to turn around and return to her place beside the bed.

"No. Come with me. Lena will watch him," Pastor Tim assured her. "He will be in good hands."

Like a lost waif, Inge allowed Pastor Tim to lead her toward the hotel restaurant. He ordered some soup, but when they brought it she could barely lift the spoon to her mouth. The restaurant hummed with voices that she wanted to shut out. Tables were filled with faces she didn't recognize. Why didn't they understand? Couldn't they be quiet?

"Inge, you must eat." He pushed the bowl closer to her.

She nodded and took a few more bites. Her eyes snapped open when her spoon dropped into the bowl.

"Let's get you to Lena's so you can lie down."

Inge followed him down the street in a stupor.

CHAPTER 72

PASTOR TIM

Pastor Tim led her through the back door to the saloon. Once in Lena's small office, he encouraged Inge to lie down on the cot. He covered her with a quilt and watched as she fell into an exhausted sleep. He couldn't imagine what she was going through. He had watched the life drain out of Karl's body last night as the doctor had tried to stanch the bleeding. The sound of the saw gnawing away at the bone rolled his stomach, but he had swallowed the bile and held the leg still.

How would Karl adjust? He was not an easy man, and this would be as hard or harder than losing his wife. And Inge would bear the brunt of it all.

I must stay here. God wouldn't want me to abandon her. He would want me to help.

He settled in the chair behind Lena's desk. It hadn't been easy to tell Inge he was leaving Taylor's Landing, but it had been a whole lot easier than this. A loose axe head had been found near Karl. It appeared to have come loose from the handle as someone swung it. They found the handle near the competition area. Had someone been practicing? Karl had been standing only a few feet away from him when it happened. No one saw anything. No one confessed to the deed. It was as if Karl had been the target.

God, why would you let this happen?

Pastor Tim prayed. He prayed for Karl, for Inge, for the boys, and for himself. The more he prayed, the deeper anguish cut through him. If only he could turn back the clock. If he had been with him, Karl might have turned enough so the axe missed him. He prayed Karl would recover from this, but he knew he would never feel whole again. Life had just settled, and now this happened. *What am I going to do? I can't leave and I don't know if I should stay.*

He slid deeper into Lena's small chair, his lanky frame overwhelming it. It creaked as he leaned forward placing his elbows on the desk. His hands covered his lower face and mouth as he prayed. How would this end? She looked so peaceful lying there. But she would wake up, and then what?

Earlier this morning he had stopped at Maggie's after he had washed the blood off his body and changed his clothes. He wanted to make sure the boys were safe. Ben and Arnie were unusually quiet, but Billy had said he wanted a funeral for the leg. Where did he come up with these things? The whole idea of a funeral for a severed appendage gave Pastor Tim a headache. And yet, he couldn't blame Billy. The boy was doing his best to deal with this tragedy in the only way he understood.

Once Pastor Tim was assured Inge was asleep, he headed back to the doctor's office. The sun was shining brightly. Somehow it would have been better had the sky been filled with dark clouds and crashing thunder. It would have fit his mood.

"Pastor Tim," Lena said as he entered, "someone needs to tell David."

He had forgotten that David hadn't been in town with the rest of the family yesterday. Yes, someone had to tell him. Maybe the sheriff would ride out there, or he could sit with Karl and Lena could go. He didn't want to be the one to deliver this news, but someone had to do it.

"I can do that," he said. "I'll get my horse."

He held the reins in his hand, feeling the worn leather. Running his hand down the horse's neck, he pushed the mane to one side. The horse sidestepped as he attempted to put his foot in the stirrup. "Quiet, girl," he whispered.

He swung his leg over the horse's back and sat quietly for a moment before kneeing her into a trot.

PASTOR TIM SAW David standing in the shade of the porch as he rode up the lane.

"Afternoon," David said. "Nice to see you."

Pastor Tim dismounted and tied the horse to the porch rail. He mounted the steps and offered David a stiff smile. "Why don't we sit?"

"Pastor Tim," David began, flashing a huge grin. "You won't believe what happened yesterday. Raven and I had the most wonderful time. We had a picnic by the river and talked–" He stopped. "What's wrong?"

Pastor Tim pulled off his hat and laid it on the bench. Sitting down he rubbed his hands together.

"David, your father was in an accident yesterday."

"An accident. What happened? Was he hurt bad?"

Pastor Tim drew in a deep breath. "The doctor doesn't know if he will make it."

David sank onto the bench as Pastor Tim related the details of the accident. The buzz of insects filled the air. Sweat trickled down his face. David disappeared into a shell, his face a pale shade of green. *How can I help the boy?*

David stood. He covered his eyes with his hand as he shook his head. He pulled his hat from his head, punched it with his fist, and threw it on the floor. He sucked in several deep breaths, then turned and kicked it off the porch. Leaping down the steps, he picked his hat out of the dirt, slammed it on his head, jumped on Pastor Tim's horse, and raced down the road toward town.

CHAPTER 73

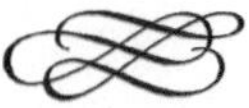

INGE

The early morning light had not yet embraced Karl's room, but Inge could make out David in the chair, asleep with his head next to his father's side. She was relieved someone had told him what had happened.

A good night's sleep and a cup of Lena's strong coffee had cleared her head, but there were still things she couldn't fathom. What would happen to this family? Karl would not take this well, she knew that, but how it would all work out was beyond her. Farming was hard, all-consuming work. It required able-bodied people to get it done. She didn't know if she and the boys would be able to manage. But they would have to—there was no choice. Eventually, Karl would be able to help some, but that would be far off. The doctor said total healing could take months if he survived at all. And if he didn't, then what would she do?

Lord, this is too much. You have to make a way for us.

Inge reached over and stroked David's hair. He jerked awake. Groggy, he lifted his head and looked from Inge to his father. "I thought... for a minute... that I was a little boy again." He laid his head back down as he reached for his father's hand.

Inge's fingers lingered on his shoulder. David's body clung to the edge of the bed, his eyes swollen and his face starkly white against his dark hair.

He leaned back in the chair, still clutching Karl's hand. "Please tell me this isn't real."

"I wish I could."

"Do you think he will live?"

"The doctor was optimistic. Said his color was better."

"What if he doesn't make it?"

"I don't know. This will be our leap of faith. Our trust in God cannot falter," Inge whispered.

Inge squeezed his arm. *Lord, I can't doubt. Not now.* But she did. Why would God allow this to happen? It just seemed that things were coming together and then this... this accident.

God, I don't understand.

David leaned back in the chair. He still clutched his father's hand. "What will we do if he dies?"

"*Nei.* That isn't going to happen. The doctor says it looks better than yesterday. That's what we must count on, that he will get better every day." Inge understood David's question. It had pounded through her head every waking moment. She refused to entertain it, but it never ceased knocking.

Reaching over, she encircled David with a hug. Would these boys survive if they lost both of their parents? That was a thought too awful to consider.

"We must pray ceaselessly and believe he will heal."

Tears pricked David's eyes. "I believed my mother would get better. I trusted, but she died anyway."

CHAPTER 74

KARL

Oh, God.

Karl sank deeper into the flames of hell.

Please. Make it stop.

But the fire in his body raged on even though he was spent. Shadowy figures danced before his closed eyes. He needed to get up, but pain pounded his body deep into the bed. He fought the blanket... and the hands that held him down. Words shuffled through his mind. *What were they saying?* Fingers forced his mouth open. Liquid trickled down his throat.

Someone was holding his hand. Even though his eyes were shut, he sensed light. A wagon clanked somewhere. His nose was assaulted by a foul odor. He tried to orient himself, but nothing made sense. Knives stabbed his leg. The pain radiated up his body. His lips were glued together. *This must be hell. And I will never get out of it.*

He moved his finger. Immediately someone squeezed his hand, and he heard a voice. *Sigrid, are you here? I need you. Don't leave me.* His eyes refused to open but he felt her hands on his face. He heard her voice say his name. *Maybe this is heaven. No, heaven wouldn't be filled with pain.*

A wet cloth dampened his lips. He tried to talk but no words came. His tongue was as dry and stiff as weathered leather. Water trickled down his throat, and he swallowed. *More. I need more.* Then it was gone. Someone stroked his head, but he tried to shake them away. *Leave me alone.*

"Stop!" Karl felt the scream escape his throat. *Please, make them stop. Someone. Make them stop.* Voices filtered through his heavy veil. "Hold him still. I have to get every bit of infection cut away." He sank into blackness.

❧

"Karl, drink this." Something dribbled down his throat. The strong, bitter taste burned, and he choked as he tried not to swallow. Hands lifted his head from the pillow. A cup was forced between his teeth. Water poured down his throat, and he gulped. Water to put out this fire that burned his body. He sagged into the bed and remembered no more.

Clinking bottles and hushed voices. His eyes opened a sliver. Shaded windows before him allowed in minimal light. Someone was sitting in a chair in front of the window. The face blurred; he couldn't make it out. A woman maybe. She was talking to someone, but he couldn't see the other person. Or maybe she was talking to herself. Why would someone be sitting in his bedroom? No, he wasn't at home. Where was he?

She was praying for him. Why? The woman stood. She was too tall to be Sigrid. Who was she? He closed his eyes and drifted away.

"Water." He wasn't sure if an actual word came out of his mouth or if it had just been a thought.

"Oh, Karl," a woman said. "You're awake."

She lifted his head, and he drank greedily from the cup, the cool water quenching the burning in his throat. Hands gently returned his head to the pillow. He tried to focus his eyes. He was so anxious to see Sigrid. She would know what to do to make him feel better. She always did. Just her presence was enough to give him a spurt of strength. The pain was always there. He couldn't get away from it. He reached for Sigrid's hand, and she gripped his fingers with tenderness. *Oh, yes. She was here.* He nodded off once again.

HANGING above his head was a yellow strip black with flies. He turned his head slightly and saw a counter with bottles. He didn't recognize anything. His head fell back into the pillow, then turned the other way. A woman was sitting in a chair by his bed, her head buried in her chest. *Sigrid! He knew she wouldn't leave him.* Joy filled his soul, knowing she was there. He blinked several times. She was asleep. Asleep but still caring for him. She had changed her hair. It was the wrong color. She was too big, not tiny like Sigrid. He raised his hand, and she startled awake.

No! Who was this? He wanted Sigrid. The woman spoke in soothing tones, but nothing consoled him. *I want my wife. I have to get out of here and go home to Sigrid.* A nauseatingly sweet but familiar scent filled his nose. A spoon poured a nasty concoction into his mouth. *No. I want to stay awake. I need to see her.* He felt himself slipping away.

SUNLIGHT STREAMED THROUGH THE WINDOWS, hurting his eyes. He lifted his hand to shade them. The woman was gone. Memories flitted through his mind like chaff in the wind, so he lay still trying to remember. They had come to town to celebrate the Fourth of July. He remembered driving the wagon. And Sigrid was seated beside him. Memories dropped in place like pieces of a puzzle. She was so sick. The funeral. Being alone. Unable to comfort the boys. No, she had been here with him. He remembered her sitting by his side.

He squeezed his eyes shut. Someone was talking. Karl's eyes sought the open door. Doctor Whipple. Why would he be here?

"Karl," the doctor said as he closed the door. "You're awake."

Karl frowned and nodded slightly. "What are you doing here?"

"Do you remember what happened?"

"Happened?" Karl bunched his eyebrows together.

"Karl, you were hurt at the Fourth of July celebration. Do you remember any of that?"

"Some. I remember driving to town…"

"Nothing else?"

Karl shook his head.

Dr. Whipple pulled a chair close to the bed. "You have been very ill for some time. I thought many times I might lose you."

Karl grimaced as he tried to move.

"You aren't out of the woods yet, but at least you're awake and in your right mind. That's a big step forward."

The doctor refused to meet his eyes. He clearly had bad news. Had someone died? "The boys…?"

"The boys are fine." The doctor cleared his throat. He tugged at his mustache. "It's you, Karl. I amputated your leg."

"What are you talking about? My legs are fine. I can feel them. The left one hurts like the devil, but it is still there."

"No, it's not." Dr. Whipple grasped his hand. "I cut it off to save your life."

Karl jerked his hand free and tried to lift himself up on his elbows. "You're lying."

The doctor ran his hand down the blanket to the empty spot. "It's gone. Right above your knee. I'm sorry."

"I want my wife. She'll get me out of here and tell me the truth."

"I'll get her." The doctor rose from the chair and stepped out the door. A woman entered.

"Sigrid, get me out..." He stared at the tall woman in the doorway. He squeezed his eyes shut. Memories hit him like an avalanche. Sigrid. Inge. None of this made sense. He tried to shut down his mind, but his thoughts penetrated anyway.

"Here, drink this," the doctor said. Karl welcomed the foul taste. Sleep would come and the memories would fade.

CHAPTER 75

INGE

By the end of the first week, Karl burned with fever, and delirium set in. His chilling screams as the doctor scraped away the infection cut Inge deeper than the knife. The smell of rotting flesh drove her to the pail near the door where she lost her supper more than once. The doctor used sheets to tie him down. Seeing Karl restrained was more than Inge could handle, and she would leave the room. Laudanum eventually allowed him a restless sleep. It was then that he whimpered for Sigrid. Inge was grateful his beloved wife had not lived to see this.

After the second week, the leg finally began to heal. Inge spoon-fed Karl broth to strengthen him, but he had little interest in food. His cheekbones protruded from his face and his eyes sunk deep into their sockets. He had been reduced to a skeleton. Determined that he survive, Inge remained at his side even when she would have given anything to run as far as she could, leaving all of this behind.

Forgive me for even thinking that, Lord.

Maggie and Gus had dropped everything to take care of the boys and the farm. How would she ever repay them? The neighbors were helpful, too. But it was Lena who had devoted much of her time to tending to Karl and caring for Inge.

Will I be able to do this, Lord? Eventually, everyone will go back to their lives, and I will be alone.

Karl moaned in his sleep. Inge was sure he still felt pain even through the opium. But it was the best they could do. Remembering how he had reacted when he broke his foot, she knew that this would not be an easy thing for either of them to deal with. Dr. Whipple said she could take him home soon, but she didn't even want to think about that.

"Lord, I need You," she cried in a ragged whisper. She curled into a chair by the window and prayed. Karl's tortured body lying on the bed frightened her more than anything else ever had in her entire life. She wrapped her arms around her chest and rocked back and forth. "I can't do this. I can't."

God, how could You allow this to happen? Karl does not deserve this, and neither do I or the boys.

Suddenly desperate to get out of the suffocating office, Inge left Karl's side. From the open doorway, she watched a parade of wagons haul goods from the riverboats. People entered the mercantile to shop, and a woman across the street gazed longingly at the bonnet in the dressmaker's window. Life went on as if nothing had changed. As if a bonnet was of any importance. Her life would never be the same, and it wasn't fair. She lifted her skirt and ran down the street, pushing her way past people. She knocked one woman off the boardwalk and didn't even look to see if she was hurt. She had to get away. It didn't matter where she went, just anywhere away from the doctor's office. Blindly she forged her way up the hill until she found herself up against a split rail fence.

"Isn't this just fitting?" she gasped looking around at the headstones in the cemetery. She clutched the top rail as she caught her breath. *In some ways, it might be easier if this is where Karl had ended up.* "Lord, my prayer was for a home and family. This is not what I asked for."

She slapped the post, ignoring the slivers that filled her fingers. Grabbing it, she pulled and twisted, trying to rip it out of the ground. "God, what do You expect from me?" Inge turned and slowly slid down the post into a heap at the edge of the fence.

The wind ruffled the leaves in the tree. Their rustling chanted *sacrifice* over and over.

I know. I offered myself.

Her choice to sacrifice herself for a family had been difficult but not beyond her. She could live with a marriage that would never be like her parents, but this was much more than she had bargained for.

I agreed, didn't I, Lord? I agreed to be a living sacrifice so others might know You, but not like this. There must be some other way. I will do anything if you heal Karl. Give him a life, a full happy life. Heal us as a family. Show me what I must do.

She opened her swollen, scratchy eyes to the calm sight of dusk. The wind had ceased, and the air had cooled. The leaves of the elm hung limp in the stillness. How long had she been here? She should be with Karl. Bone-weary, she studied the slivers filling her fingers. Listlessly, she looked up. The sun had set, but the sky was still filled with streaks of orange and lavender against the darkening background. Before the horizon completely darkened, a single star shone brightly in the deepening shadows. She felt a fleeting pulse of hope beginning to beat in this dark place.

CHAPTER 76

INGE

The weeks following 'the accident,' as Inge regarded it, had been as close to hell as she ever wanted to get. Changing Karl's dressings, cleaning the wound, allowing his verbal abuse to pound her into the ground, and trying to maintain some sense of compassion... it was overwhelming. She didn't know how much more she could take before she broke.

Karl's independent streak was going to kill him, and there was little she could do about it. He fought the crutches, though they often won. She had learned to tread carefully, trying to find a place between helping and ignoring him. He was becoming increasingly angry. Angry about his plight, angry the sheriff had not found the responsible party, angry the doctor had cut off his leg, angry about his breakfast, and angry at her. She prayed as she tiptoed around him, and she was relieved when he took the laudanum to fall asleep.

The boys tried to please their father. They took over all the chores and cared for the livestock, but nothing they did pleased Karl. It was never enough or done right. Eventually, they just quit reporting to him and went about the business of keeping the farm functioning. Arnie, the family peacemaker, sought refuge in out-of-the-way places like the hayloft. Even little Billy did not visit as much as he had in the begin-ning. Karl's harsh words had cut him deeply, and he withdrew to the cabin with Raven and David for company.

Ben's reaction to 'the accident' was a mystery to Inge. Ben, the hostile, angry child, had become patient, almost meek in his father's presence. At times, Inge could see a flash of exasperation, but he kept it under control and did his best to please Karl.

HARVEST WAS HERE. The crops were still standing in the fields. Inge suggested they hire someone to help shock the grain, but Karl would have none of it. Instead, he bellowed at every idea she proposed. Knocking her Bible off the stool was the last straw. Inge picked it up, relieved the pages were intact, and placed it out of his reach.

Through the window, she saw the neighbors coming up. She was surprised. Karl's churlish attitude had driven most of them away.

"Karl, Mr. Williams, and Mr. Hobbs are here to see you." Inge gently shook Karl's shoulder.

Slowly focusing his eyes, Karl shifted in the rocker and nodded at his guests when they entered. "Have a seat."

"Well, Karl, we thought we would drop by and see how you're doing," Ernest Williams said as he settled on the horsehair sofa.

"I guess you can see," Karl answered shortly.

Ernest touched the brim of his hat. "Well, Karl, we, that is, the neighbors want to bring in your crop for you. We thought we could cut and shock your grain, and then it would be ready when the threshers come."

Inge's hands covered her mouth to hide the joy she felt at the answer to her prayer.

Fred Hobbs chimed in. "We could easily get your crop thrashed and into the barn in a couple of days. We have a big crew. Everybody wants to help."

"That's real nice of you. I might not get around as fast as I used to, but the boys and me will get it done." He gave them a curt nod.

Seeing the neighbors to the door, Inge apologized. "I'm so sorry. He's being unreasonable." She lowered her head. "Please let me talk to him. We are grateful for your offer."

The men nodded, climbed into their wagon, and headed down the lane past the ripening fields. Inge's heart broke watching them leave. God had provided, and Karl had sent them away. How dare he be so prideful and stubborn?

Inge walked slowly into the parlor, standing just out of reach of Karl's crutch.

"We need them," Inge said. "We can't cut the grain alone."

"How do you know what I can and can't do?" Karl asked, his crutch flailing in front of him.

"You can't even walk across the room," Inge exploded. "You ought to be grateful people care enough to want to help you." Spinning on her heel, she left him sitting in the chair with his mouth hanging open.

She slammed the door and threw herself into the rocker on the porch. She could understand a man's need to care for his family, but there came a time when pride had to be set aside. How well she understood this herself. In the last year, her pride had been trampled on the ground so often it must be dust by now.

Her shoulders tensed as she heard the scrape of his crutches across the floor. Karl pushed the door open, swung his crutches over the sill, and dropped onto the bench. His breath came in short gasps. He stared at his leg and gently rubbed it.

"I'm sorry. You can't possibly know how helpless I feel," he said. "I hate this. I'm not even a man anymore." He shifted to put his weight on the opposite leg.

"Helpless? You think I can't understand what it feels like to be helpless?" She rose from the chair and towered over him. "Helplessness is all I have known for the last year."

Karl raised his hand to calm her down, which infuriated her more.

She stepped off the porch into the blinding noonday sun. Raising her arm, she pointed her finger directly at him.

"I'm afraid, Karl. I'm afraid of you, of the future, of our marriage. All of it!" She screamed the words. "I can't do this anymore." She rolled her head back and closed her eyes. "I am not strong enough. I'm done."

She began to march off but stopped, turning to glare at him, her body flushed with anger.

"We all walk around you like you are some kind of god, trying to see to your every need, and what do we get in return? Nothing. Nothing but a bunch of whining and griping." Her voice rose once again. "You want to feel helpless? Then do this alone." Her arms swept in a circle to encompass the farm. "Because that's what you will be doing very soon. No one wants to be in the same room with you, much less help you."

"Inge, wait," Karl called. "Don't go."

He could beg if he wanted. She'd had enough. She ran across the yard and down the lane. Bent over, gasping for breath, she stared at the field in front of her. *Where would I go? What about the boys? I can't leave them.*

The golden wheat waved in the breeze, the stalks bent over from the weight of the grain. It had been a good year. The rain had come when needed, the heads had filled well, and the fields were ready for harvest. She ground one of the heads in her hand. The wind blew the chaff away. She felt the seeds, full of life and waiting for another year. The grain was ready, full, and ripe. It would be a bountiful harvest, but it was a harvest she could not reap.

INGE GAZED at the field filled with friends and neighbors shocking the wheat. Karl didn't like it, but she would see to this family despite him. The harvest would come in, and he would be grateful.

She worked side-by-side with the boys cutting the grain. Even little Billy helped by toting buckets of drinking water to the thirsty workers. The sheaves would be stacked together in the field until the crew arrived with the thresher.

Inge dropped the scythe and leaned forward, resting her palms on her knees. She was so exhausted she could hardly stand up. Billy brought a bucket of cold water and she rapidly gulped down a cup. Grabbing her stomach, she doubled over. It took a few minutes for the wave of nausea to pass. She shouldn't have drunk so fast. She didn't need to be sick with all this work to be done. Straightening up, she resumed cutting the wheat.

Pastor Tim swung a sickle nearby. His white shirt was soaked with sweat. While Inge appreciated his help, she found it hard to face him. Had it been her feelings for him that had somehow caused Karl's injury? Had God seen fit to put her in her place? As much as she had longed for a husband, now she sometimes resented having one.

CHAPTER 77

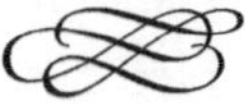

KARL

Karl seethed as he sat on the porch and watched the neighbors—and his wife—winnowing the wheat. With nothing to do, his hands hung limply at his sides, as useless as his legs. He spat over the railing. The women were busy in the kitchen cooking for the crew. He had been shoved out of his own house.

What am I going to do? The neighbors couldn't take care of them forever. And why couldn't the sheriff find whoever did this? That was more frustrating than anything. There was no reason, no guilty party, and no one to blame. It was like the axe had dropped from heaven specifically aimed at him. Maybe it had. Everyone said it was an accident, but was it? Perhaps it was retribution. But God didn't mete out judgment like that, did He?

The bitterness of being a *cripple* caused Karl's belly to burn. He couldn't even balance on the stool to milk the cow. With each attempt to do something, and with each failure, his temper raged more. Somehow, this was all Inge's fault. It made no rational sense, but he needed to blame someone.

Gus and Pastor Tim had been godsends these last few weeks. He resented them deeply. They were capable and he was not. It goaded him.

God, why didn't You just let me die? Then I could be free of this... this...

He couldn't even name what he felt.

He watched his neighbors, picking up the shocks and putting them into teepee-shaped piles. Given some warm sunshine, they would be dry enough for the threshing crew in a few days. He wanted to throw something... hurt himself... something. It nearly killed him to watch the work being done without him. He looked down at his stump. *Who am I kidding? I'll never be able to do anything. I'm a cripple! I will be a cripple for the rest of my life.*

God! Why did you do this?

He punched his leg and then moaned and writhed in pain. Physical pain somehow made him feel better than the emotions that stripped him of all his self-respect. He was a burden. He should have died. At least then Inge and the boys could have moved on. For a moment he was glad he had married Inge. At least the boys would have someone to look after them. She would be a solid anchor in their lives. He heaved a sigh of relief. When he was gone...

What was he thinking? He had considered giving up before and God had jerked him back. Was he thinking of himself or his family? Death would be easier for him. There would be no more pain, frustration, or anger. But it would be wrong to leave the boys. They had lost their mother already, and he saw the devastation that had brought to their lives. He knew firsthand how the pain could drive you to do foolish things. He couldn't hurt them like that, but what was he going to do? He could not see a clear path ahead. He couldn't even see a faint trail. All he saw was an insurmountable wall.

He closed his eyes as the waves of pain eased.

God, if you are there, then show me! Show me how to be a husband, a father, a farmer. Show me how to let this go and move ahead. I can't do it.

CHAPTER 78

PASTOR TIM

Following harvest, Pastor Tim convinced himself to visit Karl. He had helped with the harvest, but felt it wasn't enough. He was a pastor, a source of comfort for his parishioners. Unsure of what else he could do, he felt he should at least offer... what, he had no idea.

He nodded at Inge when she opened the door. She looked drained, pale, and haggard. A smile flitted across her face, but it seemed forced. "Come in, please. I apologize for the mess. I'm finishing up the last of the vegetables from the garden." She wiped her hands on her stained apron.

Pastor Tim stood awkwardly in the doorway, running his finger along the brim of his hat. "How is Karl doing?"

"He's better. He still has pain, but he is getting around on his crutches. It's good for him to get out and do something."

Pastor Tim glanced toward the parlor. "Is he here? I thought I would visit with him for a bit."

"*Nei*. He went to the barn earlier. I expect he is still out there if you want to see him."

Pastor Tim remained in the doorway. "How are you doing?"

Inge eased into a chair at the table. "It's not easy. Karl is a hard man to help." Tears threatened to fall, and she brushed her eyes with her chapped hands.

Pastor Tim slipped into a chair across from her.

"Thank you for being here," she said. Resting her elbows on the scuffed, marred tabletop, she placed her hand on her brow, covering her eyes. "I know you sacrificed your plan for seminary because of all this."

"I can go back to seminary any time." He leaned forward. "You needed help. Once Karl has regained his strength and has learned to handle things, then I will leave."

"Will he?" she asked. "Will he ever learn to handle this?" She looked at him. Her striking blue eyes were now faded and dipped in weariness.

"I don't know. It's hard to walk in another man's shoes. Or shoe," Pastor Tim said. A fleeting grin crossed his face before he subdued it.

Inge smiled too. "On a good day, it was hard to walk in his shoes. Now it's nearly impossible." She sat up straighter. "I never told you... it all happened the day of the accident, but Karl seemed hopeful that we might make a go of it, be a family. He had changed."

Pastor Tim lowered his head, embarrassed at the intimacy she shared.

Would Karl ever change? When he first came to this area, he remembered Karl as friendly and outgoing. At Sigrid's funeral, he had been enclosed in a shell, unresponsive to anyone. Most people grieved and moved on. Karl had stayed bound by his pain.

He remembered the frustration he had felt when trying to comfort Karl. The man refused to accept anything he offered. No condolences, encouragement, or comfort was allowed through. He was enclosed in a pod of pain, and he seemed to relish it. Pastor Tim couldn't understand. It was as if Karl chose to suffer, like suffering made him feel better. Pastor Tim had finally given up. He had to accept that there were some people that he could not reach. It left him feeling like a failure, or perhaps there were those that even God could not touch.

Lord don't let Karl be one of them, for Inge's sake and for the boys.

"But now, I don't think that will ever happen." She chewed on her bottom lip. "It would take a miracle."

"Fortunately, miracles are one of God's specialties," he said, not sure he truly believed even God could fix this.

CHAPTER 79

INGE

Summer slowly turned to fall. Cottonwoods wrapped themselves in layers of gold, while the plums and chokecherries flaunted deep purple and scarlet. The insufferable heat had abated, and the days were comfortably warm with cool nights. School had begun, leaving only little Billy at home. Life had slowed after the harvest, and Inge finally found time to indulge in one of the things she enjoyed most, writing to her family. With so much on her mind these last few months, she had almost forgotten the last letter she received from them telling of her mother's illness.

> October 1896
>
> Dearest Mor and Far,
>
> I am so sorry I have not written. I do hope that this finds Mor feeling better. I miss you all so much and wish I could be there to help you.
>
> How exciting that there will be a new baby in the

family. Give Sven my congratulations. We are having babies here too. My friend, Vada, had twins in the spring. And we have a young woman living close by who is with child as well.

    Mor and Far, you will become grandparents again next spring. It seems I, too, am going to have a baby. I'm excited but also uncertain of the future. I have not told you about the terrible accident that happened this summer. Karl was hurt and lost his leg. He has been struggling ever since. It takes a terrible toll on a man to be unable to work as he has his whole life. He gets better each day, and we are doing as well as we can. I pray that a new baby will bring him joy.

    Give my best to everyone.

Inge sighed. She had lied. Things were not going well. But she didn't want her parents to worry. Karl was better physically, but his frustration with his inability to do even small things ran high. His temper exploded often. She had learned to stay out of his way and let him resolve the issue on his own.

It had dawned on Inge just yesterday that she could possibly be pregnant. She couldn't remember her last time of the month but thought it might have been before Karl was hurt. She must be with child. It explained her mood swings. She was even short with little Billy. If it happened just before the accident, the baby would come in March. The whole idea of a child of her own gave rise to feelings she had never known. She had not yet told Karl. The joy she felt right now is what kept her going. Telling him could destroy that if he was not happy about adding a new little one to the family. How he could not find joy in a baby was beyond her, but with Karl, anything was possible. For now, she basked in the delight of knowing she was pregnant.

The warm Indian summer day with its clear blue skies drew her to the open doorway. Sealing the letter, Inge decided to head into Taylor's Landing. She could have a bag of wheat ground into flour, but mostly she needed to get away from the farm and Karl. A visit with Gus and Maggie would cheer her up as well. And she must stop and thank Lena for all her help. Billy could stay with Raven. While she loved the five-year-old, his never-ending questions wore on her sometimes, especially now that Karl spent little time with the boy.

The afternoon went by quickly. Inge and Lena caught up on all that had been going on in Taylor's Landing. Maggie had hugged her tightly. It felt so good to be uplifted once again. Inge was always grateful for Maggie's help and visits, but what she appreciated most was her ability to encourage Karl without ever putting up with his churlish disposition. With Maggie's resolve, Karl had gotten more proficient with his crutches and had taken to mending the harness in the barn.

Maggie's insistence that there was something different about her made Inge blush. She hoped she hadn't let anything slip that would allow her secret to get out. After picking up the flour, Inge stopped at the mercantile. She needed flannel and other sewing supplies to make clothing for the babies. Raven's child would arrive soon and would need diapers. Moreover, she could begin to prepare for her own child. What a wonderful thought, to be sewing for her own baby. Inge held the flannel next to her cheek, submerging herself in the fleecy nap.

"It's soft, isn't it?" Sam's voice interrupted her reverie. "Is there something special coming up?"

"*Nei*, oh *nei*!" Inge felt heat rise to her face. "I have some sewing to do, and the flannel is soft for Karl's leg," she added. Another lie.

"And how is Karl doing?" Sam asked. "It was such a freakish accident."

"He gets better every day. But it's a difficult adjustment."

"I'm sure it is. I can't even imagine."

You have no idea. Difficult doesn't begin to describe it.

"Well, let's measure out what you need, then," Sam said. "How many yards do you think?"

Inge gathered her goods and climbed atop the wagon to head for home. She had to tell Karl. She felt guilty about not sharing the news, and that, she knew, was selfish of her. Right now, the baby was hers alone. The thought that he might reject them both almost made her sick. Deep down, she was preparing for Karl's reaction. One moment she felt unbridled joy, and the next utter dejection.

Oh, Lord, only You can bring this family into its fullness. Let Karl embrace this new child.

CHAPTER 80

INGE

Late October had blessed them with sunny, warm days. Inge often spent the afternoons with Raven preparing diapers and other clothing for her little one, whom they expected sometime in the next month or so. Raven always had a gentle spirit, but now she seemed almost happy at times. The anxiousness and fear were gone, replaced by joy and peace. She often stroked her belly as if she were encouraging the baby. A smile would flit across her lips as she felt it kick.

God had done a miracle in Raven's life. There was no other answer for the change that surrounded her now. She had been cleansed of her past and was now full, whole, and filled with all He had to offer. Raven seemed to embrace her pregnancy. Inge would have found it frightening to face motherhood alone. More than once, it had crossed Inge's mind that she, too, could be in a similar predicament. What would she do if that happened?

"Have you thought of what you will do when the baby comes?" Inge laid out pieces of flannel for swaddling cloths.

"Maybe. A little." She blushed but didn't offer more.

"What about names? Have you decided on any?"

"Do you remember the story about the queen that saved her people? She risked her life to go before the king."

"Ja, I do." Inge was always surprised at how much Raven had absorbed from the stories she had read to Vada. "Her name was Queen Esther."

"And do you remember that the Bible said, 'She was born for a time such as this'?"

"Ja, I do."

"I want this child to be like the queen. Her name will be Esther."

"Esther is a beautiful name. But what if it's a boy?"

"It's a girl. I know."

Inge did not argue with her. Raven's mind was set on Esther and, if it was a boy, she would have to find something else.

Raven had become a sponge, soaking up Inge's advice on cooking, housekeeping, and especially childcare. They both relished the time spent reading stories from the Bible. God had created a hunger in this girl to know Him. Inge's eyes would tear up as she watched the beautiful young woman lean in to grasp the wisdom and truth of the scripture. Since their two children would only be months apart, they would grow up together. Inge embraced the wonder of it all.

"Inge?"

"Ja," Inge said.

"I... well, I... you know, don't you?"

"Know what?"

Raven looked at the floor rubbing her foot in circles. "You know. Your baby."

Inge looked up, startled at her words. "My what?"

Raven once again stroked her abdomen. "You do the same. You are with child too, aren't you?"

Inge leaned stiffly back into the rocker. Her face blanched. She didn't know what to say. She couldn't lie again. Rising abruptly, she said, "I must get supper on." Slipping on her coat, she nearly ran out of the cabin door.

Hurrying back to the house, Inge knew she had to tell Karl. There would never be a right time. It simply had to be done. She opened the door to find Karl sitting at the table. She stood stock-still. *Nei. Nei,*

Lord. Not now. I need more time.

She couldn't read his face. It seemed that he was... she didn't know... less angry, maybe.

She hesitated before she took a seat opposite him. Clasping her hands together to keep them from shaking, she said, "Uh... Karl. I have something I need to talk to you about."

He looked up from mending the leather strap in his hand.

"I know you have struggled these last months, and it pleases me that you are doing better." She drew in a deep breath. "I have news for you. I hope it will make you happy."

Karl continued to stare at her. Unreadable.

"I am with child."

Karl leaned back in the chair. "A child? You're having a baby?"

"Ja, I am having a baby." Inge sat in petrified silence, frozen and waiting for a response.

"What... when... how did this happen?"

Inge ducked her head. Heat rose up her neck. "The usual way, I think."

"I need a moment." Karl's voice shook. "Please. I need to be alone."

Stunned, Inge rose from her seat. "I'll begin the chores." She rushed out of the kitchen.

Her gut felt as if Karl had punched her. Doubling over the porch railing, she gagged as she fought for breath. Did he want this child? Would he think it was a burden? Her excitement and anticipation drained away, plummeting her into a sea of despair among a storm so great, its waves threatened to drown her.

A gust of wind nearly knocked her off the step. Heavy, dark clouds began to spit ice shards. She held her ground. The storm might batter her, but it would not destroy her. She stood taller and adjusted her stance to face the wind. The sharp snow stung her face. This child was a gift.

I choose You, God. This is Your child. An answer to prayer. I will not allow Karl to destroy this chance at a new life. All of this depends on You, Lord, not me. Only You can mend this family.

She sheltered her face with her arm and headed to the barn. "Please, please, Lord. Help Karl want and love this child. The baby needs a father, and I... I need a husband."

CHAPTER 81

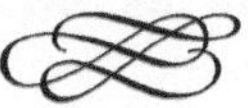

KARL

Karl slumped back in the chair, his mind rolling. A baby? It never occurred to him that there would be children within this relationship. They had not been... together since before the accident.

His mind swirled with thoughts. Inge was with child. His child. His mind reverted to David's birth. He had been so proud to be a father and to have a son to carry on the family name. He loved his boys more than life itself. Or did he? He certainly hadn't treated them with the love and care they deserved for a long time, not since their mother's death. They were the only thing he had left of Sigrid except memories.

His memories haunted the ordinary moments of his life. Certain ones lingered, and others disappeared. Sigrid was fading away, leaving him. Did he dare envision a future? He wanted to hit something or throw something to rid himself of this helplessness. He couldn't even do that.

Folding his arms on the table, he rested his head against them, his hands clenched into fists. What had life come to? The cruelty of his actions poured over him like scalding water. Pushing the boys away, his rejection of Inge, even his self-imposed suffering hit him like a felled tree. This new comprehension of what he had done was worse than the loss of his leg. It was even worse than Sigrid's death. The full understanding of his disregard for the boys and Inge sliced deep. He had cast aside comfort, advice, and wisdom from those who cared about him. He had been happy in his cocoon of suffering—well, not happy. He hadn't known how to face life without Sigrid. Cutting everyone off had been easier than grappling with the agony.

"God! If you are there, explain this to me." He groaned. "Show me what You are doing." Raising his head, he beat his hands on the table. *How am I supposed to continue? And now a baby. How will I raise a child?"* Karl grabbed the edge of the table and flipped it over. The butter dish and salt and pepper shakers crashed to the floor. He sat in the chair gulping for air. Sobs gripped his chest, but he refused to let them out. "Tell me! I demand to know."

Mercy.

Karl opened his eyes.

Mercy. Not getting what I deserve. Death. I deserve death, but You haven't allowed me that. There would have been mercy in dying. I wouldn't have to face this.

Grace.

Grace. Receiving what I don't deserve.

He wasn't worthy of this life he had been given or his family, especially not this new baby. He deserved none of it, and yet he had been blessed with it. How odd to look at the devastation in his life as a blessing. Losses had piled up on one another like stones in a wall. They had built the idol that he worshipped. He had so much, but he chose to seek comfort in the darkest part of his life. He had intentionally sought to dwell there, allowing it to mold his days and haunt his nights. Why? Had it been easier? No, not easier. Had it been because he didn't have the courage to face tomorrow?

He had been wrong. Inge had been a blessing, and he rejected her. She was an extraordinary woman filled with more grace and mercy than anyone he knew. Grace and mercy, love and acceptance—things that had once filled his life. How could he have forgotten?

"God, forgive me." Life-altering sobs poured up from his gut. The realization that God had to knock him to his knees before he would listen overwhelmed him. Life goes on, and God heals hurts and provides new joy. Sigrid often told him he could never run from the presence of God. She was right. God had hung on to him like an eagle snatching up his prey, never letting him out of the palm of His hand.

And You blessed me despite myself. Forgive my selfishness. Allow me to rebuild this gift you have given me. To make this family whole again and to welcome a new life into the fold.

He smiled as tears of joy poured down his face.

Lord, please let her forgive me. Give me another chance.

CHAPTER 82

INGE

"David. Raven. Come in," Inge said. She was surprised they had knocked. "Have a seat." She crossed the kitchen and poured coffee for everyone before she seated herself. "We were just discussing the Thanksgiving celebration next week."

She watched David fidget in his chair, leaning back on two legs, then dropping back on all fours with a thump. This wasn't like David. He was usually so calm and reserved. He slipped his hand across the table and clutched Raven's fingers tightly. Inge's stomach fluttered. She looked at Karl wondering if he sensed anything.

"We have something to tell you," David said. He pulled the chair closer to the table and reached for his cup. Finally, drawing in a deep breath, he stood. He rubbed his hands up and down his pant legs. Raven offered him a faint smile and nodded.

"I... we want to get married." He cringed slightly. Karl's face was as blank as the wall. Groping for Raven's hand, David dropped back into his seat.

Karl leaned forward and placed his elbows on the table, his clasped hands resting on his forehead, covering his eyes. The silence was more frightening than an outburst. The hair on Inge's arms rose. How would Karl react to this totally unexpected news? David looked at Raven. Her face was pale as moonlight on snow.

Inge was sure Karl would not be in favor of this. They were children, only fifteen and seventeen.

Inge slid a little closer to the table and leaned forward. "Is this what you want to do, Raven?" she asked.

David winced as Raven's grip crushed his fingers. "We've talked and prayed. We want to be married. Soon. Before the baby comes," Raven said.

"I don't suppose I can talk you out of it?" Karl asked, looking up.

David shook his head vehemently.

"Have you considered what this means? Raven comes from a different... her past has been hard. And the child will be... not yours." Karl drew in a deep breath. "These things could make your marriage difficult."

David looked at Raven before turning back to his father. "We know it won't be easy, but we love each other. I'm not asking for the world to approve, just you."

"Well then, it appears we will have a wedding," Karl said.

"What?" David stared at his father. His hands shook like leaves in the wind.

"I won't stand in your way. You are a man now and responsible enough to take care of this young woman and a child. I wasn't a lot older than you when I married your mother." Karl smiled. "Congratulations."

Inge rose from her seat and embraced David. "I am very happy for you." She beamed at him, her eyes glistening.

Turning, she pulled Raven into her arms. "We are blessed to have you become family." She backed away and wiped her eyes.

Karl cleared his throat. "I also have something to tell you." He looked at Inge, and she nodded slightly.

Karl's face flushed a bright pink. He wiped his forehead with the sleeve of his shirt.

"Well, it would seem that Inge and I are also having a baby." Karl chuckled. A huge grin split his face. "I've been blessed in so many ways." Karl reached out and clasped Inge's hand. She looked down at their intertwined fingers. "I have another chance at fatherhood," Karl said. "As well as becoming a grandpa."

Karl had changed since the night she told him about the baby, but mistrust still snaked down Inge's body. This wasn't like him. David's face was frozen with disbelief. He leaned so far back in the chair that he lost his balance and hit the floor. Smiling foolishly as he picked himself up and looked at Inge. "When?" he asked.

Inge's face lit up. "In the spring. Maybe in March."

David extended his hand to his father. "Well, that is unexpected... exciting news."

"But back to the two of you," Karl said. "When are you planning to wed?"

David looked at Raven. A pleased 'I told you so' look filled her face. Her dark eyes shone.

"We thought Thanksgiving Day would be nice. I know that's soon," Raven said. "We want to wed before David's child arrives."

Inge's eyes widened. She looked at Karl. "David's child?" she asked.

"David has been here since the beginning of my new life. He is the only father this child will ever have. My past is gone, forgotten. So, yes, it's his baby." Raven placed David's hand on her abdomen sealing their commitment to each other.

Inge's heart swelled with pride watching this young man, barely seventeen, take on the responsibility of marriage and family. David's feelings for Raven were obvious. His light touch, kind words, and the look in his eyes as he gazed at her assured Inge that he knew what he was doing. Raven blossomed in his presence. Her face lit up with his every word, her eyes followed him around the room, and she unfolded like a flower when he touched her.

David and Raven had begun their relationship under very difficult circumstances. Their youth, inexperience, the baby... it all should have worked against them. But Inge knew this was a blessed union, one that would grow deeper with time. She wasn't sure she could put her finger on the key to their relationship, except that it was filled with God's love and grace.

Inge wrapped her arms around her slightly protruding stomach. Life had suddenly become good, special, and filled with joy. Two lives in this very room exhibited the restorative power of God. Miracle didn't begin to describe the change in Karl's and Raven's lives.

Inge knew Karl's infirmity still filled him with frustration, but he was different from before. At times she could see him stop and regain control of his anger before moving on. Inge wasn't sure what to believe or expect. This transformation was not only astounding but a little confusing. Could she trust he was a new person? Ja, he was meeker. He had been keeping his temper in check and treating the boys with appreciation. And his attitude toward her was different too. Not the spellbinding love David displayed, but he was gentler and his words were kinder. He even offered an occasional familiar touch.

There was a small part of Inge that she held back. What if all of this dissolved like dust on a rainswept day? These dark thoughts bothered her. She had been down this road before and knew it could change in an instant. More than anything, she wanted to believe Karl to be a restored man. But lack of trust held her back. Would he revert to the *old* Karl? She decided to keep a wall of protection around her, just in case.

CHAPTER 83

INGE

Inge agreed that because of Raven's impending birth the ceremony should be simple—and soon. Thanksgiving was the perfect day to celebrate the gratitude they all felt.

Maggie had been beside herself with excitement when Inge told her about David and Raven. She immediately began modifying one of her dresses into a special wedding outfit. Lena donated lace to make a veil for the bride. The two women could hardly contain themselves, finding odds and ends to decorate the cabin, baking treats, and fussing over the bride and groom.

Inge had agreed to bake the wedding cake. It would hardly be the *kranskake* her mother would have made, but it would be special nonetheless. How she wished her family could be here. Inge stopped with the icing spoon in midair. Her family *was* here—her husband, her children, and her friends. Ja, she had everything she had prayed for, more in fact. She closed her eyes and allowed herself to steep in the wonder of it. Somehow giving the Lord thanks didn't seem to be enough.

Following a small Thanksgiving dinner, Inge rushed up the hill to the cabin to help with the last-minute wedding preparations. Maggie had shoved the table to the front of the parlor and covered it with a lace cloth. Gus lined up two rows of chairs to form an aisle for the bride. Red rose hips and heads of wheat tied with colorful ribbon decorated the table that would serve as the altar. Lit candles cast a soft flickering glow over the room as it darkened with afternoon shadows. It couldn't have been more perfect if it had been a cathedral.

Pastor Tim arrived with Lena just after four o'clock. Lena blew through the door like a stiff breeze. She arranged plates, linens, and utensils near the cake, pushed the coffee pot to a warm spot on the stove, and assigned everyone to a chair. Arnie and Billy were bundles of energy, unable to stay still for more than a minute. As Gus, Maggie, and Lena settled in their seats, the boys' excitement infected the entire group. Grins filled every face, whispers and giggles provided wedding music, and anticipation bounced off the walls.

David had asked Ben to be his best man. He stood near the table with David, his head bowed, shoving his hands in his pockets, and jiggling from leg to leg. Karl had spoken to the boy, convincing him to participate in the ceremony. It saddened Inge to see how much of Karl's intolerant mindset the boy had adopted. Convincing Ben that it would be acceptable for his brother to marry a pregnant Indian girl had taken restraint and patience on Karl's part. She was pleased that his efforts had worked it out.

Inge felt deeply touched when Raven had asked her to be her matron of honor. She would treasure this day for a lifetime, not just because of the wedding, but because God had orchestrated it. Why had she ever doubted that He was in control and would bring it all to fruition? He was God, after all. *Just because I can't see the end of the story, doesn't mean God hasn't worked out all the details.* She swallowed the lump in her throat as she stepped up to the altar.

With everyone present, Pastor Tim cleared his throat and nodded at Karl, who stood beside the bedroom door on his crutches. He knocked softly. Raven appeared in the doorway, looking lovely in a delicate blue calico dress. The lace veil covered her face and trailed down her back. She carried a small bouquet of red rose hips, a gift from Billy, Inge was sure. Her hair was pinned atop her head, exposing her swan-like neck. Raven radiated a fresh, innocent beauty. Her cheeks were flushed, and her eyes sparkled as she slowly walked down the makeshift aisle, holding on to Karl. David, dressed in his best white shirt and dark trousers, watched his bride approach. He stepped forward and took her hand.

"Wait, I'll be right back," Raven said, and she ran back to the bedroom. When she returned, she handed Inge the cameo necklace. Inge gasped. It was the one she had given Raven last Christmas. "You will put it on me?" she asked. "It was my very first gift. And today, David and all of you are the best gift I will ever receive."

Inge lifted the veil and clasped the necklace around the girl's neck. She had held her tears in check, but now joy poured down her cheeks. Raven reached up to wipe the tears away. Inge hugged the girl tightly, then pushed her gently toward the altar.

Pastor Tim smiled and began the ceremony. "You both began life as single individuals. After this day the two of you will become one. And God will be the head of your union. You will share pain and sorrow but also incredible joy as you walk through this life together. His blessings come to those who love Him."

He stepped back and gazed at the couple before him. Holding his Bible in one hand and lifting the other, he looked at the bride. "Raven, do you take this man to be your husband?'

She nodded shyly and whispered, "I do."

"And David, do you take this woman to be your wife?"

David gazed at his bride; his eyes were bright as he took in everything about her. "Absolutely."

"I now pronounce you man and wife. May God bless you as you share your lives together now and forever. Amen." Smiling, Pastor Tim added, "You may kiss the bride."

David lifted the veil from Raven's face and pecked her on the lips, his face turning deep red. Raven reached up and softly caressed his cheek.

"Come. Come." Lena's voice rose above the rest. "The bride and groom are going to cut the cake."

"Oh, cake." Billy was all smiles. "Can I have the first piece?"

"No, Billy," Lena informed him. "The first piece is for the bride and groom."

"Aw," his head drooped. "Shucks."

"But you can have the second piece."

Lena handed the bride the knife. Just as it entered the cake, Raven doubled over, crying out in pain, sending the slice of cake flying to the floor.

"Raven, what's wrong?" David guided her to the rocker.

Another pain gripped Raven. She gasped for breath. "I... I think the baby is coming."

"Pastor Tim, you go for the doctor," Lena commanded. "Hurry." She pushed him toward the door. "Take Gus with you. We don't need no men underfoot."

Maggie helped Raven up from the rocker and led her toward the bedroom.

Inge stood in shock as Lena shouted orders. "Inge, heat some water. Karl, take the boys to your house. David, you sit with your wife."

David looked blankly at Lena. "Wife?"

"Yes, your wife. It looks like you will be a husband and a father on the same day."

Karl put his hand on David's arm. "This will take a while. Why don't you come down to the house with me and the boys?"

An ear-piercing cry came from the bedroom. David's head spun back to the door, his eyes wide and filled with panic. "No. No, I should be here."

Inge watched David pace back and forth in the cabin, his heels clicking out a cadence on the plank floor. Occasionally he would stop to rub his hand over his eyes or claw his fingers through his hair.

She offered him a cup of coffee. "You are going to wear out the floor if you keep that up." She tried to get him to sit. "I am sure Raven is doing fine."

"But I can hear her, and she doesn't sound fine."

"Maybe you should go to the house with your father and the boys."

"I need to do something. What can I do?" David's fists were clenched so tight that his knuckles appeared frostbitten. Sometimes he was near tears when he heard Raven cry out. "Or maybe I should go see what's keeping the doctor."

"I'm sure he'll be here soon," Inge said. "Lena and Maggie know what they are doing. Raven will be fine."

Doctor Whipple arrived nearly three hours later, and within minutes the baby's cry brought David's frantic pacing to a halt. He offered Inge a shaky grin and clung to the table for support.

"Can I go in now?" he asked when the doctor came out of the bedroom.

"Give the ladies a chance to clean things up a bit," Doctor Whipple said. "And congratulations—it's a girl."

Inge picked up a pan of warm water and headed into the bedroom. She wiped Raven's face with the damp cloth and combed her fingers through her disheveled hair. Lena helped dress the girl in a fresh nightgown while Maggie stripped the bed and replaced the sheets. Once settled, Inge opened the door with the baby in her arms. "Here you go, Papa," she said.

David gingerly held the tiny bundle wrapped in flannel. "It's a miracle, isn't it?" He ran his finger down the baby's cheek. "She's perfect. Absolutely perfect."

Sitting down on the edge of the bed, Raven reached out for David's hand. "Do you still want us?" Inge could see fear creeping back into her eyes.

"Want you?" David looked at his wife. "How could I not want

you?" He placed the baby next to Raven. "You and this child are God's gift to me." Reaching out, David gently pushed the hair back from Raven's brow. "She's beautiful, just like her mother."

Inge watched the new family from the door. Incredible didn't begin to describe this Thanksgiving. She closed her eyes and prayed.

Lord, please provide this new family with all that they will ever need. May Your countless blessings be poured out upon them.

CHAPTER 84

INGE

Inge would have spent every spare minute rocking little Esther, but the Christmas holiday was soon upon them, and she had many things to finish. Karl worked on Christmas presents for the boys while they were at school. He had seemed unsure around Inge at first, but eventually, he began to pour out the emotions he had harbored alone since Sigrid had passed. Uncertain as to what to do, Inge just listened. In time she might share her feelings, too, but for now, she let Karl cleanse himself of his past.

Reactions from the boys about a new baby brother or sister had been almost predictable, except for Ben. He retreated more into himself, quieter, not even teasing the others. Arnie was old enough to know where babies came from, so he greeted this news with embarrassment. And dear Billy, as always, had a thousand questions.

"How do babies get in your tummy?"

"Will the baby suck on you like Esther sucks on Raven?"

"What if it's a girl? She can't sleep with us boys."

"I want a brother. You can send a sister back."

"What are you going to name it? I like Earl. Or Ralph. No girl names."

Inge rolled her eyes and told him to go play. She secretly hoped for a girl even if Billy would be greatly disappointed. And ja, she had a name picked out—Grace. If not for grace, she didn't know what her life would have become.

Inge didn't mind that winter had set in. She loved the bite of the freezing air in her lungs. Her eyelashes frosted, and her nose reddened in the cold as she walked up to the cabin to spend a little time each day with baby Esther. Inge wrapped her arms around her abdomen as she trudged through the snow. It wouldn't be long until she would be holding her own child.

Raven opened the cabin door, greeting Inge with a squirming bundle in her arms. Closing her eyes, Inge inhaled Esther's sweet baby smell as she clutched the small body close to her chest. What would life hold for these two children? She prayed often that God would surround them with His Spirit, protecting them, loving them, and drawing them into His embrace. "Lord, raise them up to be women after Your own heart." She knew they would make mistakes and sometimes take the wrong path, but He would be there guiding them back into the fold. He had done the same with her and Karl, as well as Raven and David. The fruits of His labor were becoming established in their lives.

After pulling herself away from mother and child, Inge stopped at the barn on the way home to help the boys with chores. It was impossible for Karl to navigate the banks of snow that covered the ground. She was surprised that he took his inability to do chores as well as he did. Inge marveled at the difference in him. Had she not experienced it herself, she doubted she would have believed it. Their relationship grew as they came to know one another. Inge found they had many things in common that they had never talked about before. Karl, too, came from a close family, and he missed them greatly. His dream to come to America had been met with familial conflict, but he had been determined to come to this land of opportunity.

The boys had created a path to the barn from the water pump, which Inge now trod carefully, avoiding icy spots. Even though the horses and cows were near the barn, they had to have fresh water each day now that the creek had frozen over. Hay was forked down from the loft, and grain was scattered in troughs for them at night. The chickens had been moved into the barn for warmth and easier care.

Inge slipped two eggs into her apron pocket, a light yield since the hens did not produce well in the winter. The boys had milked the cow, but there was barely enough for breakfast. Bossie would dry up soon, but once spring came, the birth of a new calf would fill her udder with fresh milk.

Inge stepped out the barn door, pushing the snow away so she could latch it tightly. It was nearly dark outside, so she had to pick her way carefully through the snow. Lamp light shining from the house windows carried a warm, welcoming glow. Smoke from the chimney filled the air with the faint smell of burning wood. Inge stopped and breathed in deeply, taking in the peace and quiet around her.

As she turned to begin her walk back to the house, she caught her foot on her skirt and tripped. The air whooshed from her lungs as she hit the hard snow. She lay there for a moment gasping for breath. Suddenly she felt a wetness through her skirt. *Nei*! Not the baby. God would not let this happen now. Struggling to her feet, she felt her skirt for the wet spot. Relief flooded her as her fingers connected with crushed eggshells. She laughed out loud. Then for no reason she could understand, her laughter suddenly turned to sobs.

This journey God had set her on, the one that had led her to America, to this place, and to this family had been fulfilled. Discouragement and rejection had delivered her to the brink of hopelessness, and yet she had pushed on. Why? It would have been easier to quit and go home.

Surprise—no, trepidation—suddenly filtered into this picture. Ja, she had pursued her dream. It had been about what *she* wanted, not Karl or the boys. These things had been *her* desires. She had been trying to meet her needs by herself, without truly listening to God. Her heart slammed in her chest, and her rapid breathing made her feel faint.

I was sincere in my faith, Lord. I was. How did I not understand?

Sweat poured from her body even in the frigid air.

Lord, have I been so fixated on what I want that I've gone down the wrong path?

She trembled, suddenly realizing that her desire to replace Luke and her shame at being a spinster had been her driving force. She didn't want to be alone. She had prayed, but had she really sought God's answer? She had charged forward with her own plan. What must He think of her? How could He ever forgive her?

Inge dropped back into the snow, the truth sapping all the strength in her legs. Faith was more than words and intentions. It was a complete surrender. Her will, her desires, and her pride all had to be sacrificed before God's throne. But she had wanted what she wanted, and she had expected God to provide. Intent on her needs, she never allowed God to lead her. She laughed out loud. How could she have been so arrogant as to assume God would do her will? No wonder the path had been difficult, if not impossible some days. She was walking it alone.

"Oh, forgive me, Lord. Forgive me for getting in the way and for being shallow and self-serving... all of it."

She let her words sink in, weighing on her mind. She had persevered, but had she trusted Him? She filled her lungs with the bitterly cold air. It burned yet gave her strength. Releasing her breath, she felt the shame and doubt float away with her wispy breath. Cleansing came with each exhalation. Selfishness, manipulativeness, insecurity, fear, and ja, her dream of a home and family were all let go. Exhausted, she kneeled in the snow, spent, cold, and yet refreshed.

Inge lingered on her discovery. What a superficial believer she had been. But she hadn't known anything different. She went to church and did everything expected of her. She had faith, she believed, and she read His word, but it was without depth.

"Lord make me an instrument of Your will."

The words sliced deep. The implication of a complete loss of control over her life terrified her. Could she do that? Was she willing to trust God totally? Did He really know what was best?

Inge. You are my beloved child.

Almost giddy with relief, she covered her face with her hands. Understanding and peace flooded her. Her relationship with God was now whole. She rested in Him alone, and finally, she was free to pursue a marriage relationship with her husband.

Thank you, Lord, that Your will was done, not mine.

CHAPTER 85

INGE

"Inge, is something wrong?" Karl asked. "You have been very quiet since last night."

Inge rested her mending in her lap. He was right. She had been mulling over her experience in the yard. In one moment it felt profound, and the next, it seemed improbable or even delusional. Yet, no matter what she felt, she knew it was real. She had encountered the living God on the way from the barn. It felt as if He had slain her, then raised her up with a new spirit of understanding and willingness to serve Him. Could her fear of losing the baby have created the experience? *Nei*. It was real—very real.

"I've been thinking," she said.

"Would you care to tell me what it is that has made you so... I don't know. Withdrawn?"

"I wish I could, but I am still sorting it out." She sighed deeply. "When I have put all the pieces together, then I will tell you."

"Is it something I have done?"

"*Nei*. You have been wonderful these last few weeks." She picked up the shirt she had been working on. "It has to do with me... and God."

"I might understand more than you think," Karl said. "But maybe we need to do something to get your mind off it."

Inge stared thoughtfully out the window. "Maybe."

"Then let's go cut a Christmas tree when the boys get home from school," Karl said. "It's a little over a week until Christmas, and since the weather is decent today, let's do it now."

As soon as the boys arrived from school, Karl announced the tree-cutting trip. Billy and Arnie clustered around his chair as he struggled to get up.

"Can I cut it?" Arnie asked, offering a supportive arm to his father. Karl put his hand on the boy's shoulder to steady himself.

"We'll see," Karl said. "Ben, hitch old Jenny to the bobsled, and grab the axe and some rope, too." He tousled Arnie's hair before adjusting his crutches to move forward.

"Karl, are you sure?" Inge asked. "David could help the boys get one."

"I want to do this with my family," he said. "I have so much to make up for."

Inge watched the boys race to the barn. Children were so quick to forgive. Did Karl really understand all the havoc he had wreaked upon this family in the last year? How could he possibly make up for the hurt he had caused his children... and her? *Nei*, God is working this out.

Please don't let me encumber Your plan.

When Ben pulled the bobsled up to the porch, Karl shoved his crutches to the back and easily dropped into the low seat. The horse plodded along, the sled skimming through a winter wonderland. The crusted snow was not quite deep enough to bury the prairie grass. Golden heads laden with seeds waved in the breeze. A feast for the birds with the fortitude to withstand winter in this cold, sometimes forsaken, land.

Inge led the family in Christmas carols as they snuggled close together under the heavy quilts. Their breath lingered in the air as they bellowed out the songs. Even Karl joined in, and Inge noticed he had a rather nice voice. She had so much to learn about this man who was her husband. Today she saw him in a different light. Had he experienced God the way she had? Her feelings were different, the resentment gone. She couldn't put it into words, but she felt Karl's pain like someone was twisting her heart. She had been humiliated, ashamed, and frightened, but she had never really suffered like he had when he lost his wife.

"I see them," Billy shouted. He jumped down and foundered in the snow. Ben grabbed him by his collar and pulled him back onto the sled.

"Hang on, we'll get a little closer," Karl said.

The horse lunged as the snow suddenly deepened in the coulee.

"There ya go boys. Pick out a couple of nice ones. David and Raven will need one too." He pulled the axe from under his foot. "Here, Ben. You can chop them down."

Ben stared at the axe. He took a step back, his arms hanging limp at his sides.

"Go on." Karl pushed the axe into his chest. "It shouldn't take but a few swipes to fell one of those little things."

Ben grabbed the axe to keep it from falling. He looked at his father, then back at the axe. "Maybe Arnie should do it. He's big enough."

"Do you want to try, Arnie?" Karl asked.

"Could I? Would you let me?"

"Listen to Ben. He will tell you how to do it. Hurry now. It's getting colder by the minute."

Inge watched the boys slog through the snow. They had to dig down at least a foot to get to the base of the small tree. "Do you think Arnie should be doing this?" she asked.

"He'll be fine. He splits firewood, so he knows how to handle an axe."

Inge watched as the eleven-year-old struggled to get the axe to bite into the tree. Once he developed a rhythm the tree fell quickly. A few swings brought down the second one. Billy and Arnie pulled the smaller tree while Ben toted the bigger one to the sled. Quickly tying them down, they headed home.

Karl urged the horse into a strong trot. The wind had increased, and the snow was beginning to drift. Sitting beside him, Inge pulled a blanket over their heads to protect them from the sting of the wind-blown snow. It felt good to be part of a family. It felt better to be at one with God.

"This will be a truly special Christmas," Karl said, placing his hand over Inge's. "One that we will remember forever."

CHAPTER 86

Inge looked forward to church services on the Sunday before Christmas. She could play her beloved carols for the last time until next season.

The waistline on her dress was snug. She would have to leave several buttons undone. Pulling on a heavy sweater so that her condition wasn't obvious, she finished dressing.

Ben pulled the bobsled up to the front porch. The boys lugged heated rocks to the sled and then clamored to curl up under blankets. Karl climbed down the steps and slid into the back. Inge slipped in next to Karl and carefully tucked the quilts around them both.

"Ben, let's keep this as easy and bump-free as possible." Karl grinned at him. "I want to get there in one piece."

Ben stiffened. "Yes, sir." He clucked at the horse, and they headed down the snow covered trail.

At the church, Karl slid off the back of the sled. Balancing on his good leg, he waited until Inge retrieved his crutches. She walked next to his side in case he needed her for balance on the slippery snow. Arnie and Billy raced for the church door while Ben secured the horse to a tree branch.

Karl swung his leg over the door sill and proceeded down the aisle. Just short of the altar, he settled into a seat. Inge removed her coat, gently draping it over Karl's lap. She pulled her sweater tight to ward off the cool air. Even though a fire burned fiercely in the stove, it took a while to warm up the building.

The room soon filled with neighbors and friends stomping snow from their feet and shouting holiday greetings. Gus and Maggie, accompanied by Lena, slid into the pew next to Karl.

"About time yeh got off yer duff and took that woman somewhere." Maggie jabbed her elbow in Karl's ribs. "We been missin' the music on Sundays."

Laughing, Karl clasped his side to protect it from another poke.

Seating herself on the piano bench, Inge lifted the cover from the keys. It took her cold, stiff fingers a few tries to be limber enough to play. Since Karl's accident, she had only attended church occasionally, as he was never happy when she did. But today, he had whistled a tune while getting ready for services.

Cold and lack of use had left the piano slightly out of tune. She hoped it wouldn't be too noticeable. Massaging her hands, she let them linger on the keyboard before playing the opening hymn.

"Good morning, everyone," Pastor Tim said. "And a Merry Christmas to you all."

Heads nodded as a hush stole over the room.

"Today the sermon will be taken from First John 3:11. 'For this is the message that ye heard from the beginning, that we should love one another.'" Pastor Tim closed the Bible and laid in on the lectern. "I know that these are not the traditional verses for Christmas, but I think it is appropriate for all of us." He clasped his hands and leaned forward. "Love one another. That sounds easy enough. But what does that kind of love look like?" He continued by commending the congregation for coming together and helping Karl after his accident. "Love is often hard labor. Sweat and tears. It's sacrifice." He paused. "Jesus said, 'When you do this unto the least of these, you have done it unto me.'"

Pastor Tim stepped back from the pulpit. "Christmas is all about sacrifice. God sent His only Son into this world as a sacrifice on our behalf." He stretched his arm over the congregation. "Let's remember that as we celebrate Christmas this year." He nodded at Inge to begin the last hymn.

Karl stood. He swung his crutches past the pew and stepped into the aisle. "Before we sing, might I say something?" he asked.

Pastor Tim looked questioningly at Inge, then back to Karl. "Would you like to come forward?" he asked.

"Yes, that would be good." Karl slowly made his way to the pulpit. He grasped the edges and used it to steady himself. Looking out at his friends and neighbors, he said, "I wanted to thank all of you who came to my aid during this hard time."

Inge slipped back to her seat. She swallowed hard. Grasping the pew, her knuckles protruded from her hands. She had no idea what Karl was going to do, but the last time it had been a surprise marriage proposal. That hadn't gone well. She covered her mouth with both hands. What was he doing? Her heart thudded. The unpredictable Karl funneled through her mind.

Lord, please put Your words in his mouth.

"I want you to know that I have been blessed with far more than I deserve," Karl said. "On Thanksgiving Day, David and Raven were married. Raven is a wonderful young woman and I hope you will all make her welcome. And before we even cut the cake, little Esther arrived. My first grandchild."

Murmurs rippled through the room.

Inge sighed in relief. Of course, he would want to share this news. It was probably wise to get ahead of the grapevine.

"God has done great things in my life these last few weeks. Not only has He healed my leg, but He has healed my heart. I have not been a good friend or neighbor since Sigrid passed away, but you all helped me anyway." He blinked rapidly but couldn't contain the tear that leaked from the corner of his eye. "So today, as I begin my new life with God, I would like to ask your forgiveness." He wiped his nose with the back of his hand as he lowered his head.

Inge held her breath. His confession, his contrition. Only God could have given him the courage to do this. *Would I be able to admit my mistakes openly? To confess to the entire church?* There was much for which she needed forgiveness. Her imperfect faith, her selfishness, her lack of gratitude, and her undeniably strong will.

The congregation was so quiet that the snapping of logs burning in the stove sounded like fireworks. They hung on Karl's every word. Inge couldn't look at him. His feelings were ragged and so near the surface, he might break down completely if she did.

Karl covered his face with his hand and leaned into the pulpit. Pastor Tim put his hand on Karl's shoulder and bent forward. "Thanks be to God," he said.

"One more thing," Karl said when he raised his head, his voice still strained with emotion. "I have another blessing to share with you. Inge and I are going to have a baby."

Maggie wheeled around to face Inge, her eyes shooting sparks. "I knew there was somethin' different. And yeh didn't tell me." She grabbed Inge and squeezed her tight. "I may never forgive yeh for that."

Inge's eyes widened as she watched Pastor Tim from Maggie's embrace. His face blanched, and he stepped back as if he had been hit by a swinging door. He quickly recovered his poise, but not before open-mouthed shock sprinted across his face. He clutched the back of a chair for support. She thought for a moment she saw anguish in his eyes.

Karl returned to his seat, slipping in next to Inge and grasping her hand. He looked at her with such tenderness it brought tears to her eyes. God had worked a miracle, and He'd done it without her help.

Pastor Tim reached for his notes but knocked them to the floor. He took his time retrieving the papers. Clearing his throat as he stood, he acknowledged the news. "Congratulations to you both," he said.

Releasing the lectern, he stepped back. "I also have an announcement this morning. As some of you know, I decided a while ago to finish my time at seminary." His words came slowly and with the precision of a sharp tool. "This will be my last Sunday with you."

The congregation gasped, some voices exclaiming a resounding "no" as the shock passed through the room.

"I plan to leave tomorrow and be home to spend the holidays with my family back East."

Inge's heart filled her throat. *He was really leaving.* She had put her feelings for him out of her mind following Karl's accident. Even though she had spent little time with him these last months, she knew he was there if she needed him. Pastor Tim had been her rock on many a hard day. How would she survive without him? Looking up to see his eyes filled with pain and watching her, she understood. This was his sacrifice. With Pastor Tim gone, she would be free to love Karl as he deserved.

Lord, go with him. Fill his life with every good thing. Bless him beyond measure.

"I know it's Christmas, but let's close with an old favorite instead of a carol. "Amazing Grace"." He nodded at Inge, and she moved to the piano. Placing her fingers on the keys, they refused to move. When they did, they stumbled, and she had to begin again.

Amazing grace how sweet the sound
That saved a wretch like me.
I once was lost, but now I'm found.
Was blind but now I see.
'Twas grace that taught my heart to fear
And grace my fears relieved.

How precious did that grace appear
The hour I first believed.

Ja, God's grace was an amazing thing. He had performed miracles, forgiven sins, and rebuilt lives.

He took a wretch like me...

CHAPTER 87

INGE

Christmas was fast approaching. Inge had sent Billy to the cabin to help with baby Esther. She was quite sure he would be of no help, but it gave her and Karl a chance to work on a Christmas present for the boy. Karl grabbed his box of tools and laid them on the kitchen table. Pulling a half-finished toy soldier from his pack, he began work. Using a small chisel, he formed legs and arms on the piece of wood. The detail knife in his expert hand created facial features and hands.

Inge used chokecherry juice to stain the soldier's uniform. The wood turned a dark purple. She left the legs a natural wood color but darkened his feet. Using her pen and inkwell, she drew features on the face. Billy would love these. The warmth of the fire and Karl's presence surrounded her.

"Karl, why did you give testimony in church yesterday?" she asked.

"I think the Lord wanted me to make a commitment. A commitment to Him, to you, and to the children." He gave her a sloppy grin. "Besides, I feel so blessed that if I didn't share the good news I would have burst."

She understood the need to tell others about the changes God had wrought in their lives. What a story she would have to tell when she saw her family again. So many times, she had given up, but God had filled her with the strength and faith to take one more step. But hearing this from Karl filled her with relief. And optimism.

Karl put the toy on the table and clasped his hands together. "Inge, I have something to ask you." He paused, seeming to search for words. "My treatment of you this last year has been unforgivable."

"You don't need to explain any—"

"Yes. Yes, I do. I was a miserable human being. I took out all my pain and frustration on you." Karl reached for her hand. "Will you forgive me?" He looked into her eyes. "Please."

She was dumbstruck. "Karl, I—"

"Let me finish," Karl said. "When I got your letter, Sigrid had recently died. I thought.... hoped maybe someone else could take her place. I knew better, but it was almost as if the pencil was in God's hand as I answered your letter. I don't even remember what I said."

"It wasn't much, I can assure you of that." Inge laughed. "Looking back, I fail to understand why I decided to write to you in the first place." She shrugged her shoulders. "I thought I heard, and maybe I did hear God's voice. But ultimately, I think I was trying to make my dream come true. I didn't want to wait for God to answer my prayer." She looked down at their clasped hands. "Perhaps God's hand was on my pen when I wrote to you, too."

"Well, I am glad you did." He squeezed her fingers. "And I am truly sorry for the way I treated you."

"It would seem God had His hand on both of us." She offered a soft chuckle. "Sometimes I wonder why I pray. God never answers the way I think He should. It's always a surprise."

"I'm glad you pray." He lowered his head. "I want to pray with you, and I want to teach our children to pray."

"Oh, Karl." Her heart rose in her throat. She slid her chair next to his. His arm looped around her shoulders, and he pulled her close.

"I am a truly blessed man." His voice cracked.

Laying her head on his shoulder, Inge whispered, "Karl, I forgive you." And she meant every word.

CHAPTER 88

INGE

Inge checked Karl's leg daily, but she was grateful when Dr. Whipple came a few days before Christmas to confirm that the healing process was going well. He examined the stump for any sign of infection. He also dropped off a package, which Karl stuffed into his toolbox and pushed behind his chair.

"Inge, you are doing a great job." The doctor patted her shoulder. "The leg is healing nicely. This man of yours should be up and at it soon." He put a small jar on the table. "I want you to continue to put this salve on it morning and night, and keep it wrapped."

Inge picked up the jar and wrinkled her nose at the smell.

"And, Karl, let me know how things work out," Dr. Whipple said.

Karl nodded but didn't say anything.

Just then Ben returned to the kitchen with a stout piece of cottonwood about three feet long. "I got what you asked for, Pa. What ya gonna do with it?" he asked.

Karl ran his hand over the piece of wood, his fingers stopping at knots. "I think I'll do a little whitling," he said to Ben. "What do you think, Doc? Will this work?"

"I'll be anxious to see what you come up with," the doctor said as he departed.

Taking a chisel and hammer, Karl began narrowing one end. Inge watched him work. Another Christmas present perhaps? She didn't mind the wood chips on the floor. She was glad he was occupied with something that made him feel useful.

After the doctor left, Inge and the boys filled tubs with snow and melted it to wash clothes the next day. Last winter she had done laundry for a dozen people. How had she ever managed? Of course, she hadn't been round as a barrel then either. She cupped her abdomen with both hands. What if she had twins like Vada? She wanted a baby, but the idea of two seemed overwhelming.

"Inge, sit down," Karl said. "You work too hard. I wish I could be more help."

He was right that she could use a break, so she filled two cups and settled at the table next to him. "What are you doing?"

With his awl, Karl had punched holes in various areas of a piece of leather. He studied it as if trying to envision a finished product.

"Are you making Christmas presents for the boys?" she asked.

Karl pushed the work to one side and reached for the coffee.

"Oh," Inge gasped, her hand clutching her abdomen.

"What's wrong?"

"The baby kicked." Up to now, she had felt flutters of movement, but this felt like a small cow had landed a hoof on her left side. "Here. Feel."

Karl hesitantly placed his hand on her belly and looked questioningly at her.

"I feel it." Putting his other hand on her side, he beamed like a child with a new toy. "I think it's going to be another boy. Only a boy could kick like that."

Inge placed her hands over his. God didn't make mistakes, but she was counting on a daughter.

"What are you making?" Inge asked again. The leather had taken on the shape of a giant muzzle.

"Well, it was going to be a surprise, but I guess I can tell you. Doc Whipple and I have discussed fitting me with a wooden leg. He gave me a picture from one of his books, and I have been trying to copy it."

"A wooden leg?"

"Doc says it makes it easier to get around than with crutches. He says I might even be able to get back to farming by next spring."

His enthusiasm excited her. Would he be able to walk again? He seemed so sure... and if the doctor said it, well, maybe it was true. "Can you make a leg?"

"I don't know, but I have to try." He fingered the leather straps. "This cup will hold my stump. Now I must figure out how to attach the wooden leg to it." His eyes danced as he looked at Inge. "I won't be running any races, but I should be able to manage better."

"Oh, Karl," Inge said. "Do you really think it will work?"

"Who knows? By next summer I might be able to dance you around the kitchen." A sly smile lit his face. "We'll make quite a pair... me with a wooden leg and you with a baby on your hip."

Inge's hand covered her mouth as she stifled a joy-filled sob.

Oh, Lord. I pray it to be true.

"I think I'll go into town," Karl announced the next morning. "I need to pick up a few things before Christmas."

"I should come with you," Inge said. "We will need *lutefisk* for Christmas dinner, and I could use some salt and sugar."

"There is no need to go with me. Give me your list and I'll pick up whatever you need."

"But... perhaps I should go along. Just in case..." Her voice trailed off.

"I'm not helpless. I can drive the bobsled," Karl snapped. He closed his eyes and shook his head. "I'm sorry." He reached out for her arm. "I want to do this alone." An impish smile curled the corners of his mouth. "Christmas shopping, you know."

Inge glanced out the window wondering if she should offer to help Karl harness the horse and hook up the sled. *Nei.* She had to allow him the freedom to feel capable again even though it took nearly twice as long to get the rig ready.

She walked outside as he drove up to the porch. "Are you sure you don't want me to go?" Standing next to the bobsled, she handed him a list of items she needed from the mercantile. "Hurry back. The air feels strange, like a storm is brewing."

"I won't be long." He grinned. "I don't plan to miss this Christmas."

Inge nodded and returned to the doorway. She pinched herself. This seemed too good to be true. She longed to go with him, to share the day together. Icy slivers ran up her back. Something felt wrong. Like the air was charged with energy waiting to be released. *Nei, that's foolishness. The sky is clear. He'll be home before dark.*

"Karl," Inge called as he clucked to the horse. "Wait." She ran to the side of the sled and impulsively kissed him.

Karl touched his cheek. "Well now, I will be hurrying home for more of that."

Inge smiled, glad she hadn't resisted the urge to kiss him. After all he had suffered, he needed to know love again.

CHAPTER 89

KARL

Karl waved at Inge before turning the bobsled down the lane. What brought on that kiss? He certainly didn't deserve it. But she had forgiven him. He could build a new life upon that reassurance. These last few weeks had been a conundrum of sorts. He knew he wasn't acting on his own, he felt the power of God changing him, cleansing him of pain and sorrow. He would always miss Sigrid, but the fact that Inge was here now and that he had feelings for her surprised him. Not the intensity of one's first love, but it filled him to overflowing, nonetheless. He couldn't understand why exactly, but he was happier than he had ever been. He sensed a restorative hope.

Lord, why didn't you get my attention sooner? I expect You tried. I know even You can't make someone listen if they don't want to.

He flipped the reins, encouraging the horse to move a little faster.

Karl stared at the sky, as clear and blue as he had ever seen it. A few scattered clouds edged the horizon, but the storm was far off. He should be able to finish his errands and return home before the weather changed. He didn't need to do much shopping. There was only one thing on his list. Now if only Sam at the mercantile had what he was looking for.

"Sam," Karl called as soon as he entered the store.

"Karl, it's good to see you out and about. What can I do for you on this fine day?"

He pulled Sam into a corner. "I want to get Inge a wedding ring for Christmas. Do you have any here at the store?"

Sam grasped his chin with his hand as his eyes wandered toward the ceiling. "Maybe. I recall that someone brought me one as payment for their bill some time back. Where would I have put that?"

He started for the counter. "Clara, help me out here. Remember that ring the Turners brought in before they left town? Where did we put that?"

Karl knew this news would be all over town before he even got home, but he didn't care. He wanted to give Inge something to show her how he felt. A ring was the only thing that came to mind.

Sam came out of the storeroom. "Here, I found it," he said, waving a small blue velvet bag over his head. He slid a plain gold band from the pouch. "It's a beauty, isn't it?"

It was perfect. Just what Karl was looking for. "I'll take it."

Sam clapped him on the shoulder. "It's yours."

"Oh, Sam. Do you have a pen and paper?"

CHAPTER 90

INGE

Although Christmas Eve was two days away, Inge took advantage of the boys being in school to wrap packages. Billy would be thrilled with the toy soldiers. Brown paper enclosed a warm scarf for Arnie, along with a pocketknife his father had purchased on the Fourth of July. The axe Karl had made for Ben proved difficult to disguise. Esther had a warm wool wrap, and Raven and David would receive some of the embroidered towels she had brought from Norway. But what to get Karl? Several things went through her mind, but they didn't convey the depth of feeling she now had for her husband. Maybe the baby would be enough?

The baby was a miraculous gift, one she had never expected. Her hands cupped her mid-section. God had blessed her. She would never understand the workings of her God, but she was grateful He was there.

"Hey, Mam, we're home." Billy burst through the door, letting in a blast of cold air. He had gone to school with his brothers for the Christmas party. "I have a present for you." His exuberance filled the room.

"How wonderful! I have a present for you, too."

"Where are we going to put them? We don't have the tree up yet."

"Ja, well, we are going to have to take care of that," Inge said. "Why don't you boys bring it in after you are done with chores?"

"Where's Pa?" Arnie asked, following his little brother inside.

"He took the bobsled into town. Said he was going to do some shopping," Inge answered. Glancing through the open door, Inge saw an ominous bank of clouds rapidly filling the sky.

"Ohh," Billy squealed. "Pa's bringing more presents!"

"It's getting cold out there, and it looks like snow," Arnie said.

"I'm sure he's on his way." Karl should have been back by now. She didn't like the idea of him driving home in the dark.

Inge prepared a quick supper for the boys after they had finished their chores. The wind moaned around the corners of the house, sounding like an injured animal. She paced the floor, glancing out the window periodically to see if Karl was back. It was nearly dark, and the snow was beginning to drift. *He needs to get here soon.*

Suddenly, the house shook as a powerful gust of wind struck it. A curtain of snow descended, blocking any view of the yard. Her pacing stopped as she stared out the frosted window. Surely Karl would not have tried to return in this weather. She should have tried to talk him out of going. He was a wise man, and he knew this land. He would have stayed in town. She was sure of it.

Then she thought of David and Raven. *Nei*, they would be fine. They had food and firewood in the cabin. But worry crept in anyway.

Wrap Your protective arms around them, Lord, and keep them safe in this storm.

Hours passed as if they were days. Staring out the window only increased her sense of dread, but she couldn't pull herself away. Inge ran her hand along a branch on the Christmas tree leaning in the corner, and the fresh, clean smell of cedar filled her nose. Tomorrow, Karl would be home, and they could put up the tree. She had saved the star that David had made last year. This would be a wonderful holiday as they made new memories as a family. In the morning, she would have the boys help her bake cookies.

"What if he's stuck out there somewhere?" Ben's voice was insistent. "I'm going to look for him."

For a moment Inge considered it, but she decided she couldn't risk having him out in the storm. The wind and snow continued to beat on the house, keening like a banshee as it curled into corners and crevices. The sound raked up and down Inge's spine leaving splinters of fear.

"How would you know where to look?" Her voice shook with alarm. "I don't want you lost, too."

"I'll just go to the end of the lane. If he isn't there, I'll come back."

"I said no, and you will listen to me."

Ben's fist struck the wall. He groaned for just a moment. Glaring at Inge, he stuffed more wood into the stove. The temperature had plunged, and it was difficult to keep it warm in the house.

Lord. Please, let Karl be safe.

She paced and prayed and listened to the wind shriek. At times the house shuddered from the force. *Please, please, please.*

"WE NEED to get to the barn and milk Bossie," Ben said the next morning. "If we don't, she'll go dry, and Pa will be really mad."

Inge scraped ice from the window. It was impossible to see more than a few feet. She couldn't see the barn or any of the other buildings. "*Nei.*" Her voice was shrill, keeping in concert with the wind. "We must stay inside. I can't see the barn. You'll get lost on your way."

"I could find my way to the barn blindfolded." Arrogance dripped from Ben's words. "I won't get lost between here and there." He began putting on his coat.

Inge ripped it off his back. "You... will... not... go... outside. Do you understand me? You will not."

Ben stood defiantly for a moment and then hung his coat back on the rack. "If the cow dries up, it's your fault."

Inge shook until her knees knocked together. She would not have two of her family lost in the storm. Her mind focused on Karl. He had to be safe. But her gut told a different story.

"Let's put up the tree. That way it will be ready when your father gets home." She hoped she sounded cheerful and that she could keep this gnawing feeling hidden from them.

Ben pounded the Christmas tree into a small holder and stood it in the corner of the parlor. The stove wasn't putting out enough heat to pop the corn. They wouldn't be baking any cookies either. She finally cut strips of calico from remnants in her sewing basket and helped Arnie and Billy tie bows on the branches.

A gust of wind whipped around her ankles. She heard the door slam and immediately knew it was Ben. Inge raced to the door and jerked it open. The wind and snow nearly knocked her off the porch. The cold sucked the air from her lungs. She couldn't see or breathe.

"Ben!" She screamed into the white veil that swallowed her words. "Ben. Come back." He was gone. She dropped to her knees, the snow swirling around her.

Lord, nei. Bring him back. I can't lose them both.

The wind swung the door, hitting Arnie as he stepped outside. He slipped his shoulder under Inge's arm, pulled her to her feet and back into the house. He leaned heavily against the door, struggling to keep it closed.

"Ben never would listen," Arnie said with anxiety in his voice. "He'll be fine."

Clamping her hand over her mouth, Inge squeezed her eyes shut and crumpled against the wall, frantic to save both Karl and Ben but unable to do anything.

Arnie slipped his arms around Inge's waist as Billy grabbed her leg. She drew both boys close. "Ja, I'm sure he will. He's probably safe in the barn by now." She wanted to believe that with all her heart, but she knew it wasn't so.

Finally, long past midnight, Inge collapsed in the rocking chair and dozed off. Before daylight, she heard the boys rousing themselves. It was then she realized the wind continued to hammer on the house. The storm had not passed. It was freezing. She quickly tossed kindling on the remaining coals in the stove. The wind drew all the heat up the chimney without warming the room. It didn't matter how much wood she fed the fire, the house remained cold.

Inge tried to keep the boys occupied but found herself gazing out the window and praying incessantly. The house felt like a tomb from which there was no escape. Inge doubted they could get out of the house now, even if they wanted to. A snowbank was already as high as the kitchen window. She was grateful the woodshed was full, and they had plentiful food and water, but neither would bring Karl and Ben home. She sat near the window, wiping it clear every few minutes, constantly searching the ocean of white for any sign of life.

After supper, Inge and the boys huddled around the stove, absorbing the little heat it offered. Inge wrapped a blanket around Billy and pulled him into her lap. Arnie had put on a coat. Inge offered to read to them, but no one was interested. After giving the boys extra quilts, she sent them off to bed. Well into the night, Inge stoked the stoves to ward off the cold. Covering herself, she lay down on the couch and eventually dropped into a restless sleep.

CHAPTER 91

INGE

The next morning frost clung to the walls on the inside of the room. Inge rubbed a spot free of ice on the window and gazed out on a frozen world. She found herself wrapped in silence. The storm was over. She hastily added wood to the embers in the stove. Peering through her peephole, everything was white. The wind had pounded snow into the bark of the trees, rendering the woods nearly invisible. Mountains of snow surrounded the house. Today they must care for the animals. The door wouldn't budge when she tried to open it. She considered removing the window over the sink when she heard the crunch of a shovel digging into the hard snowpack.

"Who's there?" Inge asked. "I can't get the door open."

David peered in the window. "I'll shovel it out. Just give me a little while."

As she listened to David chop away at the hard snow, Inge made coffee and brought out biscuits stored in the woodshed. The house warmed quickly now that the wind had ceased. David finally freed the door. Snow flew across the floor as he pushed it open. Huge banks lined either side of the entrance forming a tunnel.

David stepped inside. "It's freezing out there." He peeled off several layers of clothing before warming his hands with a cup of hot coffee.

"And you and Raven?" Inge asked.

"Oh ya, we're fine. It was cold, but we kept the fire burning all night." He laughed. "I think Esther is going to be a tough little gal. She seemed to thrive during the storm."

"David." Inge touched his arm. "Your Pa hasn't returned from town." A sob clogged her throat. "And Ben went out…"

"What?"

"Your Pa left the day before yesterday. He should have been home before dark." She blinked rapidly. "I told Ben to stay inside, but he slipped out when we were decorating the tree." Clutching her midsection, Inge doubled over. "It's my fault. I should have kept an eye on Ben. I should have gone to town with your Pa." It felt as if all the air left the room as she struggled to breathe.

David slipped his arms under her and settled her in a chair. "Pa probably stayed at Maggie's and Ben could be in the barn," David said. His face paled as uncertainty clouded his eyes.

"Ja. Ja, you are probably right," Inge murmured clinging to the little hope he offered.

"Have Arnie and Billy do the chores." A determined look filled his face. "I'm going to saddle the horse and look for them."

"Thank you, David," Inge mumbled. "Please be careful."

David gave Inge a quick hug. "It'll be fine." But his voice betrayed the confidence in his words.

The day crawled by as if time was caught in a net. Inge knew she should prepare for Christmas Eve, but her heart wasn't in it. She scaled huge drifts to check on Raven and the baby. Then she made sure the boys had cared for the livestock. Finally, by mid-afternoon, Inge saw a lone figure approaching on foot. She rushed into the yard forgetting her coat.

"Maggie? Why are you here? Where's Karl? Isn't he with you? And

Ben. Did you see him?" Inge's rapid-fire questions didn't give Maggie a chance to answer.

"Come, let's go inside. It's freezing out here," Maggie said. Taking her arm, she led Inge toward the house. "Where are the boys?" she asked.

"In the barn." Inge turned, facing Maggie. "Where's Karl? And Ben?"

"Ben is going to be fine. Gus took him to town to see the doctor. He probably has severe frostbite."

A sinking feeling began at her throat and worked its way to the pit of her stomach. Her legs would no longer hold her up. She clutched the table and dropped into a chair.

"Inge, I am so sorry," Maggie murmured.

"Sorry?" Her heart thundered in her ears as Maggie's words registered.

"There was an accident." Maggie rested her hands on Inge's shoulders. "The bobsled tipped over just up the road."

Inge put her hands over her ears. *Nei. This can't be happening.*

"Karl... is he... ?"

"Inge, I am afraid Karl didn't make it," Maggie said.

Gasping, Inge felt as though a rock had dropped on her chest. "Dead? *Nei*, that can't be," she stammered. "He just went to town to get presents." *Karl was dead. Nei, not now. Just when things were coming together.* She refused to accept the news.

Maggie put her arm around her. "I know, I know," she whispered, tears leaking from her eyes. She choked back a sob.

"What happened?"

"The sled was overturned. I'm not sure if they were trapped or crawled under it to keep out of the wind." She drew in a sharp breath. "Karl covered Ben with his coat and then laid on top of him. He probably saved his life."

She looked at Maggie. "The boys. What will I tell the boys?"

CHAPTER 92

INGE

Christmas was a solemn event. Maggie had insisted that the entire family join them in town for dinner. Even though she tried to make it a merry time, the air of death clung to the festivities.

"Inge, why don't you all spend the night?" Gus took her hand. "You have a lot to think about right now."

"*Nei*. I'd like to be alone." She had to think and sort this out. "But if you could keep the boys...?"

"Then let David go with yeh." Maggie wrapped her arms around her. "I don't want yeh alone right now."

The ride to the farm was unusually quiet. She tried to close the door to her mind through which she briefly glimpsed the life she might have had, but her relentless thoughts assaulted her like a blizzard. How would she survive and take care of the boys? And the baby who would never know her father.

"We will need a service," Inge said quietly. "Who'll do that now that Pastor Tim is gone?"

"We'll find someone," David said. "Perhaps Mr. Williams could help."

Pastor Tim, why did you go?

SATURDAY DAWNED without a cloud in the sky. It seemed wrong to begin a new year with a funeral, but they did. For once the wind wasn't blowing. The snow sparkled as if lit from below. Frost clung to the branches, creating a gossamer forest lining the road. The cold burned their faces as the family rode to church in the bobsled. Somehow the horse had survived the storm, and Inge was grateful for that.

She finally understood what Karl had suffered with his wife's death. This was permanent. As permanent as the frozen ground she was about to lay Karl's body in. He would not be here to love her like he might have, to parent his children, or to welcome the baby into the family. She was alone. Hope had been her lifeblood, and without it there was nothing.

Gus had taken care of all the arrangements. Inge sensed the church was full, although she kept her head down as she walked in with the family by her side. Soft whispers filled the small room. Gus had provided one of his finest caskets for Karl's final resting place. The wood gleamed as the sun's rays streamed through the window. Cedar boughs from the unused Christmas tree lay across the top, filling the air with a crisp scent.

"Let me out," Billy demanded. Inge tried to shush him, but he insisted on crawling over her to get to the aisle. Tears sprang to her eyes as she saw his tiny hand lay a sprig of red rose hips atop the coffin.

Ernest Williams preached an uplifting service to encourage those left behind, but Inge's mind was elsewhere. His words surrounded her, but she found them meaningless. She was alone. And each one of the boys hurt in ways that she could never fully understand. Billy hadn't sensed the loss of his father yet. He was curious. Where was his father now? What did you do in heaven?

Arnie suffered deeply. She could see the anguish in his eyes. Sorrow wrapped him with a crushing chain. Ben's reaction was hard to under-stand. He hobbled into the service using Karl's crutches. His feet had been badly frostbitten. Inge saw pain, but there was something else. Was it guilt? She could understand that. His father gave his life so Ben would survive. Deeper still he looked relieved, as though a heavy burden was gone from his life. None of it made sense, but she dared not ask him. David put on a good face as he tried to be the man of the family, but he was broken. He was supportive of Inge and his brothers, but he had become withdrawn. He stood alone unable to accept the family around him. It was a heavy burden for such a young man to bear.

Following the coffin to the black spot in the cemetery where the ground had been thawed by a giant bonfire, Inge felt that black hole surround her and pull her down into the pit of death.

How will I survive this? Lord, this was not my prayer. None of this.

After the graveside service, Inge endured numerous condolences. She didn't want to hear them. Somehow their sympathy felt superficial. She was glad when it was over, and the family could return home to begin life without a husband and father. She had to find a way to keep going for those who were still here.

God, You will have to be my strength
because I can't do this.

CHAPTER 93

INGE

The funeral had been exhausting. The boys had long gone to bed, but Inge remained in her rocking chair. The ticking of the clock echoed off the walls, broken only by the occasional crackle of wood in the stove. She carefully pressed the creases out of her skirt with her restless fingers.

The soft creaking of the rocker's wood frame was comforting, but her hollow body found little consolation in it.

You give, and You take away. And I don't understand. I know Your ways are higher than my ways, but Lord, please help me comprehend what you are doing.
Why would You take this chance of happiness from me? And from Karl? Especially now.

She knew that faith was an investment in God's plan. It took courage to take that step forward, not knowing what was out there waiting for her. Would she be able to do that? *Not now. Not today.*

Mr. Williams had read Isaiah 43:1-2 at the service. "Do not fear for I have redeemed you; I have summoned you by name, you are mine.

When you pass through waters, I will be with you; when you pass through the waves, they will not sweep over you. When you walk through the fire, you will not be burned, the flames will not set you ablaze. For I am the Lord, your God, the Holy One of Israel, your Savior."

Is that true, Lord?
Are You here with me now?
Because all I feel are the flames and the waves overwhelming me.

Inge picked up her knitting from the basket next to the chair. A small velvet bag lay on top of the yarn. Maggie said Karl had it in his hand when they found him. At the time, she had tossed it in her basket. Then she forgot about it. Loosening the string, she opened the bag and the ring fell out. Inge gasped. Karl had gone to town for this.

Holding the ring in her fingers, she felt joy and loss squeezing the breath out of her. If he hadn't gone to get it, he would still be alive. He would be here. They would have celebrated a wonderful Christmas. Plans would have been laid for a future together.

She couldn't put it on. She wanted to, but it would be a painful reminder of what might have been. Slipping it back in the bag she felt a piece of paper. Opening it, she recognized Karl's handwriting.

"You are a special woman. You opened your arms to things you never looked for and accepted things you never sought. Your faith persevered until God delivered me into your arms. May you always be lavished with the love you deserve, for that's where life's riches lie. You are wonderful, steadfast in your faith, and loved deeply by God and by your husband. May this be the first of a lifetime of Christmases we spend together."

Sobs clogged Inge's throat as silent tears poured down her cheeks. To be loved was the ultimate gift. Those who are loved are never alone. She pulled the ring out of the bag and slipped it on her finger.

CHAPTER 94

INGE

SIX MONTHS LATER.

The Cottonwoods released their annual flurry of fluffy seeds, creating a winter landscape in the middle of June. Every footstep raised a cloud that swirled around Inge's feet like a snowstorm. When she reached the river's edge, she settled onto a log. The mighty Missouri still raged within the confines of its banks, but the spring flood had receded. Sludge covered the ground and oozed over her shoes. Soon new seedlings would emerge and give life to this chaotic mess. The debris-filled water exuded pure power, tearing away the river's banks, leaving the trees clinging tenuously to the soil, redefining the landscape until it was unrecognizable. There was no controlling it. Life, too, was not within her control. Her only choice had been to ride out these last few months and hope for the best.

She leaned against the large tree root that angled out of the ground to form a support for her back. A small fluff of cotton landed on Grace's cheek. Inge brushed it away. The baby slept peacefully in her lap, her face upturned to the sun.

If not for the child before her, the last two years would have seemed like a dream... perhaps a nightmare at times. Thoughts formed, then slipped away before she could fully grasp them. The only memories anchored firmly in her head were of the last few weeks of her marriage to Karl. God had worked a miracle. He healed pain and sorrow and then filled them both with a genuine love for one another.

"That's what I will tell you," she whispered to Grace. "You will know your father as he was after God changed him." Sobs clogged her throat. "Your fa... father should be here to see you grow up, to celebrate your birthdays, to tease and tickle you. He sh... should be here."

As the sun rested on the horizon, it warmed Inge's face. Grace awoke and began mewling for her supper. Inge opened her dress to nurse the hungry baby. Grace suckled with gusto, her eyes absorbing every detail of her mother's face. She was so perfect and so beautiful. She had been blessed with the best traits of both her parents. Blonde fuzz skimmed her head, and her fair skin glowed, tinged pink from the warm rays of the sun. Her powerful personality surprised Inge. At nearly five months, this feisty little one had a mind of her own.

"What will life hold for us?" Inge stroked the downy hair on the baby's head. She looked deeply into Grace's intense blue eyes. "We will listen for God's whisper. For in His voice, we will find everything we need." Inge ran her fingers down the baby's cheek.

An eagle soared high overhead. Suddenly its wings collapsed, and it plummeted toward the surface of the river at lightning speed. Unfurling its wings at the last second, it grasped a fish. With heavy, ponderous flaps it slowly rose back into the sky. Astonished, Inge watched the bird fly off with the silvery fish grasped firmly in its talons. She had been hurtling toward destruction, only to have God lift her up with His mighty hand. She watched Grace squirm, her tiny fists rubbing her face.

God would always be there to lift her up when she fell, to carry her when she couldn't go on, and to whisper His words of unconditional love.

ACKNOWLEDGMENTS

To all of you who "whispered" in my ear over the years that I should write a book, you have my everlasting gratitude.

No project is ever complete without the help of many people. If you read, corrected, or critiqued my work, it was greatly appreciated. Without your help and, especially your prayers, this book would still be just a whisper in my ear.

The encouragement of family and friends is a large part of this work. You lifted me, enlightened me, and allowed me to grow.

A big shout out to Edits by Stacey, who guided me through all the technical aspects of publishing a book.

To my Beluga Pod, without your selfless willingness to coach, tutor, and guide me, I'd never have made it this far. You expected more from me each time we met, and my work got better with every suggestion you made. You are appreciated in ways you may never comprehend.

To my late husband, Jerry, who patiently waited as I spent hours in my "woman cave" working on words, punctuation, storylines, and self-confidence. You didn't always understand the things I shared with you, but you smiled and nodded anyway.

ABOUT THE AUTHOR

June D. Peterson is a freelance writer and blogger. *Sometimes God Whispers* is her debut novel. Fascinated with pioneer history, her story is set in in North Dakota where June grew up.

A former business and non-profit owner, June is now retired and lives in Boise, Idaho, near her children and grandchildren.

You can contact June at
Whisperingquill@outlook.com